MW01608361

RADICAL SURGERY

RADICAL SURGERY

WALLACE MARKFIELD

BANTAM BOOKS
NEW YORK · TORONTO · LONDON · SYDNEY · AUCKLAND

RADICAL SURGERY
A Bantam Book / September 1991

Grateful acknowledgment is made for permission to reprint the following:

"Did You Ever See a Dream Walking" (Mack Gordon, Harry Revel) copyright © 1933 PARAMOUNT MUSIC CORP. & CHAPPELL & CO. All rights administered by CHAPPELL & CO. All Rights Reserved. Used by Permission.
"Melody from the Sky" copyright © 1935 and 1936 by Famous Music Corporation. Copyright © renewed 1962 and 1963 by Famous Music Corporation.
"You're the Cream In My Coffee" © 1928 DESYLVA, BROWN, & HENDERSON, Inc. (RENEWED) Assigned to CHAPPELL & CO. INTERNATIONAL. Copyright Secured. All Rights Reserved. Used by Permission.
"Blue Skies" copyright © 1927 by Irving Berlin, copyright renewed.
Used by permission. All rights reserved.
"You're A Sweetheart" Copyright © 1937 (Renewed 1965) UNIVERSAL MUSIC CORPORATION. All Rights Controlled by ROBBINS MUSIC CORPORATION. All Rights of ROBBINS MUSIC CORPORATION Assigned to EMI CATALOGUE PARTNERSHIP. All Rights Administered by EMI ROBBINS CATALOG. International Copyright Secured. Made in U.S.A. All Rights Reserved.
"Together" (Lew Brown, Ray Henderson, B.G. DeSylva) © 1928, 1944 by DESYLVA, BROWN & HENDERSON, INC. (Copyrights Renewed) Rights for the Extended Renewal Term in the U.S. controlled by RAY HENDERSON MUSIC COMPANY, CHAPPELL & CO. & STEPHEN BALLANTINE MUSIC. Rights for Canada controlled by CHAPPELL & CO. All Rights Reserved. Used by Permission.

Library of Congress Cataloging-in-Publication Data

Markfield, Wallace.
    Radical surgery / by Wallace Markfield.
      p.   cm.
    ISBN 0-553-07423-7
    I. Title.
    PS3563.A664R3   1991
813'.54—dc20   90-27242
                    CIP

Published simultaneously in the United States and Canada

PRINTED IN THE UNITED STATES OF AMERICA

RRH   0   9   8   7   6   5   4   3   2   1

For Charlotte Amalie Black

AUTHOR'S NOTE

This is a work of fiction, begun in the late seventies when it still seemed to the author that realpolitik could not possibly beggar imagination. His occasional display of prescience is therefore altogether accidental—and so too is any similarity to real persons, real happenings.

RADICAL SURGERY

PROLOGUE

I was more fortunate than most of my countrymen; at the age of seventeen I found the one place in Russia that was without deceit and hypocrisy.
—From Leviathan's Hook, *by Pavel Gavrych*

Shortly after nightfall on the last Friday of February 1953, a blue Volga limousine, its windows showing black, entered the west gate of the Kremlin, cut sharply left, slowed, passed between the two watchtowers, and swept with sudden speed into the cold, stale darkness of a tunnel. The sandstone ceiling trickled; fat, rusty drops stained the windscreen. Yellow bulbs in wire mesh niches flamed coarsely and shed spokes of metal dust into the headlamps. Then there was a long incline, a glimpse of shaky white light. The limousine, twice scraping its exhaust pipes, descended a steeply curving cement ramp and came to an abrupt pitching stop in a thick-walled circular subcellar.

The red-headed boy cramped in the front seat between the dark bull of a driver and a slim blond man with a missing left ear chewed his tongue to keep his teeth from chattering. After eight, ten breaths he sat completely straight and still, centered his gaze steadfastly on the silvery star above the map light, and tried as hard as he could to speak proudly and very distinctly.

He said, "I am Pavel Gavrych, and there's no better Marxist-Leninist in all Moscow. If you had looked at my papers when you took me from the study house you'd have seen that I'm second secretary of the Communist Youth League for the Timoshka School District."

Opening the door on the left side, the driver exclaimed softly, "Lots of Jews in the district, Pavel. Lots of rootless cosmopolitans about."

Opening the door on the right side, the one-eared man scowled.

"Looks bad for you, lad. Way you were strutting around that study house, talking at the books. Weather like this, now—why, a good Russian, he'd be home and happy enough to warm his hands on his balls."

Pavel Gavrych lifted his eyes to the mirror, saw with relief that the half-bald rosy-faced man behind the glass partition was polishing his spectacles and smiling away; it became easier to get his words out. "I never feel cold in the study house, comrades. As for strutting and talking away at the books—tomorrow's honors day for all my districts and I'm on the program. Practicing my lecture, I was."

The partition opened, the half-bald man leaned forward, spoke to him for the first time. "And the nature of your lecture, laddy dear?"

Pavel Gavrych turned his head a little, twisted a shoulder. "Nothing much, comrade. Only a Marxist exercise," he said. "I mean to refute certain of Kunozon's ideas about dialectical materialism. Gives far less weight than he should to Russian history. Needs to see the wood as well as the trees."

The half-bald man shook his head regretfully. Softly he said, "A bit more tact and courtesy might be in order."

He stepped out of the limousine.

"Time, laddy dear."

When he had led Pavel Gavrych down some steps to an elevator with burnished copper doors and trimmings of Venetian leather, he hugged him fiercely. "Laddy dear," he murmured, "no trembling. I am Lavrenti Beria, and my ways are the heavy-handed ways of Russia's policeman. If I filled you with so much fear it's only so that what comes now will seem all the more glorious."

Then he moved back, extended a rigid forefinger, and lowering his voice almost to a whisper, said, "Do straighten up."

Masterful.

There is room for the Central Committee in his chair, yet he appears to fill it completely.

Stiff backed, he breathes so quietly that he appears more sculpture than man, and his immobility controls this huge hall, all the mighty persons in it, and perhaps the stars and planets as well.

Are you smiling at me, my Stalin?

And Pavel Gavrych squinted.

No, he is not smiling, but neither is he grave; his eyes are lidded, nevertheless he is watchful; he is intensely concentrating, sunk into profoundest thought, but he looks indifferent to all findings.

There is a tremor to his neck; the skin is fallen and crosshatched with wrinkles; the collar of his tunic gapes.

He is older and smaller than I would have him; his hair is gray; his moustache is as white as sugar.

He. Mine. Ours.

Who has never been before and will never be again.

And in brainless exaltation Pavel Gavrych murmured, "Stalin."

"Come now," Beria said mildly, patting him on the hand and preceding him under the gilt and ivory arch onto an expanse of rug that showed dragons and skimming birds of prey, steering him around lamps as tall and broad as Cossacks toward the head of the immense oblong table.

Pavel Gavrych thought, I shall never again take such pride in my existence, in the movement of my every muscle, in my singularity.

Now Stalin stirred; all the mighty persons at his table turned vague and shy and gave him earnest silence.

Now Stalin folded his hands, crossed the right thumb over the left, blinked, and opened his eyes fully.

Black, deepest black.

Discerning eyes.

Casual and majestic; sorrowful and jubilant.

Now Stalin curved his mouth into a friendly smile and in a voice that had echoes in it, said, "I feel the boy loves me, Lavrenti."

Beria replied, "Feel it, feel it, Koba."

"Koba," said Stalin, tipping his head. "When you call me Koba, Lavrenti, it touches my heart." He put a hand to the hilt of his ceremonial dagger. "A Georgian hero's name. A name I took in my shining youth. A magic name, and you will see why. Fifteen, I was. But man enough to deny God, czar, and weeping. Who has seen Koba weep?"

Pavel Gavrych thought, Here I am, and at this moment nothing in the universe is more alive than I.

Addressing a chandelier, Stalin said, "The sound of that name is one of my few pleasures. But they will not use it. Why not?"

He paused, whispered to himself, nodded, circled a finger at his temple.

"Fear. And they're right to fear. How right they are! Why are they right in their fear? Because those who speak the name reveal their true feelings to Koba. As I said, a magic name."

He marched his feet against the floor.

"Let me hear the name."

He swished his hands at the table, dilated his nostrils, and took a long, slow, powerful breath, as if to take something down into his soul.

"Let me know who loves me."

Some of the mighty persons in the front answered with a tinily audible "Koba." But then, compelled by the clamor of those behind, they sent the name beating and ringing through the hall like the smiting of cymbals.

Stalin closed his eyes, opened them just a little.

"Well, Lavrenti," he said. "Well, well, well, Lavrenti. Do you see how things are?"

"Am I not your guardian eye?" said Beria.

He swung slowly around, thrust an arm at the table.

"Comrades," he called ruefully, "only wait and learn how disagreeable life can become."

With a throb in his throat, Stalin said, "They oppress me. How they oppress me with rancor, guile, malice." He added a second later, "And bad ideas."

There was immoderate laughter; Stalin, with a scowl, stopped it abruptly.

"I feel, I sense that nineteen here—nineteen love me less than they should."

"Nineteen at the very least," declared Beria.

He walked over to the chair on his right. A thin-faced woman with a tight black bun flushed, paled, compressed her lips. For an instant she examined him as intently as a jeweler with his loupe, then she looked off into the far distance.

"Lena, Lena," Beria said, "savor each breath. Embrace your husband ardently, ardently. Fill up on pleasure."

"I see rancor, guile, malice honing her face," said Stalin. "Gotten sharper and sharper it has. Like the point of a weapon. Nasty eyes, too. They want to make a quick end of me. Know a thing or two about quick ends myself. Been many a quick end for Koba's enemies, quick as summer lightning. Thousands, tens of thousands. Wish I

could call them back now. Oh, yes! Wouldn't they have love enough
to go around!"

He turned his eyes on Pavel Gavrych.

"Comrade."

He clucked his tongue, swayed slightly.

Pavel Gavrych thought, May my solidarity be great enough.

"Comrade, do you see how things are?"

"He sees, he sees, Koba!" cried Beria. "Clear-sighted enough to
love you. Listen to how he loves you!"

He took a piece of onionskin paper from his breast pocket and
passed it to the thin-faced woman.

"Read, Lena."

She smoothed the paper with nervous fingers. " 'Pavel Gavrych,
sixth form, Timoshka Central Institute' "—for just a second her voice
was dim, hoarse with humiliation, then it began to ring strongly—
" 'Herewith a few words from a student's heart on the occasion of
my Chairman's seventy-third year. A curse on those dull, flat, mediocre opportunists who diminish his stature by perverting his blind-
ing truths into safe and comfortable truths. For their solidarity is not
great enough. Myself, I swear that if I had wisdom for a thousand
Lenins, wisdom enough to discern a single error in the Chairman's
teaching, this error would still be more precious to me than all the
truths under our sun, our Soviet sun.' "

There was a gust of acclaim.

When all the noise died Stalin extended both arms, beckoned.

Pavel Gavrych thought, I can never again be as other men.

And Stalin put a hand strongly on his shoulder, turned him a little,
looked at him with grave intensity.

He asked, "Do you understand why you are chosen, why you are
here?"

Pavel Gavrych thought, At this moment I am grown a day older
in history than even the mightiest at this table.

"You are chosen, you are here so that Koba can soften his feelings,
his awful knowledge of how things are. See, you are a shining youth,
a shining youth. Lavrenti did well. And when has he not done well?
Who knows me better? Who serves me as well? Oh, yes. I need only
think of vinegar and Lavrenti's teeth are set on edge."

Beria said, "Could I be otherwise?" He strode the whole length of
the table, then back again, then stopped suddenly before the chair of

a stout man in a black suit of Western cut and screamed into his face, "Am I not Koba's guardian eye?"

Stalin drew Pavel Gavrych closer, gave him a brilliant wink.

He said, "Nothing in the world is kind or fair. The burden of rancor, guile, malice, and bad ideas is intolerable. Who sleeps deepest and sweetest? Those who learn to tire themselves with hard and ruthless action. Those who understand that hammers must not stop falling or blood flowing. Shining youth, this is how things are. Life is difficult, men are imperfect. One learns"—he put a finger to his moustache, frowned; a vein grew full and hard on his forehead—"What does one learn, Lavrenti?"

"One learns," said Beria, waving at the other side of the table, "to measure the back of each ear for a bullet."

Then Stalin sat loosely in his chair, his expression pondering, his lips working in silence. At last he said, "Ossip, Ossip Miutin, let's have a look at you."

An elderly flatfaced man with muttonchop whiskers lifted himself up, bowed his head deeply.

Stalin extended his right hand, worked thumb and forefinger as if squeezing a trigger.

"Fart, Ossip. Why don't you fart? A wise man farts when mortality sniffs his asshole."

The flatfaced man took his seat, said, "Koba, ah, Koba," and ground himself into the ruddy leather of the chair.

"Can't hear you, Ossip."

Sitting upright the flatfaced man hoarsely whispered something.

"Doesn't fart, doesn't talk. Rancor, guile, malice, and bad ideas stick in his throat. How will you answer the fundamental demands of the masses, Ossip? When they want cows you'd give them gramophones. A fine example for my shining youth."

Stalin's fists slammed down on his thighs.

"Shitball, make way—make way for those who love me. Give my shining youth your seat."

The flatfaced man hastily rose and walked off on tense legs. When he had reached the gilt and ivory arch Stalin marched his feet against the floor and cried, "Hey, Ossip shitball! Ossip ratpiss!"

"Koba . . . ?"

"And who is to carry the chair? Let those who are to be swept into history's dustbin serve those who love me."

The flatfaced man scuttled back to his chair.

"Koba, ah, Koba," he said.

He turned, sank his knees, felt for a position, tipped the chair onto his back, staggered forward a few yards, rested.

"Come, Ossip Miutin, Ossip shitball, Ossip vomit!" said Stalin. "Carry it as I've had to carry you all these years. Let your balls drag on the floor."

Once more the flatfaced man moved the chair, rested.

"Put it to my right," said Stalin. "Can you find the right? Hey, Ossip Miutin, Ossip theoretician, Ossip scholar, could you find your cock with both hands?"

And all at once Stalin spat into his palms.

He stood up, ran at the flatfaced man, bumped him away with his belly and took hold of the chair by its arms.

"Look and see if Koba can still deliver a blow."

He raised the chair over his head, walked slowly backward, and set it down easily to the right of his chair. Then he clasped Pavel Gavrych under the arms and swung him into it.

"Made your point, made your point, Koba," said the flatfaced man. "I see your point. Point is well taken."

His arm half rose in greeting.

And rounding his shoulders and letting his mouth hang low he crossed the great hall and vanished.

Stalin sat down.

After a while he said, "Lavrenti, guardian eye, how many heads turned to look after Ossip?"

Beria, pacing back and forth, held up one, two, three fingers.

"Only three?"

Stalin's eyelids throbbed.

He said, "Oh, my." He raised supplicating hands and in a voice that carried undercurrents of melancholy and nostalgia said, "Was it so very hard for the rest of you to remember that in his prime Ossip was a man of grace and charm, flash and wit. Wrote like an angel, he did."

His laugh was short and faint.

"Won't his confession be a pleasure to read!"

Then he pushed some hair back from Pavel Gavrych's forehead and smoothed it down.

Then he pulled Pavel Gavrych's chair a little closer to his chair.

"Well," he said, "and when Lavrenti took you did he talk of your crime?"

Pavel Gavrych thought, Father, Mother, Marx, Lenin, Life, Space.

"Lavrenti," said Stalin, staring down at his shoes, "when was he born?"

Lavrenti took a few steps, stopped. "April 1936." He clenched a fist. "Fifteen April 1936."

"Well, do you see?" Stalin gave Pavel Gavrych a sidelong glance. "See how things are? You'll still be a hot young ram when I'm dry and cold in my grave. And that—shining youth, is the very worst of crimes."

He let out a whoop of laughter; and Pavel Gavrych, when he found breath, laughed too.

After a few moments Stalin clasped his hands and struck himself on the breast.

"Comrades," he cried thickly, "was there ever such a host? What a poor host I've been."

He rounded his eyes and shook his head.

"To keep you sitting here with empty plates for—Lavrenti, how long has it been?"

"Three hours and twenty minutes, Koba," said Beria. His hands flew to his head. "Can't understand why nobody spoke up."

"No matter, comrades, no matter." Stalin patted his stomach, his ceremonial dagger. "Promise you a regular love feast, I do."

"Hasn't been a meal like this since"—Beria ticked off something on his fingers—"why, I'd have to say since the Doctors' Plot."

"Comrades, are we hungry?" Stalin demanded.

There was a flowering of applause from the table.

Chuckling, Stalin returned the applause.

Beria said, "How wise you were, Koba, to suggest that the comrades skip lunch." He extracted a cartridge-shaped whistle from his shirt. "Whenever you're ready, Koba." He put the whistle to his lips, tapped it against his teeth. "If you can, comrades, leave room for the pies. A foot thick and swollen with cream."

"All the same, comrades," Stalin said thoughtfully, "let's not forget that there's no joy sweeter than a deferred joy."

And slowly, and with many pauses, he began speaking of his world outlook.

He took care to remind all present that practical political techniques were conceived—but how were they conceived? Only on the basis of what is possible, what is necesary. Can we, he asked, understand the nature of revolutionary programs by what they promise, what they say? Of course not. As he had told George Bernard Shaw on 23 July 1932, revolutionary movements must be defined not by what they promise and say but by what they do.

When he had spoken of these and related matters for thirty-five minutes he addressed himself to the national question.

For the abstract internationalism which seemed to be demanded by Marx, he insisted, had always foundered on the rising tides of nationalism. His solution, to this day confounding sectarians and dilettantes, consisted of a daring and original stroke. What was this daring and original stroke? Well, if the comrades were to understand his answer they must also understand how much he owed to Lenin's teachings, and he summarized and quoted from these teachings at some length.

Then he passed perhaps fifteen minutes in silent meditation.

After this he asked for comments, and when a soft cheer of awe moved upon the table he stood up, raised his hands above his head, and said gently, "Well, comrades, shall we eat?"

And Beria blew his whistle.

A little later, as he boned some steamed fish for Pavel Gavrych, Stalin told him, "Don't be ashamed, shining youth. My mother did the same for me. And cut my meat as well. Oh, ay, oh yes, how she spoiled me. Saying, 'Blessed head, beautiful head, how is such a blessed and beautiful head mine? What am I to do about those little hands, those little feet, those sugar candy fingers and toes? Made to be tasted and nibbled they are. First a mother must nibble them, then a mother must bite them, then she must eat them. I must eat them all up . . .' "

He put down his knife and fork, nodded, and stayed silent for a moment. Then he said, "See how things are, shining youth? Man's nature . . ."

He picked up his fork, dislodged a small square of fish, halved it, blew on it, and put it to Pavel Gavrych's lips.

"And what is man's nature? Brutish, at bottom most brutish. See, do you see, shining youth? Why, even at his kindest, even in the midst of loving thoughts he must think also of devouring."

—

After the eleventh course Stalin said, "Lavrenti, guardian eye, how many heads turned to look after Ossip Miutin, Ossip shitball?"

Beria, pacing back and forth, raised one, two, three fingers.

"Once," said Stalin, "I asked Lenin why he seemed happiest in the company of small children. Told me it was because they had not yet failed him."

His laugh was short and faint.

"It's said I poisoned him. No such thing."

A glaze of perspiration suddenly covered his face; it turned white and hard red in patches.

"In the end Vladimir Ilyich died of bad ideas, bad ideas."

One eyelid closed, twitched, began beating like a heart.

"Denied myself weeping after Mother died. Had to weep over Vladimir Ilyich's coffin though. Unseemly not to. Begged pardon of Mother and pulled two hairs from my nose to start the tears."

He moved his feet, moved them again as if he had taken a misstep.

He opened his mouth, his tongue flittered.

"Still deliver a blow, comrades. Wait, only wait. See how things are soon enough. Life is difficult, men are—"

He gripped his hair.

"Dustbin. His-his-tory."

He winced, gasped, rocked quietly back and forth.

And Beria was over him, whispering, pinching a pill out of a tiny packet.

Stalin whispered back, closed Beria's fingers over the pill, sent him off with a soft cuff on the cheek.

For almost half a minute Stalin sat crouched, making small snarling sounds from deep within his throat.

One side of his mouth was fallen and a little twisted, one hand was frozen in a gesture of denial.

Then he blinked brightness back into his eyes, braced his shoulders, and shouted, "Only a headache, comrades. Not done me in yet." He nudged his chin closer toward the table. "I've things in mind, no fear. Such things—oh my, oh yes. But they must wait for another time."

And Beria was back with several steaming rolled-up washcloths.

He opened one of them and fanned Stalin's face with it.

But Stalin looked uneasily at him, shook his head, said, "Guardian eye, keep watch, keep watch."

They whispered together briefly.

Beria said, "Laddy dear."

Stalin said, "Shining youth."

Pavel Gavrych stood up.

Stalin silently directed him to take a second washcloth.

"Put one behind my neck," he said, "put the other over my head."

Before long his eyes were closed and he was sighing with utmost satisfaction.

Then he shook his head heavily, opened his eyes, thrust his hands under Pavel Gavrych's nose and said, "Take them."

And when Pavel Gavrych had taken them Stalin said, "Young hands, strong and loving hands."

He moved Pavel Gavrych's hands to his temples and patted and pressed them.

"Shining youth, shall I test you on Marxism? Oh yes, Koba must test you on Marxism."

He patted and pressed, patted and pressed.

"Marx tells us there are two forms of wages. The two, let me hear the two."

Pavel Gavrych answered, "Time wages and piece wages."

He covered Pavel Gavrych's hands with his hands.

"And how did Marx say capital came into the world?"

Pavel Gavrych answered, "Oozing blood from every pore."

Stalin teased Pavel Gavrych's knuckles with the palps of his fingers.

"Being—what determines man's being?"

Pavel Gavrych answered, "It is not the consciousness of man which determines his being, but on the contrary, it is his social being which determines his consciousness."

Stalin spread the fingers of Pavel Gavrych's right hand.

"Comrades," he cried out, "a toast! Toast our shining youth!"

In a single wavelike motion all the mighty persons rose and raised glasses.

And with both hands Stalin lifted up the thumb of Pavel Gavrych's right hand and bent it back from its socket; and he took a grip between the knuckles; and pursing his lips and frowning in concentration as if threading a needle, snapped the bone.

"All the stronger when it heals," he murmured over Pavel Gavrych's quiet moan.

Then he marched his feet against the floor and with a little snarl said, "You'll outlive me anyway."

The dark bull of a driver said, "Watch out for the rootless cosmopolitans, Pavel."

The one-eared man said, "Nine good fingers left. Enough to play with yourself."

They lifted Pavel Gavrych out of the limousine, set him down on the first freezing step of the Timoshka study house.

Just before they drove off Beria opened a side vent, stuck out his head, and called out, "Luck, much luck and success in tomorrow's lecture, laddy dear."

How long Pavel Gavrych sat, whether he fainted or simply slept very deeply he scarcely knew. But when he opened his eyes in the expectation of utter darkness he saw the pale blue streaming of first daylight. And then, becoming more clearly aware of pain, he moved the thumb a little, and the sound of the bone rasping in its socket was nearly as frightful to hear as to feel.

He would remember walking fast, running and sobbing and glimpsing through his tear-blinded eyes men and women whose faces were docile, placid and neutral as water.

He would remember that when he halted some of these people and showed them his broken thumb and tried telling how he had come by it, they looked at him as if to say, "Why, this is why you are a Russian, this is what comes of being on Russian earth."

He would remember feeling numb and nauseous and having to concentrate on each step.

He would remember murky redness devouring the daylight and the start of snow.

He would remember that when he was two versts away from his housing complex he came upon some snow sweepers, that among them was a dwarfish crook-backed old woman.

He would remember that she was grumbling because someone was teasing her by sweeping snow into her boots.

He would remember that she shook her broom at the sky and gave thanks to God for leaving her strength enough to do her work, and do it well enough to incur the spite and envy of others.

He would remember that as he drew near she had swept a path for him, and so quickly and wonderfully well that he impulsively kissed her.

He would remember that she smiled, and lifted her broom like a scepter and said, "Whatever work thy hand findeth to do, do it with thy might."

And many years later, when Pavel Gavrych was ready to change and confuse things in Russia, he began with those words.

ONE

At 5:53 A.M. on that unseasonably mild November morning when he was to have his first knowledge of Pavel Gavrych, the President awakened powerfully heartsick. So when Eunice, looking serene and humble and filled with adoration, sang, " 'Love is everywhere, its music fills the air,' " he set his teeth against her and did not sing back. He lay silent, supine, pursuing an intuition, a feeling that he must catch and hold a line of thought before it slipped to the back of his mind.

The morning mist imprinted itself on the windows of the Edith Wilson Room like the marks of a claw.

The spikes of the rising sun struck the triple mirrors above Eunice's makeup table and empurpled them.

A twitch in the President's eyes spread to his cheeks and to the right side of his mouth. He took a breath, expelled it harshly, and tried as hard as he could to connect himself to the chain of being, calling in despair upon Father, Mother, and Nanny Dora. But when he could not quite bring forth his feelings to them, he cried out silently to JFK.

"Jack," he began, "I had, I think I had a nasty dream . . ."

In his fake light-hearted Irish lilt JFK answered, "Whist, laddy-boy, 'tis all in your mind."

"I feel as if I'm not connected to the chain of being or the human condition . . . as if, by Jesus, everything had been made for the MBAs, as if they have charge of the human condition."

Then as Eunice tapped her teeth with a thumb a fragment of his dream returned to the President.

Cassette, there was a cassette.

Which he'd been obliged to kneel before and kiss.

A cassette no bigger than the breadth of his nail.

"And yet," he told Jack, "it contained all the world's knowledge. Dying to turn it on, but I knew better. A premonition that I'd bring about some terrible misfortune. An economic catastrophe. Hands off or . . . or, by Jesus, this country would go back and back to guilds and vassals and workshops."

"Boy-o," said JFK, "pious platitudes will soon be the only major American industry. Sure, now, and haven't we cornered the market on cant and rant? While our smokestacks vanish we'll be telling people, 'Your vote counts . . .' "

Eunice scratched at the sheet and made a soft *oooh* sound and then her louder morning sound of warmth and comfort and mild hunger.

But the President flashed her an awful look.

For he was just then asking JFK if he was truly a good man.

"Far better than most," Jack answered kindly. In a subdued and downcast voice he added, "And perhaps a wee too good to be president."

"Because in my dream the name of that cassette was Hunaru. And when I saw it I went wild. Aflame with rage. Wanted to blow them to hell. If I'm a good man, even a reasonably decent and moral man— by Jesus, Jack, I had them set for extermination. Them, them! The Japanese, the Koreans, the whole Pacific Basin. Couldn't bear it, killing me. In the dream I kept saying, 'I can't bear it that in no time, in eyeblink time history has gifted brown barbarians with the power and glory, the lovely servility and stupidity and work ethic of two long, hard American centuries.' "

"Oh laddy, laddy," answered Jack, "and what was it I'd be telling you away on back when we made the sorrowful talk of young senators? Do you not recall how oft I'd tell you that the economic realm is the devil's realm?"

Gazing steadfastly at him, Eunice sang, " 'Ever Thy name, Ever Thy glory.' "

By night I wipe out an easy fifth of mankind, the President thought, and by first light I'm preparing myself to put aside principle, to be altogether at home in an office, maybe a world, that smells of greed and hypocrisy. Still, still—now somehow there's always that 'still'—her old down-home hymns do me good, sweeten my spirit.

And so the President sang back, " 'Ever this soul riseth to Thee.' "

Shadows fell across the needlepoint stool, the Leporello spinet, the fruitwood breakfront, the Grand Banks fire screen.

There were footfalls in the corridor and the clink and clash of cutlery from the downstairs kitchen.

"Let me tell you, Eunice"—the President brought a fist down heavily on the mattress—"the economic realm is the devil's realm."

She stroked his fist over and over, waited, then nodded vigorously and breathed out a yes. Finger by finger she unlocked his fist and when she had slid her palm under his palm she went on to say, "Why, that is ever so well put."

"Foundering . . ."

The President gazed at Eunice and Eunice gazed back, her eyes bright and fixed in profound attentiveness.

The President moved and said, next to Eunice's ear, "Foundering on economics and economic necessity. And you know I did my reading. I kept up—by Jesus, I tried to keep up."

"Oh, you did. Goodness, you most surely did."

"Schumpeter, Keynes, Hobson. The Swedes on how to handle poverty. Poverty, Eunice! The urban poor, the factory poor, the rural poor. Tawney or somebody called them 'the laboring cattle,' and that phrase, that image, wore me down and the guilt near killed me. During the campaign—no, I never told you this, Eunice—midway, during the northeastern swing, I seriously considered giving my money away." He stretched his neck up on the pillows. "Couldn't, Eunice. Couldn't, couldn't. Not in three lifetimes."

Softly and a shade shyly Eunice murmured, "I do rightly believe I remember that northeast swing and your . . ." A moment passed. ". . . most worrisome behavior." Another moment. "A three-week interval of non- . . . of abstinence. One-sided abstinence."

The President stared hard at her. Must you? he silently demanded. Please don't follow this line, this biologic-erotic line which I can't, I never could handle.

She seemed to understand at once, for her throat flushed. Then she clapped her hands soundlessly and in a high, plaintive, interrogative way said, "Economics?" Her color receded. "*And* the poor *and* 'laboring cattle' *and* Tawney, Tawney was the last name you mentioned. Test me if you like. Followed everything, every last little word."

"Shhh," said the President, writing in the air. "Don't mix me up now."

"Test me," whispered Eunice. "Poverty, go on." Then she stayed silent.

"Must you do that? Did you have to, have to? Yes, you had to," the President grumbled. "Just when I have a point you . . . ah, by Jesus."

Then it seemed to the President that his mind was speeding, storming, that the thread of a thought, a bitter but essential thought, was stretched dangerously tight within him.

He struck his breastbone and pressed and pressed himself for this thought till at last a figure was inscribed onto his mind, and the figure was 5.9.

He put a quick hand to Eunice's shoulder, cried, "Five-point-nine. Don't let me forget it."

In a conspiratorial voice Eunice answered, "Five-point-nine, and I most surely won't."

On the farthest wall the glass over a photo of the old *Mauretania* flamed.

The sound of birds pecking, drilling at the ventilator resonated.

"The MBAs and the CEOs"—the President's eyes grew fluid—"if I could . . . straight down to hell, the farthest pit."

He became aware that he was biting a knuckle, and he wondered, Since when have I picked up Harry's habit?

"A bullet into every last ear."

"Five-point-nine," Eunice ventured in a low voice. "Only reminding you."

And something occurred to the President, something that pierced him with pleasure. Yes, high time I took Harry by surprise, he told himself. For once, only once. By Jesus, why not? Give him a taste of my annihilating emptiness. My turn. Surely my turn. I'll make it the first order of business this morning. Coolly, quite coolly, before he can pull me along in the wake of his news I'll say, "A small favor, Harry. Oblige me." I'll say, "Instruct your people to send upper American management straight down to hell, the farthest pit." And before he can top me, before he answers . . . oh, he'd answer, "Indeed, sir. And why not the entire corporate community?" I'd turn him aside with talk of Nell. I'll say, "Those rumors, Harry. On the tongue of every wife in this administration. Is Nell in hospital?"

Eunice fumbled for his hand, missed, found it, gripped hard.

"A bullet into every last ear," he repeated.

"Five-point-nine," Eunice repeated.

And the President picked up, saying, "The point I want to make, Eunice, is that economics . . . economics cuts you off from God."

"That is ever so well put."

"Now the figure, the statistic, five-point-nine, stands for this month's unemployment rate, and"—the President stopped his breath for an instant—"and it's nearly three tenths of a point, a percentage point higher than last month."

Eunice looked toward him, apprehensively polite. She nodded and seemed about to speak. The President pressed her hand for silence and said, "Every tenth of a point, Eunice, stands for close to one hundred thousand workers. So, therefore this month we've got three hundred thousand more workers unemployed than we had last month. Workers?" He gave a wild, panting laugh. "Did I say 'workers'? Oh my, oh no! Ought to have said 'laboring force,' Eunice. That's the term out of the Wharton School of Business straight . . . straight to the mouths of the MBAs and CEOs. Properly cold, properly clean and bland."

"New names for everything," said Eunice.

"Crazy. Beyond—by Jesus, absolutely beyond my power to understand. Because, you see—follow me on this, Eunice, only follow along—see, it's outdated, no longer relevant to feel sorry for those three hundred thousand unemployed."

"New feelings for everything," said Eunice.

"I'm required to serve a higher good. Did I say higher? No, Eunice, the highest, the highest, and it's called 'economic necessity.' What's more . . ."

Eunice had a finger on his forehead and she was gently tracing a vein which had grown full and hard. Then she looked at him gravely, earnestly, and she murmured, "Well, but you're *my* highest good."

"Eunice. Ah, Eunice, Eunice, Eunice," declared the President, and he checked the impulse to say, "You do weave a different cloth of thought."

"Now continue. Where you left off was—and I loved it and I

followed along your every well-put point and phrase and your last words were 'What's more' and a second before that—"

"What's more," the President rushed in, "on the day those three hundred thousand poor bastards were officially added to the unemployment rolls . . . Up and up and up! On that day the market climbed, fifteen points I think, and though I had about as much to do with it as you did I made it big with the MBAs and the CEOs and the Wharton School of Business. Suddenly they were calling me clear-sighted and tough-minded."

He was deeply silent, and into this silence Eunice spoke. "Time they did, for that is most surely the truth."

"Is it?" the President said, as if the words had been shaken out of him, and he made a negative sign with his hands. "Do you, can you honestly believe I . . . I and my consultants and my advisors . . . ? Ah, Eunice, we can no more regulate this economy, we have less control over it than a minnow, a clam has over the movement of the seas. No answers, Eunice. How—by Jesus, how can we have answers if we're not even sure of the questions? Like . . . We're like General Allenby on the western front. 'No plans,' he told his staff. 'We shall improvise.' "

"You'll do just fine," said Eunice, her eyes shining. "You're a gifted improviser."

The sun moved slowly from the windows and settled high and straight along the burnished arms of the Spanish grained-oak rocker.

In the downstairs kitchen water ran and drawers were opened and a timer buzzed loudly and several voices joined in the hushing.

By some trick of light the Leporello spinet seemed to have moved closer, but the photo of the old *Mauretania* looked a little farther away.

From the corridor there was the shuffle and hiss of shoes.

Motes of dust floated slowly around the topmost shelf of a glass-faced cabinet and gave the porcelain figurines of shepherdesses a silvered aspect.

A vacuum cleaner started.

The whir of cooking appliances seemed close and hard.

Floorboards creaked in the corridor, the shuffle and hiss of shoes advanced, stopped, and there was a restrained rapping on each of the double doors. After a moment, like the first notes of a spiritual, came the fine basso drone of George, the pantry master.

"Newspapers waitin' on you and breakfast be in fifteen minutes, Mr. President."

"Well?" answered the President in utter coldness.

God forgive me, he thought, because I know he's standing there and waiting on my morning pleasantry. But what am I to do if I can't bear his colored-folk diction? His loyal houseboy way of chuckling and rubbing at an invisible rabbit's foot?

He heard George clear his throat, clear it again.

He thought: urban poor, rural poor, three hundred thousand, laboring cattle.

And for their sakes and for the sake of human relations he made his morning pleasantry.

"Well, by Jesus, George, is it morning already?"

Then Eunice, as usual, sang, " 'Blue skies, smiling at me.' "

And the President, as usual, sang back, " 'Nothing but blue skies do I see.' "

For it was 6:25 A.M. and time to admit the day.

Light-headed but dim, aflame with thought but also without spirit, without heart, the President shucked off his pajama top, tensed and relaxed, tensed and relaxed his body, extended his arms straight up so that he would have no purchase and leaped lightly from the right side of the bed onto the exact middle of his exercise pad.

While he took his thirty deep breaths he prayed, as usual, "Ancient of Days, Sir, Thou who has seen fit to immerse me in the crazy clutter of this century, these present times—ah, help me handle it."

And while he jogged in place he considered this century, these present times, and he addressed himself, as usual, to the task of sorting out crazy clutter.

And while he did his push-ups he whispered aloud as usual, covering some of the matters that astonished or bewildered him. With the expulsion of every third breath he whispered, "Market forces" . . . "Capital" . . . "Processes and products" . . . "OPEC" . . . "Toxic waste" . . . "Conflict of interest," and the words imparted a kind of design upon the day.

His pores opened.

He felt . . . steadfast.

He felt . . . valorous.

So when Eunice preceded him to the bathroom and stopped and stuck out her tongue at what she beheld in her makeup mirrors he very nearly said, "Don't. No need. Why, by Jesus, even in the morning light your color is healthy perfection. Never saw you make an ungraceful movement. And I'm pretty damn well satisfied with your parts, quite delighted in fact."

But all the same one current of his mind was running on into another channel.

All the same he felt unpleasant intuitions.

And though he responded amiably to Eunice's chatter, he was wondering what he might expect later from Harry.

For he had sensed some obscure trouble behind Harry's clear, cold voice.

"Odd, unlikely events, Mr. President."

Eunice was at my side and jiggling my elbow and mouthing, "Nell, ask . . ."

"Russia, sir."

But I was half asleep and there was a problem with the scrambler and before I could get the words out Harry rang off.

"Odd, unlikely events, Mr. President."

And I'll be most likely carried along in their wake.

Or in Harry's wake.

They took breakfast in the C-shaped alcove on the pale beech table Father had given him for his World War I trench warfare maps.

After they'd had their fresh fruit cup and their fiber and their Thursday boiled egg, the President allowed himself a second cup of Kona coffee, and when Eunice looked questioningly at him he said, before he could stop himself, "Today I want to be especially awake, wakeful."

She blew a kiss and said, "No worrying now. You're having a blue dew-honey apple kind of day, I know you shall."

Then they took up their newspapers and for perhaps three minutes they talked less and less and for a very little while not at all.

Eunice had *The Washington Post* and she was sighing and clucking her tongue.

He had *The New York Times* and he worked his way toward the editorial pages as though toward quicksand.

He read Anthony Lewis, who wanted to know where the unorthodox voices were and when they would be heard and who would anyway listen.

He read Tom Wicker, who speculated that modern American history might well be a tale of failed journeys to the wrong places.

"Moral," he murmured, putting a forefinger on "moral indignation," then "moral imperative," then "moral order." "By Jesus, how would they manage, where would they be without that word?"

Eunice leaned forward, tightened her lips. When the President met her eyes she looked away, stared incredulously out the bay windows, shook her paper and cried, "Only one little second . . . May I, may I? That Chevy Chase murder. He confessed the whole thundering thing."

The President nodded curtly and rapidly.

"I knew. Oh, I most surely knew. His jawline. They always have these jawlines, they . . . That's all." She touched her shoe to his shoe. "No more. That's all."

She seemed elated and the President pretended not to notice that when she turned the page she started rocking and her elation faded.

For he had spotted his name near the foot of Flora Lewis's column, and he was puzzling away at the lines, "between the thrust of global realities and American politics falls the shadow of his Middle East policy."

Then Eunice pulled down his arm and held it down.

"I am ever so pissfire angry." She flung away his arm, fell back breathless. "So *furious!*"

The President waited.

Eunice gazed long and steadfastly at him. "She *is* sick. Most surely."

The President nerved himself to say, "Nell?"

"Every blessed one in the group sensed and felt and talked and worried over Nell looking like she was near being lifted onto a cross. See, women turn a little mean about another woman's internal physical frailties. Close to gloating. Not exactly that. Maybe not *gloating*. Maybe more, 'Your turn now, my turn next.' "

The President waited patiently, tiredly.

"Oh, but not a blessed word from dear Harry, precious Harry. No sharing, no confiding, no syllable out of place or a sign to caring friends."

All but pleading, the President said, "Enough. Isn't that enough?"

Then Eunice motioned toward the floor, where the paper was. "The tiniest little item," she told him in an embittered voice, "way down in the comings and goings section. That Mrs. Nell Porlock, wife of Harry Porlock, one of the President's intelligence advisors, has been moved from Cedars of Lebanon to Bethesda Naval Hospital."

"Well . . ." the President said, and he put his hands on the back of his chair. "Did they say—" he began, ending only with, "No, they wouldn't, they never do."

And Eunice said, "The wing?"

And he said almost simultaneously, "Which pavilion?"

He decided to allow himself another half cup of the Kona coffee, and this time Eunice looked at him as if into an image of still water. Before she could look away he said, "No need to think the worst. Doesn't have to be *that* pavilion."

"Surely not," she answered.

And she reached so suddenly at his cheeks that by reflex he flung back his head. She smiled away his whispered "Sorry," waited till he had swallowed the last of the coffee, then said, "Am I awful? Am I as mean in spirit as all the other Washington wives? Talking the nastiest way about Harry . . ."

He set down his cup. With a special ringing schoolboy certainty, he said, "Harry's a compulsive repressive, Eunice. By training and profession, of course. But also . . . Also by birth and breeding which tells you, never stops telling you, that strength is in silence, in restraint of feeling. And he knows it, admits it. Remember what he once called himself? By Jesus, you laughed and laughed. Remember? 'A state-of-the-art Wasp.' "

"Only man in your cabinet who can make me laugh. And I do rightly believe now . . ." She rested her face sideways on her wrists, raised it, pondered. "See now, I do suppose I'm simply a woman who's thundering jealous of her husband's best friend."

"Best friend," the President repeated. And a sense of well-being reached suddenly at his heart and he said with manly humility, "Yes, he is my best friend. Because he is that, only because he is, Eunice, and only because Harry knows better than any man alive the burdens I carry, he's held back about Nell."

Eunice bent so far forward that the President had to blow a strand of her hair away. "That was ever so well put," she said, "and you make me mortally ashamed of my mean spirit and my wifely jealousy."

Presently he pushed away from the table, rose, extended his wrist at Eunice and tapped his watch as usual. "Five of seven," he said.

Then he added, as usual, "Time. Time to assume the seamless cloak of authority."

And Eunice answered, as usual, "Bet you'd look so very nice in a cloak."

All the way to the double doors they held hands, and the last thing he said to JFK that morning was, "Can't push her too hard or delve too deep, but I'm pretty well satisfied, Jack, I wouldn't want her otherwise."

In the subground level of the West Wing, between the Communication Center and the Situation Room, was the study the President had designed and furnished in the style of the private railway car that had shuttled Marshal Foch to the Vermelles sector during those terrible times in 1915. It was long and tubular, with fluted columns on each side and dark wine Aubusson carpets underfoot. On the vaulted ceiling angels and devils were engraved, and also knights heaving and striving against one another and bowmen unloosing arrows into the flanks of horses.

"Drapes open, sir," said the blond agent with the rimless sunglasses.

"More light, Mr. President?" said the balding agent with the tortoiseshell glasses.

"Those, just those," murmured the President, indicating the stained glass coach lamps Father had given him when he recovered from that chest thing.

Then he said, "Thank you, boys," and on the balls of their feet they left the room, closing the ebony and gold door so slowly and quietly that he could scarcely hear it.

For a little while the President paced about, looking only straight ahead in the half light at the glassed case of rifle-grenades and gas helmets and trenching tools.

But suddenly there was an orange glimmer over Nanny Dora's tea service.

A long shadow broke across Mother's wicker flower basket.

And Harry Porlock entered, saying, "Marshal Foch, poor man, was once seen spitting at a crucifix in his railway car."

The President answered, "Well, by Jesus, Harry, he too lived in dark times."

He opened the drapes all the way, started to raise the scalloped Honteaux shades. But the worn old silk curled, snagged on the rollers, and when Harry sped over to help and they stood shoulder to shoulder the President sneaked a close look at his long bald face. Yes, the truth about Nell is confessed there—oh, there, in a certain darkness under his eyes, and there in a tension, a clenching about the cheekbones.

"Was it Foch?" Harry was smoothing the shade down on his side. "Wouldn't let his generals talk of casualties."

Suddenly the President caught something else amiss.

A piece of button over Harry's monogrammed shirt pocket was gone. Chipped.

Well then, well then, how long must Nell have been sick? And in what awful pain?

"Foch or Joffre," said Harry.

Almost certainly long sick, almost certainly in awful pain. For Nell would never tolerate that bit of missing button. "Before Harry goes off," I heard her say many times, many times, "I make him stand inspection. Walk round him three times clockwise, three times counterclockwise."

"More likely Joffre," said Harry.

And they went to the spindly-legged Directoire table to start that morning's business.

I'll never get used to satellite photos, the President thought. To their clarity, their appalling, invincible clarity.

"What fooled the sensors was the accumulated body heat," Harry said.

"I can see how, yes."

"Nearly as many bodies massed there as in a standard Russian combat corps."

"But these are children. Only children, Harry."

"Nevertheless . . . odd, sir."

"Nevertheless . . . unlikely," said the President.

Locking his breath like a diver, then expelling the exhausted air in the heavy, ardent way he would expel it when he had that chest thing, the President gazed down at the children.

They were in immense lines.

Though the photos had been shot at different times of the day and in different weathers, they were always in immense lines.

Though some shots showed men on horses bumping against them and men on motorcycles riding dangerously close and men on foot chivvying them with long sticks or poles, the children appeared uniformly tranquil and in possession of themselves.

Though in some photos it was deepest night and in others murky sunshine, many of the children, the youngest as well as the eldest, had both hands raised at the sky and seemed to be pointing out, one to the other, things about the sky.

"This"—the President raised both his hands in the same way— "Why are they . . . ?"

"They see, or believe they will soon see, a special light."

The President said, "Ah," as if this were perfectly natural.

"A 'light of many colors' the Russians call it."

And what light—there was a clutch at the President's heart—ah, what light, he reflected, do America's children look for?

"A piece of superstition," Porlock said softly.

"Superstition," the President said, just as softly.

"Since the fourteenth century, Russians have believed that this light, mysterious and majestic, announces, oh, 'better things to come' might be the translation, or perhaps 'the arrival of happier times.' "

Porlock bit a knuckle.

"Happier times, at any rate, for the Russians."

He lowered his hand, rested it momentarily against his monogrammed shirt pocket, rubbed and rubbed at the chipped button. His vivid, explicit blue eyes diminished, darkened. Twice he started to speak and twice his voice took flight. The President leaned toward him in perplexity and appeal and stifled sorrow and mouthed, "Harry . . . ?" But then, seeming to will himself into a state of energy and lucidity, Porlock recovered his balance.

He gave the President a prolonged look and said, "There's a song Russian children are lately singing. How the new light of the sky keeps them filled with heroism and high purpose, with peace, sympathy, brotherhood, and purest joy."

Might catch on here, the President mused as a hard stroke of despair went through him. Yes, oh yes. Perhaps when our last piece of infrastructure is rusted out and . . . and America's children have marched off to kick the last grandmother to death.

Then Porlock pointed with a rigid finger at the photos.

"These are the children of Kharkov, and they were the first to sing it. Heard next in Moscow, Leningrad, Kiev, Smolensk." He gave way to a short, harsh laugh. "Each time a library was closed."

The President's brows went up. He foundered and faltered out, "Come on, come now, Harry. *Each* time . . . ?"

"Each time, sir," Porlock said, describing a spiral with his fingers. "In Moscow. In Leningrad. In Kiev. In Smolensk."

"By Jesus, peace!" The President scowled with distaste and anger. "And sympathy and, what, purest joy. Then I suppose bang and smash, wreck and ruin. What goes on nowadays? Because I hate to picture that happening to libraries. Even Russian libraries." He glanced at an angel in the vaulted ceiling, then at Nanny Dora's tea service and Mother's wicker flower basket. "But I suppose nowadays wreck and ruin is the universal language of children."

Porlock watched him.

The President momentarily closed his eyes. " 'Hooliganism,' isn't that what the Russians call it? Ah, the word's not good enough, not nearly good enough."

"Indeed not, sir, not nearly enough." Porlock continued to watch him. "However"—he stopped his breath for an instant—"there was no hooliganism. Or about as much as babes might commit in their nurseries."

To himself the President said, "I'm glad of that. Even if something's about to come down on me, at this moment I'm glad." On the verge of blurting it out he checked himself, thinking, All right, so you have soft feelings, a heart in your breast. And what has that to do with statecraft? No—management! For I'm more manager than president.

Then in an implacable, remote voice Porlock spoke out.

"In each library they caused to be closed—in Kharkov and Moscow and Leningrad and Kiev and Smolensk—the children would maintain a silence so prodigious that one could hear the pneumatic hiss of the doors opening and closing as they were admitted. No matter if the district managers had ordered the thermostats turned down and they exhaled vapor—they were happy and hopeful, they were rising to a higher plane and earning their way to a glorious reward."

His eyes lost focus for a moment. The President saw him slide his fingers up his shirt, toward that chipped button. But he caught himself in time and holding his body rigid, went on.

"The girls curtsied, the boys bowed when they whispered their requests to the librarians. 'A magazine, sir, a book, madam, to help with my theme.' "

"By Jesus, I can just imagine the themes, the anti-Soviet themes." The President could not help laughing. "If they had to close the libraries . . ."

Porlock bent forward and, smiling a little, said, "I'm afraid that in all Soviet history you would not find themes that better served the state. Absolutely sound, sir, in outlook and ideology. Such 'people's hero' subjects as 'the collectivization of agriculture'; 'literacy in the Uzbek Republic'; 'Stakhonovism, its glorious beginnings'; and my own favorite, 'toward a new definition of democratic centralism.' "

The President blinked blindly several times. "Well, then, they were using the libraries lawfully. And if they were, I fail to see, I absolutely fail to see, Harry."

"Nor did I. But as I came to understand from"—Porlock seemed to be considering something—"at the moment I'd best call him a colleague . . ."

And Porlock very suddenly stamped his feet, made a furious fist, and in a voice which was altogether unnatural to him, a coarse, overbearing voice which resonated like a drumhead, said, "How can an American understand?"

He rolled his eyes, he flailed his arms.

"May their eyeballs bleed and the glue drip from their guts. Our Soviet sons and daughters, our immortality, our hope, our future did not come to use the libraries but to overuse them . . . to milk and bleed them and suck them dry of books. Do you wish to find a book? Easier to find a smile on a Muscovite face."

He humped his back, he let his underlip droop.

"And everything lawful. Oh, scrupulously lawful. As if every child had mastered Daghestan's *Elements of Soviet Jurisprudence*."

He pulled his ears.

"But somebody did master old man Daghestan. The five volumes, double columns on each page. And mastered it and simplified it and wrote it out so clearly, so seductively that it would enchant the youngest and the dullest."

He pulled his cheeks taut.

"And they would not leave, the goat dugs, the afterbirths. Though hosed with water cannon. Though forced to remove gloves and shoes. Though allowed no food, no comfort stations, they kept their lines. In stinking zero weather they kept their lines."

"In zero weather," the President involuntarily repeated. He shrugged, submissively, thinking, Yes, I have that . . . that oppression I'd get before my chest thing. Oh, yes, something's about to come down on me.

Then Porlock was speaking in his own voice.

While the President had another long look at the photos, at the extraordinary expressions on the children's faces—defiance? arrogance? intractable certainty?—Porlock said in his clear, cold way, "Somebody's brought their hearts to a boil."

"Touching in a way. You can see their expectations, Harry, their . . . stupendous expectations here." The President tapped the photos, sighed deeply, and raised his face.

"Stupendous?" Porlock put a hand to his lacking scalp, nodded as if to say, "The word will do." For a short space the two looked at each other, then Porlock said, "And somebody, sir, has taught them a stupendous truth. Taught them, as I came to understand from my colleague, that a government is most endangered when its laws are absolutely obeyed."

"Well, we're in no danger here," said the President. But his tone was not as scoffing as he had intended.

"Lord have mercy upon such a government."

"Oh, and those who serve it. Those who"—the President's voice wavered as he quoted JFK—"who must render unto Little Caesar that which is Little Caesar's."

Then a stir of uneasiness passed over him.

"There's one thing, Harry." He drew up his brows. "Their purpose, the purpose of the children. What is it they wanted?"

"The very question I asked . . . my colleague. He told me, as I remember"—and Porlock was once again speaking in that coarse, unnatural voice—"Dear old friend, it did occur to us to inquire. In Kharkov, also in Poltava and Belgorod and Novorossiisk. In each city, from each line we chose ten children. 'What do you want? You will tell us what you want, what you want.' The oldest and the youngest would bow and curtsy, bow and curtsy, and answer—always they answered, 'Russia.' "

In a near whisper the President said, "Is that all?" He tried to pass his next words off as a joke. "No more, no less. Russia."

Porlock was silent.

Then, a little vexed, the President murmured, "No need, we've still plenty of time." For Porlock, to his surprise, was looking at his wristwatch.

Clasping and unclasping his hands, Porlock said softly, " 'I have no precious time at all to spend, nor service to do, till you require.' "

And the President fell into considerations of the children, the Russian children, and soon he was moving one finger around in a circle and he was locking in on a thought.

He said, "Now if they wanted nothing more or less than Russia, if that was always their answer—wouldn't that be enough . . . ?"

"Indeed. Good thinking, sir."

Porlock's wristwatch clicked, belled; he touched the stem and silenced it.

"Should have been more than enough," the President said. " 'Russia.' Sure, with that answer the authorities had them, and absolutely. No, not for hooliganism but for—"

"Obstructionism," Porlock finished.

He rose, went to the window, squinted out, and said abstractedly, "There's your new kitchen man taking delivery from Teasdale's. Powerful chap, oh my. Hoists a case of baking potatoes in each hand."

Then he took a few short steps before the window, gave a little push at the drapes, at the Honteaux shades, turned, murmured, "Obstructionism," and sat down. Eyes fixed and large, mouth sunk at the corners, he examined the President at length.

The President, his gaze hard, unmoving, cried, "By Jesus, Harry!" He was going to say, "A new kitchen man! Fascinating, duly noted! Now, may we move along?" or some such rough thing. But he stopped and took into account another source for Porlock's distraction. And so he sent him a silent message: "Is your mind on Nell? Are you ashamed to show that you too have soft feelings, a heart in your breast? Let loose! Share! Give out! Speak up, speak up! Did I ever restrain myself with you . . . ?"

But Porlock, with utmost reserve and deliberateness, only said,

"Obstructionism, indeed, sir. One of my colleague's most favored charges. He gave me to understand, in fact, that under ordinary circumstances he would have used it as a pretext to lock up a few hundred wolf cubs from each city. Putting them in those special cells he calls 'Turkish heaven.' A few days, perhaps two weeks on bare springs under the dazzle of naked bulbs would have finished those infernal library lines which he had started to see in his dreams; in one dream they were stretched across the centuries to antiquity."

He turned a glance to the door. Once again his look was distracted and once again the President kept silent, thinking, "He's anticipating a message, a summons, some news of Nell."

Then Porlock continued more surely, "Unfortunately, my colleague confronted a rather unforeseen circumstance."

"Ah," said the President, stretching out the sound. Though he did not stir an inch he felt a prodding in every particle of his being.

"No room for children in Turkish heaven, sir. Or any other cells. Somebody, you see, had managed to get them filled."

"Ah," said the President. In weariness and rage he thought, Well, then, let it come down. Let it, let it!

Then the door opened. The balding agent with the tortoiseshell glasses put his head in.

He said, "Your snacks, sir."

And the blond agent with the rimless sunglasses also put his head in, and he said, "A basket of buns, a pot of coffee, Mr. President."

"Hope they'll do," Porlock told him quickly, lightly. "I took the liberty . . ."

With a pleasant light in his eye, he added, "My thought was . . . oh, that another cup, a fourth cup of the Kona coffee you favor might be in order."

"Well, why not!" exclaimed the President. "Libraries closed, jails—what?—filled."

Then he shook his head.

"A fourth cup of my Kona?"

He uttered a bark of laughter.

"How the blazes did you know I had three—three this morning?"

Porlock's eyes contained all the comment that was necessary. They seemed to say, "Why, sir, because I know how your mind works."

Intent on this, the President did not immediately notice that a man had come into the study, moved aside the photos, and set down a tray. It was only when the man, with a cadence and intonation he could not place, said, "Why so many colored in his kitchen, Harry?" that he shot up and turned to look.

A Neanderthal head.

A bearish belly.

In his mouth steel fillings.

And Porlock, pouring a precise half cup of coffee for the President, introduced him.

"My colleague, sir. Colonel Arkady Stepanchov, KGB Central, Moscow."

"A hard day I had in your kitchen. Too hard for aging apparatchiks. The good cheer of your colored, in particular a certain George, has crippled my health."

Stepanchov, massively crowding the table, lifted his shoulders as if to ease his breathing.

"To be sure, your Harry promised a safe house. And what house is safer than the White House? So I forgive him his irony. Little friend, everything is forgiven. In my present state I also overlook how you shorted me on our prisoner exchange in Norway. Two more gays I shall want next time, if there is a next time."

Breathing in a massive rhythm that involved his whole body, he smiled at the President.

"Sir, a poor joke. From established habit I contend—always I must contend against your Harry's irony."

He wound his arms around the back of his chair.

"This winter more irony than grain in Russia. They go about saying—but how can an American understand?—that Aleksandr Kerenski has been heard from and he demands a recount."

Then the gaze of his Eskimo eyes turned inward.

He swung his hands loosely and spread his fingers out in a gesture which the President read as concession, resignation, surrender. And all at once Stepanchov became to him a little less the rudimentary peasant, a little less the blunt-browed fear maker.

"Take assurance, Mr. President, that I do not come to . . . turn. Sell out. More or less, I am content in my function. The function of an aging apparatchik. Ideologies, talk of means and ends, bore me. What use is talk of means and ends to us, Harry?"

"Indeed, none," said Porlock. "None whatsoever. After all, Arkady, nowadays there are only means."

"How our mutual friend would appreciate you!" roared Stepanchov. "He too is a lover of books. Likewise irony. Imagine the contest! Oh, he'd match you book for book, irony for irony."

"This mutual friend. Now, by Jesus," the President flung out, "is he the one . . . those filled jails. And does he have anything to do with the children, with . . ." He hunted for the phrase. "Their hearts, did he bring their hearts to a boil?"

But Stepanchov declined to answer directly. "Though I am pregnant with news, Mr. President"—his large head twitched—"I must deliver it my own way. From established habit, as an old apparatchik."

And with a drop in his voice, in a drab, measured, stolid tone that sounded to the President as if he were reading out a charge, he said, "Some fifty-five hours past I emplaned from KGB Central, Moscow, to Perekop for ostensible purpose of consultation at our Psychic Research Center about recent behavior patterns among children and other citizen classes. An aide, one of many currently more loyal to me than to our government, arranged a navigational error that brought me to Finland. Contact was there made with Harry Porlock, who ordered my immediate fly-out without knowledge of your rulers or your media. I arrived some thirty hours ago and in Langley fulfilled my true purpose. This was direct delivery into the hands of Harry Porlock a taped interview with a certain master printer in Sverdlovsk, one Boris Valentin. In his Langley laboratories, admittedly superior to ours, he could perform voice stress tests and such, satisfy himself."

"Boris Valentin is normal," Porlock murmured. "Resolutely normal. Someone, as you Russians say, 'at home in his soul.' "

"Should my purpose be considered traitorous? Who knows anymore?" Stepanchov distended his bearish belly, rubbed his eyelids. "If considered upon return traitorous"—he was playing to the President—"I will claim sufficient punishment from those two shifts in your kitchen among your coloreds."

Then he boosted himself up from his chair and went about the study.

He paused before the glassed case of rifle-grenades and gas helmets and trenching tools.

At length he said, "Though I am without absolute confidence in the understanding of an American, these Great War articles must count for something. I think they count for something, yes."

Whispering hoarsely, he shambled over to the President and kissed his cheeks.

He took his seat, turned his head toward him like a tank turret, and sighted along his forefinger.

"Before speaking of Boris Valentin, master printer in the city of Sverdlovsk, I have a personal curiosity to ascertain if you have knowledge of that city's name from former times. From"—he swung the forefinger at the glassed case—"those times."

"Ekaterinburg," said the President, remembering to put a "Y" before the first syllable and to bite down hard on it.

"So. That too must count for something, yes."

Stepanchov showed his small stub teeth, his steel fillings. He tucked his chin down.

"Then as to Boris Valentin the following must be related, Mr. President. Therefore, there . . ."

He roused himself and speaking with the utmost deliberateness said, "Three weeks ago, on a Wednesday, Valentin entered the Fifth Auxiliary Police barracks of Sverdlovsk, southeast sector, precisely at midnight, proceeded to the sergeant's desk, kneeled, and banged his head against the floor. Upon rising, he reported a mysterious affliction which called for imprisonment. An affliction of thoughts. Anti-Soviet thoughts. Then he related how this morning, at six A.M., he had decided to walk where he had never walked—northeast, to the top of a hill where he saw, in his words, 'A sir, a swank, a majestic type whose face could've been on my old dad's rubles.' "

Though the President was listening with entranced solemnity, though he kept his face stiff, devoid of personal regard, he nevertheless felt a keen, sweet piercing of fraternity at the way he'd remembered that "Y" in Ekaterinburg.

"According to Valentin, the sir, the swank . . ."

Stepanchov shook himself, stretched and stretched till his joints popped. Then, holding out his arms to the President, he said, "No, no, fatigue will not make me inexact. I retain Valentin's words precisely. They were as follows. 'The sir, the swank, stood and frowned like I was a hundred years late. Fine posture. On the short side and handsome. Beautiful beard.' "

"All the kings of Europe wore such beards," the President whispered.

"Boris Valentin approaches. The sir, the swank, wants to know if this is indeed Sverdlovsk, once named Ekaterinburg. 'No other,' says Valentin. They talk of times past—of the Winter Palace and the czar especially. They talk of silly, stupid Nicholas. How he was vain, weak, wife-ridden. How he wanted only to be left in peace to swim with his officers and review his cavalry and wear his seventy uniforms."

"But history was waiting for him," the President whispered.

"Side by side they went through a bit of woodland, and the sir, the swank, stops to point. 'In that house,' says he, 'a merchant, Ipatiev, lived. In the basement of that house Nicholas and Alexandra and their children and their servants and their doctor and their spaniel, Jimmy, were shot.' "

"History was waiting for them," the President whispered.

"The sir, the swank, talks of a sickly son, of four girlishly vain father-loved daughters, of how poor Nickie's mind was more on them than on how to grind his heel into the neck of Russia. Streaming tears, he gestures at Valentin. 'Boris, is it not time to take pity?' There is wild wind, broken sunlight. 'Boris, will you not kiss the hand of poor Nickie, your Daddy's czar, Nicholas the Second?' A single branch breaks into flower before Valentin's eyes. He falls into a dead faint. Awakens confused, awakens changed. Voices banging away in his head. And the things they say! 'Boris, we've broken our eggs and made our omelettes, and though we're choking and strangling on them let Lenin's name live forever and ever.' "

"Lenin's supposed to have been personable and charming," the President said vaguely. Then in a louder voice he said, "Doesn't count for much, no. History . . . he couldn't fight history any more than the czar."

"They arrested Valentin, of course. Within the week three state psychiatrists sent down their diagnosis of sluggish schizophrenia. By which time"—Stepanchov laughed immoderately, stopped abruptly —"all the cells in Sverdlovsk and in twenty-nine other major cities were packed with those who had bedeviled the police with tales, word-for-word tales of an encounter with poor, vain, wife-ridden Nickie, czar of all the Russias."

He rose, walked twice around the table, so wearily that his feet seemed scarcely to leave the floor. Stopping at the glassed cabinet, he gave the President a prolonged look.

"Sir, can an American understand how there is in Russia such a one as makes omelettes without breaking eggs?"

And he breathed out the name, "Gavrych."

"The one who . . . brings hearts to a boil." The President made his face austere, judicious, assessing, and he said, "Gavrych, Gavrych," so that the name might be set in his head.

"This one, sir, finds a method to exhaust our leviathan. Impaled on his hook, his leviathan's hook, we are powerless in the way a state must not be powerless. No means to order or regulate. No means to foresee. Mercy upon the state which cannot foresee, which must fear a surfeit of iron on Thursday and a cold forge on Friday."

The President wrinkled his forehead, obliquely searched Stepanchov's face for signs of guilt, dissembling. At last he thrust out the flat of his hand and said, "Your Comrade Gavrych is a powerhouse, a kind of force, and he brings hearts to a boil. Granted. No argument there. Only you don't, you simply don't hook the likes of your state with—by Jesus, not with children and bare libraries and packed prisons and tales of the czar. No." He said the last word mildly, but with careful distinctness. Through his teeth he added, "And just why, what exactly can't your state foresee?"

"More a matter of setting limits, sir," said Porlock in a voice that was strange to the President. "Most dangerous when a state can't set limits. One might make an analogy to human cells and cancer."

"For an aging apparatchik talk of such bleak physical processes . . ."

Stepanchov gave a mock shudder, blew on his hands, chafed them.

Then, eyes lidded, bumping twice against the table, he went to the President, bent close on trembling legs, and cried, "To overdo is the Gavrych hook."

A moment passed, another.

"To shake out an explanation, to unloose my Stalinist temperament . . ."

And Stepanchov fell into his chair, breasting the table so heavily that a coffee spoon jumped from its saucer.

"Therefore—therefore, Mr. President, accept as fully as possible into your imagination the existence of a working class whose history . . . like oxen, it is a history of complete passivity. What is war and what is peace to them? In war, in peace, their destiny is to be used as a natural resource is used."

"Dark times," said the President. He saw that his hand had moved across the table toward Stepanchov's arm, and he abruptly raised it and made it into a fist. "We live in dark times."

"From their minds they have uprooted what is the most necessary and natural thing to a mind—the pathetic, the forlorn but most powerful assumption that one day will be somehow different from the next."

"Tedium," the President ventured.

"But tedium is their refuge from truth. The famous Russian quest for God," said Stepanchov, "has become a quest for tedium."

And the President thought, Why, I'm no novice to tedium. In tedium there is the truth of America. On my northeast swing, between Batavia and Buffalo, tedium was imprinted into my being. When I went among the crowds—God forgive me, but even plain and simple consciousness was beyond every last one of those tens of thousands. Blind—no, unseeing. Like bats in a cave, like stones. Boarded-up factories and boarded-up faces. Willed oblivion, willed ignorance. I had an unholy desire to test them, to see if I might rattle them by saying that the Indians had won. Instead I said, and with all my heart, all my heart, "Better that a rich man serve the interests of the poor than a poor man serve the interests of the rich."

Then he quelled his thoughts, his useless, insupportable thoughts.

He compelled his mind to take fresh hold on the here and now.

With a proud, strong presidential scowl he said, "The Gavrych hook, then. I'm trying to imagine . . . pressing my American imagination to understand. 'To overdo,' you said, 'is the Gavrych hook.' But merely to do, to stay on the earth has to tear all hell out of your populations as I see it, as you've certainly made me see it. Merely, by Jesus"—he was once again overcome by memories of those tens of thousands—"to go to bed, to wake, to keep the breath of life from hour to hour is enough, more than enough to ask of them. How then . . . ?"

His voice trailed off.

"What's left for them to overdo?"

Stepanchov answered serenely, "One thing only, Mr. President. Work!"

And he pantomimed digging, hammering.

"With the overdoing of work, Gavrych confounds authority. With his parody of Marxist-Leninist logic, Gavrych pushes everything to a madhouse extreme which wrecks the machinery of state. From ancient Bible nonsense he strikes a real spark, from milking and bleeding new meaning out of such words as"—he tugged Porlock's cuff—"if you please, Harry, his Bible words. Reading and retention of Bible words is alien to a Stalinist temperament."

" 'Whatever work thy hand findeth to do, do it with thy might.' " Porlock crossed his legs elegantly. "Pity the ancients didn't consider man's perverse eagerness to deal himself blows."

But there was turbulence inside the President's ears, and several kinds of intuition stole over him, and he realized that he was nodding and shading his eyes.

He sat upright. "Then for those who . . . who become en-Gavryched," he said, "it's everything in excess."

"Excess, excess!" said Stepanchov, lifting his voice almost to tenor. "A cascade, a torrent, a Niagara force of demented excess from every laborer in every miserable Russian hole and corner."

"Workhorses," the President whispered.

Cold certainty touched him like the hand of a ghost.

And he thought, Amen. So be it. It comes down. The harsh trying, the bitter cup of history, statecraft. Jack, how I long to be worthy! If they will let me, Jack, if they but let me. Buddy, boy-o, intercede that they may let me. For their reach is great. From the devil's domain, from the economic realm they lay fast hold on me. The CEOs and MBAs compass me round and I am full of trouble from them.

But meantime he pondered and reasoned away; meantime his mind took giant steps, quantum leaps; meantime he improvised thrilling new policies, foreign and domestic.

And Stepanchov was saying, "Excess of production will shut down a factory as easily as scarcity. Engines which do not stop consume oil, coal, electricity as a Ukrainian consumes curses. What data, what plans and systems can come from the corpses of computers? Under way, sir—oh, a stupendous human action is under way."

And Porlock, making a face of false dismay, said, "Yet another of Russia's stupendous human actions?"

Then, as if in afterthought, as if to pass it off, the President murmured, "One thing. I'm rather curious about one thing . . ."

Take care, he told himself. Smooth and easy and artful.

For he had no wish to show that he was worked up, that his heart was aroused, that he was in a state of enthusiasm.

Therefore he looked idly at the vaulted ceiling, locked in on a bloodied knight.

Casual and remote, transmitting no messages from his face, he said, "Your military now."

With a clouded glance, a practiced, lidded glance, Stepanchov answered freezingly, "Our Russian forces."

The President thought, I'll risk a pathetic joke.

He said, "Yes, your Russian forces," and went on to say, "if they're still yours." He considered smiling, but he did not have it in him to smile. "No excess from them? None . . . en-Gavryched?"

Stepanchov released a pent-up breath. "At this moment," he cried out thickly, "perhaps my last such moment, I am altogether Russian. I, Arkady Iosif Stepanchov, have longings to fill myself with bullets, you with disinformation. Therefore, therefore . . ."

He bowed his head for a moment. He brought his hands down hard on his thighs.

His mouth shut sternly. His lips twitched.

To Porlock he said, "At this moment I crave to shed tears. Patriotic tears, free and copious."

To the President he said loudly, but not quite shouting, "From border unto border both regular militia and reserves make outcries of 'peace, sympathy, brotherhood, and purest joy.' As to supply . . ."

The President thought, Ancient of Days, how I've lucked in! If it be Thy will I'll do battle for America's multitudes, for mankind!

". . . Send Russia your Great War articles, sir. For our spare parts will be gone before the New Year."

Then Stepanchov put his head on the table and shaded it with his hands.

He raised it an inch or two and said, "Sir, fatigue does not render me forgetful. There is one thing more."

He opened his mouth, got out the word "gift."

By the time the President had leaned close to listen, he was fast asleep.

After a few silent seconds the President said, "By Jesus, why not?"

And he poured himself a full cup of Kona coffee, and he drank it down cold.

While Stepanchov snored sonorously something seemed to shine in the President's mind, and he was connected to the chain of being, the human condition; and in a kind of intoxication he dedicated himself to the rural poor, the urban poor, the laboring cattle.

He felt an exultant laugh coming on.

He held it down to a smile and said, "Momentous, Harry, momentous."

"Indeed, sir." Porlock bit a knuckle. Then in his clear, chill way he asked, "But however will we manage in a world that might be safe, a world of rhyme and reason?"

"All the same, Harry . . ."

Stepanchov stirred.

". . . Momentous, Harry, momentous."

Porlock's wristwatch clicked, belled.

He silenced it and said, "Of course, sir."

Stepanchov shook himself like a wet dog. "Time, old friend?"

Porlock nodded, touched his chipped button. "I envy the sweet sleep you'll have in Moscow."

Then Stepanchov took both the President's hands and said, "There is the matter of a gift, sir. From factions in KGB Central favorable to Gavrych."

Blood glowed in the President's face.

"A good-faith gift to you and America. When fully rested from travel, also the ordeal of your coloreds, I will choose it myself."

"Why, then, all the more pleasing," said the President. "It will remind me of a certain aging apparatchik of Stalinist temperament."

They were squeezing each other's hands when the coach lamps flickered twice, then twice more.

"That will be your transport, Arkady," said Porlock.

Stepanchov pulled himself to his feet, took a step, turned to the President.

"Sir, I have no fear of being misunderstood if I render what is a commonplace farewell for Russians—that I would wish upon you what you would wish upon me."

And he went out the door.

HOUSE ETHICS SUBCOMMITTEE, 9:45–10:20 A.M.: "Tomorrow Alex announces his resignation," said Cornelius Saddler, R., North Dakota.

"Now if he had a letter from you . . . Standin' tall and proud when he reads it out . . . ," said Haspell Gwinn, D., Connecticut.

"A simple humanity letter. Sorrow, regret for one mistake, lapse, indiscretion. But friends and pals forever," said Dwight Willingham, D., Alabama.

"Now I'm wondering," said the President, "and I continue to wonder—what's Alex worth?"

"Give or take, more or less . . . one-three, one-five," said Fritz Turnell, R., Delaware.

"Never fails," said the President. "And it always beats the shit out of me."

"What does, Mr. President?" said Emery Vorys, D., New Mexico.

"By Jesus," said the President, "for the sake of some landscaping; a GAS-7 job for his wife . . . When they sell out . . . Always for so little. Time and again, time and again, always so little."

"Alex's district is a defense district," said Fritz Turnell, R., Delaware.

"And when you represent a defense district you fall into the defense district outlook," said Haspell Gwinn, D., Connecticut.

"About your letter—doesn't have to be more than ten lines, fifteen," said Dwight Willingham, D., Alabama.

"I'll do two, three pages. Why not?" said the President. " 'Whatever thy hand findeth to do, do it with thy might.' "

"Sure thing," said Emery Vorys, D., New Mexico.

"What's more," said the President, "I'll do the same thing for any of you when the time comes."

And they all had a good laugh on this.

SPENCER HEINTZ, CHAIRMAN, KIMBALL INSTITUTE FOR STRATEGIC STUDIES, 10:25–11:15 A.M.: "Under normal-average worst-case condition pass-along decision would have to be set at or within four minutes by NORSTAD and presidential hold-loose decision in five minutes optimum-maximum."

"A madhouse extreme," said the President, "which wrecks the machinery of state."

SENATOR VICTOR ZANKEL, NEW YORK, 1:10–1:55 P.M.: "I'm talking no less than eleven thousand jobs, Mr. President. I'm talking ripple effect on a totally absolute defense-oriented area. I'm talking good-bye, goodluck, Long Island."

"I hear you," said the President. "I get the message."

"When I visited the plant I got scared. How do you not get scared when you see the elite of the work force, I'm talking their top engineers, pushing apples and pencils at you?"

"Dark times," said the President. "They're in for dark times."

"Sir, these are my constituents. And it's not fair, it's not right, it's not equitable to kill what they have. I'm talking of not merely security but about a prideful spirit that comes . . . Goddam, it comes from feeling and knowing that you're assembling and designing and manufacturing and putting together the best fighter plane in the world second to none. What they feel is why should they have to make way for a cost-efficient tomorrow?"

"Here, now, this minute," said the President. "Always the short-term interest."

"Mr. President, who thinks above and beyond his short-term interest? Back when I was an assemblyman I had a two-year term, so I thought in terms of two years. Now I'm a senator with a six-year term so I look at things from a larger perspective—a six-year perspective."

"Yes," said the President. "I see your point. I do, I most certainly do."

BARNARD (BUCK) MACKENZIE, EDITOR IN CHIEF, *HERE* MAGAZINE, 3:20–4:10 P.M.: "We'd like yours to be the last words in the last paragraph, sir."

"I'll speak out," said the President, "and I'll say . . . I'll say what a pleasure it is to speak out in the pages of *Here*."

"The theme of the issue is 'the me-ing of America.' We hope to x-ray a generation which has had to nurture and bond itself into an era of ambiguous peace, painful peace, an era of precarious, nerve-rattling balance between peace and war."

"I'll say," said the President, "I might say that peace is not a growth industry."

"It won't be the whole picture of America. Thank God, there is no whole picture—and certainly not the whole picture, the broad canvas of the left wing or the couch liberals or the herd of independent minds for whom the times are always out of joint. We'll cover a nation which is finally free from the hangover of internationalism and the helpless, energy-sapping, sentimental guilt over a starving, slaughter-house world we never made and couldn't possibly save even if we spent the next century on a universal New Deal."

"Why, then I'll say," said the President, "that the light of self-interest is shedding over these dark times."

VIDEOTYPE GREETINGS TO ROGER ESTABROOK, CEO, ELVAC COR-PORATION, 5:15–5:25 P.M.: "Good evening, Roger.

"I'm immensely pleased that you and the Elvac Corporation are being honored tonight with the Freedom Award of the Democratic Legacy Foundation.

"This event underscores for me the powerful partnership between two American giants—a giant of the business community and a giant of human rights.

"For both Elvac and the Foundation have striven to fulfill the dream that brought our fathers and grandfathers to this land—the dream of an open society and an open workplace, wherein people of all races, all faiths can become whatever talent, character, and oppor-tunity combine to make them.

"And from the very first, Elvac has looked beyond the boardroom, beyond the quarterly report and the year-end statement, and out to the broader, deeper communality of nations and societies. It has met, it continues to meet the awesome challenges of this century with a passionate commitment to a moral standard that makes man, not profit or loss, the measure of all things.

"Keep up the good work, Roger. And God bless you all on this memorable night."

EXERCISE, 7:20–7:35 P.M.: When he had done his first mile on the Exercycle, the President stopped and swallowed hard and sighed, and when he glimpsed himself in the little magnifying mirror his face looked fierce and lonely.

He did a half mile more, and then he sought to declare himself to JFK, but he felt choked up and thick, and all he could manage to say was, "Momentous, Jack, momentous."

And during the next three miles he said this again and again, and each time the Exercycle bell sounded he would whisper, "peace," he would whisper, "sympathy," he would whisper, "brotherhood," he would whisper, "purest joy."

Whiffs of sugary warmth came in from the ventilators.

A brown-orange burl in the Leporello spinet watched the President coldly, wickedly, like the eye of an octopus.

Through the bay window he saw the moon, and it seemed to consume more light than it gave.

The noises of his respiratory tract turned ragged and irregular and stertorous, and though he raised himself up on the pillow with great care and gentleness he nevertheless awakened Eunice.

She looked at him so coyly and so ardently that when he had breath again he said, "Would cuddling be enough?"

She took his hand, touched it to her cheek. "I do rightly believe cuddling would not go altogether unappreciated."

Presently he was abstractedly stroking the underside of her left breast and he was saying, "There are things I'd like to do in the way of history and statecraft, but I'm worried about the people."

He moved to her nipple, and when it was erect he said, "By Jesus, if only we had a parliamentary system. Then I could dissolve the people and elect another."

Eunice tensed and quivered and scratched the sheet, the pillowcase.

"By Jesus, Eunice"—he warmed his hand between her thighs— "the things I have in mind are momentous things. Social programs from sea to shining sea. Good-bye rural poor, good-bye urban poor, good-bye laboring cattle."

"You are my own sweet master planner," said Eunice.

And presently she sang, " 'If we'd only love, if we'd only care.' "

And the President sang back, " 'Baby, it could save so much wear and tear.' "

2

Walking with small steps, mincing ballet steps, Stepanchov prowled up and down and back and forth along the frost-hardened cellars of KGB Central's new annex, stopping and squatting a little before the tall steel vaults that housed the "Deviant" and "Neurasthenic" archives to scratch his back against a protruding bolt. Then, half blinded by tears of cold, he lengthened his stride for some thirty paces, went under the Romanesque arch into the zigzag courtyard, scuttled past the outdoor toilets, took the five flights to the American Studies Bureau at a brisk clip, and stood stamping his legs before the narrow gloom of a cubicle.

"Irena, Comrade Irena," he whimpered, pushing through the plywood gate, stepping over the twine-bound volumes of Armbruster's *Colonial New England*, and blundering against the cluttered iron desk. He sat down on a high stepstool, stood up, swayed his wide hips as if dancing. Feigning a cough, he put a question to himself.

"Stepanchov, why is there rancor and regret in your organism?"

And ruefully, speculatively, he answered it.

"Poor apparatchik, only because you have seen the future and it works on your nerves."

Though he followed this with violent sobbing sounds, though he wriggled out of his sheepskin greatcoat and let it fall to the floor, the slender, huge-eyed, braided girl dressed all in black took no notice of him; intensely, silently, she bracketed and starred and underscored some flaking pages with a yellow felt marker.

First warming his hands on a canvas-jacketed pipe overhead, Stepanchov put his forefinger to the tip of her nose, her brows, her braids, gave her a forlorn, doting glance, and said, "Comrade Irena Nikolaevna, hear the prophecy of your colonel and chief."

He moistened the forefinger with his tongue and rubbed and rubbed at an ink spot under her right eye.

"I foresee a time when that fine full bosom will heave in happy distress, erotic distress. Your libido, released by Gavrych from the tyranny of the state, from Marxist doldrums, will seek connection and transcendence and fulfillment through the flesh. In the throes of what Americans call 'casual sex,' also 'affairs' and 'quickies,' you and yours will make tinkly talk, praising each other's parts and performance, at the end crying out together. . . . But what would you and yours cry out together? Perhaps, perhaps—"

He stiffened, shivered, and embraced the air.

"Solidarity forever."

"I think not," said Comrade Irena, holding her felt marker gracefully aloft. "The crying out of 'solidarity forever' contains too much syllabic weight for the spontaneous physiological circumstances you describe." After a moment she made a movement with her mouth. "The cry of 'solidarity forever' is further inappropriate because it is the title of an American working-class song of pseudo-folk origins, aforesaid working class aspiring to little more than trade-union consciousness."

Stepanchov pulled her braids. "Orgasms!" he exclaimed, speaking the word with a terrible, brutal bitterness. "Thoughts of profound, volcanic, indefinitely protracted orgasms will be on your orderly snow-queen mind—thoughts fed from copious readings in the many and various American periodicals directed at your gender. I must tell you, Irena Nikolaevna"—he raised his hands, as though he had done everything possible to spare her—"that such periodicals of orgasm-achievement methodology are read even by American coloreds of your gender."

He squared the edge of her tea-scalded desk blotter.

"Read at such times as they are not occupied inventing their history."

"Should Gavrych assume power," she answered, dipping her head like a bird going after seed, "coupling will be of less interest to my gender than consumerism."

She took a green felt marker and crossed it over a pair of foot-long shears.

"In the periodicals of . . . the American periodicals to which you make reference . . ."

She reached for a ruler and measured her hand.

". . . the common usage for the desired end of ideal coupling procedures is 'climax,' though such restrained and ideologically conservative periodicals as *Reader's Digest* prefer the phrase 'mutual satisfaction.' "

Stepanchov gripped his right wrist with his left hand, squinted, and set his feet apart like a marksman.

"Why is there no pity to her gender?" he asked a rusty sprinkler in the stonework ceiling. "None, none, none!"

"The biology of my gender," she said, "is tyrannical, absolute, and altogether without pity." She slapped down the ruler. "The biology of my gender is Stalin, not Gavrych."

"Take pity on a poor apparatchik, an aging functionary. For he has seen the future and it works on his nerves."

Irena was silent for some moments. Then she said with a look of pride and casual, benign indifference, "Ever his way, ever his way. When overwrought he oppresses my gender."

"Once released," Stepanchov rushed to say, "the raging torrent of your lust will compel you to demand of your partners nothing less than simultaneous orgasm."

"America," said Irena, losing breath and coloring, "has unsettled him. He is furthermore in the extremity of indecision."

"You will glean the paperback writings of American sexologists for guidance in what is called 'foreplay' and 'arousal,' and by the time your poor partners are done obeying your drill-sergeant directives, done diligently tinkering with your parts, they will have forgotten their original purpose."

"Ever his way, ever his way," said Irena. "Perplexed and furious, he oppresses my gender, endeavors to shame me. This is displacement of rage, this is his old brutal habit for release of tension. But what"— she showed Stepanchov her palms—"what feeds the rage and tension? What really is in his mind?"

Stepanchov's voice broke as he cried, "On your feet, Comrade Irena Nikolaevna!"

But Irena was shaking her head and her face altered as if a very low light had come on behind it, and she said, "Yes, he is confused and reluctant over the gift he must make the American president. Oh surely, certainly, he is in an agony of spirit. His Stalinist temperament, his old devil raises mountains in his way."

Then she jumped up and they stood facing each other across the desk.

"Ah, the pitilessness of her gender, the wickedness of her mouth."

Stepanchov put his forefinger close to her throat, drew a quick, straight line across it.

"Oh surely, certainly"—Irena leaned forward so as to whisper—"the moral man and the Stalinist devil wrestle within him. They carry on internal civil war over the good-faith gift to the American president."

An angry yellowish radiance rose in Stepanchov's eyes. His ears flamed. He suddenly began to yell. "Pitiless creature! She smirks—a schoolmistress smirk though beneath and below she is rank and dank from the lustful fluids of her gender!"

"Three weeks since his return from America. Far past the time for his good-faith gift. And Gavrych—for sure, for sure, Gavrych presses him."

Snorting through distended nostrils, Stepanchov flogged the canvas-jacketed pipes overhead with his fists. Then he took up Irena's ruler, balanced it in his palm, and hurled it like a lance over the partition.

There was the urgent scraping of chairs, the hollow iron unison of ponderous file drawers shutting all at once.

"For sure Gavrych presses and presses him," Irena sang out, twirling on her toes about the desk. "He would know why America is not now celebrating and extolling Russian generosity."

Five massive, matronly clerks, looking pleased and easy, watched now with folded arms outside the plywood barrier.

"May your parts and apertures engorge with tumescence," Stepanchov croaked at Irena.

And stamping his feet at the five clerks, he cried, "To work, to work, nose pickers. Take up the archives, comb the encrusted dossiers till your fingers bleed, till Trotskyite ghosts come howling out!"

One by one they turned, one by one they pulled down their ravelly coat sweaters and scuttled off with gruff, mannish whispers.

Irena stood looking at him, waiting, rocking a little on the edges of her galoshes. Neither spoke for a long while; then she said in a calm and implacable and oddly compassionate voice, "What does my colonel and chief fear? Why, only this, only this: the demons from his hellish past, the thought that there remains in him now a part of what he was then."

Stepanchov's hand went up and touched Irena's cheek.

"The bloody-minded sinner repents," she said solemnly. "The old bird of prey strains to hatch a dove."

Stepanchov's eyes sprang full of tears; he dropped his hand; he stood straight-legged against the desk; he looked as if he had journeyed a great distance.

"How well she reasons," he whispered.

A sob leaped through him.

"And how well she prepares her anatomy for the Gavrych era. All, all is in readiness—from breast to buttock."

He filled his lungs with air, he leveled a forefinger.

"Raise the dress," he rumbled.

"Happily," she murmured, "we are accustomed to the subtlety of his methods."

In a single move she had the big-skirted dress up, over the cotton lisle stockings; disdainfully, she bent and removed what was left of each knee elastic with thick knots.

"Those knots"—Stepanchov made a bashful face—"like cow dugs."

She answered softly, indeterminately, "But when the Gavrych era is upon us . . ."

For the flicker of a second Stepanchov smiled. He shut his eyes and said, "Why, I foresee . . . panty hose. Perhaps . . . blue jeans."

Both smiled.

"Well, then," said Irena, showing him her palms, "the rage and tension . . ."

"Over. Done," said Stepanchov, putting his hands into the waistband of his trousers and scratching himself.

"My colonel, my chief, has exorcised his demons, settled on his good-faith gift?"

"He has, he has," said Stepanchov, smiling and scratching away.

Then his hands came out from the waistband of his trousers and he was stamping his feet and pulling his ears.

"To the files, to the files," he shouted. "You will find me three, no less than three Jewish scientists, outstanding, shining!"

"And who is better than Orlofsky?" she demanded fiercely. "Vidyon Yezel Orlofsky!"

Irena walked around the desk, started to go past him. But Stepanchov stopped her with two wet kisses.

"Yes, send for Orlofsky," he told her. "But send also for War-Horse."

She returned his kisses, and presently both were laughing and laughing.

3

Bearing Lenin's mummy on his back, he entered the United States capital of Washington, District of Columbia. Pavel Gavrych, smirking, presented him to the American intelligence community: "Here is Vassily Turakanych, war-horse of the KGB. His is the last face many of your best operatives have seen."

Thousands cheered.

Nevertheless, he heard his father mocking him in Jewish singsong.

Why, just for that, Turakanych decided, I'll give them the names of every Soviet agent in America.

But I am the war-horse of the KGB.

His eyes filled.

He drew breath, sighed out the first hundred names.

Oh, shit. Lenin's mummy had begun to stink. Hide it in my dacha. Wash it in the waters of the Black Sea. My dacha, my Black Sea, my five-, six-, seven-room dacha on the Black Sea waters . . .

What a dream. Father, of all people, making Jew sounds.

And Vassily Turakanych lay still for a moment, listened to the cries of early bathers, blinked away the fatty white spokes of sun. Bad light, evil light all this week. A malignant chill to everything. Unsuited to the Black Sea in late summer.

Father making Jew sounds. Where had he pulled out such sick, repulsive stuff?

KGB's war-horse. Stepanchov's phrase, entered on my evaluation when he advanced me three ranks right into Moscow Central. Gave me that fine little Furadini pistol. Embracing me. Saying, "Shoots low and to the left, but no harm leaving them with one testicle." Putting both my hands on his heart. Saying, "Come, Vassily, between us we'll make the state wither away."

Elena stirred, captured the blanket.

Nineteen clean kills to my credit. A file like the Angel of Death.

Elena made a noise, freed a leg, scratched a thigh.

Yet on the last day of my life I am connected to nothing in Russia.

Elena took a fetal position.

He smiled at the sight of her.

Then a strong suffocating pressure rose up to the root of his tongue.

Wife dear, he silently declared, iron necessity forbids disclosure of my plans, opening of my heart. While it is the punishment of eleven hells not to leave behind a note, an outcry against Gavrych, I simply won't trust that open potato-face of yours. One quick look and Stepanchov would read you like a handbill, cause you loss of pension, dacha, Moscow flat. Kiss our sons. My feelings are no longer inflamed against them. Good luck to them, good luck to all of Russia's young with their stupendous Gavrych truths. But some day, no fear, Russia will once again take note of her Vassily Turakanychs. Do you think I killed my nineteen for nothing? That I have no understanding of mankind? It's as Father said: "The sun will fall three times before men learn to spare each other." Bless the rearing he gave me. When I was unruly he'd drag me to the coops, slaughter a chicken, rub my eyes with the carcass. For with the children of Russia only blood teaches good manners.

He leaned toward the light, squinted at his watch. A quarter to six.

Elena coughed, smiled, slept on.

I myself will be the cleanest kill of all.

Connected to nothing in Russia.

Making America a present of our best Jew-brain.

Wife dear. Silly spendthrift hen. For the sake of your winter strawberries, your white asparagus, I deny myself the dignity of a bullet.

Tell the West, says Stepanchov. Believe, only believe how things have changed, says Stepanchov. Peace, sympathy, brotherhood, purest joy to America.

But, Stepanchov, if I could leave behind a note I'd make you understand I hate earth, water, air because America has them.

He rose, used the toilet, stood on the lid to have a good look at himself in the medicine cabinet mirror. Fifty-two was fifty-two, of course, and something in his face showed the beating he'd been taking since Gavrych. But that thick, coarse, bristly Turakanych hair still swirled in all directions, he had the teeth of an Eskimo, his body—oh, shit.

A fat-weakened bureaucrat's death for such a strong-looking, well-hung man.

He stepped down, opened the medicine cabinet, took out his razor case.

A coronary.

He opened the case, dug under the red plush lining, found the capsule.

Stepanchov, you might have handled Orlofsky yourself. I pleaded, practically kissed your feet. Such a grand joke, one of your lovely ironies to have me catering to a Jew.

He stretched his lower lip, popped the capsule under the gum line, went back into the bedroom.

Stepanchov almost weeping with laughter. "Vassily, ho ho, Ukrainian mule, it's time to tell the West. Show me, ho, how your heart, ha ha, overflows to the Jews, to America, to mankind. Feel, only feel, Vassily. Peace, sympathy, brotherhood, purest joy."

He stood over Elena, moved his feet apart; touched, fingered, pressed himself; warmed both palms on the quivering blood-gorged length of it.

Elena opened her eyes, stared, shook her head, moaned out, "No."

He grabbed her hair.

Good dirty fun for Stepanchov. When he gets the death certificate he'll talk of dogs in heat, Ukrainians on leave. How I never got enough of Elena.

He said, "Take me into your mouth."

War-Horse went red in the face, boys, tight in the balls at the sight of wifey.

He pushed against her lips.

Always ran home for lunch, boys, to get his slap and tickle.

Elena lifted her eyes to the ceiling. "He drains me. Thinks we are twenty again."

"Then only use the tongue," he pleaded. "Last day of leave."

Giggling, crawling up from the sheet, Elena said, "Only the tongue, yes. Some rest at least for my . . . parts."

But presently her lips closed around him and she was moving her head from side to side and lashing his scrotum with her hair.

If there's afterlife, I'll find the Jew in America, circumcise him at the throat.

"Are the parts rested now?" he said. "Yes, they'd best be rested now, yes."

He turned her, forced her onto her stomach, threw the bottom of her nightdress up to her waist; pinched, slapped, squeezed her buttocks till she assumed the position of a cow about to graze.

What was Father's expression? Jews—no, sparks—sparks fly up-ward, misfortune follows from Jews.

He took a half step forward, aimed himself at Elena's labia.

"Like a bridegroom," he heard her say.

To please Orlofsky, Stepanchov cuffed me like a schoolboy. Called me "stupid," called me "turd," called me "peasant prick."

"Like two bridegrooms," he heard Elena say.

Nineteen kills to my credit. Took down every operative the West sent against me. But he made me apologize to a Jew.

He thrust, missed; he raised Elena by a hip and a buttock; he humped his back; he thrust again; entered.

Elena closed on him. Cried, "Bridegroom!" Cried, "Love!"

While Orlofsky sat and smiled away with that fat Yankel mouth I had to prance and caper and put on a penitent face. Saying, "May you live two hundred years, butter both sides of your bread, find pleasure from the goods and services of America. What an error I've made! How shamefully I've treated you! A few smacks from a good Russian knout would benefit a blockhead like mine. Can't imagine how it happened."

Elena hissed, whimpered; dilated, contracted.

Saying, "If there's an afterlife, Comrade Orlofsky, I'll be at your feet in Jerusalem. Believe me, and here's my Ukrainian hand on it; in all Russia you'll not find more respectful admiration for the man of science. A good thing, this life of science. Better than putting a seed in the ground or a nut to a bolt. Real taste, our Pavel Gavrych. Knows what's good. Gives America only the best. A brain like yours."

He took Elena's ankles; lifted her, rocked her.

Elena rolled her buttocks, clicked her teeth.

Saying, "I'm a victim of my untidy desk, Comrade Orlofsky. Froze my wits, all those files. But Russian life is lived by files."

He dug his chin into the base of Elena's spine; reached around for her breasts; clutched, kneaded, twisted.

Saying, "Files are not my medium, Comrade Orlofsky. Hope I drown in paper if there's afterlife, that's how terrible I feel. Turns out I had your file all the time. Well, but a few hours in a detention cell doesn't appear to have harmed you. No rough handling, I hope. If you'll be so kind as to give the particulars about any rough handling I'll have those responsible shitting green water. Take my Ukrainian hand; have a kiss before you're off to America. . . ."

He paused, arched his pelvis, snorted.

Saying, "Off with you, Jerusalem beak. One less Jew now to worry Russia."

He took Elena's knees; opened her wider; still wider; came slamming in.

Saying, finally, into Orlofsky's face, "Good-bye and be damned, kike head, devil fucker."

He heard Elena scream; sigh, croon.

"Peace!" he snarled. And, "Sympathy, brotherhood, purest joy!"

Stepanchov would snigger, whoop, roar. "Boys, with Vassily a case of prick wants, heart won't. Dogs in heat, Ukrainians on leave. Used to run home to get some slap and tickle. Ten days at the Black Sea, must have topped her like two bridegrooms. Fifty-two is fifty-two, dogs in heat, Ukrainians on leave . . ."

And thinking, Safe now, my pension, my flat, my dacha, he bit down on the capsule.

4

FROM THE JOURNALS OF HARRY PORLOCK: Coffee and sweet rolls this morning in the Oval Office. Enjoyed free and easy discourse with the President, the luxury of galloping off in all directions, climbing like alpinists from thought to thought. For this has always been our way of approaching the heart of things.

And so the President began with Tom Mix.

"Harry, do you remember what Tom Mix used to say when he had that radio show? 'Straight shooters always win.' Now Harry, it really beats the shit out of me. By Jesus, are there just no more straight shooters? Or did they just stop winning?"

I told him that we would find the answers in history, that we would always find in history what we wanted to find.

He spoke next of Nanny Dora, his British nursemaid.

"The sort of voice, Harry—one of those sweet, those tinkly voices you expect to come out of a music box. Trained me to knife, fork, potty, and good vowel sounds. Pulled me out of chest weakness with coddled eggs and flannel vests and readings from Macaulay. Always began with the same lines. 'William Henry's slender frame was shaken by a constant hoarse cough and Cruel headaches oft tortured the Prince of Orange. . . . Yet through a life which was one long disease, the force of his mind never failed, on any great occasion, to bear up his suffering and languid body.' "

He was readying himself to speak of Nell, I thought, and so I diverted him. I told him that Macaulay's admiration was misplaced, that the Prince of Orange should not have played the game of power without the necessary vigor.

He was before long assessing the national mood.

"Everyone—by Jesus, everyone's waiting for the end. Programmed for failure, chasing ruin. Did you read Hans Schweibel in *The Wall Street* fucking *Journal*? 'It may be that we have overlooked the moral superiority of being a second-rate power.' And you should have been at Kennedy Center yesterday for that oratorio. 'Oh, Ethiopia, oh, famine gutted, forgive us our shopping centers.'"

I told him that a flick from the switch of hard times and Americans would relearn the moral superiority of their object-hungry consumption-minded ways.

He complained that America was now ungovernable.

"Like I'm presiding over some kind of national group-therapy session. All the coalitions are falling to pieces. Even if I wanted to sell out I wouldn't know to whom. Any little stability is from the Teamsters or the Mafia. Blood in every eye. Unrest in the cities. Shoddy goods, emptying farms. And everyone in a state of excitement. Third-rate minds on ten-speed bikes of consciousness."

I told him that Rome, during her most glorious centuries, had employed this dangerous energy in middle-sized, low-risk wars, that she would allow no decade to pass without at least two such wars.

He wondered if his powers of compassion were not being exhausted by the inordinate demands of our age.

"There was a time—by Jesus, Harry, there was a time when the plight of migrant workers crippled me. When they first took me to an inner city I hid my face and I broke down in front of the press. With all my heart I cried and with what voice I had I said, 'Ladies and gentlemen, brothers and sisters, proclaim, honestly, you have to proclaim unto the land this shame and abomination. It's a message, a portent. If God smote the four corners of our national house and made fear visit unto us I wouldn't be a bit surprised.' Nowadays—nowadays, I have to think in starving continents before I shed a tear and the last time I said 'holocaust' I didn't feel shit."

I told him that however sensitive his nature, there was little any president could do for suffering mankind save to maintain an air of gentle earnestness and decent, manly courtesy.

At this point he mentioned Pavel Gavrych.

"Plenty of smarts there, Harry."

"An intelligent and sensitive man, sir."

"He writes like a fucking angel."

"Indeed, sir. The pleasure in reading him comes not only from the cogency of his thought but also from the elegance of his style."

And we spent a few moments discussing these lines from Pavel Gavrych: "Since 1946 there has been a family tie, an incestuous bond between America and Russia. In a special sense they need and complete one another, like razor and wrist."

Here, seeing that the President had grown somewhat pensive, fearing some reference to Nell, I hastened to take charge of the conversation.

I told him that the permanent war economy was not his fault.

I told him that America's wealth and strength depended upon living in fear of Russia.

I told him that Americans had come to see the whole of life as a Russian conspiracy, that the sudden absence of such an outlook would deprive them of sanity and stability.

Though wholly in agreement, the President expressed the hope that straight shooters might one day win again.

Then he wanted to know how I proposed to handle the matter of Orlofsky.

Because he had such a downcast, dreading look, I did not answer directly but spoke instead of how we were both merely job holders, assigned a shaky moral and social order not to do right, not even to do something called "duty," but merely to do.

He gave an odd smile and quoted a remark made to him by John Kennedy: "Boy-o, what do we do about our inner lives?"

I observed that in this shaky moral and social order our inner lives were best left to our dreams.

When he had laughed under his breath, I told him that the Orlofsky matter would be handled by a special group, a group I like to think of as "the Listeners."

He made an immediate connection with his schooldays. "By Jesus, sure, listeners. That's what we used to call the people who were absolutely forbidden to sing at Sunday services. Because their voices— awful!"

"And so it is in a sense with this group," I said. "One might say

that the right tone, right key and pitch, will always elude them however they try. They're . . . incomplete. Unfinished in some essential
human area."

And nothing was said of Nell. I was able to end the meeting with
some gossip about the polymorphous sexuality of a certain Pentagon
wife.

Because he felt unaccountably depressed after Harry left, because it
was a drab, overcast, rust-colored morning, the President seemed to
sense the presence of JFK with singular force. And though he should
have been using the time to prepare for the National Security Council
briefing, he sought to awaken his heart from a host of unquiet
thoughts.

The back of his neck and his cheeks went hot and he struck himself
heavily upon the breastbone and he blurted, "A few minutes of your
time, Jack, if you can spare them. For I'm harried by worries. That
mood, that seizure, that old awful morning grief, that nothingness
mood is upon me."

"No fear, laddy," said JFK. "I'll see you through. Don't I always?"

"By Jesus, he makes me feel—" With a trembly forefinger the
President scribbled something in the air. "Against Harry I feel weak
and incompetent. No, unfinished—unfinished, like one of his listeners.
There's nothing I can do or think or say that can possibly take him
by surprise because he's long since read and defined me absolutely."

"Boy-o, boy-o," JFK answered slyly, "you'll not be the first president to feel that he has no share in the life of this republic."

"Misgivings," the President said to himself. And to JFK he said,
"Last night I had awful misgivings about this Orlofsky business. One
way or another he'll be crumpled up in—what's Harry's phrase?—
'in the hand of necessity.' All last night I couldn't fight off a thought
that when it happens, the crumpling . . . By Jesus, he's Jewish, and
. . . and will he wonder if it's happening because he's Jewish?"

"As to that, laddy," JFK told him in tones of exquisite protective-
ness, "there's no statesman alive who has less to fear from judgment
by our common Judeo-Christian God."

"Grateful, Jack," said the President. "Most grateful." And his eyes
filled up, and he felt somewhat contented and more at peace with the
morning.

5

To: Harry Porlock
From: Byron Wagonside
Re: Code Name Beau Geste

Delighted to learn that I'll be having "some small role" in the Orlofsky pickup. However small, I regard it as the kind of valuable field experience which will certainly serve to augment my in-depth understanding of the Gavrych caseload.

Warmest personal regards from my father, who speaks no less often and fondly of you.

━

"This is Dr. Annalee Goldensteen, and I am not in my office. Please wait for the chime before speaking. As soon as you hear the chime, leave your name, message, and phone number, and your call will be returned."

"Byron Wagonside here. I saw the ad for *Coping* in *The Washington Post*, 9/23, and I wanted, in my capacity as former patient, to express the hope that it, *Coping*, achieves a status of best-sellerhood or best-sellerdom, whatever."

"This is Dr. Annalee Goldensteen, and I am not in my office. Please wait for the chime before speaking. As soon as you hear the chime, leave your name, message, and phone number, and your call will be returned."

"Byron Wagonside here. Buzz. In my former-patient capacity I have to say how pleased I was to be turned away at the Book and Author Luncheon in the Shoreham Hotel, 9/30, because of the overcrowding. Warmest personal regards and enjoy your forthcoming High Holy Day or Days."

"This is Dr. Annalee Goldensteen, and I am not in my office. Please wait for the chime before speaking. As soon as you hear the chime, leave your name, message, and phone number, and your call will be returned."

"It's Buzz, Dr. Annalee. Shalom on being a full Literary Guild selection, and as of 10/5 I've been in great pain and would like to set up an appointment involving therapy resumption on my part."

"This is Dr. Annalee Goldensteen, and I am not in my office. Please wait for the chime before speaking. As soon as you hear the chime, leave your name, message, and phone number, and your call will be returned."

"Byron Wagonside here. Buzz. I wanted to add that pain is pain, whether you're a superstud or a dry twig, which is what Natalie calls me customarily after I service her. What do you think? Isn't pain the same for an anal-retentive compulsive repressive as it is for a spontaneous person or a natural child such as Natalie? My emotional agony when she sounds off makes me no less want to climb walls than her failure to achieve multiple orgasm."

"This is Dr. Annalee Goldensteen, and I am not in my office. Please wait for the chime before speaking. As soon as you hear the chime, leave your name, message, and phone number, and your call will be returned."

"Byron Wagonside here, and I'd like to know how much openness I should take from Natalie. When Daddy was over last Sunday and she had to do her business and was really tinkling away a storm she opened the bathroom door all the way and—and during her drying process she stepped halfway out to participate in the conversation."

"This is Dr. Annalee Goldensteen, and I am not in my office. Please wait for the chime before speaking. As soon as you hear the chime, leave your name, message, and phone number, and your call will be returned."

"Byron Wagonside again. Buzz. Relations between Daddy and Natalie are causing return of that slightly spastic colon. His last visit—jumping melonballs, Dr. Annalee, a doggone disaster. Though I went into long detail beforehand explaining the importance of avoiding overt displays of affection, she never left off continually rubbing and ear blowing. When I uncorked the wine, Gevrey-Chambertin 1975, she kissed me in a manner where her tongue must have been halfway down my throat. Also, whatever Daddy said—Do you mind if I anyway talk into your dead line from the necessity to release painful anxiety? Okay, whatever Daddy said—that he believes an American character exists and will be always equal to whatever is demanded of it; that every Veterans Day he goes to Arlington Cemetery and recites 'The Battle Hymn of the Republic,' all six stanzas—jumping melonballs, she'd answer teasing and close to downright snippiness. She kept offering him canapés of high sodium content, though I had repeatedly briefed her on his coronary infarction of 2/11, and don't tell me that her constant offering wasn't to deliberately remind him of his clearly declining health. Okay, I would be less than fair and distorting if I claim that Natalie is the sole cause of Daddy's inflamed feelings against me. He thinks I lack heroism and am the runt of our forebears' litter. I tell him, 'Daddy, I can't leave a leg at Antietam to please you. Or chase Pancho Villa across the Rio Grande. I couldn't command your squad on Utah beach and you couldn't evaluate the intelligence community's handling of a general strike in Milan!' But he's my daddy, and he gave me, during my formative years, a happy childhood, and I'm in pain, and try to fit me in next week, please, jumping melonballs, please, please try . . ."

6

Dear America:

Hi!

Listen guys, gals, folks, excuse me for getting on your backs with yet another piece of Vidyon Orlofsky correspondence. But the American Studies people here at Moscow Central won't lay off until I demonstrate a more swinging mastery of colloquial English than I have hitherto displayed. Therefore let's hope this dry run training exercise turns out less along square side.

Hi and Hi and Hi!

If I employ the above word again it is only because I dig it absolutely. Of all the salutations your obedient servant Orlofsky has been turned on by, none send me more fully. What a gasser of a word, what a turn-on sound! Small and simple, free and easy and carrying overtones of farms and filling stations and frankfurters; these last named are also referred to as "hot dogs" and "red hots," depending on your geographic locale.

Okay, friends, shall I tell it like it is and from where it comes?

Off the top of my head out of left field, I'd say that the flip-out far-out tendency might be rather deeply embedded in the U.S. life and life-style. Such, at any rate, are the vibes received from many concentrated hours of eyeballing background films of a documentary nature on Uncle Sam and related matters.

One scene from such a film I shall describe in support of my far-out contention.

I recall a city, and the narrow sidewalks and immense causeways of this city. A good strong sun pours light, yet as far down as one can see streetlamps are on. Sewers steam. Cars are double- and triple-parked, and some have their front wheels mounted on the curb.

There is a small crowd.

Oh man, oh brother!

America, like, wow!

What is, what gives with these people?

For their expressions—if the graves of the world cracked open I would expect such expressions on the faces of the dead. Terror and rage were dominant, but I also caught shadings of spite, malice, wrath, and barbarous suffering.

A moment later the camera moved back, and I saw that these were only some pedestrians halted by a traffic light.

From this brief glimpse I fully dig why your poor queer poet, Hart Crane, has said, "Ride the subways /And behold ten thousand deaths in each eye."

I realize too that my friend Semyon Andreyev had his head straight and knew his U.S. urban habits stuff when he cautioned that a bump, a jostle, or even a touch is enough to overload the circuits of nerve-rattled American metropolitans, that one can be turned into a corpse for the sake of a parking spot.

What's more, oddball flashes of berserk and blowtop behavior are manifested also among your rurals. While I don't mean to put down hick-hayseed type, it appears that such a type may decide to wipe out his entire family very much as he might decide that the time has finally come to trade in a balky tractor.

Nevertheless, America, I am in less fear of your switchblades and shotguns than of your rock and disco music. While I have made a massive effort to get with it, I detect in your Top Forty only unfocused complaint and lamentation. All right, okay, there is protest. A sort of protest, protest of a sort. Your singers, your composers are demanding—but what are they *not* demanding? More than they have, if I get the message. Yet how much more, and more of what? Love, to be sure, though in this clamorous call for love—or is it unrestricted copulation and getting off one's rocks utterly?—I hear bad news.

Blind, destructive disgust. High on despair. Like, you know, resign and surrender. Like, you know, Don't command and be sure not to obey. And all those primal screams, those sexual gruntings—a voice-vote from the children of Caliban, a unanimous monkey howl for nonstyle, nonelegance, nonculture, nonorder, nonreason, nonlanguage.

While space remains and with time on my hands, I might as well shoot down a few other American aspects which bug me or fall outside my comprehension. Among them:

Your need to feel that your men of wealth are at bottom melancholy and go about saying, "Yes, but money after all isn't everything."

The fact that no society has ever demandèd less from its young.

A belief that for every experience there is always, there must be, some adequate response. "Once again," you will say of the stacked corpses at Buchenwald, "grim evidence of man's inhumanity to man."

Your desire to be left alone and in undisturbed possession of your lives and your property; your belief that this is peanuts to ask.

But never mind.

Forget, screw the above.

For even if I appear to be giving it to you with both barrels, I feel bliss from every pore. I say, Right on, America. While in various small ways you may be a grand pain in the neck, balls, and ass, you remain hot stuff and A-OK in my book.

Look, you are possessed of a certain sweet-tempered dopiness which renders you immune to murderous ideologies; you have not yet made life like a desert for your citizens; and your desire to be loved among nations does you credit. These things, together with images of Pacific beaches and something called "soft ice cream" grab me and reach me truly where I live.

Honest, the willingness, the gladness with which I take my chances on you, America, are no better summarized than by your wonderfully affirmative word, Sure.

Am I ready for the whole bit? Ball of wax?

Sure.

Can I take on and make sense of Big Macs, Sears catalogues, jeans, mixed drinks, the way-out incidence of infidelity and divorce, fender-benders, gays, and something called "milk shake"?

Sure and Sure and Sure!
All good wishes, warmest personal regards, up your Establishment!

Vidyon Orlofsky

P.S. Call me chicken, but I am as yet unable to overcome jitters at my impending duel with the waves. Yet, however lacking in stomach, I shall bust a gut playing out the assigned role of dissenter-defector. After all, your intelligence community has in recent years suffered a lousy press, and if films of Orlofsky jumping ship help restore your spooks to superstar status—well, why not? Besides, America, I understand, I dig from readings in Hemingway and others your tradition of courageous physical action. If a little manly melodrama achieves for Pavel Gavrych fuller national coverage from your thrill-happy media, if you can survive the ugly Orlofsky puss on Dan Rather prime time—look, no sweat.

O.

1

As agreed, the Soviet trawler *Akipomoff* silenced its engines two hundred and three miles due west of Norfolk.

Orlofsky, a small pug-nosed man with a graying goatee, climbed to the bridge, breathed deeply of the bracing air, and raised haunted, beseeching eyes at the sliver of moon.

Makharenko, the second mate, lifted him, squeezed him, set him down softly, and crooned, *"Nozdrovnya."*

Two seamen belted him into a tufted flotation jacket of urinous orange.

Blowing kisses off his fingertips, murmuring effusive thanks, Orlofsky moved dreamily to the rail.

And froze.

Makharenko, with operatic gestures, pantomimed the jump, the cleaving of the water, the paddle and kick to the surface.

Orlofsky sought to say, *"Nyet,"* managed only strangling sounds.

The American motor launch approached, wheeled in a tedious circle.

Orlofsky waved and held up one finger.

Someone in the launch raised a bullhorn, croaked, "Go" . . . "Forty seconds" . . . "You must" . . .

And all at once Orlofsky was overcome by a strange sweet languor. Why, look now, he longed to answer, you should consider and make allowances for my landlocked ancestors. Rabbis, money changers, cobblers, ritual slaughterers, cantors, and such. Understand, please, that they oppress me, that they ride my back, they tear at my liver and would drag me to the bottom of the sea.

"Breaking contact" . . . "Returning" . . . "Now" . . . "Unless" . . . "Must" . . .

Orlofsky backed off, ran at the rail, and worked a foot over it.

But a schoolboy phrase jogged his memory: "Mighty are the Don and the Vistula, but mightier still are the oceans."

And he withdrew the foot.

Then Makharenko, sighing, grumbling, took him by both ears, turned him, and barked into his face, *"Zhid!"*

From force of habit Orlofsky flinched; instantly Makharenko scooped him up and flung him over the side.

His first taste of the Atlantic thrilled him.

Why, Gavrych is right, he reflected, making masterful wading motions. The weak are never absolutely weak.

And when the Americans fished him out of the sea he was smiling tranquilly and enjoying utmost clarity of mind. Listen, he silently exclaimed to the long dead, Hey Mendel and Nachim, Hey Laib and Pinya, did you watch? Should have seen that jump I took! How perfectly I arched my body, how I remembered to clamp my jaws and lock my breath, how I stiffened my legs and reared back my head! . . .

But all the same, hiccups distended his diaphragm.

And as he stepped aboard the American minesweeper *Dover Jones* he sucked air, bit his tongue, and fainted dead away.

They put me in *sickbay*.

Upon a *bunk*.

There I am *sacked out*.

For I was *groggy, woozy, pooped*.

But now I am filled with comfort. My heart is lifted, I am at perfect peace, and I feel *super*.

"Super," Orlofsky said aloud. "I feel super."

"Splendid," he was answered. "And you must hold on to that feeling."

Not fully roused, Orlofsky pressed his eyes, opened them. Iridescent specks troubled his vision. The rough cloth of the turtleneck garment they had given him twisted under his arms and those workpants pinched. He felt chafed, itchy.

"As Mark Twain put it," he heard, " 'Stranger, welcome. For here, with us, you shall dream other dreams, and better.' "

Orlofsky brought his head forward, squinted.

Haloed by a sunbeam that pierced the porthole, he beheld a tall, spare, bald man on the elderly side with vivid blue witty eyes, sharp nose, lively mouth. Meticulously dressed in a rich brown linen blazer, matching ascot, and intricately tooled boots of unborn calf, he sat straight backed, legs jauntily crossed on a low stool near the surgical cabinet, beaming and chuckling away at Orlofsky.

Mildly surprised—he had somehow anticipated a taciturn, crewcut Yankee in wide-wale corduroys—Orlofsky raised himself and doffed an imaginary cap.

"Orlofsky," he announced. "Vidyon Yezel Orlofsky. One who"— he sneezed, whacking his head on the side of the bunk—"One who presumes to think of himself as physicist of consequence but who would happily enter your socioeconomic mainstream under any capacity."

"And I," said the American, pleased and easy, "am Harry Porlock."

He came over, made room for himself on the meager mattress, and shook both of Orlofsky's hands.

Orlofsky, face glowing, said shyly, "I have knowledge of your name, Mr. Porlock, and connect it with the highest American places and personages."

"Only another civil servant," Porlock answered.

Orlofsky peeped into his eyes. "Stepanchov"—he looked around, lowered his voice—"Stepanchov believes you were his most worthy or worthwhile antagonist."

"There was a time"—Porlock chuckled—"we played a dangerous game or two."

He bit a knuckle.

"Now I'm of the age when it's enough to know, like Lear, that 'Men must endure their going hence, even as their coming hither.' "

He coughed thickly.

" 'Ripeness is all.' "

He blinked away some suspicious moisture from his eyes.

"But you can't know, sir, how the flavor and savor of this clandestine operation restores . . . The stimulus of the field . . . Only to hear Stepanchov's name . . . lengthens my life."

"Long wear and hard use to you!" Orlofsky cried with elation. "As we say."

"Spare me such a blessing, sir."

"One should not rush into eternity, as we also say."

"Would you have me"—Porlock gave a mock shudder—"endure yet another administration? Yet another set of bellicose academics with impoverished scalps and luxuriant beards?"

Orlofsky combed his goatee with his fingers and laughed nervously.

Porlock laughed too. "Shouldn't be at all surprised if they're awaiting me when I pass through the gates of death. Still sleeping their stupendous liberal sleep."

After a brief silence Orlofsky said, "I begin to understand and dig more fully why Gavrych advised me against acceptance of an American university post. How he scorned or scoffed at the notion! He said, " 'My friend, my friend, have you not already suffered sufficient insult and injury?' "

"Delicious," Porlock whispered. "He has a way of putting things."

"A beautiful person," Orlofsky whispered back.

"What a fineness of tone and temper."

"Gavrych is totally with it. He"—Orlofsky drew a jagged breath—"he enjoys the capacity of reaching where one lives."

"Though I've only seen bits and pieces of *Leviathan's Hook,*" said Porlock, "there are passages spelled out in my mind with letters of flame."

"His head is straight. He knows the universal score and I am fully into him."

And sitting cross-legged, lightly holding his knees, Orlofsky breathily said, "Remember how Gavrych characterized this century?"

A spasm of delight went through Porlock. "Indeed. As a tale told to frighten children."

Orlofsky clapped.

Then Porlock, after a warm panting laugh, said, "Shall we trade Gavrychisms?"

"By all means, you bet, and you're on." Orlofsky hugged his arms. " 'There is always some unpleasant surprise in store for mankind.' "

A sorrowful sweetness passed over Porlock's face. " 'Though left alone in the universe, which one of us would not soon be hungering for a bit of private property?' "

" 'Science makes everything possible,' " Orlofsky returned. " 'Politics makes everything permissible.' "

" 'The commonest' "—Porlock socked his brows—" 'Coarsest,' rather . . . 'The coarsest materials and the crudest machines are exalted in industry. Only the worker is debased.' "

" 'God has made all the phenomena of this world subject to limits; he has thus far refused to do the same with the state.' "

" 'What is it' "—Porlock raised his hands—" 'I would teach America?' "

And both together said, " 'Despair.' "

Porlock studied him with his vivid blue gaze. "We're well matched, sir."

Orlofsky murmured his thanks.

"And well met."

"As we say, those who are enriched from the same source are no strangers."

"It will be a pleasure, Vidyon, to see America through your eyes."

Smiling dimly, Orlofsky said, "Old cinematic memories have made me very high on your American horses. Your ponies, your mounts, your Old Paints and Old Dans. Wonderful creatures, very swell beasts. Or so it seemed to me in my youth."

"And what a youth it must have been!" Porlock pumped Orlofsky's hands. "Calculus at five, if I remember your file; *Principia Mathematica* at nine."

"Your American horses fought off—but what did they not fight off? Grizzlies. Wild stallions. Back-shooters or bushwackers."

"Indeed, indeed, Vidyon. All they wanted was the chance to use their teeth on a cowboy's bonds, to pull him out of quicksand, to kneel so that he might mount when wounded—"

A knock sounded on the swing door.

"One long leap," Porlock said with elaborate, unhurried ease, "took them across chasms. And if called upon, Vidyon, they rode double. Oh my, oh yes, they pursued the work ethic."

A fair, bland, open-faced young man carrying an overloaded clipboard put a foot inside the sickbay, coughed discreetly, and said, "Isn't it time?"

Porlock shook his head. "Thank you, Buzz. No, Buzz."

Paper crackled as the young man riffled through his clipboard.

"We're in American waters and it should be—"

A rubber band snapped and flew across the sickbay.

"—time."

"Good morning, Buzz," Porlock said pleasantly.

"Jumping melonballs," murmured the young man. A cheek quivered. Then he shrugged one shoulder and closed the door behind him with mild force.

"A good lad," said Porlock, "but given over to the administrative side of things."

He bit a knuckle.

"Hungry?" he asked abruptly.

Trying to seem casual, Orlofsky fluttered a finger.

Porlock went to a white wall phone, dialed one digit. "Galley?" He nodded and waved at Orlofsky. "Some weak tea here. And junket. And a scoop of cottage cheese, too, small curd."

My first American breakfast, Orlofsky thought bitterly.

"Perhaps some hard candies. Unfilled and in assorted flavors."

I had yearnings for flapjacks, bacon rashers, yellow cornbread.

"Whatever fruit juice you have, though no more than two ounces."

Coffee strong enough, as is said by their cowboys, to float a pistol.

Porlock hung up.

"Easily digestible, high in protein," he said.

He smiled at Orlofsky and Orlofsky smiled back.

"I'm looking ahead, Vidyon, to your receptions and state dinners. Best build gradually to our overrich American diet."

"Good thinking," said Orlofsky. "A light repast—right on!"

Dawn was flooding the small library when Orlofsky entered to prolonged applause.

Flustered, he grabbed his goatee and bowed at the furled American flag.

"I would express the immensity of my gratitude to those who assisted in the planning of this endeavor or enterprise. Peace, sympathy, brotherhood, and purest joy. As you know, I am following the custom, Russian and American, of bearing a gift to the host. This gift, the Zaisan Process, comes also from the Russian people or peoples—"

He wrinkled his nose at Porlock.

"While Process is my pet brainchild, my baby, I shall follow the enjoinder of Mr. Harry Porlock, who advises that I save myself for forthcoming interviews from your Dan Rather and other commentator anchormen. So, therefore, okay, may it help keep America's boilers full, even as"—he touched his left side—"as my heart was full when I found on my breakfast tray that small batch of blue violets."

There was applause, cheering, and then Porlock started him forward with a soft shove, saying, "Going counterclockwise, we have Ab, short for Abner, Beddoe, ends with an 'E.' Ab, who keeps track of the Soviet scientific scene, predicted your Order of Lenin three weeks before it was announced."

Orlofsky bumped against a big, chunky, hearty-looking fellow, felt meaty, comforting hands on his back.

"Still going counterclockwise, Vidyon, this long drink of water, this good old boy here, for obvious reasons called Tex, is Chester Pomeroy. Tex, well, Tex enjoys investigating such factors as the behavior of crowds—these factors, I daresay, which make for the massing of the masses."

"Pleasured, mightily, mightily pleasured, suh." The voice filled space, the gold-brown eyes warmed and penetrated.

"You already know Byron, call him Buzz, Wagonside. Buzz, as I've said, handles the administrative side of things."

Some peculiar, twisting distortion in his face froze Orlofsky's ears; when he risked another look, though, Wagonside was smiling.

"And this is Penelope Oxbridge, who's done some fine stuff for us on the uses of tedium in performance alteration. Penelope—I respect her wish not to be called Penny—is on leave, though we're hoping to make it permanent, from the University of California in Berkeley."

Through a constricted throat Orlofsky said, "You are of or from California?"

"Like most," she answered, "a transplanted easterner dissatisfied in the midst of paradise."

"California," he murmured, secretly examining her pale, fine-boned, elongated head with its single massive braid.

"Another transient mourning the absence of seasons, the high cost of dentistry."

"If you please," said Orlofsky, fighting down an unseemly lick of desire, "I solicit information about Disneyland. A recreational area of unusual, perhaps astounding, dimension located, as I am given to

understand, near the intermediate-sized city of Anaheim in the aforementioned state. Be assured"—he gave her a stricken glance—"that
I am in earnest and tell it straight. I am somewhat less than a swinging
bachelor and have no wish to come on strong or, as we say, to pull
your nose."

"Not to worry." She took his wrists and drew him a little apart
from the others. "Go ahead, yes. Disneyland."

"Then tell me this. This." He broke off. "To be sure, Afonka
Volisetev was a scoundrel. A bigamist. Where Aeroflot had offices he
had wives."

She answered, "I see," as if she did.

"All the same, five years on your coastlines surely taught him a
thing or two about American life."

"Of course," she said earnestly.

Under some Mercator charts, inhaling the odors of soap powder,
rancid fat, and lubricant that poured through a ventilator grill, Orlofsky bent his knees and rose on his toes as if about to sprint. "Americans . . . Afonka was convinced utterly . . . workers and peasants,
holders of wealth, wielders of prodigious influence, the simplest and
the wisest—among them one idea, one notion, one conception prevailed. That there are prime movers and supreme manipulators at the
bottom of American things. That they are the source of great events,
great events. That they can change matters as easily as sharks do their
direction. Okay? Well, Afonka would from time to time ask representative Americans to name those they held to be at the bottom of
things and the source of great events. But he was deported, then
imprisoned—a matter of embezzlement, to say nothing of the aforementioned bigamy—and so I never came to see his listing of those
prime movers and supreme manipulators."

"A shame," she said, looking at him with deep interest.

"Yet a little before his troubles Afonka sent me a most splendid
and diligently detailed map of your Disneyland. He had marked off
an area between the House of Fun and the Cave, or Caverns, of Peter
Pan. 'From here,' he wrote, 'they command.' "

Orlofsky swayed in his tracks.

"A piece of nonsense. Playing me for a sucker. How could it be
otherwise? All the same I am compelled to ask if it be so."

She whispered, "No."

"What an Afonka. Oh, what a scoundrel," said Orlofsky with a half-sad smile. "Well, okay, he was even in gymnasium a formidable wag. The most cunning of tricksters."

"Not to worry." She gripped his fingers. "He knew, as you said, a thing or two about American life."

She seemed on the verge of saying more when Wagonside stepped forward and held out his clipboard.

"You suck," she said, and slapped the clipboard out of his hands.

Wagonside made a weak, nasal sound. "Jumping melonballs, I would call that a disproportionate reaction."

"Enchanting," said Porlock, rapping Orlofsky's arm with soft knuckles. "You've made me feel the bite of that Moscow wind."

"He tells a wonderful story," Wagonside said.

The one they called Tex tugged an earlobe and rumbled, "Sir, I'd be pleased, mightily pleased, were you to honor us with your continued recollections of Mr. Gavrych."

"You don't dare stop now," exclaimed the one they called Ab. "Dearest Lord, you were climbing nine—nine flights to Gavrych. You were burning matches—and I love the way you put it—'initially for illumination, then, alas, for warmth.' "

"Sure," said Orlofsky, straining back and against the sling chair and kicking his heels like a swimming frog. "Sure. I was, okay, like I was breathing vapor and simultaneously perspiring. At even-numbered landings I rested. At odd-numbered landings I held private conversations with myself. Such things as, 'Orlofsky here, a reasonably well-placed scientist, a prudent bachelor of fixed habit, a cold stone of a man dreading intensity of feeling. All the same I am turned on to whirling ecstasy.' And, 'Orlofsky here, and I have this unshakable conviction that *Leviathan's Hook* could have been written by only the purest of souls.' And, 'Orlofsky here, a craven churl who thinks twice before visiting what remains of his mother's grave lest he be charged with covert Zionist contacts. . . .' "

" 'A craven churl.' Lovely! First-rate!" cried Porlock.

"America, sir," said the one they called Tex, "shall presently be celebrating a great physicist *and* a great phrasemaker."

"He has real . . . *kulturny*?" Wagonside underscored something on his clipboard, at the same time checking his watch.

Orlofsky released a pent-up breath. "My first sight of Gavrych—

I had the impression of a horse. A thoughtful horse. A horse immersed in contemplation of the equine condition. Something in his walk, his gait, as though he were attached to an impossible load. And by way of greeting—this was his greeting: 'Orlofsky, I must know about Jews. You must make it plain to me. What is it like to live in continual expectation of the world's wrath?' And this, on my word, was his most commonplace remark. For in that hideous furnished room—a desk of greening wood, thready carpet, lamps that consumed more light than they gave—he reached me utterly. Like, wow! Bared and unbuttoned me. Like, everything in my life made such great good sense. From the smallest amount of my smallest day I was all of a piece."

"A pure soul, as you say!" exclaimed the one they called Ab.

Wagonside said, "I had a political science instructor like that."

"We talked. No, he—he talked!" shouted Orlofsky. Aware of his loudness, he wrinkled his nose. "With the herring and slivovitz he led me through a hundred years' thickness of disaster. Cecil Rhodes dreaming in continents. Bakunin and Nechaev announcing that man is something to be surpassed. The Paris Commune. Verdun and Tannenberg. Lenin scribbling slogans over the linens of some Zurich cafe. Gandhi smiling as if at the wearisome joke of human expectations."

"Gavrych offers a powerful reminder," said the one they called Ab, "that as the range of our missiles increases, so too must the range of our ideas."

"Oh, everything sucks," Penelope was muttering. "Existence sucks too."

"And yet"—Orlofsky looked at her, pacified his goatee, looked away—"I must make plain that there was in Gavrych—deepest despair, you bet. Nevertheless—a certain merriment. And patience, such patience. Small children, you see, were in and out of his room, pulling his hair and knotting his shoelaces and emptying his pockets. To please them he imitated the sounds of forgetful computers, headless hammers, corks refusing to leave bottles, arrows returning to bowstrings. Then, as he sent them off, he flipped me, he blew my mind. He told them, 'Obey, only obey. Fulfill the quotas. Exceed the limits. Whatever work thy hand findeth to do, do it with thy might. Become drunk on labor!' Well, on my word! What manner of dissent was this? And when I left to catch the last autobus I was sick at heart. In the pits. Descending those nine flights I was giving it to Gavrych with both barrels. 'Oh, friend Gavrych, are you one of those charlatans who, as we say, wears an eiderdown hair shirt?' And, 'Friend Gavrych, with such dissent what need have we for affirmation?' Put Gavrych from your mind, I decided. Let Russia remain Russia: the butcher block which outlasts the butcher. But within that year, as you know . . . Wild stuff. Mind-blowing rumors. Library lines. Prisons jammed. Printers in Tiflis who set up a chant of 'Do and overdo!' and chained themselves to their presses. Then, out of Minsk—thermal glove liners. Enough, it was said, to maintain Russia till the millennium. Then from the Caucasus and the Urals—what a quantity of steel cable and fan belts and copper tubing! But where was the rolling stock to transport them? The containers to package them? Well, I began to understand and get with it. Sure, you bet, and how!"

He was still talking, voice up a notch to hide the rumbling of his stomach, when Wagonside tiptoed out of the library. Porlock, biting a knuckle, watched him go.

Iron buoy bells clanged.

The deck trembled underfoot from the pull of the anchor.

Through broken clouds the sun burnished black bridge trestles, played on chrome and glass, gave distant sheds the look of silver artillery shells.

Gulls steered back and forth, back and forth, and it seemed to Orlofsky, as he blinked and wept, that they were crying, "Norfolk! Norfolk!"

His heart hammered.

A humming, a purring, a benevolent agitation, began in the depths of his diaphragm.

Closing his eyes, he conjured Leatherstocking and Billy the Kid shooting gold nuggets from the beaks of bald eagles. Somewhere in the Dust Bowl, John Steinbeck and Upton Sinclair broke bread with oppressed workers and peasants. Young Abe Lincoln blew pining notes into his mouth organ, then dropped a single rose upon the grave of Nancy Hanks. At the wheel of an ancient flivver, Henry Ford gave chase to the Keystone Kops. Along a secondary road Charlie Chaplin and Jacqueline Kennedy walked bandy-legged toward a forlorn horizon.

"Well, then, hi, and hi and hi," he whispered to America.

From under his turtleneck garment he removed an oilskin envelope.

"If it please God," he told all present, "I touch these for the last time."

And he withdrew his black and tan labor book, then his black and orange labor passport.

"One nevertheless feels," he said. "Strangely, one does feel, one does feel."

He sent his documents sailing into the stiff breeze.

Then Porlock cried out in a cracked voice, "Vidyon!"

And Wagonside was upon him, razoring his left sleeve.

"I want you to know, Vidyon," Porlock said, "that I delayed matters so you'd have your chance to see America."

And Wagonside said, "Negative effects are contraindicated, and you'll be fine."

To all present Orlofsky lamented, "I come to you with the Zaisan process."

To Porlock he screamed, "Why I would have saved America—but what sums would I not save America!"

"Jumping melonballs," said Wagonside, as he sent the needle sliding in, "hundreds of billions maybe."

The last voice Orlofsky heard was Porlock's: "This is what Marx called the contradictions of capitalism."

TWO

8

FROM THE JOURNALS OF HARRY PORLOCK: The alarm clock failed to go off. After all these weeks it seems I am still unaccustomed to setting it myself. Awakened late into a dark, blustery, rainy morning, dressed and shaved hastily and arrived wet and chilled for the nine-twenty staff meeting. Spent much of the time staring out the streaming windows while I droned away like an instructor who has given the same course too many years. A blessing when the coffee cart came.

Then a call from Nell.

Her first word was "thymoma."

She went on to say, "Nell Porlock has thymoma, an enormous mass in the breastbone region near the anterior mediastinum. In time, before too long, I, Nell Porlock, will be presented with my due bill from the nitrogen cycle."

I began, as usual, in a bantering tone. "Really, Nell, no rush as I see it." And as usual, I could not sustain it. "You're a wonderful woman, Nell. I'm proud to have you as my wife, proud to participate in your existence, proud that . . ."

But she was eager to tell me about her "first time" exercises.

"Harry, for the first time in my life, I, Nell Porlock, am paying attention to sparrows. Meticulous observation, you see, is part of the program. Now, outside my window, on the cables which hold the Bethesda Naval Hospital banner, are many sparrows. If I listen I can hear their wings beating strongly. I'm holding the phone a bit away so you can hear them too. Do you hear them? Do you understand how they are linked to the chain of being?"

I waited a moment before answering dramatically, thrillingly, "I hear them and I do understand."

"I'm now throwing away some tissues. My calling attention to this is important. The idea, they say, is to stress the dispensability of material things. Once we terminals accept the dispensability of material things we can move on to broader themes, such as an understanding that the species is enhanced by the sacrifice of individuals. We enter a higher realization, we're prepared to accept—"

Death, say death, I silently begged.

"—a summons from the firm of Null and Void, a walk at the side of Brother Sleep, a ride with the Courteous Coachman."

I suddenly hear jovial noises behind her, then, "How we doing today, Nell?"

"It's Dr. Hurster. Must hang up. Come early, early, early this afternoon."

After a while I went to the firing range. Thirty-five rounds with a Smith & Wesson. Cursed God under the blast and concussion till my throat was raw and gradually brought myself under control.

By the time I returned there was a message on my desk from Nell:

Always push and hold RESET BUTTON *(the green) on alarm clock. Saddlesoap only for your boar's hide loafers.*
Stop by Dr. Hurster's office. Some forms to sign. He's looking forward to meeting. Time, high time for it.
If you fail to remarry, I, Nell Porlock, thymoma, promise to pursue you throughout eternity.

"Why, Nell," I murmured, "nothing would give me greater pleasure."

Dr. Hurster.

Hefty, pink-faced, goat-bearded.

With meaty ears, hair like unstranded rope, nostrils spread wide, and an audible whistle to his breath.

"I'd like you to look at a terminal group session. They'll be doing IR's. IR's," he adds reverently, "are 'irrational thoughts.'"

From a deep armchair behind his one-way mirror I watch a tiny old woman wearing a furry neck brace cane her way over to a potted plant to strike at its leaves.

A teenage boy circles her in his wheelchair and cries, "Granny Julia, speak up. Speak up, Granny Julia."

"This IR of mine"—she strokes the leaves again—"see, now, I do imagine they'll be puttin' this plant topper my coffin so's to make the lid press down on my nose."

"No way," says the teenage boy. "Flowers are what they put. Flowers, is all."

He hugs her about the middle.

Around this time I switch out the lights over the mirror.

Dr. Hurster stares at me for some word. When none comes, he spreads his fingers over his tie, says, "Being supportive, that's what it's all about."

A breath whistles out of him.

"From the first session we teach them and train them to an understanding that, what's the saying? that man is born between urine and feces."

"Is he?" I answer. "I find that no cause for celebration."

And I sign the forms permitting Nell to visit the hospital mortuary with her group.

"Long as you're here—"

He searches his desk, shakes out several pieces of Nell's blue stationery from an accordion-pleated envelope, sets them before me.

"—only need to initial this."

He pulls down air like a diver about to submerge.

"We're doing another press run of the 'Death and Dying' brochure, and your wife's pain meditations would be an invaluable addition."

And I am presently reading:

God watching the world on TV—would he require a laugh track?
How strange that both my night nurses eat white raisins.
Why not dolls that die?
After a certain time, there will be no mail for me.
Certain words suddenly beautiful to me—linoleum, trolley, davenport, shears, bonfire, awning, coverlet.
After a certain time, there will be no calls for me.

*Both my night nurses eat white raisins and pretend to write down
the names of books I recommend.
God as a game show host would*

Presently I pull the rest of Nell's stationery from his fingers, slide
it into my briefcase, and walk to the door.

With a gaseous expression he opens it for me. As I start along the
corridor he calls out, "You'll have to be more supportive."

Nell was sleeping so deeply that she did not feel my weight on the
bed or my touch to what radiation has left of her hair. Twice she
moaned, spoke broken words, and raked her breast as if trying to lift
the heart out; both times her wedding band slipped down to the second
knuckle. Death, like a malignant cosmetician, seems to be highlighting
her very worst features—trying a touch of brown on her upper lip,
a few veins for her large sculpted nose, clotted yellows and squiggles
of blood to ring her pale freckles.

Then an arm flew up, her body shook, and she came awake.

She began to laugh and said, "Oh, my, these late afternoon naps."

I said, "Slugabed."

She propped herself up, knees raised girlishly under the blankets.
"I think"—she moved one finger around in a circle—"I think my
body is telling me, and please don't press the point, Harry, that we
must reach each other with meaningful conversation."

She closed her eyes a moment.

"For example, the matter of children. There's Harriet in my group,
Harriet Menkes, tuberculosis of the spine, who makes me very cross.
Never a session when she fails to ask why I didn't adopt. I've been
quiet till now because it's impossible for a terminal not to sometimes
feel that when this-is-it-time comes sons and daughters in multitudes
should be, oh, flinging flowers."

All I could think of to say was, "Rest, Nell."

"But tomorrow I mean to tell Harriet that we were always a very
self-contained couple, that the child was never the meaning of life for
us, that—"

A moment passed; she apparently thought of one thing, then said
another.

"—that I could never relate to fingerpaints and pediatricians and, oh, jungle gyms."

I only nodded; it was the first time I had ever heard her use the word "relate."

"There're also the small resentments which I should start discharging because they tend to be magnified in the minds of terminals. Do you know I never saw that much, not nearly as much as you, in *Moby-Dick*? I wish you'd never told me that I left faucets running. I wish you'd encouraged me to keep up with my old friends. I wish you didn't know the history of every bloody city in the world. I wish I had some secrets from you. I wish, I almost wish—"

She dwindled off.

"—there was more."

Suddenly she winced. What crossed my mind, and with consuming bitterness, was that I could bear her grimace of pain more easily than her look of abject submission.

A good half minute passed.

"There's much to be said in favor of it," she declared.

I waited another half minute before saying, "It?"

She urged up into her face a squirty little smile. "This concept of unpacking all your bags. Shedding," she rushed to add, "traveling light."

I said, "Oh, yes?"

"As though"—Nell pushed back into the pillows, stroked the binding of the blanket—"well, as though one must flee before the coming of the barbarians to the city of Necropolis in the kingdom of Nether. Along the way one sheds, oh, everything. Till there is only . . . organism. The husk of minerals one has borrowed from nature. Because one—who is specially privileged? Billions upon billions have . . . These are the terms . . ."

Then her arms turned downward, moved wide on the bed, and she drifted into sleep.

"The city of Necropolis," I whispered, "the kingdom of Nether."

I wondered why my hand was in the air. But after a while I realized that I had been close to slapping her.

The night nurse found me on my knees. "Aw now," she said. She padded over, her soft, heavy front bobbling, and raised me. "A hard, hard time," she said. "But Nell . . . she's somethin' else. Comes night and some patients . . . Never her. Character. A fine person, a honey and a real darlin'."

"Thank you."

"Keeps her group goin'."

I turned on her and snapped, "But all the same she'll be as dead as a doornail."

Then I kissed the very ugliest splotch on Nell's forehead and stalked out.

Back in a heavy snowfall for some night work.

At a quarter to one a call from the President and an invitation to Camp David.

He talks and talks, trying as usual to stave off sleep. Then in a caved-in voice, "Harry."

A sudden deep silence.

"What's your thinking, Harry?"

His teeth click.

"Our way of life, this society, American civilization, you know . . . Could we make it without a permanent war economy?"

I refrain from answering.

Presently he inquires after Nell. "What's the story? In hospital?"

"One of those interminable women's ailments," I reply, and he is gracious enough not to press me.

9

That night at Camp David, as he had many nights before, the President went to his little movie house fifty minutes early so that he might think things through.

"Selected short subjects, sir," said the blond agent with the rimless sunglasses.

"Running time under an hour, Mr. President," said the balding agent with the tortoiseshell sunglasses.

"That will be fine, boys."

He bounded over to his grand old Da Cintre recliner, gripped both arms, and after a wavering moment, mounted in one light leap.

"All the way back tonight, Mr. President?"

"By Jesus, why not?"

He sank back and down, crossed his wrists like a corpse. He whispered, "God. I to Thee. Unto all nations. Righteous, righteous."

Soon tears of fatigue sprang to his eyes.

And under the cover of the projection booth din he began addressing JFK.

Saying, this time, "Old buddy. Stud. Cocksmith. How do I get out of this clutch? What a beating I'm taking. In perils by mine own countrymen, in perils by the heathen, in perils in the wilderness, in perils among false brethren. You'd hardly know me. Lost my clean jawline, my lank Henry Fonda look. Something's happened under my eyes."

The blond agent with the rimless sunglasses brought him three Perugina chocolates.

The balding agent with the tortoiseshell sunglasses brought him a package of assorted nuts.

And when they had walked off as if with pebbles in their shoes, when the tea-colored lights had twittered and dimmed, the President resumed his entreaty.

"Old buddy. To whom I was an inconstant friend. Pardon. Overlook. For I am between nothing and nowhere. They dump on me. My base of support is eroding, my programs turn to shit. Nothing seems altogether true or clear. I try to spend twenty-five minutes a day on *The New York Times,* but for all the good it does me I could be chained by the neck and watching shadows in Plato's cave. Protect. Pity. Intercede. Suggest, please, some viable policy. Help me push a bill through committee. One bill, I'll settle for . . ."

And then the Merrie Melodies came on.

And he put a Perugina chocolate into his mouth, sucking it very slowly.

And by the time he reached the rum-flavored center he had decided, after complicated doubts, to accept the Adlai Stevenson Medallion from Liberty House.

I'll speak out plainly, he reflected, about the need for plain speaking.

Twelve to fifteen minutes underscoring the need to stand tall but not stiff necked before the world.

I'll tell them we must launch not missiles but dialogue. I'll use the word "moral" three times, work in a "God and man" phrase. Then, with my head bowed, with that rise, that valor, in my voice, I'll ask—

"No Bugs Bunny," he reminded the projectionist.

—for their prayers, their support. The support of their prayers.

He finished the second Perugina chocolate, then the third, then he was pulling apart the packet of assorted nuts and picking out the filberts.

A circle of blackness enclosed Tom and Jerry.

Presently Donald Duck was tearing down endless closed doors to get at a dripping faucet.

And in his mind's eye the President saw Harry Porlock plucking at his trouser leg from under the dais.

Then Harry would say, "Now, Mr. President?"

And he would cry, "Now, Harry, now!"

And when he and Harry had kicked over the dais, spilling baked Alaska and demitasse on everybody, they would spray the Liberty House crowd with a hundred rounds from concealed Uzis, and he would deliver a last message to America. "This is what you get for living out your lives without praise and without blame. For chuckling when Walter Cronkite chuckles. For your healthy affirmation and common sense. For believing that healthy affirmation and common sense will see you safely through history."

But light suddenly hit him full blast.

"Thermidor entering B Gate for check through, sir."

"Thermidor given Sector 9 routing, sir."

And the blond agent with the rimless sunglasses set the recliner at one hundred and three degrees.

And the balding agent with the tortoiseshell sunglasses put a brown-and-gold folder into the President's hands.

He broke the cloudy gutta-percha seal and took out the slick faxed pages.

Attached with Scotch tape was a three-by-five card carrying a single handwritten line: "You are by now out of Perugina chocolates—Harry."

Uttering a high nicker of glee, the President began to read.

"In effecting the Orlofsky transformation our purpose is to have in reserve yet another example of Soviet duplicity should Gavrych's strength prove greater than our present estimate."

"Transformation" means they used drugs, the President reflected. Really, I should feel something more about that. I should feel something!

He read further.

"Orlofsky believes himself to have been a class-five journalist assigned to the Leningrad biweekly magazine *New Collective*, for which he wrote a regular 1,000-word feature called 'Large Thoughts and Small Matters'—colorful vignettes which most often communicated the ideas, sentiments, and styles of behavior of working-class types. He believes further, that Pavel Gavrych sent him here to take a simple, human measure of the common experiences of Americans. Orlofsky was to report regularly on his findings to the President so that he might better understand the heart and mind of the people, better understand how far he dared take them along the road to disarmament and—"

But now the blond agent with the rimless sunglasses was whistling into a walkie-talkie.

And the balding agent with the tortoiseshell sunglasses was saying, "Thermidor coming through Checkpoint Valvelifter, sir."

By Jesus, you'd think—blood stormed the President's head—surely you'd imagine that I'd be used to Harry by now. That these feelings would stop. This . . . criminal joy.

Sighing like a sleeper, he started to skim. He lingered over "Orlofsky means to meet with you one day and discuss the making of a healthier society" and "Together you will start working out a list of what is to be defended and preserved, what is—"

Then a shadow fell across the page.

Then a Perugina chocolate bounced onto his lap.

Fighting down a tickle of nervous excitement, the President raised his face. "Well, Harry," he managed to say in a tone of mingled authority and affection. "Well, well, well, Harry."

And struggling for casual irony he next said, "Hooray for our side."

Porlock smiled a half-angry smile.

"Indeed, sir. But which side is that? How long, sir"—with consummate delicacy of gesture he passed a hand across his barren scalp—"since there were sides?"

It came to the President that there was something . . . something autocratic, despotic, to Harry's baldness.

"Once, Mr. President"—Porlock shed his dove-gray Chesterfield, stretched and twirled his white silk scarf like a strangler—"there was a time when one chose. Truly chose."

As if hairy mankind owes him an apology.

"God or Satan. Church or state."

Makes me think of Dr. Moriarty.

"Charles or Cromwell."

Or those great adversaries Bulldog Drummond and the Secret Six went up against.

"Harry," the President said, pursing his lips, "about Orlofsky's . . . transformation. Now it strikes me there are some issues, weighty issues involved."

"Indeed, sir."

"Moral problems. Problems of a moral and ethical nature."

Porlock bit a knuckle.

Then the President asked if Nell was getting back her strength; and

Porlock mentioned a minor infection which seemed to be persisting; and they discussed how Porlock was managing with household matters till it was time for their swim.

The blond agent with the rimless sunglasses fed a little more chlorine into the pool.

The balding agent with the tortoiseshell sunglasses softened the overhead lights.

And when the President had done his hundred yards he said, "Was Orlofsky as gifted as all that?"

"One of those wizened prodigies, sir, which Russia seems to have in oversupply."

"When I was nine"—the President chinned himself on the diving board—"I built my first model airplane."

"For each perfect grade," said Porlock, "Orlofsky received an egg from his mother. This would be 1932, perhaps 1933."

"A Handley-Paige bomber. Three wings and the wildest tail assembly you ever saw."

"What it must have cost the poor woman! Kulaks were opposing collectivization, slaughtering livestock. Couldn't have been ten thousand hens in all Russia."

The President chinned himself twice more.

"I was all *Hell's Angels* and *Flying Aces* and . . . ah, by Jesus, Harry, how fast, how fast the time goes."

"Only a few decades apiece, sir." Porlock's mouth flickered.

"Listen,"—the President submerged, made blubbery noises, then surfaced and treaded water—"that process of Orlofsky's . . ."

"The Zaisan process. Pity they didn't allow him to name it for his mother."

"And what in the blazes is it, Harry?"

Porlock scratched at his brows before saying, "Ultimately, sir, an infernal nuisance."

He laughed badly.

"West of the Rockies there's all this molten rock—magma—a few miles down in the earth's crust. Rather like the entrance to hell. Temperature close to two thousand degrees Fahrenheit. Energy enough for the next five centuries if our drilling equipment could overcome the problems of corrosion and extreme heat."

Porlock lowered his eyes as if to spare the President.

"They tell me that the Zaisan process overcomes these problems, that it could allow us to live wonderfully well within our energy means.

"They tell me that certain of our larger enterprises would see little point underwriting massive investments in the sublimely complex and costly techniques of converting coal into high-octane fuel. . . ."

Porlock raised his hands.

Seconds passed.

Then the President said, "When I was running for office I figured— now, of course, my father always warned me that I'd have to learn to take capitalism without sugar—but I still figured, by Jesus, that within the system . . . within the system I'd do good and wise things."

He slapped the water.

"*O sancta simplissimus,*" said Porlock sadly and gently.

The blond agent with the rimless sunglasses led the masseur away.

The balding agent with the tortoiseshell sunglasses blew talcum dust off the cots and set the sunlamps for eleven minutes at low medium.

"Listen, Harry."

The President turned and opened his eyes into Porlock's face.

"If I have it straight, we're worried about losing energy investments that would amount to . . . what? Forty billion? Or a big fifty billion?"

Suddenly he was squatting on his cot.

"Losing them . . . their loss would kick the shit out of the GNP and naturally the unemployment rate . . ."

His fingers went up and up.

"Now that's merely on the basis of a lousy forty, fifty billion."

He hopped off the cot and jogged in place.

"A pain in the balls. Let's say a *grand* pain in the balls."

Now no muscle moved.

"But . . . but if *it* happens, Harry, if the Russians start really fucking around and one of these days, and right now it could be any day . . ."

"Indeed, sir. Any day, sir."

"They'd disarm, honest to God disarm, and we'd have to go along. And the military budget for this year alone, this year's military budget is one hundred and ninety-eight billion, not counting military-related expenditure. Not counting, Harry! Then we cut the size of the armed forces and we won't need all those civilian employees, of course, of course. Figure—have to figure on another million for the labor force to absorb."

Suddenly he threw himself on the cot.

"Harry."

Porlock bit a knuckle.

"What's your readout on Gavrych? I mean, if, as, and when. I mean Gavrych and us. Gavrych and his influence and impact and effect on . . . things."

"A first Soviet strike might be a bit more beneficial, sir."

And the blond agent with the rimless sunglasses came with a tray of various fruit juices.

When the sunlamps were off Porlock asked the President if he had received the recent communications from Orlofsky.

"They're crazy," said the President. "Although . . ."

"Although, sir . . . ?"

"He has his eye . . . At times, Harry, he has his eye on . . . real stuff."

"At times, sir."

"All nonsense, of course. Till, by Jesus, it stops being nonsense. It just stops, it stops, and I start reacting, responding."

"I understand, sir, that he believes he will one day be at your side. As an advisor giving you insights into the—how does he put it?— 'the ultimate realities of the American commonplace.' "

"Poor son of a bitch."

The President drank down some grape juice.

"Poor son of a bitch," he said again.

Then he drank down another glass of grape juice.

"We live in dark times, Harry, dark times."

"Indeed, sir."

10

"This is Dr. Annalee Goldensteen, and I am not in my office. Please wait for the chime before speaking. As soon as you hear the chime, leave your name, message, and phone number, and your call will be returned."

"It's Byron Wagonside, Dr. Annalee. Buzz. I am in the emergency room of Cedars of Lebanon Hospital, 900A Midvale Avenue, Chevy Chase, and the doctor has taken five stitches behind my head. The reason I am here under a suspicion of possible neurological damage is because of being struck with a shoe tree, the heaviest wooden kind, by Natalie. Furthermore, she has also done something to me in a careerwise security-risk sense whose future harmful effects are such that I'll be lucky if the Peace Corps will have me. Anyway, I hear a clicking, so in the event of being disconnected I want to cancel next week, maybe next month, as I have to pursue on an absolutely unofficial-leave basis what is left of my painful career. Also, I have to chase after Natalie and—and I think my nose is starting that anxiety bleeding again, all I need, jumping melonballs . . ."

—

Eyes Only: Porlock
        Re: Unauthorized absences of Wagonside, Alton Byron;
             and Dowdson, Carol Natalie

Pursuant to instructions we have changed status from Discreet Inquiry
to Amber Alert.

II

This is being written in the five-story annex recently built by the Komitet Gosudarstvennoy Bezopasnosti eleven-and-a-half kilometers southeast of Moscow's Sheremetyevo Airport. (So, at least, Comrade Irena tells me.) But though I'm in the hands of the KGB, though I'm deeply frightened and filled with monstrous intuitions, I feel also supremely alive—wide open, wonderfully conscious, prepared for once to take a good look at the actual. There'll be no universalizing this big close room, this cumbersome metal desk where I sit, this corridor with its colossal filing cabinets, no analogies to the human condition or the power of the state. Right now the proper study of mankind is Lewis Buntline.

So let's hear it for abject helplessness.

And for the obdurate truths which abject helplessness scrawls on the soul.

Among these truths:

1. I am forty-seven and have not fulfilled my early promise.
2. Most everything interesting and significant happened to me twenty years ago.
3. Because I have a round face, a gap-toothed grin, and a nutty belly laugh I'm conned into believing myself tender and giving, a sweet guy.
4. I have failed wife, son, country, numerous editors, and the massive majority of my students.

5. I have by slow degrees turned myself into the kind of academic Rotarian who publishes a novel every three years to nail down his tenure.
6. I cohabit with coeds.
7. The forty-seven-year-old protagonist of my work-in-progress is a tender, giving academic who cohabits with coeds and mails them quality paperbacks inscribed, "You are the best thing that has happened to me in twenty years."
8. My last coed said

Never mind.

As usual, I'm being selfish.

For if I don't leave myself with a few squeaks of dignity and self-respect the KGB will have nothing to violate.

Besides, it seems

"Seems I'm running out of paper," Buntline muttered, jumping up.

A brawny, hay-haired man with a twisted lip and pitted cheeks bounded over.

"Susyatin, I," he said in a baying basso.

He opened a misbuttoned, double-breasted jacket, hiked up ballooning trousers, wiggled his thumbs near Buntline's eyes.

"Is there need"—he hooked his thumbs under the collar of Buntline's turtleneck and pulled him close—"to empty bladder?"

"No," Buntline answered, after thinking about it. "Only some paper."

"To wait," Susyatin instructed.

He went to the low plywood barrier and grunted into the corridor.

Buntline sat down again. On what was left of his last page he noted:

When he had those thumbs on me, when I was brought close to that depthless face

Question: Was it Gavrych who stirred my heart and pushed me on this quest? Or a loony longing for one spectacular fling of true suffering?

All the same, Comrade Irena, Colonel Stepanchov, I promise to bloody the next brute who puts a hand on me. Fair is fair. Am I not pouring myself out? Have I feigned innocence? Whined for somebody from my embassy? But you must allow me to touch bottom in my own way. I insist, I

"Poor Professor Buntline."

Comrade Irena was beckoning and smiling across the expanse of desk.

"And how must you think of us."

She came round and set before him pads of thick green paper, two fat nickel-plated fountain pens, and sharpened pencils in a cherrywood box.

"I should have understood how insufficient were the supplies for one who is a writer and teacher."

"See here"— there was a bold glint in Buntline's eyes and he pumped up one of his belly laughs —"do you consider me a writer who teaches or a teacher who writes?"

Comrade Irena showed neat small teeth.

"What charming irony of phrase. How wise is Colonel Stepanchov to anticipate pleasure of reading."

"Really? Well, I appreciate that and I'll try to give him my best." And then with a glance of candor Buntline added, "Though surely he must be surfeited with confessions."

"Confessions? Not so. Who has used such a word? What Colonel Stepanchov would have from you—"

She sat down on a corner of the desk and spoke earnestly to herself in Russian.

Finally she said, "A personal history. Did I not explain that with adequacy?"

"So you did," said Buntline. "But I was somewhat tuned out. And on the distraught side."

Distraught or not, he longed to say, I took to you immediately. Didn't you notice me suck in my belly and brace my shoulders?

"Once again, then"—Comrade Irena tossed her hair in a solemn, silly girlish way that sent a pang of lust through Buntline—"to your personal history. Colonel Stepanchov would appreciate these things: One, how do you place yourself within the American socioeconomic context?"

By adroit use of eyes, nostrils, and respiratory rate, Buntline began transmitting subliminal sexual messages.

"Two, was there an involving, official or otherwise, by American government with your enterprise?"

No less than ten minutes' free play with those breasts. For if small boned you are certainly stacked.

"Three, description and clarification of events which brought to your attention Pavel Gavrych and his writings."

Nibbles to each finger. With special emphasis on those ink-stained knuckles. Intake of breath.

"For this personal history sincerity, self-criticism, and straightforward—"

Suddenly Comrade Irena had him by the hair.

"Do you ail, Professor Buntline? How your hands shake!" She pressed his head down. "Place between knees."

Obeying, he sent out a last subliminal message: My life doesn't understand me.

"Have you need of doctor?"

He put a fist to his face, murmured, "Is there a metaphysician in the house?"

She smiled vaguely. "Yes," she said, "Colonel Stepanchov will have pleasure from you."

Then she tapped his knee.

"To work, Professor Buntline. To work, to work."

It was not until she had entered the corridor that Buntline remembered to say, "Thank you."

Comrade Irena burst out laughing.

I'm a middle-aged novelist, Buntline wrote, everlastingly seeking a climax.

He struck this out and started again.

Have you read Gavrych's comments on Lyndon Johnson? "The grosser the nature," he concludes, "the more is it susceptible to noble impulses." Same here, same here.

But you might as well hear about my wife, Enid.

She is a big, fair, clear-eyed, heavy-moving Hoosier.

She is of the lawn-loving, poll-watching, PTA temperament.

She is given to saying, "Believe in the *Consumer Reports* and thou shalt save."

But in my own way I love her.

When I think that Enid is not immortal, that fifty and fibroid tumors await her, my sinuses clog.

Then why is the emotional climate of my household about as healthy as Agamemnon's?

I'll give you an idea.

There was a morning in our kitchen when Enid had just used a no-frills brand of cleanser on the Formica. It pleased her powerfully. She danced around, clapped hands, and I was moved.

I started to say, "My dear."

But then she was pouring heavy cream into her coffee and loading her English muffin with sweet butter.

I said, "Fat cow."

She answered, "Minor talent."

I said, "You will never lose weight and you have turned my life to mud."

She answered, "You are a minor talent who can't even change a washer."

Then she spat into my hair and I flung the butter dish at her Sierra Club calendar.

Our son Chris stopped us.

"See here," he drawled in the way I have always detested, "I am speaking on the telephone."

It's not his fault if he affects me like the prolonged scratching of a nail on slate.

When I ask myself what I want of him the answer is always, "A surprise."

I'd better explain that at seventeen Chris has three scholarships to choose from, that he's honest, reliable, and somewhat on the innocent side, and I imagine the world could fall into worse hands.

But there are no surprises in him.

If I ask for his feelings about eternity he sucks a pencil and says he would rather hold off till he's taken at least nine elective credits in philosophy.

If I say, "Chrisee, the earth is cooling down and so too is humanity," he announces that Stanford has been doing excellent work in body temperature.

If I take a chance on openness and direct appeal, if I try . . .

—

Only just then Buntline was gripped from behind.

As his feet cleared the chair he heaved, twisted backward, and glimpsed that hay-head, that brute-nose, that Susyatin.

Susyatin made soft, snoring noises.

"Lay off! Off!"

"Only to go—"

Susyatin set him down. "To void. Pass water. Long sit write." Susyatin let him have a look at his watch. "Sit write, sit write. Hurt bladder, hurt kidney."

"This is a matter of principle," Buntline roared.

"Empty bladder."

"I'll be giving mind and soul. With pleasure. But it's my bladder—"

With a very short thrust at the midriff, with only the tips of two fingers, Susyatin took the wind out of him.

Buntline needed two minutes over the urinal to start his water. When he did, Susyatin applauded and said, "We have sorrow for our roughness."

"Look," Buntline told him, "a totalitarian is a totalitarian."

Maybe a month before I took off, he wrote, I climbed upstairs to Chris's room and sat whistling beside his work table like a nervous bridegroom.

13 Rue Madeleine, starring James Cagney, was coming on TV, and I wanted him to watch it with me.

"Chrisee, let's have a little I and thou. Let's eat sesame nuggets and watch Cagney."

He looks at me, and in that look only his intelligence is involved.

"Have you ever seen Cagney? I bet you've never seen him, Chrisee."

His "I don't know" is a single uninflected syllable.

I take his hand and open it finger by finger.

"Now here's the thing. I—I and mine lost the straight way. We have no right or somehow can't bring ourselves to say, 'Child, this you must believe.' But I can give you Cagney. Which is something. What say? It must surely be worth something."

"I'm really not interested in movies on TV," he answers, "and it's not my fault if you lost the straight way."

I went out of my skull.

By his hair I dragged him to the den. Then I dumped him on the couch, pinned him with my weight, and force-fed him sesame nuggets.

Downstairs the living room was filled with Enid's League of Women Voters chapter.

I went down among them.

Yowling, " 'Tremble ye women that are at ease; and gird sackcloth upon your loins.' "

Only that's not why I took off. Not really, not altogether.

For next morning my chairman called.

"Lewis, about the Max Wister thing. At this point, Lewis, the thrust of our thinking is that his strengths don't quite suit the present needs of the San Francisco State English Department."

Now Max Wister is important to me.

He gave me my first book to review when I came to New York, bought me my first espresso.

Comrade Irena, Stepanchov, I was Midwest, a grind, a cornball, a meathead. He was New York. Hip, complex, political, embattled, cranky.

All the same he made me feel like a prince of the avant-garde.

And I wanted to do something for him.

They were starting to undercut him at Columbia University, giving him bonehead courses and a basement office which shook from the concussion of the subway.

During this time his literary quarterly folded.

A conglomerate took over Emmereich Books, and the new senior editor fired all the consultants.

And late one Friday afternoon some teenagers jumped him in his office.

He lost eighty percent of his hearing in his left ear and there was liver damage.

Also he was burned out, worn down, without presumption.

Never mind.

Whatever he's lost, Max could still dazzle.

And even during his interview, when I was sweating with boredom, Max showed wit and said significant things.

So I thought it was in the bag. When I drove Max to the airport I was spilling over with delight. "Max Wister at forty-three thousand dollars is the steal of the century and they knew it, I saw they knew it. Oh, this is it!"

But on the boarding ramp Max muttered, "Sport, I blew it."

I felt my heart shake.

"Shouldn't have told that Edmund Wilson story. Stale. Dated. Didn't even tell it too well."

I said, "We'll get the magazine going again."

He answered, "Sure, sport."

I said into his bad ear, "I love you."

He answered, "We'll talk."

He squeezed past me and I watched him board.

I thought that something very essential to life had just passed out of him.

Is it any wonder I was clobbered by my chairman's call?

Three days later I reopened Max's case with the Budget and Personnel Committee.

They had me wait in the corridor while they voted. But through the transom I caught the four nos from my colleagues and the "Definitely not!" from my chairman.

Something discharged in my chest.

I threw open the door, I yowled, I sprang into the room—

But my ankles have always been too thin for my weight.

And a tendon gave way.

This sent me slamming into a chair, the chair skidded, I skidded with it and was caught square in the head by a window plant.

A Kaiser Plan clinic was nearest.

Dr. Kabia Sethi, a sensitive, courteous little Hindu, took care of me.

Instead of sutures he used a butterfly clamp and was sloppy about irrigating the wound. I soon had a dangerous fever.

His insurance company offered a settlement and I wound up with twenty-nine thousand dollars.

My lawyer thought I was out of my mind not to go to trial.

"Forget it," I told him. "The times are out of joint, nobody has immortal longings, and I can't abide another six months of this country."

But here's the truth.

During my fever I dreamed continually of Max, and he was trying to tell me that death would soon have him.

I became embittered in advance.

I foresaw a chilly little service attended by failed poets and ancient ex-radicals and two sticks of type without a photograph at the foot of *The New York Times* obit page.

Those and similar thoughts wiped me out and finally drove me from America.

Neither Enid nor Chris rode to the airport with me, and when the cab came and I tried to hug them—

Never mind.

I had my mind on Paris, also on a certain Ronica Gildersleeve who would have been my next coed if she hadn't gone off to the Sorbonne.

It will be four weeks next Thursday, if I have a next Thursday, that I met Natalie Dowdson.

Inside of our first ten minutes I said to her, "Whatever develops, you are the best thing that has happened to me in twenty years."

She immediately took my hands, kissed the palms, and answered, "Don't let me fall in love with you."

I'll take it back a bit.

About an hour out of Kennedy, when I was on my way to the magazine racks, I spotted her in the aisle seat hunched over some papers. A perfect Middle American sweetheart. Slender. Deep breasted. Dark golden hair. Eyes like a workhouse waif or a child concubine. She was snapping the points off pencils and scraping with her fingernails for new ones.

I said, "I'm a middle-aged writer everlastingly looking for a climax."

"Hey, wonderful!" she said.

Then she gazed intently at my fly. "In your writer's view, do you think"—she peered at her papers—"that there's an affinity between oppressor and oppressed?"

Comrade Irena, Colonel Stepanchov, this was my first knowledge of Pavel Gavrych.

I counted off a dozen heartbeats before saying, "Bless you, girl. I'm really taken with you."

"You're a spontaneous man with wowee reactions," she said, never lifting her eyes off my fly, "and I'll bet you'll be good for me."

She scooped up her papers and stowed them into a tote bag between some hefty Russian-English dictionaries. She snapped the point off another pencil.

"I'll finish that in Paris," she said, and her eyes swam out of focus. "My alumni magazine asked for an update and I'm trying to tell it like it is."

She wanted me to know she was lying, and I can't describe my pleasure. Really, is it me? America? I mean . . . most of my extramarital coupling starts off with some imbecilic lie. Oh, what an anthology of nitwit pussy narratives I could compile! Those prefuck sympathy builders! Tisha's rape by a stepfather; Mimi's clinical death during a tonsillectomy; Leatrice's dead twin . . .

However, we were soon heading into deepest Atlantic night under a single blanket, and we slept and stroked and with our mouths pressed together went, "Hello there, hello there." A little past Iceland, though, she whimpered and drew away.

"Buntee, do you want to make out with me?" And before she had drawn breath: "Buntee, how would you react and what would you do if I used your toothbrush?"

"It would represent to me the *summum bonum.*"

"Mary Mother, how I hoped you'd say that!"

And she plunged her tongue into my right ear.

A flight attendant pushing her food cart down the aisle stopped, wagged a hand over us, and giggled.

"You two believe in satisfying only one drive at a time."

This broke me up. But Natalie shivered.

She told me, "My curse is on the way."

A little later she bit my lower lip. "It's two weeks off. And when I fly I'm always late.

"The way that stewardess said, 'You two!' It crossed my mind, uh-oh, she'll remember you, and so I crapped around about my curse to cover a disproportionate reaction of free-floating anxiety and, Mary Mother, listen, listen!"

She breathed as if her lungs were not large enough.

"I sound just like him."

She took a swing at the air.

"Mr. Compulsive Repressive. Mr. Father Love. Mr. Shoe Tree."

She blew breath up into her face.

"He wanted me to go for consciousness raising. Too much effing consciousness as it is. When the end of time comes mankind will still be gibbering, 'I didn't relate to my peer group, I had impossible ego goals, I held back, I overreached, I underachieved . . .' "

I said, "I like that."

"Not mine."

"Whose?"

"A mad Russian with bad thumbs."

And I was overtaken by queer presentiments.

But Natalie rattled on.

"Buntee, I have to get air back into my tires. Sweet Buntee, there's a wild hair inside my head."

She wept into her hands.

"That Buzz, that Buzz!"

What a case she built against him!

During foreplay he might whimper, "We're losing India," or "Kiss off Europe, concentrate on China."

Bed was a battlefield or a kindergarten. He was bad ball. Low on gas. Yet she didn't mind. Not exactly, not really. She'd think NOR-STAD, NATO, ground zero. Then power.

"Mostly power. Buntee, I had the whole military-industrial complex inside me."

Meanwhile the sun was climbing from the sea to our port wing. And pretty soon the captain banked to give passengers a look at the French coast. Then everybody got busy with passports, vaccination certificates, and such, and we did the same.

That's when I saw a State Department ID in Natalie's billfold.

I was confounded. For all along I'd imagined her at part-time jobs in boutiques or record shops or coffee houses.

"What do you do there?"

All she would say was, "Coffee serving."

We stayed at the Hotel Nirveau near Père Lachaise Cemetery, and by our fifth day I expected to be laid under those evil-looking locust trees alongside Hugo, Zola, Balzac, and the other illustrious dead.

For I had constant low back pain and my prostate felt lumpy as a potato.

But Natalie was drugged with love.

Comrade Irena, Colonel Stepanchov, in writing this I feel gross, low, a real shit. For Natalie had a good heart and wanted more than anything else to please me.

I understand now how she worked to change herself.

What did it cost her, I wonder, to stop barking orders like a sexual drill sergeant? To stifle that throaty, "Mary Mother, fuck me, fuck me, fuck me hard and hard"? To leave off hammering my head and raking my back?

At the time, though, I was set to cut and run.

Till the morning of our sixth day, when Natalie said wistfully, "I think I'm most likely some kind of fugitive."

I answered, "I too, I too."

"Buntee, I did something that's sinking in, yessiree, it's coming down on me like a busted house."

And then with scrupulous diction she said, " 'Good-bye Grover's Corners . . . Good-bye to clocks ticking and sleeping and waking up.' "

And then in her own voice she said, "I was the best Emily Gibbs they ever had, and they were always putting on *Our Town*. I loved high school. I think this is a fucking fine country and I love it and would never hurt it. I once loved it so much I cried when I heard Walt Whitman was gay."

Twenty minutes later she put before me bits and pieces of Gavrych's writings.

They grabbed and shook me up so that I nearly turned my weak ankles again.

Also I thought, "I have to get this to Max. This will have him on his feet and back to his place in the world. What an introduction he could write, what a fusion of political insight and literary sensibility. Oh whoopee, can it be that good might come from my horny ways?" And more of the same.

Now I'll try to tell you how Natalie came by those pages.

About a week before her curse, a time when her moods were always wild and adventurous, she recited twenty minutes of *Our Town* into a cassette tape recorder and played it during sex with Wagonside.

Whereupon he'd truly tuned in. Rang the bell. Flooded the basement. Rained on the roof.

She said, "El smasho," he answered, "Jumping melonballs."

But days later she discovered that he'd erased the tape.

And filled it with birthday readings for his father from Charles Beard.

"Buzz, why couldn't you use another tape?"

He got on his back.

"You are a piece of Washington ass without family feeling."

He flogged the floor with his buttocks.

"You are a dumb GAS-5 cunt and you think only with your snatch."

Comrade Irena, Colonel Stepanchov, Natalie is a quick, strong girl.

And so, when Wagonside rose she butted him with her stomach, hooked a leg behind him, and smacked him hard on the nose.

She saw blood. This somehow stirred her further against him, and she picked up one of his shoe trees and knocked him senseless.

Then she packed a bag and left.

She recalled that while driving away she was screaming, "Washington hurts! America hurts! Take off! Save yourself!"

And so she returned to Wagonside's flat for her passport.

He was on the floor and in a bad way.

But by the time she got her passport he had found strength enough to wheeze, "Beats having to ball you."

Then he heaved his clipboard at her.

She caught it on the fly and fled with it.

That clipboard, that clipboard!

Thicker than his dick and more essential to him.

And so Natalie cruised around Washington feeding memoranda, progress reports, and such into the Potomac, the Anacostia, and Rock Creek.

The last batch she meant to impale on a spike at the north gate of the White House.

Only she noticed suddenly that it was a mix of Russian and English.

She noticed a line: "Man is the only species in nature with a capacity for self-hatred."

Riffling pages, she noticed also the words "creature" and "death" and "savage."

These pages she stowed away in her tote bag.

On the flight to New York she read further and remembered feeling more settled and thoughtful than she had any right to feel.

At Kennedy she considered mailing back the material, postage due, to Wagonside.

No, she decided, let him seethe and boil and suffer his constipation.

After all, she'd taken an adult education year of Russian. She would finish the translating and have it sent by diplomatic pouch.

And so she bought a hefty Russian-English dictionary from the bookshop in the Aeroflot building.

But I had distracted her on the plane.

"Sweet Buntee, you had such a big fat hard-on."

I phoned Max that night.

"Max. I'm in Paris."

"Not what it used to be, sport. Never was."

"Max, armor yourself against despair."

"I have thumbprints on my glasses."

"Something is under way, Max."

"Can't think of a reason to clean them."

"I'll say no more, but something is under way."

Then Natalie and I went walking.

I was giddy with thought.

Near the Tuileries Natalie started to fade and lag. I parked her on a bench and wandered off among the stone and bronze beauties.

To Eleanor of Aquitaine I said, "Lady, help me purge and restore Max. Help me turn him on to Gavrych as I'm turned on. I'll send him—what do you suggest? Give me a sign. Bond a little of your wisdom onto me. Maybe the section about the Russian fascination with suffering? Where Gavrych says that suffering has altered nothing. Has taught Russia about as much as the cleaver teaches a carcass."

Then Natalie came after me.

"Buntee," she said, "it's going to rain. Emily Gibbs died in the rain and my nose is running."

But it never really rained. There was only an incessant damp which fell cold and miserable and smelled of wet dog.

After three days of this Natalie said, "When it's over eighty percent humidity I achieve only clitorals and Gavrych is too rough to translate on just clitorals."

So we flew to the Andalusian province of Spain.

In Torremolinos we had a happy week roughing out Gavrych on the habits of tyrants.

Here Wagonside caught up with us.

It happened five days ago, just after sunrise.

Natalie and I were alone on the beach, capering and squirting wine at each other because she'd translated eleven lines of Gavrych. One phrase, though—"There are things must have their turn in the world"—we never got to complete, and I'd give anything to know what things Gavrych meant.

Sweating and wheezing in a heavy blue double-knit suit, Wagonside came wading through the sand.

"Yo, everybody; everybody, yo."

Natalie lobbed seashells at him.

"I'm Byron Wagonside," he said.

Looking at him, I was compelled to think of Chris. Handsome but flat. Fervent but dull. Clever but dense.

He said, "Sir, you have something of mine."

Then he kicked sand at Natalie.

Natalie was first on all fours. Then her hands were over her ears.

He said, "You have something of mine, sir."

A very thin noise came from Natalie.

He said, "Be grateful, sir, that you're dealing with me. There are those . . . They'd have seen fit . . . Jumping melonballs!"

He pulled Natalie to her feet. She wouldn't take her hands from her ears.

Working his jaws as if he were cracking a tiny seed he said, "They know how to prolong the sensation of drowning for twenty minutes."

My ankles wobbled.

"They can do it with six drops of water."

And I handed over the Gavrych papers.

Then Natalie whimpered and bumped each of us with a hip.

"Jumping melonballs," Wagonside said in a flat voice. "Isn't she a great piece of ass? A real thumper?"

An odd dreamy smile crossed Natalie's face.

And Wagonside marched her toward the coarse dune grass.

I walked a little behind, snarling with hatred and weakness.

Then an idea took hold.

"Yo, Wagonside. Wagonside, yo."

He turned and said, "Six drops of water, sir."

I raised an imaginary phone to my ear and in a prissy Princetonian croon said, "Lewis Buntline here, Mr. Undersecretary. Shan't be more than half a mom'. Bit of a security leak. Suggest a peekyboo at the Gavrych file."

Natalie put her cheek to Wagonside's and kept it there.

"Shouldn't be surprised if it's signed out to a certain Wagonside, Mr. Undersecretary."

Then my ankles gave way.

"Easy, sir," said Wagonside.

He walked me about till the pain passed.

"In Mexican standoff situations," he said, "we're trained to come to terms."

He looked down at his loafers as if they were burning.

"What do you want?"

"The Gavrych manuscript," I told him. "All of it."

His face expanded.

"The manuscript is called *Leviathan's Hook*," he said listlessly. "If you want the rest I'll endeavor to give you ways and means of bringing it out, sir, with minimal risk from—"

And he pointed, Comrade Irena, Colonel Stepanchov, straight at North Africa.

"—Russia."

Natalie sucked his ear.

"Could have brought it out last October. Only I didn't think it was worth shit. Too doggone much liberal arts lingo, and I was never strong on liberal arts."

"But you're very good on detail," Natalie told him.

In London I had to go to Globemaster Tours on Edgware Road and meet a certain Anthony Montcrieff.

He was a plump, rosy, bald little squirrel of a man, and so cordial, so civilized that I hated belittling him.

Neverthless I went by Wagonside's instructions, saying after tea, "Can't you speak up? No wonder you people lost the Empire."

He twinkled and gave me an answer.

" 'When Earth's last picture is painted and the tubes are twisted and dried/When the oldest colors have faded and the youngest critic has died/We shall rest, and, faith, we shall need it.' "

"Great!" I cried.

For all he really needed say was " 'The youngest critic has died.' " But he was a gentleman, he had a giving nature, and I hope Comrade Irena, Colonel Stepanchov, that I do him no harm by naming him.

In a phlegmy whisper he said, "World could stand a good dose of Kipling, don't y'think?"

Then he came round the desk and slapped my back.

"You'll be doing the two-hundred-fifteen-pound Moscow Intourist week and putting up at the Rossiya Hotel. Excellent heavy sausage. Black bread's deteriorated. Greens start vanishing this time of year. Stay with the fine smoky cabbage."

He wagged his head like a bird on a branch.

"Coupon packet includes three days' prepaid auto rental. Best avoid driving on your own. Nothing much to see, anyway. Do your Lenin's tomb, your Basil Church, your Bolshoi, your Fabergé eggs, and Romanov bric-a-brac."

He opened an ancient-looking ledger.

"One thing more. You'll be having a distressingly noisy WC at the Rossiya. Or missing a bath plug. A spot of bad plumbing, at any rate. Be sure to make a ghastly row about it, there's a good fellow."

He folded down a souvenir calendar and pushed it into my pocket.

"You're set for Welbeck House on Tottenham Court Road. Best we can do for you during the cricket matches. Beastly food. Open sandwiches and half a paper napkin."

I waited till my Russian visa came through before calling Max.

"Heart and truth will be had, Max."

"My name's misspelled in the university directory."

"Transcend, Max."

"Still haven't cleaned my glasses."

"Something's under way, Max. New heights are appearing. My word on it."

"Shouldn't have told that Edmund Wilson story, sport."

Thirty-six hours of Moscow were all I had.

At the Rossiya Hotel I found a plumbing problem just as Anthony Montcrieff had promised. Right after breakfast this morning my radiator started throwing off water and steam.

I cried, "Good show, old spymaster!"

And remembering Montcrieff's instructions about making an awful row, I really threw myself into it. By the time I saw the service chief I was shedding tears of rage. I even broke his yardstick across my knee. He was a nice old guy, too, and when he bent for his yardstick I noticed a crooked spine.

Ten minutes later a man wearing coveralls, a burlap apron, and a bandolier of clinking tools let himself into my room. Though he had a lean face he carried a huge belly like an altered tomcat.

"Hullo."

And he put a penknife to the radiator valve, gave it a quarter-turn, and stopped the gush.

"Needs a new valve, actually," he said looking very fatigued.

"I feel like Kim," I said.

He buffed his nails on the apron.

"Oh, you English were so right to call this the 'great game.' "

"So we did. So we did."

Suddenly he fingered the lapel of my jacket.

"Might get yourself something in wide-wale corduroy. Lots coming in from Bulgaria. Excellent goods. Nothing at all like your Muscovite shoddy. Goes directly to commission stores."

He snapped a loose thread from my buttonhole.

"Gorki Street, fifth exit, where it runs into Kutuzovsky Prospekt, has one of your best commission stores. You'll want Mitya. Do please tip him. Handsomely, if you can manage it. Wages only one hundred thirty-five rubles the month, apart from our pittance. Fellow's been to some trouble on your behalf. Hours microfilming your Pavel Gavrych. And handstitching the stuff under two thicknesses of collar yoke. Bloody awful on the eyes."

We shook hands.

"Rumors about your Gavrych. Has a following they tell me. Passing his book about by the thousands. Underground press and such. Might want to wait a month or two, get y'self a copy easy enough."

I told him there was a friend, a good friend, who couldn't wait.

The Rossiya doorman assured me that the fifth exit of Gorki Street where it runs into Kutuzovsky Prospekt fell within the nine-ruble taxi district.

But when I arrived the driver demanded double because it was raining.

We came close to blows. In fact, we were stamping around each other in the street, howling, shoving, swinging powderpuff punches.

And that's why I first thought I was being arrested for hooliganism.

"Stepanchov wishes that you shall have a real Russian tea," said Comrade Irena.

"To eat, to eat," Susyatin bayed, showing off the trays of pirogi, caviar, grated egg and green onion, smoked fish and seeded cakes.

Comrade Irena said, "Stepanchov will himself express in a time of no more than a quarter hour the pleasure he has had from your statement. I am on his behalf empowered to say that many things will then come into a higher clarity for you."

"Doubtless," whispered Buntline.

And with streaming eyes he added, "It'll be handy learning how much pain I can take."

Normally he hated dawn, and there was, besides, a thin drizzle. But Buntline felt such a flow of peculiar energy that he wheedled Comrade Irena into parking her ZIL below the Karmeni Bridge and walking the last kilometer to the Rossiya. And though he risked turning an ankle on the slick paving stones, he took long, sweeping strides, head up, hands linked behind him.

"Your color is so rich, Professor Buntline. Do you presently have thoughts of Gavrych? Or is your mind with coeds?"

Blushing deeply, she added, "This was teasing only."

She went on to say, "In their teasing Russian women bring customarily a lacking of grace. In particular this may be true of those trained to Marxist-Leninist perceptions. Like myself."

She put a quick hand to his shoulder.

"See here—"

And Buntline spoke out with sudden force.

"—I'm not sure I'm the man."

Comrade Irena's brows rose, her eyes turned moist and brilliant. "I should say yes, Professor Buntline. I should certainly say yes."

"I'm not . . . at bottom I'm not political. In fact, Max—"

There was a broken sunlight now and the sky was clearing itself. Two batches of clouds collided, merged, and Buntline watched the wind sculpt them into George V and Nicholas II riding a single skinny horse.

"Max," he picked up, "claimed that I'd have forgiven Stalin the pact and the Moscow trials and the labor camps if he'd had a superior prose style."

"This is not the view Stepanchov holds."

"And do I really want to change things?" He pressed hand to hand. "There was a time I did. But now I make no demands. Not really. Not like the old breeds. They had standards. My Aunt Clarissa once claimed there soon won't be an American alive with courage enough to send a restaurant dish back to the kitchen. When I wanted to know what special present she wanted for her ninetieth birthday she said, 'Grandeur, dear boy, grandeur.' "

"You should talk of her to your president. Oh certainly you should."

Comrade Irena wrinkled her face.

"Yes, I have utmost belief in your ability to transmit Gavrych's teachings to representatives of American power."

"We have an ambassador," Buntline told her stumblingly, "you have an ambassador. We have a Congress, you have a Supreme Soviet. Why me?"

She answered, "One, circumstance has favored us with an eloquent American at the service of no special interest. Two, what you have revealed under unpleasant but necessary pressures are true feelings of most admirable friendship and loyalty—to your Max Wister if not to your wife. Three, on both our sides there are such as Wagonside— carriers of clipboards, paperworkers, clods, to whom the permanent war economy is meat and drink. Which one should speak for Gavrych? Four, I have the belief that Stepanchov clings to established habit and takes a private happiness in surprising and pulling the nose of one who in Washington is his counterpart."

"I'm being used," Buntline grumbled.

Comrade Irena twisted a finger at him. "As to that, I note in your dealing with student coeds an absence of saintliness."

Trying to work himself into a rage, Buntline said, "I'll back out. Don't think I wouldn't."

"Were there no difficulties to these student coed matters? In our universities there would be difficulties, though these difficulties may to an extent be a function of our housing shortage."

Comrade Irena clicked her tongue and as if in afterthought said, "Do not change your mind, Professor Buntline, though in fairness I have no true belief you hold such an intention. This would distress Stepanchov, and from established habit he could not restrain himself from causing you comparable distress."

"Those eyes," Buntline exclaimed. "And he was being amiable."

"There is further this. Properly concerned officials of Washington will soon be knowledgeable that there is a Professor Buntline, and he carries significant news. Likewise your media. Already you are a media event, and have been such for the last several hours."

All Buntline could think to say was, "Really, I don't go along with

Max. I wouldn't have forgiven Stalin. However well he might have written I wouldn't have forgiven him."

"Yes." She made a gesture that stopped just short of his arm. "Yes, I hold such a view of you."

After a while Buntline said in a cracked voice, "At this moment I feel . . . I simply *feel*."

"And so you should, Professor Buntline. So you should." Comrade Irena gave him a vivid glance. "How well you have done! For your Max Wister the guarantee of introducing *Leviathan's Hook* to your countrymen. For your English connection, your kindly and courteous Anthony Montcrieff, safety—though I must tell you that he was never in danger, that over the years Stepanchov has used the poor gentleman very much as he needed and saw fit. For yourself—"

They were near the Rossiya now, but she hung back.

Blinking and twisting her neck and shoulders, Comrade Irena said, "There is in his chapter nine an observation by Gavrych which has light to your personal situation as I view it. 'Man's capacity for wretchedness is not diminished by unrestricted gratification.' "

She touched a finger to his forehead.

"This too was teasing only."

"See here," said Buntline, bringing up one of his belly laughs, "I'm glad the KGB is an equal opportunity employer."

"What is 'equal opportunity employer'?"

"See here," he said again.

"See here," she mimicked.

He rose on his toes and filled his lungs.

"Comrade Irena," he said, "I don't suppose . . ."

She answered, "To wife, Professor Buntline. To wife, to wife."

And they smiled at one another.

"See here, see here, Professor Buntline," she began. Then she paled and an expression of austerity and severe primness settled on her face.

"There are hours only to your plane departure. And I am one of those . . . There is a saying, and for such a saying there is a reason . . . He who holds the wish to please a Russian woman must . . ."

And she shook his hand.

"Comrade Irena," he said, "tell me this." He trapped both her hands and brought them together in a clasp. "What in blazes will it feel like? How will it be for you and Russia, after a thousand years of repression?"

"How will it feel? It will feel sympathy, brotherhood, purest joy. To some extent also it will feel—"

She pulled away her hands.

"—like this, Buntee, Buntee, sweet Buntee."

Then she kissed him and murmured, *"Dozvedanya, dozvedanya, dozvedanya."*

12

When they had drawn as close as they could in their aluminum walkers Dr. Hurster said in a soft voice, "Comments? Anyone?"

He adjusted the pulley lamp so that they might see better.

Harriet Menkes, tuberculosis of the spine, rocked on the edges of her furry slippers. Then with a slow wagging of her head she said, "He must have been . . . Sort of shows on his face to me . . . A sneaky, nasty person."

Loretta Osterburg, pancreatic adenoma, gave her a harsh, freezing glare.

Gertrude Sazar, hemochromatosis, gasped, crossed herself, and said, "There's our little Harriet. Oh, if there's a rotten word to say, it'll come from her mouth."

"From her mouth"—Loretta raised her walker, slammed it down on the cork floor—"and with her last breath."

Nell Porlock, thymoma, spoke up, saying with brightened eyes, "Harriet was increasing the . . . the petty viciousness of people to make departure from the human scene easier."

"Hell I was," said Harriet. "If it comes to the petty viciousness of people"—her voice rose a notch—"no need increasing it with those two around."

"Yes, that's our little Harriet," Gertrude said to Loretta.

"Darling mouth on her," Loretta said to Dr. Hurster.

"Don't want to lose sight of today's point," said Dr. Hurster. "We're down here primarily to—to what?"

"To learn to apprehend," said Nell, "that man is essentially a biodegradable substance."

"Right," Dr. Hurster answered gloriously. "And very good."

"Right, yes, very good, yes," Harriet croaked.

"Who forced you to come down here?" Loretta asked Harriet.

"I just . . . wonder"—Harriet tittered—"I don't suppose, no, of course not, we couldn't be jealous. Could we be jealous?" She held her lip an instant with her teeth.

" 'Course we are," Loretta answered blandly. "Every reason to be jealous. We're jealous of your . . . that gorgeous sick-bed attire. Those fashionable outfits."

"Her bed jacket with the split seams," Gertrude cried gaily.

"When did your children last visit?" Harriet demanded. "Because mine don't miss a day. Not a day I don't have my children. Mine take turns driving in from Trenton and Wheaton and Dover and Philadelphia, and they bring me—"

"Harriet," sang out Nell.

Harriet bit the tip of her tongue.

"No, Harriet," Nell exclaimed.

Harriet looked suddenly meditative and heartsick.

The elevator bell pinged, the door opened, and two male nurses dragged a cart of bloody bedclothes behind the brickwork pillars.

Then Loretta said, "Wouldn't you think . . . ?"

And Gertrude said, "Considering our circumstance. Circumstances being what they are for us . . ."

One male nurse could be heard admonishing the other for "disrespect" and a tasteless joke about cold cuts.

"I would think," Harriet said to Loretta and Gertrude, "that considering our circumstances—why are we so absolutely locked in to what we are? Far as I can see, I'm still what I was, and if God returned me a year from now I don't imagine anything on earth suiting me the least bit more or me being the least bit easier on people. Still, listen, jealous or not"—she burst into laughter, stopping only when she momentarily lost hold of her walker—"I am feeling love. I love you all."

"That's the ticket," said Dr. Hurster.

"Welcome, welcome, welcome back," said Gertrude.

"We love you, love you," said Loretta.

"Harriet," cried Nell, "be bathed in golden realms."

Then Dr. Hurster moved over to the next wheeled stretcher and uncovered the corpse.

"Comments? Who wants to start off with a comment or an observation or a feeling? Anyone?"

Nell spoke first.

She said, "I see in his face no sign of sorrow or anger. He has a very English sort of face, and I imagine he may have thought of death as an English pub keeper, a kindly but firm English pub keeper with an eye on his customers, an eye on his clock, a kindly, tactful English pub keeper who sticks to the rules, and once eleven o'clock comes won't be swayed from calling, 'Time, gentlemen, ladies, time, time, time . . .'"

13

"I had every thundering right to know," said Eunice.

"Drop it," the President said, opening his hands.

"Thanks to your precious thundering Harry I was humiliated personally"—Eunice threw a cotton swab at him—"and affronted as First Lady."

"Nell's dying, by Jesus, but you're affronted." The President stared at her brutally, wonderingly.

"If I'd known, and I had every thundering right to know as Nell's friend—"

"Shit you had."

"—I wouldn't have been reminded of a certain awful thing, you know what thing, a thing that maimed my childhood."

The President did not treat this as needing an answer.

"Walking in unawares and expecting la-de-da talk about D and Cs and such with Nell. You just tell Harry I am so thundering pissfire angry at him I could spit."

"Well, don't be," said the President. "Harry's a very private person and it's not as if you and Nell were cookies-in-bed close."

"One little look at her"—under the pallor of makeup Eunice's face darkened harshly—"I straightaway knew what she had."

She took a thin pearl choker and an Elath stone on a fine silver chain from her jewelry box, held them at her throat, then out toward him.

"Gee"—he frowned— "I don't know. They're both . . . Though

neither is . . ." He drew a slow, deep breath and under it murmured, "Umm, no. No."

"What is visited upon mortal flesh surpasses my understanding," said Eunice. "So thundering . . . Oh Lord God, Thou knowest."

She pushed an orange stick into her cuticles.

The President applied a little lanolin to the snarled ends of his back hair.

"Least saw Nell alive. Least gave her such consolation as I could." Eunice pulled in her chin, blew powder off the plastic cape that covered her shoulders. "More than I could do for Papa, poor Papa."

Eunice pointed at his shoes. "There."

"By Jesus." Wrapping a towel tightly around his palm, the President blotted away some drops of lanolin.

"Walking in on Nell gave me such a thundering fright. Memories of Papa, poor Papa. Pangs of déjà vu."

"Nell's dying, but you get pangs."

Eunice rubbed estrogen skin lotion into her extended throat, into the backs of her ears, into the base of her hairline; what was left on her fingertips she very slowly and teasingly stroked into the President's sideburns.

And while his eyes dreamily closed, while he gasped with satisfaction, he silently called upon JFK.

Saying, "Old buddy. Pal. A hint, a sign from you would go a long way. For I still want to fulfill my assignment in history. Do you think they could stand straight talk? Suppose I spoke out and—but what do I say if I speak out? People, America, hear me. I must ask you— but what do I ask of you?"

"They never truly knew what caused Papa to hemorrhage."

She sprayed cologne on her wrist and sniffed it.

"Walked in, Cousin Luren and I, and doctors and nurses were around and doing things to him. Turning his head this way, that way with their red hands."

"People, America," the President silently declared, "can you change your ways? Your spoiled child ways of eating, wearing, using . . . ?"

"Appeared to me as they were tearing away at him, and the floor shone, just glowed with blood, poor Papa's blood."

She stepped near the President, turned, hunched her shoulders.

Careful not to touch her hair, he slowly drew the plastic cape over her head.

Children of the permanent war economy, be not like the dumb driven cattle. Look at yourselves! You've had five fat decades of filling your stomachs and closing your minds.

"Never did get to see him again. Only as a corpse three days later. Tuesday, that was. Come Thursday and I had my first curse."

Eunice moistened a finger on her tongue, tilted her head, touched an eye, came away with a loose lash.

Let me take you through these dark and cynical times. Give me the chance and I'll fulfill my assignment in history, I'll do good and wise things.

"Only eleven and not another girl in my class had her curse, and sure as blue tarnation I believed—know what I believed? what awful thing? the thing that maimed my childhood?"

Together we can rediscover our national soul, get back to unfinished social business.

"My blood and poor Papa's blood. His life ends with blood and my womanly life begins with blood, and to me there was a connection and no one could tell me otherwise, and it was more than I could rightly bear."

Eunice nodded, blew a kiss at herself in the mirror, nodded again.

The President went to the door, opened it, and to the blond agent with the rimless sunglasses said, "On our way."

He extended an arm to Eunice; she smoothed or pretended to smooth a wrinkle along the yoke of his collar, then took his arm.

Working together with belief and purpose we could make heaven jealous.

The balding agent with the tortoiseshell sunglasses opened the door fully for them, and they heard many voices below in the East Room and the soft, sweet sound of mixed saxophones and violins.

Eunice nodded, tapped his wrist, moved ahead.

But if I may speak the truth—forgive me, people, America, children of the permanent war economy, but this is the truth: By Jesus, I've no more faith in you than you have in me.

Keeping one and one-half steps behind Eunice, the President, heavy with unshed tears, prepared to greet Mr. and Mrs. Lewis Buntline and their son, Christopher.

COUNSELOR: I would be pleased to hear about him, Vidyon.

ORLOFSKY: Zashilov, Georgi Zashilov was his name, and what I shall lay on you is no jive. Perhaps a womanizing cocksman. Perhaps even a murderer. Certainly a mystic, of a far-out mind-set. In the seventeenth century he went about Russia talking Kingdom of God stuff to the serfs and badmouthing the nobility. But they were happy to keep him in business.

COUNSELOR: Because he was a holy man?

ORLOFSKY: Because where he went, to whatever hole and corner, misery and despair were not seen again among the small-fry masses.

COUNSELOR: I imagine, like many seventeenth-century Russian mystics, he preached to the poor that violent hatred of the present is the gateway to ecstasy and rapture.

ORLOFSKY: The poor had less interest in his ecstasy and rapture than in the costly wines he would hide a few versts behind their villages. They thought him otherwise a posturing fool and named him "Wine Hider."

COUNSELOR: What brought him to mind, Vidyon?

ORLOFSKY: Yesterday, traveling to an Elktown junk-food place favored by my good buddy the driver for soft ice cream, I saw a man leave his broken-down car and walk off to seek help. This was on your I-95, which has no lack of hustle-bustle traffic or fuzz. Why then, I wondered, was my good buddy laughing and snorting at this man and saying, "parts city" and "chop chop"?

COUNSELOR: He meant, I would imagine—

ORLOFSKY: Spare yourself breath. For ten minutes later, returning from my junk-food blitz and once again on your I-95, I saw what was left of the car. A shell, a husk, a cadaver, a gutted automotive effigy. Four of your blacks, still wielding dismembering tools, called us rude names when we slowed down to eyeball and presently came alongside us in a vehicle of many colors and covered with such scatological commands as "Eat shit." By the blasting of their stereo, the waving and high signs, the style in which they saluted us with their beer cans, I could see they were well pleased, in bliss, gloriously bonded to your pluralistic society. Okay, then and there I was socked by an inspiration. Do you wish . . . ?

COUNSELOR: I do.

ORLOFSKY: Let your president learn from Georgi Zashilov. Let him become, so to speak, a wine hider. Let him—but I am in excess of mental dazzlement. . . . Forgive if I seem lacking in the lucidity department.

COUNSELOR: Oh, but please continue. And no apologies necessary.

ORLOFSKY: Right on, then. So . . . so I imagine I am not soft in the head to maintain that after two-hundred-plus unsouling years your blacks are still stuck at a minimal level of caste and class? Still sad and dreary and worn down from the push of all the currents that run against them? Still the sickly children of your national nursery seeking to suckle and nurture?

COUNSELOR: Sound enough, Vidyon. All too sound.

ORLOFSKY: Your billions of welfare dollars, your housing projects, your voting rights, your public health clinics leave them unsatisfied. And what should your blacks be satisfied about if their leaders demand everything in general from nothing and nobody in particular? The black leader message is, "Blood and bombs in the streets but also the benefits of order and organization." The black leader message is, "Unlimited social progress without society." What they want will not be found in their American diaspora, perhaps not even on this earth.

COUNSELOR: You have little hope, then, of a change in the essential black condition?

ORLOFSKY: No way. What I would offer the President is an outlet for the unused and dangerous energy of your blacks, an escape valve to let off some of their inner confusion.

COUNSELOR: Sip a bit of that juice, Vidyon. Your blood sugar . . .

ORLOFSKY: With minimal budgetary drain he can give America some short, peaceful times by a now equivalent of wine hiding. Let him abandon, close by your great metropolitan centers, a few hundred fine cars that can be dismembered by the black artists of chop. And why not increase their joy, announce a contest and cash prizes for those whose dismemberment and chopping is swiftest and most artful?

COUNSELOR: Clever, Vidyon. The idea will be on his desk before long. I'll see to that.

ORLOFSKY: Should success follow, as I believe it must, your president might be knocked out by another Orlofsky thought—to scatter in strange American places purses and pocketbooks containing valuable baubles and charge cards and such for free-and-easy spending, also—

COUNSELOR: He'll take to it, I know. But what about a bit of that juice, Vidyon?

15

OPENING STATEMENT: Earlier this week I brought you—and America—together with the man who helped open up a new era in personal diplomacy. For I wanted you—and America—to know Lewis Buntline as I have come to know him, to understand the nature of the mission he undertook and performed so wonderfully well with the guidance and, yes, the prayers of our government.

Now I shall try to give you—and America—some deeper understanding of the enormous events in the Soviet Union which compelled that mission, and of Pavel Gavrych, whose writings and teachings profoundly influenced those events.

The Soviet system is presently beset by unparalleled internal difficulties, by stresses and strains, cracks and fissures, of such magnitude that its ability to function as a viable society is clearly threatened.

This has come about without bloodshed, without incitement to the kind of popular uprising or civil disobedience whose consequences have come to weigh too heavily upon us all.

For Pavel Gavrych gave the Soviet people a new instrument of struggle.

"Let us," he said, "obey to the utmost and with an air of unthinking conviction."

"We shall accept submission," he said, "with the delight of a child accepting a new toy."

"Through our absolute consent," he said, "they shall be denied everything."

"How shall we wear them down?" he said. "Only by exceeding their demands."

"Those who carry placards," he said, "those who chain themselves to gates, those who write and paint what is forbidden only enslave us further."

This is the doctrine Pavel Gavrych called *dachnyetism,* or "negative affirmation," the doctrine Soviet authorities derided as "political vegetarianism." Gavrych himself they viewed as a harmless crank who would serve them well with his opposition to the dissidents.

Yet within two years it was clear that Gavrych understood the facts of Soviet life better than the dissidents.

One of these facts, for example, is the chronic shortage of telephones.

Thus, in the outlying districts of every Soviet city there are tens of thousands who live in huge new apartment house complexes constructed so hastily, so shoddily, so irrationally that no thought was given to the installation of telephone cables. At all hours hundreds stand in line and wait a turn at the one or two public phone boxes which must serve an entire complex.

One day there was no such line in any city.

And not a single call was made.

In Moscow, Kiev, Leningrad, and Odessa people simply wrote . . . and wrote . . . and wrote letters to friends and relatives, to newspapers and magazines, to clerks and commissars. They exchanged recipes and passages from the classics. They commented on articles and editorials which had either never appeared or had appeared months before. They requested that searches be made for imaginary records in bureaus that had been destroyed during the Nazi invasion.

Soon there was a shortage of stamps. Mailboxes were padlocked or simply removed from the streets. Police cordoned off post offices. Millions of pieces of mail lay undelivered.

This was *dachnyetism*—negative affirmation.

And before long the Soviet government faced a curious tax problem.

Now the Soviet tax system is a remarkably complex and inhuman one—yes, even more complex and inhuman than our own.

[Laughter]

Should, for example, a resident of Rostov be found in a fraud he must personally appear at Voronezh, hundreds of miles away. He thereby suffers twofold punishment—for the fraud, of course, and for absenteeism from his job as well.

About eleven months ago computers in seven different tax districts began picking up a singular pattern.

Fraud? No, officials couldn't call it fraud. They would have to call it—but just what could they call it?

For about three quarters of a million Soviet citizens were guilty of an offense—or was it an offense?—which no Soviet statute covered.

Overpayment.

Never less than three rubles, never more than ten.

Dachnyetism—negative affirmation.

But it was too late to reprogram the computers, which by this time had printed out three quarters of a million forms summoning three quarters of a million taxpayers to their district offices for interrogation.

And within a month, as we estimate it, the Soviet Union lost some three-point-seven million workdays.

Then Soviet managers and planners were suddenly celebrating a dramatic increase in the production of high-quality steel from the Donets Basin.

And just as suddenly the celebration stopped.

Yet steel production was still climbing.

But where was the high-quality coke to keep blast furnaces going at such capacity?

It would be on its way soon—well, as soon as certain newly opened mines in southwestern Siberia received shipments of certain overdue safety devices.

It would be on its way as soon as—well, as soon as railway cars could be transferred from the Ukraine, where they were already in short supply because of an unusually heavy harvest.

It would be on its way as soon as—well, as soon as the planners and managers had recruited more miners for southwestern Siberia, redesigned the safety devices, and improved the roadbeds on the rail line between the Ukraine and the Donets Basin.

Dissent? Opposition?

Only if zeal and diligence were offenses.

Only if work itself was an anti-Soviet activity.

Had not Gavrych said, "Through our absolute consent they shall be denied everything"?

Now the final phase of *dachnyetism*.

All at once workers presented their trade union councils with this petition: "We urge restoration of the labor policies and practices instituted by Stalin as a means of awakening sluggish proletarian consciousness. Only the most stringent measures can inspire us to harvest ever-new fruits of labor heroism for the final victory of socialism over the forces of reactionary imperialist expansionism."

Ironically the government had to resist.

For how would America and Europe and the People's Republic of China react to a new emphasis on sacrifice? Would they not see such heroic measures as preparation for impending military adventurism? And what if the Soviet Union's own armed forces saw it the same way. If they were less than pleased by thoughts of their own Vietnam? Or nuclear war?

While the government debated, hundreds of thousands of university students were spending their midyear recesses on agricultural collectives.

Miners demanded increased quotas.

Textile workers stayed at their machines and chanted, "More, more, and still more!"

Government workers contributed three extra shifts a month.

Soon Gavrych was invited to the Supreme Soviet.

He was asked, "What is it the people want of us?"

"Russia," he answered.

The wage base was immediately raised. Workers could change jobs at will. Interior passports were no longer required for travel between cities. Farmers now had the right to sell as much of their surplus as they wished. A new tolerance toward religion was proclaimed.

On the day these reforms were announced eleven of the Red Army divisions on the Chinese border rejected all military leaves.

Though there had been no call-up, reservists started reporting to their bases.

And there was a new petition: "Let workers and peasants remain firm in their resolve to withstand those who weaken our collective will to sacrifice for Leninist principles. We ask for nothing that does not further these principles. Only through the unity of the party and the people, only through renewed socialist self-denial can we demonstrate what our enemies can expect from us."

Within weeks the Supreme Soviet was compelled to enact even farther-reaching social reforms.

Within weeks it was giving evidence of a new, a profound change in its posture toward the West—a change which Lewis Buntline set forth and summarized so powerfully and eloquently when he faced you—and America—earlier this week.

Now I'll take your questions.

Q. Mr. President, Senator Rademacher alleges this in the advance text of a forthcoming *Symposium* article, that the United States was not—I am quoting—"not quite as surprised and delighted as it appeared by Mr. Buntline's news. Indeed, it had for some time been aware of and alarmed at the growing influence of Gavrych and *dachnyetism* in the Soviet Union." Our State Department, he argues, far from supporting and far from using its moral authority to advance the Soviet people's efforts to achieve full human rights, prevented the Voice of America from broadcasting any news involving Gavrych. In his view, it is his view I am advancing, the State Department and the intelligence community on two different occasions made unofficial, secret contacts with highly placed members of the Soviet government, at both times warning it, the Soviet government, that it was underestimating Gavrych and should take more effective measures against him. Do you care to comment on these issues, the issues raised by Senator Rademacher?

A. I do, yes, I certainly do. To start with, I categorically deny and brand as false and untrue these stories of secret contacts with the Soviet Union. Now as to whether the State Department was *aware* of Gavrych—of course it was aware. It is the business of the State Department and the intelligence community to be aware of developments inside the Soviet Union. But what supportive action should it have taken on Gavrych's behalf? And would not such supportive action constitute meddling in internal Soviet affairs?

I believe, however, and I want to speak to this point, that Senator Rademacher's article raises a crucial and compelling issue which disturbs me much more than his unfounded accusations. Because the danger of these accusations is that they aggravate and intensify the mistrust and suspicion sapping America's will and energy, America's faith in its institutions. It is time, high time, that we curbed our excessive national appetite for—yes, there is no other name—for paranoid drama. Indeed, I wonder now if Senator Rademacher has forgotten what he once told a freshman senator anxious to investigate the secret conspiracy of the day: "Son, isn't the real world dangerous enough for you?"

Q. Have you as yet formed a judgment, sir, about the merits of *Leviathan's Hook*? Also, what effect do you think the availability of the book in the United States may have on Soviet-American relations?

A. My own belief—and this is based upon a translation which had to be prepared rather quickly and without emphasis on literary value and qualities—well, it is certainly not too much to say that Mr. Gavrych is motivated by a deep and profound concern about the awesome and agonizing problems of this century.

Q. Mr. President, the secretary of state in his news briefing of Wednesday last stated that this country is prepared to offer every assistance to the Soviet Union toward the establishing of democratic forms and institutions. Can you at this time expand on his statement and the nature of the assistance?

A. Our thinking on the matter is, this is how Secretary Kinsolving and I are assessing the future course of democratic development in the Soviet Union—we foresee, given the history of the Soviet Union, a long history during which democratic forms and institutions never had the chance to take root and flourish, that it will be confronting immense problems, complex problems, as it undertakes the transition to a freer and more open society. Our purpose during this transition is to develop the most effective ways and means of providing to the Soviet Union whatever guidance and counsel it requests—and I can tell you we are already receiving such requests—from our storehouse of democratic experience.

Q. May I further explore this matter, sir?
A. Certainly. Please do.

Q. Secretary Kinsolving declared that his intent was to call upon the best minds, leaders of business, labor, education, religion, Americans from all walks of life, to participate in what he termed "an ideological Marshall Plan." At the same time he mentioned a proposed budget of two million dollars for the plan. My question is whether such a relatively small budget is consistent with a project of the complexity and magnitude you describe.

A. If you think it through I believe you'll conclude that at this point Congress is clearly in no mood for large appropriations and will want to know, properly and rightfully, that maximum effectiveness will be forthcoming from each dollar. To that end our proposed budget is a realistic budget, given the congressional mood, and Secretary Kinsolving has appointed a uniquely qualified person to serve as a liaison with Congress in this matter. He is Byron Wagonside, and though his name may be new to some of you, I have confidence that his unique and extraordinary administrative and organizational abilities will make him a vital link between the executive and legislative branches.

Q. Mr. President, Senator Rademacher's forthcoming article contends that in the event the USSR abandons its historically aggressive global aspirations, this administration has contingency plans, including deliberate violation of Soviet air space, to maintain international tensions at their present level. Do, in fact, such plans exist?

A. None exist; none are even remotely contemplated. And I still say, regrettably, that if anything is designed to maintain international tensions at their present level, it is Senator Rademacher's article.

Q. Mr. President, the longings of the Soviet people for an improved living standard will certainly compel the Soviet government—this is the consensus among Kremlinologists—to shift priorities and allocate the bulk of what is presently spent on defense, perhaps forty percent of its gross national product, to a consumer-oriented economy. My question is—really, it's twofold: one, do you envision a similar cutback in American defense spending; and two, in the event of such a cutback, would this not mean, would it not make available additional funds for social welfare programs?

A. We shall of course meet cutback with cutback, disarmament with disarmament. And we shall of course continue to work to improve the condition of those Americans who have been relegated to the purgatory of poverty and prejudice.

Q. Mr. President, I wanted to return a moment to *Leviathan's Hook*. Would you care, since it is to be shortly brought out in this country and since it will undoubtedly be a major publishing event, can you give us your view, your estimate of American reaction?

A. As I said before, Mr. Gavrych strikes me as an original thinker with a uniquely individual way of writing that compels attention even in translation. Of course, he writes as a Russian out of his Russian experience, and it may be, I wouldn't at all want to predict this, that an American audience could find his outlook puzzling at times, puzzling or confusing.

Q. Could you go into this aspect, your difficulties, that is, a bit further, Mr. President? Because you did say earlier this week on the White House lawn that Lewis Buntline, among his other services, the phrase you used was, "that among his other services he brought America a universal work by a universal man."

A. I did say that, and I assure you I feel now as I did then. I would not take anything away from that statement or from Mr. Gavrych. But I do feel—and the First Lady felt this too—that even in those sections of *Leviathan's Hook* which are meant to carry universality— well, even some of these sections might put unnecessary difficulties or obstacles in the way of a reader, an American reader. For example, this comes to mind, Gavrych tells about the plight and the problems of Russian farmers, the peasants, as he personally observed them during his youth. I found it moving, I found it stirring, and I for one learned much that was valuable about the appalling and dreadful agricultural conditions of that time, the time of his youth. However, Mr. Gavrych finished with a statement, now this is from memory and on the basis of translation, he concludes, "By its very nature rural life commits an offense against humanity." Well, I wonder if that is a point of view, an outlook which our farmers, which Americans from our heartland—and the heartland of America is a rural heartland— will necessarily appreciate.

Q. Sir, Professor Robert Bowers, executive director of the International Education Congress, openly charges that our State Department has given American colleges and universities reason to believe that any invitations issued to Mr. Gavrych would be looked upon with great disfavor. Is this true, Mr. President, and if it is, could the motivating factor, as he maintains, be the government's reluctance to bring Mr. Gavrych and his principles of *dachnyetism,* or negative affirmation, onto our campuses?

A. Now it should be obvious, I think, that the internal situation of the Soviet Union at this time is so unstable and uncertain that any kind of invitation to Mr. Gavrych ought to be deferred until at least the holding of open and free elections. The State Department quite properly advanced this view to the International Education Congress and put forth arguments in favor of a policy of wait-and-see prudence and restraint. As to whether this government feels *reluctant,* I believe that was the word used, about exposing our campuses to *dachnyetism,* or negative affirmation—well, I was not reluctant in my opening statement to explain it fully and fairly to America on prime time. Oh, and one thing more. I would not be at all reluctant to see some of Mr. Gavrych's methods endorsed on our campuses. Yes, I can assure you that nothing would please me more than to witness Americans overpaying their income taxes or striving to improve work performance and productivity so that our goods might more effectively meet competition from abroad.

Q. Mr. President, Lewis Buntline has announced that he plans returning within the next several weeks to the Soviet Union. I wonder if he will in any way or capacity be acting on behalf of our government.

A. Mr. Buntline travels this time entirely as his own man. The understanding I have from him is that he plans only to deepen and enrich his understanding of Russian culture and cement some of the valuable personal friendships he formed on his last visit.

Q. If I may stay with this, sir, the matter of Mr. Buntline's trip to the USSR, he does say that a visit with Mr. Gavrych is high on his agenda. Have you given thought to what you yourself, given the opportunity for such a face-to-face meeting, might say to Mr. Gavrych?

A. Can't think of anything better than his own statement, statement or declaration—"Peace, sympathy, brotherhood, and purest joy"— which to me, my mind, sums up the essence of our common Judeo-Christian heritage.

Q. Mr. President, the wire services are carrying a report that Mr. Buntline will receive a special award from the United Nations to be designated as the Human Community Award and that you will be invited to make the presentation. Can you tell us if he is in fact to be so honored and if you would accept the invitation?

A. My own understanding is that such an award is being very seriously considered and discussed and if invited I would certainly do everything possible to be on hand for the ceremony. In any case I'm delighted at the prospect of Mr. Buntline receiving world recognition. This recognition—and I want to explain why it's especially meaningful, especially significant—vindicates and justifies one of the lonely and solitary decisions I had to face up to as president. For the time was ripe, the moment was at hand, I knew, to achieve a historic breakthrough in our relations with the Soviet Union. I asked myself, what bold step might we take, a step which would underscore to the Soviet Union our openness and sincerity and high purpose? And I wondered, what if we were to attempt a piece of precedent-shattering, innovative, human diplomacy, what if we were to send them one who would represent no special interest, one who commanded the eloquence and imagination to surmount the barriers of ideology and speak as an American for all Americans? Well, one day Secretary Kinsolving presented me with a book. It was the novel *Once,* by Lewis Buntline. I knew, I felt after reading that superb piece of Americana that I would have to talk with this man and—well, the rest you— and America—know. As I said earlier this week, what Lewis Buntline did he did because he believed he had to, because he believed someone had to, yet what he did is now part of mankind's enduring chronicle.

Thank you, Mr. President.
Thank you, ladies and gentlemen.

16

Then toward the end of January, after a late dinner in the Edith Wilson Room, the President, bending and straightening and still breathing through his nose at his twentieth sit-up, mentally drafted yet another possible answer to Pavel Gavrych's third private communication:

I am delighted, believe me, to know that the Soviet Union may presently be entering the Gavrych era. How I wish, sir, that I might share your generous hope for "love and restoration," for the transition from a world which stinks of death to one in which your principles of peace, sympathy, brotherhood, and purest joy are supreme. All the same, I fear you still fail to understand how the power of what you call the "old politics" prevails in America, or the cruel and monstrous problems we would face if total disarmament emerged as an imminent possibility. . . .

Propping himself up on his elbows, he thrust his chin toward Eunice and told her, "Has to be twenty-five sit-ups now and I'm still breathing through my mouth, still."

She came over to the mat, tickled his face with the sash of her peignoir, and answered, "That's because way, way down inside, you've made a gentle and loving decision to watch—"

Her next words came in a rush.

"—Cary Grant, *None but the Lonely Heart,* where he cries!"

The President got to his feet, thinking, There's no justice or mercy in my decision, but the decision is absolutely not. Oh, innocent, sweet-tempered Eunice, whose love for me is prodigious and steadfast, I have need to take a stand. Let the cross of statecraft and history be borne upon you and Cary Grant. For something nasty, baleful, malignant is at large within me.

He shook out his legs; he ran in place; he threw out two jabs, an uppercut.

Then he put his hands on his hips, and unprepared for the hard, savage beat of his voice, said, "By Jesus, no Cary Grant! Can't stand his . . . he's all prissy elocution and he doesn't move, he jiggles around, he dances like . . . I always expect to see a horse collar around his neck. . . ."

He had to wait a long time for a very short answer: "Mean."

She moved her mouth like a famished baby.

The President waited again, momentarily working on a secret message to Gavrych:

Do you know nothing, sir, of our skimpy, our pathetic rate of economic growth at present? Disinterest, sir, disinterest and disdain have long marked my efforts to push this government toward serious study of the economic consequences of disarmament.

"What a flaming mean man you are," said Eunice.

She made a small noiseless clap with her hands; she moved closer to him; she tossed her head so that her hair came flying into his face; she raked her fingernails down the length of his fitness suit.

"I do rightfully suppose that you have a most particular need to deny me a bit of simple pleasurable escape time, and I do rightfully suppose as I can endure and accept this need."

Her face was puffy with rage, her breathing shaken and irregular.

"I do rightfully concede, willingly and gladly, that your blue-black funky meanness was made needful somehow by a long and trying politicoeconomic day."

"The longest," the President whispered, barely able to bring the words out. "The most trying."

Eunice began to tramp around the room, knocking against the Leporello spinet, flinging open the bathroom door, thumping in to flush the toilet, then advancing upon him and smiting her breastbone.

"The longest, the most trying," the President whispered again.

"However, you know my honey-gold feelings about Cary Grant," Eunice was saying, "and I do rightfully resent what you were doing."

He moved forward, nodded a little to show Eunice he was listening to her. But he had started another message to Gavrych, he had decided he would sound off, give way, cry out:

I must tell you, sir, that this has surely been the longest and most trying day of my administration. Reading the reports from my Council of Economic Advisors made me feel simple and stupid and helpless and fearful. As if I'd been forgotten in an abandoned house. As if the premises of my life were part of a cosmic joke. As if I'd been born too late in the day to make a difference. Understand, sir, I beg you to understand that time and technology have conspired to make conversion of our defense industries perilous and disgraceful for any American president. They'd blast and curse me, sir, they'd blow me away with wrath and scorn.

And Eunice was holding him and sagging a little; for a moment he feared she would fall to her knees, but she righted herself.

"Please let go," she said, though he had not touched her.

She walked backward, fell into the wing chair near her makeup mirrors.

"I don't rightly care that thundering much about your Cary Grant comments," she said. "No, what gets me to feeling like rotting flowers, like there's no bottom for my feet, is the knowing that when you willfully please you can . . . can pull my inner self out and make me into an emptiness, into a silly-nilly storm-tossed creature."

"By Jesus, Eunice"—the President mustered up an air of shame and dismay, far more than he felt—"you're overreacting. Let it pass. Easy on the chaos and anarchy."

I am told—no, assured—I am assured by my advisors, sir, that there is absolutely no peacetime use for the exotic materials and esoteric production systems of modern armaments, that any pathetic effort to convert them to a consumer economy would result in chaos and anarchy.

He walked to the wing chair, leaned a little toward Eunice, considered an amiable touch to the underside of her breast, settled instead for a kiss above her right eye.

She humped her shoulders, planted her fists on her knees, expelled so powerful a breath that her makeup mirrors misted. Then she pushed herself up and said, "Principle."

The President thought, Yes, she weaves a different pattern of cloth. I suppose Cary Grant is as much principle to her as full employment is to me.

"Principle," she repeated, shaking her fist. "Hear now, you despoil my feelings of wanting to watch a movie with you and sharing and easing your long, trying day—"

"The longest, the most trying, Eunice—"

He thought, A day of annihilation and emptiness, a day of resignation and surrender.

"—and I need to see gunmen and cowboys and private eyes."

She quieted him with a glance, with the pain in her eyes. "I have honey-gold associations with Cary Grant and *None but the Lonely Heart* and—and the sharing of these associations is a matter of pride and shining spirit and bedrock principle tonight."

How devious and dirty I have become, the President exclaimed to himself, how crazy and mean. If history and statecraft oppress you, don't take it out on her. Give in.

"My Cary Grant associations"—Eunice gazed at him as if he had returned from a long voyage—"are colored balloon and attic trunk and *Black Beauty* associations, blossomy girlhood associations."

Ah, you cruel, miserable, pricky bastard! Can't you give in to her, the President reflected. Will a stand on this matter, this tiny, inglorious matter turn you into king of the mountain, give you the brass and balls to stand against the money men, the words of faith and fervor that choke in my throat when I hear their whispery fanatic boardroom talk?

But the malign, the infinitely malign was at large within him again, and he said in a shy and sorrowful voice, "Associations . . ."

For he was remembering something from Jack.

Guilt.

Womankind.

The silent, the ominous power of guilt in womankind.

He put the flat of his hand to Eunice's breast, and it came to him: "Womankind is born aswim in guilt, boy-o. Foundering in the knowledge of what they must do to mate and breed. No sin, no indiscretion they can't imagine committing."

He withdrew the hand, paced around the chair, and said, "By Jesus, Eunice, I also have associations about you and Cary Grant and something . . . way back, long ago . . . something you let slip. How you and a certain boy went to a Cary Grant movie and while you were watching it with him you . . . down below, there, you became wet, wet to the skin, and later . . ."

He thought, Depraved.

He thought, Unclean.

He thought, Is this the wicked way the world uses the weak and loving and especially gentle?

But all the same he finished in a perfect throb of manly righteousness.

". . . later, after the movie, the Cary Grant movie, you did something oral to that boy."

Eunice put both arms on his shoulders, pulled herself out of the chair; she whooped with astonishment and joy and urgently shook her head at him.

Then she held him away from her, and her face seemed to shine.

At length she said, "A man's memory . . . ever so unreliable . . ."

"I suppose. I know." The President focused his eyes a little away from her. "Jealousy." He stroked the edge of her back from shoulder to waist. "Stupid, pointless jealousy." He moved away, spread his arms as wide and flat as he could. "But, by Jesus, that's me, that's how I am. My nature. Powerless, absolutely powerless against it."

At a certain point of this long and trying day, sir, when I was given to understand that such firms as General Dynamics, skilled only in high-cost, high-specification operations, would need decades—decades, sir!—to adapt successfully to low-cost, low-quality production and normal factory methods, I felt powerless, absolutely powerless. Like a bear cub in a pit, a puppy in a thunderstorm, a child in a world where nothing imagined is true.

"Why, near as I remember," said Eunice, pointing her index finger upward near her ear, "and a woman's memory is turn and turnabout and colored and affected by womanly biology—hear now, the only oral thing I did till age nineteen was kiss."

The President thought, I feel no shame. Only . . . only a quick, painless shock at what I'm capable of, a dread.

"Mind now, sulky jealous creature"—she gripped his fingers, gave him a look of hungry tenderness—"it was for no lack of opportunity or continual pestering by a boy named Bradley who told me and told me it was as natural as a kiss."

". . . how I am, Eunice. My nature. Jealousy."

Don't you suppose, sir, that I wish a secret meeting? That I could bring you news of how we have planned thus, we have planned so, that we are ready, as you put it, for "the transaction to humanity"? But our only plans, decades of plans, marvelously detailed plans, are for the contingencies of conflict. Ah, what could I not tell you of these contingencies! How ready we are for the permutations and combinations of military circumstance should you move against us near the polar ice caps. . . .

"The jealousy of a man," said Eunice, "is love's burden. The jealousy of a man, my cousin Bettina May would always and ever say, is the heavy trunk he carries up and up the endless staircase of his life." She moved so close that she stepped on his toes. "I am most heartily proud of your jealousy and I therefore love you all the more."

We have lived too long in dark times, sir. The mighty fortress of our bureaucracy—ah, if you knew, only knew, its might!—functions not for life but disaster.

Then Eunice was sobbing into his fitness suit.

Then she led him to bed and made him close his eyes; and even before she instructed him to open them he knew by the doomful soundtrack that she had chosen *King Kong;* and a little after his first sight of Skull Island, he fell into sleep; and he dreamed of old actors and actresses whom he could not identify; and they were telling him they were glad to be dead, glad not to see what had become of America, a colorized America.

17

FROM THE JOURNALS OF HARRY PORLOCK: An explosion of temper with Nell last night.

There are passages in *Huckleberry Finn* she enjoys deeply, and I was reading one of these aloud to her when she began to rub and grind against the back of a hand until the ball of her thumb was spotted with blood.

I turned, whispered, "Nurse"; she only stood and shook her head.

Nell gave me a beg-pardon smile and silently directed me to continue reading.

I read, " 'When I lit my candle and went up to my room that night there set Pap—his own self! . . .

" 'He was most fifty, and he looked it. His hair was long and tangled and greasy and hung down, and you could see his eyes shining through like he was behind vines—' "

"Harry," Nell said, with the relic of a voice.

"Time we had some sodium pentathol," I said, wiping a string of saliva from her mouth.

"No," said Nell.

"Sodium pentathol," I told the nurse.

She gave me a message with her mouth and eyes I could not interpret.

"Dialogue," I heard Nell say, "please skip to the dialogue."

I read, " ' ' "You're educated, too, they say—can read and write. You think you're better'n your father, now, don't you, because he can't. *I'll* take it out of you. Who told you you might meddle with such hifalut'n' foolishness, hey?—who told you you could?" ' "

Nell said, "Now do the cows."

I read, " 'He took up a little blue and yaller picture of some cows and a boy, and says:

" ' "What's this?" '

" ' "It's something they give me for learning my lessons good." ' "

" 'He tore it up and says, "I'll give you something better—I'll give you a cow-hide. . . ." ' "

Nell caught the hair of her temples and pulled.

She moved as if to tear herself from a hook.

"Put her under," I told the nurse.

But she only walked forward one step, clicked her teeth, turned, slapped the wall, and said, "Don't you know she's my darling? Don't you think I would?"

"I'll not"—Nell caught control of her breath—"shall not go under."

"She, she herself," the nurse whispered.

"I'll have nothing, nothing, nothing take away what pain gives me," said Nell.

"What pain gives you? Oh, Nell, it gives you—" I pointed at the blood on the ball of her thumb, at the hairs she had torn from her temple.

"I have . . . realizations. Realizations, Harry."

"You have pain. And pain offers no special blessing."

"It's the truth," said the nurse. "Only what I've told her."

"The realizations that I have—are my legs covered? Yes, I see they are—my realization is that pain, pain if it's borne well, will make known . . . oh, things."

"Things, yes," I said, trying to laugh just a little.

"*Insights* into things."

"That's a honey," the nurse told me. "Lord in heaven, that is a honey."

"Pain is a teacher," Nell said carefully.

She held her hands out; I could not force myself to take them.

"Better," she said defiantly, "than Socrates."

I only shrugged.

"Better than Jesus."

"More *Huck Finn*?" I asked, a shade formally.

I read, " ' "I'll learn people to bring up a boy to put on airs over his own father and let on to be better'n what *he* is. You lemme catch you fooling around that school again, you hear? Your mother couldn't read, and she couldn't write, nuther—" ' "

"There now, yes," Nell cried. Though her chin was trembling and she breathed as if the air were filled with steel filings, she went on to say bravely and wonderingly, "Momentous, Harry. Momentous, momentous. Everything connects. I see for the first time in my life that . . . he . . . Huck's father isn't wicked or nasty. He's only living the life which happens to be possible to him, and he believes Huck should do the same. Why, he's trying to tell Huck as best he can, oh, 'This is what you are, how you stand before the world. Neither of us is special. You can't have things your own way or do whatever you want to do, and you should have known better than to try.' And he's wise, don't you think he's wise, Harry?"

I sat completely straight and still. Watching her bite the heels of her hands I felt sorrow and scorn for every moment of well-being we had ever had.

"How everything connects, Harry, and how momentous, momentous, momentous it is, and what good sense it makes. Huck's father is a creature, but he sees clearly. As a creature sees. Clearly, Harry, and with unspoiled eyes, in the same way as—why, a bird, a rat, or a snake. Nothing obstructs the vision of a bird, a rat, or a snake. No expectation of justice. For them only blind nature. It's not kind or fair, yet it's not unkind or unfair either. It simply is. Impartial as water."

After a moment I said, "Perhaps." Then I could not keep myself from saying, "No."

"She's all that's good and fine," said the nurse, "and she's spoiled me for all other patients."

"I, Nell Porlock, thymoma, am no special case. No right to ask that the weapon aimed at me be diverted. Existence wields an ax, and if the ax falls existence owes me no accounting."

I could bring nothing out.

"Yes, I've been like Huck in hifalut'n' foolishness. Believing that I was born under a sign of grace and couldn't be touched by the ax because—"

She struck her neck, her breastbone, as if she would strike herself off the earth.

"My turn now. I'm a full member of the human race. Momentous, momentous, momentous, Harry."

Then I became aware that I was opening and closing and bending her *Huckleberry Finn* back.

And when I heard the heavy old vellum spine crack I rose, raised the book high over my head, smashed it to the floor, and stamped on it.

At breakfast this morning Mrs. Altsheler, the new housekeeper, came in to ask me how I thought she was handling her work. She is a tall, rather heavy woman with a withered left arm and a step so tired, so shambling, that I imagine her to be husbanding her shoes. Because she is marred and suggests, in her embarrassing humility, a failure suddenly fallen upon good times, I had no heart to mention a certain seediness about the house, an absence of established routine.

Instead, I told her I was deeply pleased at the way she had taken charge of matters.

She faltered out that she was still learning her way around and wanted to put her energies into what counted.

She handed me some folded sheets of loose-leaf paper and a tiny ballpoint pen.

Better if here and now she saw in black and white where she stood. For in some houses you were hated the second you walked through the door. Hadn't she learned these many years that—?

She made a throat-stopping noise and walked off. For a while I sat listening to the drag of her feet. Then I took up her pen and wrote.

"My compliments. Hall closets never better organized. Capital idea discarding all those wire hangers. Window plants thriving."

Suddenly I felt a hot drenching in my chest. "Well, this is what it is, what it all comes down to," I said aloud, though I had no clear idea why. And I wrote:

"Consider, Mrs. Altsheler, that the dying may owe us something. But what? Surely not serenity. I think that through the dying we must relearn our own fear of death. But those who allow themselves to be folded into the grave like infants into bassinets—believe me, I welcome your ideas.

"A good touch, moving the toaster to the table.

"You are the first housekeeper thoughtful enough to remove laundry pins from my shirts.

"If we do not pity ourselves, Mrs. Altsheler, whom then shall we pity? If we do not fear death, what then shall we fear?

" 'Curse God and die,' Job's wife told him.

"What fine iced coffee you make! Is it the confectioner's sugar?

"But do the dying owe us something?

"Believe me, I welcome your ideas."

Nothing of consequence accomplished at the morning meeting. A narcotic dullness has settled over us. We try to be ironic about Gavrych, but we are past the point of irony.

Though it was time to call Nell, I spent more than an hour at the firing range. Some moderately good clusters with a Walther P-38 rebored for parabellum shells.

Dr. Hurster took his time coming to the phone, and when he did his "Yes" was so nearly inaudible that a hard stroke of fear went through me.

"Nell," I ventured.

"Yes." Now he spoke out strongly, and his voice rang with pleasure in itself.

"Nell's not picking up her phone."

"Well, no."

Carefully, evenly, I said, "I wanted to be sure that everything is all right."

He did not see fit to answer immediately.

"Is everything all right?"

"Nell is all right."

"Then why isn't she in her room?"

He took an official tone. "We encourage our terminals, physical state permitting, to store up whatever events they can for departure time."

"Departure time." I gave way to a short laugh.

"Our language," he said deliberately and dryly, "might have struck you as, well, less comical if you'd seen fit to attend our panels and seminars and lectures, if you'd shared experiences with other terminal mates."

"Dr. Hurster, may I say—"

I fought down a blind, destructive disgust.

"—thank you, and I'm glad everything is all right."

A little later Nell called.

"We lost Harriet Menkes, tuberculosis of the spine."

"Last night, Nell . . . As to last night—"

"We were in the solarium planning a memorial. There'll be readings, so you must bring my Oxford anthology of English verse. Try not to crack the spine."

"As to last night—"

"You see, Harriet and Loretta Osterburg, pancreatic adenoma, were always—oh, Loretta believed nothing on earth exactly suited Harriet except my readings. I'll read, Loretta will mend one of her bed jackets."

"Nell, what do you want of me?"

"Only my Oxford anthology."

"You have me on the outskirts, Nell. If I come near—but there's no coming near."

"Perhaps some Ezekiel might be in order. 'Son of Man, can these bones live?' "

"Nell, I want the right to give you comfort. Even if it's false comfort. And last night—"

But her phoned clicked off.

Impossible to resist any longer.

I'm done.

Nell has prevailed. She leaves me with only a desolate kind of pride in her strength.

Tonight Nell announced that she could no longer abide the grind of the electric motor which adjusts her bed.

Head back, chin trembling, she took hold of the bars and tried to bring herself fully upright. When I went to help she clashed her teeth, gave me a short, hard, vindictive look.

And she took hold of the bars again.

I said, "Enough, Nell."

She tightened her grip.

I grabbed her hands and pushed them from the bars.

"Do you want pain?" I demanded, putting forth all my strength. "Take it, then take it and be damned!"

Nell smiled, closed her eyes, and gave birth to a scream.

Moments later I told the nurse that Nell would now accept sedation.

She came forward, embraced Nell, then me, and wet me with her tears.

I did not tell her that I, in return, had agreed to enroll in the "Death and Dying" program for terminal mates.

For Nell's sake I transformed myself into an ideal recruit.

Early this morning I strode blindly into Dr. Hurster's office, contorted my face, and for a few silent seconds stood before him, dissembling remorse.

Presently I sat down. I looked straight into his eyes and said, "Please."

He thinned his pulpy mouth.

"My feeling—" I clenched my fists.

"*His* feeling!" Dr. Hurster cried.

"—positive. An end to cheap cynicism."

"I'm obliged. And damn glad. For Nell's sake," he added pointedly.

"For Nell's sake," I repeated.

"This whole damn time—departure time—couldn't give an inch, no sir."

"God forgive me." In an ecstasy of humiliation I went on to say, "Inhuman of me. And merciless."

In a sudden burst of inspiration I clasped my hands and pitched forward to my knees.

"All right now." Dr. Hurster came round his desk. "You're going to be all right."

He stooped, took me by the elbows, and helped me to my feet.

"Everything is all right, everything will work out, everything will be fine now." With a pleasant light in his eye he patted my shoulders. "Everything, everything, everything."

THINGS TO DO
1. Engage Nell in open, detailed discussion of funeral arrangements.

   2. Imagine that it is the day after Nell's death. Draw up agenda for this day. Concentate on routine, humdrum activities.

   3. Settle in advance number of annual visits to Nell's graveside.

It was my turn to give support today.

I drew Gene Siampa, a stumpy man, about thirty-five, with angry skin and carious, tobacco-stained teeth.

Dr. Hurster set us face-to-face on the floor, under the eyes of the group.

"Gene's problem," he announced, "is a fairly universal one, and I think it'll do us all some good to get the benefit of fresh thinking from Harry Porlock, our new terminal mate."

He sat down on his bridge chair and rapped the wall behind him. "This time round, Gene, let's be, oh, I don't know, open and vulnerable, really tuned in to"—he flapped a wrist at me—"to what I bet will be waves and waves of support from Harry."

And Siampa began.

"When our big girl was born—we have only Melissa, but I call her 'the big girl'—I made a sacred promise in church that Melissa don't get touched. No hands. Now the thing is, Melissa is very advanced. She'll come out with things you don't hear from any average eleven-year-old. Well, Melissa's feeling—as she puts it, her *insight*—is, okay, that her mommy went into the hospital out of . . . spite. Mommy was always *man-if-estly resentful* of her prettiness and superior intelligence and advanced reading scores."

Siampa shook his body like a wet dog.

"Brings home a report card last night—lowest mark was 'outstanding.' I say, 'Melissa, call up Mommy and tell her your marks.' I say, 'Don't you want to make Mommy happy now? The both of us have to make Mommy happy now as she is very sick.' Here is her exact answer: 'Truly, my interest in her situation is minimal.' I then cracked her one. In the face. Okay?"

He scraped his right hand against the floor.

"Go, Harry," Dr. Hurster said briskly. "Gene's cried out, you support."

I opened my arms to Siampa and we embraced.

"Harry—"

Dr. Hurster squatted beside us.

"—what's your feeling?"

I told him that something prodigious was being inscribed on me. He smiled at me and I smiled back.

"That's it. That's the ticket, Harry."

A breakthrough of sorts.

Today, for the first time, my terminal mates asked me to join them for breakfast in the hospital cafeteria. We went down in the elevator with a crowd of young girls, high school seniors I gathered from their giggly, quick-running chatter, come to be interviewed and tested by the nursing school. There was a long stop at the lobby for more girls and we were pressed so close that our arms were pinned.

"Cute little bunch," Siampa whispered. Aloud, he said, "Good luck, everybody, on your tests." And after a pause, "I volunteer hereby in case you have to practice alcohol rubdowns."

Dan Ebert lifted his big ball of a head and snorted. "Whoa," he cried. "Down, down boy."

Siampa's cheeks darkened. "What are you talking . . . ?"

"Ah, gee," Ebert said, "the injured innocent."

Alex Turkel, his narrow, shrewd, rosy face twisted in laugh wrinkles, said, "I envy Gene. I—by now I'm like the sultan's son. You know the joke. The kid inherits the father's harem, and though he knows what he's supposed to do he's not sure how to begin."

"I," Siampa insisted hotly, "am not looking to begin anything."

"I'd need blueprints," Turkel mused. "By now I'd need blueprints."

Nothing further was said till we were in the basement and lined up at the cafeteria steam table.

Then Siampa told us, "As my terminal mates you ought certainly to know that my horniness"—he shook his head as if to shake loose the next words—"is wife directed."

"And we do," said Ebert.

"My God, of course," said Turkel.

Siampa moved one finger in a circle and addressed it. "My standards are not so low that I'm seriously looking for action with high school stuff. When it comes to putting it between the sheets I have been spoiled. My Roseanne spoiled me. My Roseanne had a highly terrific instinct toward sex and I could not keep my hands off her.

There's a picture they have of our table at my niece's wedding, it shows me copping a feel. We were then in our ninth year of marriage."

There was a long pause. Then he picked up a tray and said with authority, "Well, I think I am going to order. I think I am going to have French toast, two slices, with—screw the cholesterol—that ham."

He seemed deeply pleased when we one by one announced that we would have the same.

THINGS TO DO
1. Give Nell a cassette tape recorder. Encourage its use, as departure time nears, for oral letters to herself.
2. Remind her that obituary notice for winter issue of alumni magazine is due next week.

A cold, drizzly morning which miraculously warmed and brightened. The day appeared to fit Ebert's mood, and the pleasure he took from the weather was all the greater because he was the only one in the group who had not overdressed. He was playful, exuberant, and so eager to speak that he stammered at first. For his wife, he announced, was with it, in focus, ready to take a good cut at the ball and clear all the bases.

Turkel also wanted to report progress. His wife's compulsion to keep her feet covered at all times had passed. What's more, she was lately finding comfort in thoughts of a net, a kind of safety net such as firemen use. It was being held by her parents, and she believed that when termination time came they would call out, "Jump, child; now, child; now; we're ready for you, child; we've always been ready."

And Siampa had better news about his daughter. He was handling Melissa along the lines laid down by Dr. Hurster, and she was responding nicely. By now she understood that because she was an outstanding and exceptionally gifted girl, Mommy, at great personal sacrifice, has decided to give her special instruction. She would learn things only the strongest and bravest and brightest girls learned.

Dr. Hurster thought this might be the right time to start stressing the idea that when Melissa grows up she too would have a funeral, she too would be the center of attention, the diamond of all eyes.

The cancer has entered Nell's bones. Tonight she pulled me onto the bed and, with a tinge of pride, gave me the news. "Why, I'm swimming in the stuff. Down to the metatarsals. Doesn't happen *that* often with thymoma. I must have a talent for metastasizing." She kissed me on the cheek. "Looks like I found my medium. I'm a cancer artist."

"How . . ." I found my voice again and said distinctly, "How long till departure time?"

"They give me"—she made a self-effacing gesture—"oh, eight, ten weeks. Brings us to late April."

"Late April will be fine," I said.

"A splendid time," she repeated pleasantly. "Just before"—she gave a mock shudder—"the networks start their summer reruns."

"True enough. Good thinking. Although," I rushed in with too much eagerness, "if you could possibly manage a few more weeks . . . wouldn't go altogether unappreciated, you know."

A few seconds passed.

Then in a voice of rising valor Nell said, "I have a silly compulsion to fill myself on facts lately. Pointless, irrelevant facts. Did you know that in William Blake's time the average Englishman consumed forty quarts of gin? A year? A lifetime?"

Then she watched me with apprehensive politeness.

I took her in my arms and rocked her.

I told her as much as I remembered about the cult of Virgin worship, the age of Constantine and the rise of the English public service class. Though she was soon overtaken by exhaustion and fell into a heavy sleep I continued to whisper away until I myself dozed. Somewhere around first light the noise of a low-flying plane awakened us. Nell's brow twitched, her eyes were fluid.

"On New Year's Day, 1845," she said shyly, "Victoria and Albert distributed joints of beef and portions of plum pudding to three hundred and thirty families."

"Five years later," I replied, "the price of illuminating gas in London was reduced to four shillings per thousand cubic feet."

Then I took her hand and in silence we watched a rather disappointing sunrise.

—

Dear Mrs. Altsheler:

Did I disconcert you with my staring yesterday? No need to have become flustered. I should have told you earlier that the sight of a woman at certain household tasks is a source of delight to me. Goethe, I believe, says somewhere that the devil grows wretched whenever a dirty surface is made clean. In any case, my compliments; believe me, when you lift a rag you are closer to heaven than I shall ever be. Mrs. Porlock has a similar gesture.

But if we do not fear death, what then shall we fear?

A late snack with the President, then a stroll around the White House gardens. Though it was the mildest of nights the President's teeth chattered and he shivered in his cardigan as if he had been touched by a ghost. He started suddenly to jog and shadow-box, then he picked up some pieces of gravel and tossed them at the nubbled trunk of a wonderful old cypress.

"Four out of six, sir," I said. "And a good, strong, balanced follow-through. Follow-through," I added, "always seemed to elude JFK."

But he only walked ahead fixedly, and I kept two and a half steps behind him. I could hear him sniffing and blowing on his hands, a sign that he had ideas to proclaim. We had just passed under the ornamental scrolls of the birdhouse when he stopped so abruptly that I caught the heel of his shoe under the toe of my own. In his cheeks and temples nerves twitched.

"Need some feedback from you, Harry."

"You shall have it, sir."

"I'm thinking of putting together a prime TV event. Sort of a happening."

"Intriguing," I said.

"Still roughing it out, Harry, but the idea is to let the cameras in during a cabinet meeting. Everybody talking away. Gavrych. New Gavrych vistas, new Gavrych course, new Gavrych priorities. The usual bullshit cantata. Not a word from me, though. By Jesus, Harry, I'm sitting easy and relaxed. No, not exactly relaxed. More like . . . reposed."

"The repose of one who is strongly in charge."

"I'll have a 'Can you believe this?' expression. Then I'll open up with a down-home appeal to America. Don't do this to yourself, America. Hang on to the status quo. Ideas will only fuck you up. You can't handle Gavrych and his egghead crap."

"Splendid," I said.

"Leave them with the idea that it's all a Russian trick anyway. Finish off with a quote from Lenin. By Jesus, Harry, doesn't even have to be a real quote. I've been thinking about this. Something along the lines of, 'If Marxist principles fail to bring Western capitalism down, we shall give it a good dose of our Russian mysticism. Weaken it with peace, sympathy, brotherhood, understanding, and purest joy.' "

"Bravo," I said.

"America"—he had to lower his voice to control it—"Thank God you can always convince America that everything is a Russian trick."

"Thank God."

We walked on. The President looked so powerfully heartsick that I elected not to tell him the Russians had begun bulldozing the gulag labor camps and airlifting the prisoners to the Crimea for rest and recuperation.

When we reached the flower beds he recalled that Nell favored early jonquils, and he sent me home with a good-sized batch.

Passing the hospital gift shop this morning I heard a knocking at the window. It was Siampa. He met me at the door, pulled me inside. "Come say hello to my big girl, to my Melissa." He went toward the back of the shop and caroled, "Hey, where is she, where's my pumpkin?"

A small, white-faced girl with round, luminous eyes and auburn bangs that followed the vivid curve of her forehead stepped around an island of assorted hard candies and advanced toward us calmly and surely.

"Don't ever call me 'pumpkin' or 'peanut' or 'pussycat' or 'princess.' "

"Okay, Melissa; okay, Melissa Theresa," said Siampa.

"That's how all fathers talk in sitcoms. Sitcoms"—she tossed her head theatrically and addressed us both—"are situation comedies."

"Melissa," said Siampa, "come and meet a friend of mine. I want you to meet Mr. Porlock."

"Mr. Porlock," she said, "I apologize for that bratty scene." Though she had a slight lisp it only set off the patrician elegance of her tone. "I suppose it was principle, 'P-L-E.' "

"You could not do otherwise," I answered solemnly. I nodded, and found myself prolonging the nod into a bow. "My compliments, 'L-I-M.' "

"Now listen, Melissa," said Siampa, starting then stopping a soft swipe at her bottom, "can we step on it? Mommy's waiting."

"I'm afraid I haven't picked out my present yet."

"May I be of some small service?" I asked. "Come, m'lady." I drew and flourished an imaginary blade. "Perfumes? Colognes? Twixt the two of us, I warrant, we'll find a gift to your mother's liking."

"He's fun," she told Siampa accusingly. "But you see," she told me, "I was referring, 'E-R-R,' to *my* present. The present's for *me*. A bribe," she added wickedly.

Siampa colored. "Why do you call it a bribe?" he said, kissing her above the eye. "Oh, I know. Oh, sure. Because it's a show-off word."

"It is a bribe"—Melissa sniffed, but not to clear her nose—"so I will not divulge to Mommy that she is leaving me with mastectomy anxiety for the rest of my life, so I will talk only about my lima bean plant and my soap sculpture and starting negative integers, two 'E's."

"See," Siampa told me, "they're smart and they're brilliant and they even so have to go through their hoity-toity phase; they have to disagree. Anyway," he said to Melissa through his teeth, "will you please pick out something? Mommy's waiting for her big girl. You can imagine how she's looking forward to your first visit. And don't forget, we have to see Dr. Hurster—"

"H-U-R-S-T—"

"He has to write out a pass because you're under fourteen. How about that? You're getting special-case treatment from Dr. Hurster."

"Dr. Hurts-her."

"Five minutes more? What do you say?"

"Oh, dear." Melissa extended her neck its full length and made a movement with her mouth. "Five minutes, three hundred seconds. However shall I manage? Such an embarrassment of riches, two 'R's, two 'S's."

"Ay, faith," I murmured, " 'tis a veritable bazaar, two 'A's."

"Are you always such fun?" she said.

I bowed and as Melissa curtsied I pinched her nose. She let out a peal of laughter and cried, "Not fair!"

"I'm fun," I said, "but I'm not always fair."

She took my hand and drew me along. I helped her choose a book of mathematical puzzles, then a small red-beaded purse, then an origami starter kit. Near the stationery counter she let go my hand. "May I tell you something?" Her eyes clouded. "On the elevator I am going to be . . . oh, very insolent. Bet I get a pair of clogs out of it. Okay?"

With amusement and sorrow I answered, "Okay."

"I imagine I'm a monster. Do you think I'm a monster?"

I shook my head. As Siampa came doggedly forward, moaning, "Melissa, how are we doing, please?" I touched her bangs and said, "No monster, but you are a bit on the greedy side."

"Not greedy. Not really. Only sort of acquisitive, 'A-C-Q.' "

She took a box of poppy-colored stationery and skipped over to Siampa. When I caught up she was already giving him a hard time with her shrieks of "Dr. Jerk-ster" and "Dr. Burst-her." I had an impulse to applaud, to shout, "Well said!" But I only murmured, "Melissa, watch the mails."

She whispered back, "For a present?"

I nodded.

"My clogs are going to be royal blue and I'd love a proper accessory, two 'C's, two 'S's."

I had in mind at first a certain Gustave Doré sketch, *King Death*. Then, as Melissa pulled at Siampa's sleeve and pointed to her left sneaker, as he squatted and pulled its tongue taut and fished out the loose shoelaces and tied them with a double knot, I decided on one of Nell's antique dolls; she was, after all, only eleven years old.

Last night I dreamed of our first director of research, Minna Rostek. We are in our old headquarters, in Wheaton, and Minna is busy at her archives. "Don't you understand that it's over?" I say. "Nothing can be the same anymore." Poor thing, she does not know about Gavrych, I realize. But all at once she puts into my hands a mimeographed pamphlet, and by her terrible look I understand that she has given me the means of prevailing against Gavrych. "What's required of me?" I ask. Minna only shakes her head and runs off. "Is it something so hideous," I wonder, "that she has no heart to tell me?"

Then I have a powerful presentiment that whatever it is will come as no surprise, not really, and I awaken.

Turkel's wife has suffered a stroke.

Departure time is imminent.

He confesses to the group that right now he has no clear impression of who she was or exactly how she was connected to his life. Only her long illness is fixed in his mind.

Dr. Hurster had us all lay hands on him in support.

He told Turkel to take it year by year and work up mental pictures of the times he and his wife had prized most.

Turkel remembered that late one afternoon, probably in August 1969, when they were vacationing on the Chesapeake shore, they'd found a gold-plated Zippo lighter in the sand.

Around that time, it occurred to me, I had been instrumental in the downfall of my first government.

Turkel had no more pictures till 1976, the fall of 1976. For it was a significant season, a season when he and his wife had seen the changing of the leaves in Vermont, taken a half-dozen flying lessons, joined the Fruit-of-the-Month Club, found a marvelous old brass bed near Syracuse. But he could turn up nothing, absolutely nothing for 1977 or 1978.

The very same years, I was thinking, when I authorized production of a chemical agent which promised to destroy the Russian winter wheat crop, recruited homosexuals and deployed them in the most intimate circles of Capitol Hill, funneled tainted rice and counterfeit ration books into Cuba.

Turkel suddenly sobbed. And I, brooding over that plainer, simpler time when I stood for the lesser evil, shed a few tears also.

A charming thank-you note from Melissa Siampa. She encloses a Polaroid snapshot of herself in new royal-blue clogs. There is a PS:

"Do you still think I'm acquisitive? After studying three dictionary definitions I've decided definitely that I'm merely fulfilling an irrational need for objects. Whilst on the subject of words, another question. Yesterday I left my mother's room a few minutes before Daddy and waited for him outside in the hospital parking field, Area G. Dr. Hurster was just pulling into his reserved spot. When he left, I took a piece of loose-leaf paper, I folded it lengthwise and put it under his left windshield wiper so that upon his return he will have a heart attack from the initial impression that he has gotten a ticket.

"Question.

"Is there a word for what I did? Is it a word that describes something that is more than mischievous and less than evil?"

I sent her an astrological bracelet and a box of scented soap.

THINGS TO DO
Condolences to Turkel.

Nell is fantasizing visits from the dead.

Last night her mother came by.

They talked of the American Kennel Club, the seediness of Vineyard Haven, Central American housemaids, outdoor weddings.

Then her mother suddenly frowned.

"Nelly, you haven't told me what you're doing here."

Nell did not answer.

Her mother drew a deep breath, said, "Well, Nelly, well," and gave her a glance of surmise.

Nell nodded ruefully, affectionately.

"All the same, Nelly, that's really no reason not to keep those nails of yours buffed."

Here Nell began to giggle.

Then she was swept by such waves of coughing that the nurse made her take some oxygen. Within minutes she was asleep and the nurse turned on the TV.

Though I had her raise the volume twice I could still hear Nell's breath—the heavy sucking sound, as if her lungs were foundering in ooze.

The resident monitoring her vital signs mentioned pneumonia.

"One of those crazy new strains," he said. "Hasn't even been named yet."

This morning, in the middle of things, our new terminal mate passed out and Dr. Hurster halted the session. With time on my hands, I decided to stop by the Social Service Department and see what was holding up Mrs. Altsheler's appointment at the allergy clinic.

The office was in the hospital's oldest building, a cumbersome limestone construction with wired windows, a broad staircase of ruptured concrete, and a canopy hanging on a great chain that leaked rust. I had a long wait for the elevator, and when it came a painter sprang out and swished a crusted drop cloth at the crowd, mostly working-class black. "Out of service," he muttered. "Twenty minutes, practice how to snatch a purse."

Some people showed fists and made rude lip noises. Then I heard my name called. A heavy, short-legged woman in a blue hospital smock drew me off to the side, near the remnants of a phone booth. When she saw I had trouble placing her she raised a hand and moved the middle fingers as if they were the blades of a scissor.

"Carmen, Mr. Porlock, Carmen the beautician. I seen you plenty time when I do your missus' hair."

I nodded and smiled a little at the memory of her musical chatter, her way of clicking her teeth like castanets as she worked.

"Fine lady, your missus. Tell her why I don't come is I give up business." She slapped her thighs. "All time on feet bust up the veins. I get a phlebitis. Now plenty sick leave, plenty holiday. I got it good."

But then she wrinkled her face and gave me a gravely examining look.

"Mr. Porlock, why you here? What I mean—a nice classy gent with them hillbillies from the projects."

I told her I was here only to do a favor for my housekeeper in the Social Service Department.

"My pleasure to help." She put an arm to my back and pushed. "Lissen, we go in style."

Crunching bits of broken soda glass underfoot, I followed her down the corridor to a bank of elevators stenciled EMPLOYEES ONLY. We rode up to the fifth floor and stepped directly into the Social Service Department, a vast airless room with a multitude of backless benches

which were already so filled that children in underclothes squatted
on the floor. It seemed to me that among these people every human
kind and condition were represented, every want and deficiency, every
disease testing flesh and bone.

But Carmen moved me along, pointing out all the transistors blaring Latin music, the variety of costly shoes, dresses, and hairstyles on
some of the women, saying, "Plenty spongers here, Mr. P. Take like
blind horses. I got stories, boy—"

She stopped herself and waved both hands at a gloomy-looking
fish-eyed man who stood before his cubicle of an office twitching his
neck and shouting, "Forty-two, next is forty-two." When there was
no answer he fingered the base of his throat. "Forty-two. *Adelante.*
Wake up, will you move?" He lowered his voice. "Hell with you,
then. Don't come. Don't ever come. For my part—"

"Hey, *guapo*," Carmen cried, "when you let me give you a nice
razor cut?" She squeezed his cheeks. "Jack Drexler, I want you meet
Mr. Porlock here. Classy gent. He need a little help. Couple minutes,
good for you, give you a rest from them hillbillies."

"Rest in my grave," he grumbled.

I said, "Perhaps I've come at a bad time, a busy morning."

"Every day here is a good day for suicide," said Drexler.

Carmen threw a kiss and sauntered away, her soft figure shaking.
Then she whirled and yelled, "Say hello to the missus. Tell her maybe
tomorrow I stop off, I bring something for her split ends—"

"Carmen," somebody sang out, "what I got split your end good!"

"Here you can forget civilization," said Drexler, as he led me into
his office. "Hope you don't get pellagra, Mr. . . . ."

"Porlock. Harry Porlock."

He pulled a folding chair near an overhead fan whose blades turned
so slowly I could count the revolutions. After silently directing me to
sit he said, "Coffee?" Though I shook my head, Drexler cried, "Forget
it, excuse me," and kicked his desk twice. "Can't heat the water
anyway on account of yesterday they ripped off my electric coil." He
shivered or twitched. "Beats me how they do it. They come in twisted
up with arthritis and in a second, an eyeblink, they have the casters off
your chair. We gave up air conditioners because they found a way of
getting to the compressors. Marie Nivers, she's three doors down—"

Drexler turned his hand inward and stopped himself. "So? A little . . . A little help, Carmen said."

I started to give an account of Mrs. Altsheler's allergies, of how her doctor wanted certain tests only clinic specialists could perform. But Drexler cut me off. "Excuse me," he said, "if I know the rest by heart. She can't get an appointment. Three months till she gets on the waiting list. Backed up. Overloaded. You can imagine"—he opened the office door a crack, squinted out, closed it softly—"with whom."

He sat down, pranced in his swivel chair.

"However—however, Jack Drexler, formerly the kind of social worker who thought humanity was his caseload, will pull her folder and red-tab it. Means rush. Unethical as a kick in the balls. Because it also means some inner-city lunger gets fucked."

I said, "Oh, no need, no need."

"*I* need." Dots of blood appeared in his eyes. "I'm entitled. I owe them. And how I owe them! For my electric coil. For the words they wrote on my wife's picture. For my migraines, my spastic colon, my diverticulitis. Listen, it's three years since I used a toilet here because I never know when I'll find a fetus in the booth. Yes, sir. For my part, they can all . . ."

"Hey, *guapo!*"

And Carmen charged into the office, clapping her hands flamenco style.

"*Mira que pasa!*"

Drexler jumped up. "Has to be a cockfight," he cried. "That's their latest. Am I right? What else? Already had our miscarriage for the month. Or maybe an OD. Hope so, could use a real nice OD. . . ."

"It's Otis," said Carmen, taking a wrestler's stance.

"Whoopee, Otis Griswold!" Drexler collided with my chair as he ran to the door. He turned, beckoned to me. "You don't want to miss him, please. This is a performer."

"Strong"—Carmen made a fist—"like a rock."

She swung open the door. Drexler waved me forward, saying, "Won't see my seat cushion again. Costs me every time Otis carries on. But he's almost worth it."

Then he boosted himself up on a bench and called, "Otis, yay, Griswold, what's the problem?"

Over the metropolitan din I heard a sonorous, "Good morning, Mr. Drexler."

And though Carmen was clamping my arm and shaking her head,

I twisted away and climbed up beside Drexler to have a better look.

In the midst of a crowd gathered around some overturned benches stood a broad stocky black man, the color of burnt coffee, who would have been handsome except for a twisted nose. Though his wash pants were skimpy, riding too low on his waist and leaving his middle naked, he carried himself with style; even when he scratched away at his haunches I caught a certain arrogance, a princely disdain for appearances.

And he appeared no less interested in me.

For he said, "Mr. Drexler, I sees we got us a guest." And to me he salaamed, saying, "Do you be engaged, sir, in the highly worthwhile vocation of social worker?"

I could not refrain from answering, "I now and then think of myself as one."

"Performance about to begin. Would please me"—he clasped hands and hung out his red tongue—"if you two gentlemen was to descend."

Advancing upon our bench, Griswold, with a thrust of his arms, cleared a space, and Drexler and I stepped down.

"Gentlemen," he said, "I ax your permission to set forth some few grievances for your compassioned social work judging."

"Sure, you bet!" exclaimed Drexler. His face was radiant.

In utmost calm, almost languidly, Griswold said, "The union doctor have lifted my card. He tell me, 'Otis, no more scaffold. Suppose there come on you a dizzy spell from twenty story up? Could happen any day with what you has inside that big head.' Now what I has, Mr. Drexler and guest, go by a cancer name I forget. No matter. Otis Butler Griswold only a little bit human jelly, and death don't twist my gut. No shame to the book of my life. Way I figure is . . . Why, Otis Butler Griswold, your aunt raise you good and you done the same to your only begotten son, Tully, though his momma walk away when you get yourself cancerized. Tully be of valuation to me, gentlemen, and on death event the last face I means to see be his. Only not in no ward, not 'mongst the likes of sink-pisser retards who's happy to suck rat dick for a couple dollar-bags. Excrementals all, they—"

A man heaved against him and threw a punch. Griswold caught the fist, swung him around, and cuffed him hard in the face; he fell without a cry.

Then Griswold walked into the crowd, thumping his chest, bawling, "Monkeys, little brown monkeys!" He stopped to gaze at a dwarfish, long-armed woman with orange hair and skin eruptions that empurpled one side of her small flat face. "Lookey here," he said, moving around her with short sidling steps. "Don't this be the ugliest monkey you ever see? Uglier than a chimpanzee asshole." He dangled his arms. "Bet she do day work on a monkey farm."

He reached out and ripped her bright print dress from neck to waist.

She hung back dumbly, trying to cover herself. But Griswold slapped her hands away, jabbed a finger at her unshaven armpits. "Way I figure, gentlemen, this ain't no fit company for Otis Griswold on his death event. I ain't no illegal alien looking to suck the country dry."

"Damn right," said Drexler. "Don't I know your record, Otis? You've paid your dues, paid your dues." Though he spoke out somberly, there was a derisive twist at the corners of his mouth.

"Way I figure, gentlemen, is how on death event Otis Griswold have himself one them private rooms in the main pavilion where he never need see the likes of chimpee monkeys—"

He turned to the woman and made as if to spit into her blemished face; this time she ran, wobbling on her absurdly high heels.

"Private room, main pavilion," said Drexler. "No more than you deserve."

"Twenty, twenty-five floors up," said Griswold, "so's I has a view. And nurses! Not like them grunts they has in the wards."

"Otis, Otis," Drexler cried, "no need to tell me how they staff the wards."

"Fetch respect when my boy walk in. Kinda thing mean a lot when you be fifteen."

"All for your son, isn't it?" Drexler sighed from the heart.

"All, sir."

"To be so close, to feel so much!" Drexler sighed again.

"Figure you understand."

"You and I, Otis—" Drexler raised his face emotionally.

"We do got this understandin'. Yes, sir." Griswold came shuffling over and touched Drexler's hand. "And for that understandin' I thanks you. Always been square with me, Mr. Jack."

He clasped Drexler around the waist and for a moment they stood nose to nose. Then he lifted him, took a short run, and threw him with both arms. Drexler went crashing into a water cooler. As he reared up on all fours, Griswold pushed him down and put a foot on his face.

"Look to me"—Griswold raised his foot—"as you in need of guidance and counsel. Like the good book say, you brought low and cast down."

He scraped his heel on Drexler's nose.

"But not near as bad as if you was laying cancerized in the wards."

Then I heard *"Aquí"* and *"Venga, venga!"*

Police were fanning out now from the elevators. An oxlike plain-clothesman cried, "Otis!" in a fat-hampered voice and shook a pistol at him.

"I got a surname," said Griswold.

"Freeze! Now, cocksucker!" The plainclothesman closed one eye and sighted.

"Shit I will." Griswold laughed explosively. "Come on, man, favor me with a bullet." He crouched and capered around. "Be a blessing. Dead anyway. What I got to lose?"

Nothing, I thought, absolutely nothing. Something moved in my chest, an awareness came over me and my head rang with a silent shout: Lord have mercy on me!

And Griswold, prancing from side to side, was saying, "Waste me. Blow me away. Put a slug up my cancerized ass."

But the plainclothesman had his gun holstered. There would be no firing, I realized, no chances taken on a wild shot or a ricochet in such a human thickness. Then, glancing around at the police, I saw how they were husbanding their rage, how they were bound to deal with Griswold.

Therefore I edged out of the crowd, moved past the police before they thought to stop me and stood before Griswold. In a soft voice I said, "This is foolish, Mr. Griswold. Do believe me."

He answered, "Take off, old man."

I stepped back, pretended to stumble over Drexler, then to right myself, and with the edge of a hand struck Griswold behind his neck, just over the occipital bone. He went to his knees.

By the time the police were frisking him, though, he had shaken off my blow.

"Hey, old man," he called over his shoulder, "you the one hit me?"

"My apologies," I replied, "but I did want to spare you a very long hospital stay." And as he was led off I added, "In a ward, Mr. Griswold, in a ward."

I see no need of cataloguing the pathetic little indecencies I uncovered in Jack Drexler's life.

Early this afternoon, when I told him the tax assessor had no record of the second bathroom he'd added to his house, he dropped the charge of aggravated assault against Griswold.

By nightfall, Griswold was released to my custody.

As I drove him away from the station house I said, "After dinner, Mr. Griswold—and I understand you favor seafood—I should be pleased to take you to the hospital's main pavilion, to a suite on the twenty-ninth floor. Yours," I added, "in return for a certain small service."

"Best tell me the service," said Griswold.

After I did he slapped the dashboard, snickered, and said, "Old man, you be one helluva social worker."

The Romans never understood the disease which afflicted their legions in 44 B.C. in the Spanish town of Cartela near the Strait of Gibraltar. Lucretius tells us that it turned men wild and crazy, that "Many, as the last tainted blood poured from their nostrils, went into the town with their weapons and slew whom they could."

This morning, a little after five A.M., Nell died.

She looked more simply bashful than anything else. It was the look, I think, of a schoolgirl who has been praised by her teacher for preparing her lessons well.

18

Though the President had deliberately lingered in the tub, though he had read and meditated and pretended to doze, Eunice, drenched by moonlight, nevertheless awaited him before the mullioned windows.

By Jesus, he thought, I'll probably have to end up servicing her anyway. Yes, and here in Camp David with her curse just past she'll expect a hot time. The big bang. One come after another.

"Hail deepest night, eternal woods," said Eunice in her throatiest voice. "Hail mysterious forest, endless vistas."

"Hundred forty-three allergenic acres is all," he muttered, holding his rancor, hardening himself against considerations of the trouble she must have taken painting on that Munich harlot face.

"I feel as thundering right for this land as"—her hands were on the flesh of her hips—"as those blue junipers."

"Well, and so you are," he couldn't help saying. To himself he declared, "By Jesus, do you honestly think this paperback chatter, this verbal fancy fucking, makes you twenty again? Please knock it off! Will you ever knock it off? Because he's a writer you were talking the same ripe magnolia way to that Lewis Buntline. And couldn't you have included his wife? Wasn't I tense enough at the reception?"

"Hark, unseen bird life. Hark crows and woodpeckers and chickadees and"—Eunice turned her eyes upward—"jackdaws. Jackdaws or warblers."

She was silent a moment.

Then, shakily, "Now I do believe that was a jackdaw. I learned all the bird sounds from Papa. Poor Papa. 'Catch-a-fox' is the chickadee cry, but the jackdaw is 'Click-a-lick-a-lock.' "

The President answered her as he always did at Camp David.

"Never was anything like your ear. What a good ear you have!"

She took the tassels of his bathrobe and tried to pull him against her.

He stiffened and scowled.

"Only want to tie some love-knots," she said. "Poor Papa always let me put knots into every little thing. Eunice love-knots. I'd be climbing all over him and jumping and pounding down. One time now—oh, one time I got to crying. Cried and cried so! 'Papa, when I'm a big girl I'll be too heavy to be doing this.' 'Why, you're my big girl now,' he said, 'and come time when you're *that* big I'll be long gone.' And he was, so he was."

"Yes." The President set his teeth, nerving himself to say, "Why don't you pray God you don't have to take the beating Nell took? Are a few weeks of self-denial too much for you? Vain, silly creature! Dumb cunt! Only thing that bothered you at Nell's funeral was seeing that plastic grass they use nowadays. Don't you know, care to know, that I'm at the end of my rope?"

He said, instead, "Yes, you're the First Lady now."

Then she was on her knees under his bathrobe.

"And you're my commander in chief," he heard her say.

"Eunice, there are things on my mind. Annoying things."

". . . that executive branch is *ever* so powerful."

He stared out glumly at the stars.

To some melody of her own Eunice sang, "I shall do with him what I want, what I will. . . ."

And the President's pajama bottoms fell, though he never felt her touch the buttons.

Looking down, he saw Eunice working with skill and purpose, and his blood responded.

Then with a single fluent and supple thrust of her body she was on her feet.

He stepped out of his slippers, shed his robe, and kicked away the pajama pants.

"Shall I touch my president here? And here? And here?"

"Wherever, wherever," he answered. Nitwit twat! Selfish bitch! he was thinking. Couldn't manage to squeeze out a few more tears at Nell's grave.

"Then he must touch too."

He slid a finger between her legs and she gasped and rode the finger and locked her thighs and drawled, "Why, you nice thing!"

Both laughed together.

And when they had kissed Eunice stood on her toes and scooped up her breasts and teased the President's mouth with the nipples and said, "Oh my baby, a virtuous woman is worth more than jewels. Is she not unto her husband as shield and buckler?"

He answered as usual, "Shield and buckler, tit and ass."

"Shall"—Eunice closed her eyes and ran her tongue over her teeth—"shall we let the power of love prevail?"

Swinging their hands they went to bed, turning out lamps on the way and moving the hot-line computer a few inches so that the frigid green light of the screen would not fill their eyes.

Then in darkness and quietude the profuse night noise beat and pulsed and sprang upon the President's nerves.

He heard a frog grunting, "Gavrych!"

He heard the vindictive locusts gibber, "Peace! Sympathy! Brotherhood! Purest joy!"

He heard a rooster scream, "Orlofsky! Vidyon, Vidyon!"

He heard crickets peeping, "Bendix! Raytheon! General Dynamics! Farewell, farewell!"

And Eunice closed on him and put him into the hot puddle of her body.

"Oh Lord, Lord, Lord!" she cried.

"Jesus, by Jesus," he returned.

He thought, For every three-hundred-million-dollar cut in arms spending Oscar Furtgang claims nine thousand workers would have to be absorbed by the private sector. If I understand that ratty little kraut, deflation will hit us like all ten Egyptian plagues. The way he tells it every other breath an American draws is defense related.

Eunice moaned into his mouth and he moaned into hers.

She raked his back and he chewed her hair.

She clasped his neck and he pounded her buttocks.

"Did I lose you? Are you out?" she cried.

"Ah damn, ah darling, ah quick," he said, guiding her hand.

He thought, But I had a glimmering, a presentiment back in the Senate. My first real bill, my maiden speech. And I glowed. I blazed. "Do we dare presume that the cold war is eternal, that this nation shall be forever fixed on the unalterable course of containment? No, I cannot tell you disarmament looms on tomorrow's horizon. Yet if the day of disarmament should come upon us and we have not prepared—I tell you I tremble at that day of economic chaos and social upheaval."

Eunice did a grinding thing and he did a pumping thing.

She scratched the sheets and he slammed the pillows.

She made whimpering sounds and he made hushing sounds.

She cried, "Saviour sweet!" and he returned, "By Jesus!"

He thought, Appealed for a long-range study of ways and means to prepare for disarmament. I needed—what did I need? Three, four paid consultants, a batch of high-minded graduate students, chickenshit funding. They called it the Plowshare Bill and murdered it in committee.

"Shall I go on top? I'll go on top!" cried Eunice.

"Absolutely," he returned.

He thought, At this moment I'd love to let it all come down!

Eunice cried, "Honey love!" and he returned, "Dearest darling!"

Then Eunice dilated, contracted, came! and the President, after counting off ten long pumping strokes, did the same.

The President caught up to Rose Kennedy on the fifth floor of the Texas School Book Depository.

She took his hand and with throat-stopped Irish charm crooned, "Whist, lad, how I've wondered why at this hour we're weakest and nearest death. Yes and might it not be because at this hour Peter denied his Lord?"

He sensed the whirring start of the phone, but he battled to hold a shallow sleep.

"Have I told you how Jack loved old newsreels? He'd look at the faces and say, 'Mother, these people were there!' "

But the phone, at the peak of its volume, prodded him sharply awake, and he opened his eyes to the mother-of-pearl dawn.

These people were there, the President thought. Is that important? Must be important, should be important.

Only when Eunice kissed his belly did he realize that he had spoken aloud.

"I'm here." She fingered his pubic brush. "I'm important."

He pulled away and raised a fist. "Poor Papa, dear Papa!" he started to yell. "Oh, your sweet tail-chasing papa! Bird calls, no less. Did he ever teach you his Dade County gimmee-gimmee kickback bird? That pious shitkicking peckerwood cunthound, that . . . grafter," he finished weakly.

And he went to answer the phone.

Eunice was weeping freely and quietly when he returned.

"Papa," she began.

Then, covering her ears she screamed, "I shall never again, never again hear a single thundering word against him. And I do rightly . . ."

But the President kissed her heartily on the mouth and smiled down at her and for the first time in many weeks sang, " 'You're the only star in my blue heaven.' "

Sniffling, Eunice sang back, " 'And you're shining just for me.' "

Nine minutes later she used what was left of her breath to say, "Had to be Harry on the phone, just bet that was Harry, oh, you and Harry . . ."

Though a jeep was waiting, the President sprinted the fifty-three yards to the Little Theater. "Knocked off nearly two seconds, sir," the blond agent with the rimless sunglasses told him. "And without a warmup."

"Well, sir," the black man said, stepping a little away from the body, "it do appear as the book of your life be about closed now."

He put a bloody fist to his temple in a mocking salute and smiled into the camera.

"Old man, you truly be one helluva social worker."

Beaming and chuckling, he stooped, took the body by the wrists, turned it, and set it facedown over the low cement barrier that was stenciled RESERVED FOR DR. HURSTER.

As the camera pulled away from the parking lot the President glimpsed, through the distortions of twilight, the electric-blue towers of a huge complex, and these looked familiar to him.

When the screen went white he said, "Now, Harry, isn't that Bethesda? Where Nell . . . ?"

"Indeed, sir," murmured Porlock. "One of those very painful coincidences."

The Little Theater lights came on.

"Sonuvagun"—the President whisked a fist through the air—"but he really had some great moves. Didn't throw more than eight, ten punches. Placed them perfectly, too. Kidney-groin-mastoid, kidney-groin-mastoid, then a couple in the larynx. And without rushing. That's the thing my martial arts instructor used to stress. 'Never rush. As if you have all the time in the world.' "

"Pity our people had to keep driving about to block off the entrances. Made for poor quality in the close-ups. There was the bit of business at the beginning when he took Dr. Hurster by the beard and had him kneel. Not a word said or a blow struck, but—but all the same the poor wretch had the look of one who understood that death was inescapable. And imminent."

Porlock smiled dimly and examined his nails.

"Altogether his own idea. Improvisations on a theme, one might say. Yes, Mr. Griswold is a most gifted improviser."

"And eloquent, Harry."

"You've a good ear, sir. One or two of his outbursts . . . Almost worth committing to memory."

"I'll tell you this, Harry: the sonuvagun got to me. By Jesus, for a minute, a second . . . that stuff about holding back on a cure for cancer. Said to myself, 'You know, I wouldn't put it past them, not at all.' Then I realized"—the President's breath came out shakily—"*I'm* one of them."

"Mr. Griswold is somewhat on the paranoid side. Nevertheless, sir, there's no escaping the feeling that somehow in his paranoia . . . oh, it's rather as if . . ."

"And how, Harry!"

"As if he spoke for the representative American."

"Dark times, Harry. We live in dark times."

"Well said, sir."

The President expelled a stifled groan.

"It burns my balls, Harry."

"It, sir?"

"Everything, I guess. By Jesus, Harry, everything either burns my balls or throws me into confusion. Confusion mostly. Nothing in the papers seems true or clear to me anymore. I try to spend twenty-eight minutes a day with *The New York* fucking *Times,* but for all the good it does me . . ."

There was an interval of silence.

Then the President described a slow spiral in the air, shook his head, and exclaimed, "Hurster!"

"Dr. John Franklin Hurster," said Porlock.

"Now somehow"—the President ran a finger along the hard bone of his nose—"somehow I connect that name with HEW."

"What splendid recall!" cried Porlock. "And HEW it is. Appointed last year as a consultant. Handled, as I remember, some of the more melancholy aspects of the aging process."

Then the blond agent with the rimless sunglasses brought two mugs of Earl Grey tea.

And the balding agent with the tortoiseshell sunglasses brought two plates of Scotch shortbread squares.

Keeping his eyes thinly closed the President thought, I should be feeling profounder things.

Presently he and Porlock left the Little Theater and climbed the long, slow, winding rise to the duck pond. As he listened to Porlock, as he began to understand more clearly where he was being guided or driven, he looked at the last tired stars and wondered why something wasn't happening in nature. At the very least, he thought, the flowers in this part of the world should be withering, sap should stop rising in trees, and a bloody sweat should break out over the face of the earth.

But all the same a good strong sun was rising and beating and beginning to warm the mortal bleakness within him.

He said, "Dark times, Harry. By Jesus, we live in dark times."

Eunice sang, " 'When evening is done and dancing is through.' "

The President sang back, " 'Moonbeams will shine on roses and dew.' "

Almighty and everlasting God, he prayed, King of Kings and Soul of Souls, should not the burden of this be more intolerable? The sorrow more crushing? For I am oppressed by serenity.

Opening a clean page in his logbook he wrote:

Harry's Principal Points:
1. *Spirit of self-sacrifice strongest in those who have least to lose.*
2. *Who has less to lose than the terminally ill?*
3. *Next year America will have no less than 700,000 new cancer patients.*
4. *A splendid resource. An abundance of Griswolds. Down and out, over a barrel, submerged and alienated and dispossessed, no money in the bank. And harrowed by strong family feeling.*

Eunice sang, " 'Shall I be your true love and will you agree?' "
The President sang back, " 'Down by the green bushes to tarry with me.' "

5. *Actually doing them a favor. For them murder will be therapy. To say nothing of providing a decent middle-class future for their dependents.*

Eunice sang, " 'The trees are getting high, and the leaves are growing green.' "
The President sang back, " 'The time has gone and past my love that you and I have seen.' "

6. *Best follow Harry's advice and think of this as a kind of social work.*

But just to play it safe, he silently prayed, "Ancient of Days, if it please Thee to let this bitter cup pass from me, if it please Thee to let me off the hook, it would not go unappreciated."

THREE

19

MOSCOW, FEBRUARY 23, 1993: The first dispute of the day between Viktor Belyushkin, minister of culture, and Pavel Gavrych started southeast of Semyon Square, a short distance from the renovated Dovzhenko Ciné, where many hundreds of Americans pressed about the small grassy island under the marquee, comparing cameras, exchanging sweet potatoes for sausage, *Herald Tribune*s for paperback novels, now and then singing plaintive cowboy songs to soothe the restive children. For just when they'd left Belyushkin's ancient Fiat powerful gusts of unexpected wind had brought freezing snow and snapped the new power line that was to feed the marquee, lighting the name of Luke Tyler in blue and the letters of *The Last Gunfighter* in alternating gold and bloody bronze.

"Yes, I am altogether without surprise," said Belyushkin, shaking out his small legs, slapping ice from the kinky filaments of his sparse hair. "How should I be surprised? Yes, this is the luck your Lewis Buntline brings."

He squinted, nodded, gestured with an open hand.

And there was Buntline, a little outside the marquee; and he had mounted a toddler on his shoulders; and he was prancing and slapping his behind and rearing his head like a horse; and though two overalled electricians were warning him away from the sparking power line he went blindly, dangerously close; and then Irena Nikolaevna forced her way forward and stopped him and led him away by the nose.

Belyushkin laughed, whooped. "A shame. How fitting if he had suffered the electrocution of his film gangsters."

"Belyushkin," said Gavrych, moaning the name, "may a long life lie ahead of you"—he took Belyushkin's muffler by both ends, pulled down on it, then rolled it up into a ball—"but I must say, regretfully, regretfully, that you would make a fish thirsty, a dog rabid."

Belyushkin winced, trembled.

"Continue to belittle me," Belyushkin said, the hard, black shells of his eyes altering strangely, taking on an aspect of love. "Piss on my counsel. Does it warm you? Then good! Then more, more!"

Gavrych blew on his thumbs, said lightly, roguishly, "Perhaps Stalin's hands reach out from the grave to break them again."

"In such weather he wears—who knows what he wears?" Belyushkin expelled a confused, immense groan. "A garment? A shroud? Yes, in such weather it will be your shroud."

"A Luke Tyler garment. A hero's garment. An American garment for those who value free movement and endless frontiers"—Gavrych took three steps backward, hulked his shoulders, brought his head a little forward—"for those who fulfill themselves in single combat, who have no need of gold, who are relaxed in the face of tension."

The wind changed; snow, in mild, fat flakes, began to spin down again; children opened their mouths to it; and several held hands and plopped down and rose, plopped down and rose, and made vehement, happy noise.

"Belyushkin," said Gavrych, now singing the name, "this garment, admittedly of thin cloth, cloth totally unsuited to this morning's weather, is known as a duster. This duster, I am given to understand, was favored by American drovers of cattle, by Luke Tyler as well in his film displays of snakelike gunmanship—"

"Who has given him this understanding?" Belyushkin rested his forehead against the Fiat. "Whose counsel does he heed? Lewis Buntline, hedonistic child-man, academic anthropoid!"

"Are there tears on your cheeks?" Gavrych pulled Belyushkin up by his muffler.

"Snow, snow only," Belyushkin sobbed.

They looked at each other's shoes.

They listened a while to pigeons contending under the marquee for potato skins, to the shy, shameful chatter of the Americans waiting to use the chemical toilets.

Then Gavrych engaged Belyushkin's eyes.

"See first"—he pointed—"to removing the windscreen wipers. A good Muscovite can make them levitate into his hands. For the world is not quite a soft place."

But the blades stuck fast. Belyushkin croaked, "This is the luck your Lewis Buntline brings."

Lighthearted but melancholy, sternly authoritative but affectionate, Gavrych declared, "In our youth you excelled me at dialectical materialism, showed me, step by step, how commodities develop into money. But now you resist altogether an understanding of the playful theater which relaxes Americans in the midst of tension and prevents them from coming to the bottom of themselves." He cuffed Belyushkin's cheeks, embraced him, pushed him off. "To give you such understanding it would likely take a Stalin to break your thumbs each day. Nevertheless I must try."

The electricians whistled; there was a whish, a snorting start of power; there was some applause as the name of Luke Tyler came alight; there were boisterous, good-humored boos as a spray of golden sparks fell from it.

Belyushkin laughed, whooped.

"May they burn a path from Lewis Buntline's gapping teeth down to his indiscreet, inconstant genitals. Let each spark—"

But Gavrych silenced him.

"I hold the view that in his desire to cast off the hold of Europe the essential American inhabits an endless frontier, a Great Plains of the mind, a bare landscape. History is fixed for him at some point ten years after his Civil War, a time when the reign of civilization had not yet displaced his belief in the importance of personal bearing, of graceful carriage, of the importance of style while facing dangers."

With a proud scowl Belyushkin reached over, buttoned the top button of Gavrych's thin garment, grumbled, "In its impact upon human nature and destiny, in everything save the spilling of blood, our Civil War surpassed theirs."

Gavrych kicked a little snow at him, stared warningly at his thumbs, gave him a swat, went on in tones of fortitude and forgiveness:

"I hold the view that the essential American demands now and forever from his public personages the bearing, the carriage, the style before danger of a Leatherstocking or a Luke Tyler, that now and forever he awaits such a one as will set things right and quell the modern Redskins and renegades."

He paused, nodded as if conferring with himself:

"Though such a one wears a commonplace guise, a country-boy mask, he must let the populace know that he is invulnerable to what afflicts ordinary American flesh and bone. He does this—but how does he do this, Belyushkin!"

And Gavrych opened the top button of his thin garment:

"Woe to the television personality who will not stand bareheaded in the most inclement weathers, the American president foolish enough to use an umbrella or wear more than a Yankee smile in these weathers."

Grieved, brooding, Belyushkin said, "May Lewis Buntline contract the respiratory infection for which you are destined."

Now five more electricians arrived, and while they set up a portable generator they joked with the crowd, and one passed out loaves of bread from a string basket, and another, in a Mongolian fox coat and baggy paratrooper's knickers, was letting children turn his pockets inside out.

"The playfulness, the theater." Gavrych focused his clouded eyes a little away from Belyushkin. "You will not understand the importance of playful theater to Americans." His brows rose and sank, and he spoke quietly and slowly. "Is it too much for you to understand America's sparse mental landscape? Are you still the pompous study-house boy training himself on universals?"

"Pompous!" Belyushkin cried. "It was not I—not I who tried vainly, vainly to grow a proper military moustache."

"Their eyes are forever fixed on deportment. Therefore, I shall bear myself with free and easy democratic deportment. Unhatted, in my thin garment, I announce myself immediately and in full as one who will not make them put their fingers on political and social sore spots or warn them how weakly they are anchored to their national existence. What they are most comfortable with, I will be: a pleasant primitive, a quaint evocation of the American little man."

Now the electricians had the generator started, and it caught and held, and pigeons flew away from its kerosene fumes, and one by one all the letters on the marquee were alight, and Buntline was trying to

R A D I C A L   S U R G E R Y

lift Irena Nikolaevna by the waist, but he slipped and a toddler pranced off with his hat.

"In their comfort, Belyushkin, they will surely ask, How can such a one possibly have been touched by the alien, unhappy aspects of Russian history? Oh, such a one, they will surely know, will not burn them in the subterranean fire of fanaticism. In his cultural furniture there is no metaphysics, no walking among gravestones, no moping in corners, no kissing the earth."

And Gavrych blew on his thumbs, faced toward the marquee, went forward. When Belyushkin lagged behind he stopped abruptly, laughed through his nose. "Be with me now in playfulness and theater," he said. "Forward to what they will surely call the Gavrych era."

They linked arms, walked.

And Gavrych's face was wrapped in good humor, but Belyushkin sucked his lips.

He moved along wearily and without spirit, and several times he stepped into snow and had to hitch up his trousers.

The wind screamed; Belyushkin screamed above it, saying how he would have gladly carried Gavrych single-handed in a howdah.

Then they were seen, recognized, and Gavrych applauded the crowd.

He raised his left hand and waved it in the gallant, sporting way Luke Tyler would wave to a schoolmarm or a wild stallion, and there was exquisite, reverential silence.

But the donkey engine faltered, spewing kerosene, and the alternating gold letters on the marquee went out.

"Do you see?" Belyushkin whispered into Gavrych's ear. "This is the luck your Lewis Buntline brings."

Whereupon Gavrych kissed him twice, blew mightily on his thumbs, and whispered back, "Playfulness. Theater. The ebullience and spontaneity that conditions Americans to believe the world yields to ebullience and spontaneity."

Then he bent, scooped up a big handful of snow, packed it, and lobbed it straight into Belyushkin's nose.

While cameras swung around and snapped and snapped he did this three times more, and presently most of the many hundreds were calling the name of Pavel Gavrych, and by the time he had signed the first Polaroid print the marquee was fully alight again.

ARLINGTON, TEN DAYS LATER: Mrs. Altsheler spooned marmalade over Porlock's Wasa crackers, and as she nearly always did in the morning, talked aloud to herself.

"Today I got his eggs right. Outside hard, but a runny yolk. Still left grime on the shell, I'm sure. Wouldn't you think my fingers were clean? Mother's problem too, and never was a housekeeper to match her. Might be when I brought in the papers and magazines my hands were still wet from the sink, and a bit of print ran off on them."

Porlock bent back his copy of *Here,* meticulously smoothed out the creases with the handle of a spoon. He looked keenly at the cover, murmured, "Daresay it's the recycled paper, Mrs. Altsheler. Nell had much the same complaint. 'Recycled paper and recycled thoughts,' she'd say."

"So much strange news these days," said Mrs. Altsheler. She had lifted the creamer to brush away some crumbs; suddenly she set it down as if the weight were unsupportable and moved her withered arm close to the cover of *Here.*

"Indeed." Porlock bit a knuckle. "Perhaps one must turn inward to discover the real news."

"Excuse a silly question, but"—Mrs. Altsheler squeezed past the back of his chair, squatted a little to better see the magazine—"people are people . . . everywhere. Especially in . . . today's modern world."

"Yet another liberal fallacy," Porlock said, his mouth twisting derisively.

"But here's this Pavel Gavrych, a person, a Russian, and"—she squared the edge of the magazine—"even though I know there's all that snow in Russia, I never realized Russians might play in it or throw snowballs."

"A somber people, Mrs. Altsheler." There was a pleasant light in Porlock's eyes. "You've grown accustomed to seeing them massed in some huge, gray public square."

Then Mrs. Altsheler went round the other side of the table to the pantry closet and fetched out her *Joy of Cooking* and her lavender Merry Menus pad and her balky old Parker fountain pen. She waited till Porlock roused himself, murmured, "Do, please, of course," and dropped into a chair beside him.

"Veal?" she asked herself. "But I don't believe Mr. P. likes veal all that much, and God's mercy, let's not forget the awful way they get veal, what's done to the calves."

After some moments she looked so longingly at the magazine that Porlock said, "Do, please, of course," and passed it to her.

She held it against her chest.

"What's *The Last Gunfighter* about, Mr. P.?"

"Why, horses and guns and cattle, Mrs. Altsheler. About a man"— Porlock cleared his throat—"who must do what a man must do."

"Will this be the first time the Russians see him? Luke Tyler?"

"Indeed. The very first, Mrs. Altsheler."

She set down the magazine. Her mouth became loose and soft.

"Has to be an old Luke Tyler movie, and that makes it grand for the Russians."

"Grand, Mrs. Altsheler?"

She slapped herself lightly in the face with her withered arm.

"Because they won't have to see him grow old. No stooping, no lines in his face, no hiding a belly."

By the time she was at the sink the red tinge had left her eyes, and she said in her erratic, animated way, "If you would, Mr. P., write me down your thoughts for tonight's dinner."

"I anticipate a long day," said Porlock. "Therefore something hearty." He laughed lightly. "Something western."

"Only write it down, Mr. P. I'll be leaving with you for the shopping and I'll need a list."

Then Porlock took the Parker pen and the Merry Menus pad. He printed, CASSEROLE, ANY KIND, AND ASPARAGUS, STEAMED, WITH YOUR FINE VINAIGRETTE.

Then he turned over the pad and on the cardboard he printed LUKE TYLER, and under this he drew a little humped mound, and over the mound he drew a slanting rudimentary cross.

20

Mr. Luke Tyler
Rimrock Ranch
South Meseta Road
San Jacinto, California

Dear Mr. Tyler:

Two of your old stunt men doubt you'll want to see me, and so does Cappy Briggs. He thinks you'd "sooner piss into a high wind." But this was said after I came on a bit strong and made the mistake of calling him "a director's director" and the "Eisenstein of the badlands."

As you can see, I'm not trying to misrepresent myself. I know I embody everything you stand against—I'm a feminist, a cineast, a spear carrier in many left-wing causes, and—my ex-husband's term— a lethargic fanatic.

But you are a figure, a personage with whom I must deal, and not only because I've gotten a grant from the California Arts Council to undertake a study of Western films and film heroes. Does it make sense to you if I say you're a splinter in my mind which I must either absorb or eject? That you're both beloved and despised to me? That I can simultaneously condemn your politics and grieve over each new line of age in your face?

But will you see me anyway?

>Sincerely, hopefully, imploringly,
>Margot Freeman
>
>1883 South Dunsmore Ave., #307
>Los Angeles, California

—

"May I call you 'Luke' immediately?"

"Sure, Sis."

"And I'm Margot, one 'T,' very hard on the 'G,' and this is tape one, side one."

"Figures."

"My daughter has to click her teeth to say it. When she says it. Hey, what figures?"

"Way I look at it, Sis, everything at my age and stage just about figures. One lung, four wives, seven kids, hundred ninety-three pictures, and that's not counting serials away back when. Here on in it's only retakes. Then freeze frame and fade out. World gets a little worse every day, Sis. Best leave it before your hammer falls on an empty chamber."

"That sounds . . . oh, like *Powder Valley. Powder Valley* and you're Wes Pardee taking a last challenge from that young gunslinger."

"Well, how about that!"

". . . and you're putting me on."

"Like Cappy said, you got good bones."

"Bet that's not all he said."

"Where does a creeping socialist spear-carrying lefty get herself such good bones?"

"From things traveling through her lymph glands and . . . and what else did Cappy say?"

"Said your mouth's too wide, your cheeks are lopsided, and you carry less beef than Billy the Kid."

"Oh."

"Said I ought to see you anyway."

"Yes."

"Might get to find out what a sinny-ass is."

"That's 'cineast,' and I'm not sure you want to know."

"Figures."

"Margot Freeman, tape one, side two, with Luke Tyler in Rimrock Ranch. Impressions of living room to come later. Sort of . . . sort of a private railway car ten years after the Civil War. But a mix of styles . . ."

"Four wives, Sis, four decorators. Got a kick out of decorator three. He'd say, 'Dearie, don't be so feisty. Maybe *we* know what's good.' "

"When you drove me around—yes, I'm changing the subject, yes, I do support gay rights—you asked me how I thought it happened. Then you dropped the subject. Whatever the subject was. Can we start there? Didn't you want to make a point?"

"One lung, four wives, seven kids, hundred ninety-three movies is all."

"Seriously . . ."

"Still won't tell me what a sinny-ass is?"

"I'm being serious."

"Least tell me why that there writer lady wouldn't shake hands."

"After your testimony before the HUAC!"

"Cute when you get riled up. Hundred percent eyes."

"Given your position, your politics, she had every right not to shake your hand."

"Hell, politics or not, people ought to shake hands."

"Did you really say to her, 'Put 'er there, Red Menace'?"

"Sis, you're talking nineteen fifty-two, fifty-three. Last thing I remember, last thing I want to remember, Eisenhower was daddy to us all and Cappy'd call me up and say, 'Stud, move your ass down here. I'm birthin' a movie.' Sozzled when I got there. Maybe not a word for two hours. Then, 'Stud, suppose now, suppose we took us this couple of over-the-hill gunslingers down on their luck. They team up for some bounty hunting. Only the hardcase they're after turns out to be their best friend.' He'd shut up, and pretty soon I'd come in with a notion, and pretty soon we had us a movie. Fun . . . We had . . . fun."

"Joy."

"Bet your good bones on it, Sis."

"Although the theme of the Western—always a certain melancholy."

"Stopped having fun after Eisenhower. Whole damn country stopped having fun after Eisenhower."

"No matter what, there's melancholy because the Western hero is always defeated by civilization. He can never really defeat the sodbuster or the cattle baron or the banks; he has to be bested by civilization, the encroachment of civilization."

"Sis . . . ? About that there writer lady. Now instead of going over and trying to shake hands—you don't suppose I should've just up and maybe kissed her?"

"Let's drink to tape two, side two, to sunlight, clean water, black bread, natural food, alternative cancer therapy, Pavel Gavrych, peace, sympathy, brotherhood, and purest joy."

"And Eisenhower."

"And Eisenhower."

"And creeping, socialist, spear-carrying sinny-asses and good bones and hundred percent eyes and nineteen twenty-three."

"Nineteen twenty-three?"

"Cappy's favorite year. Way he tells it, weren't so many bad ideas around."

"One lung, four wives, seven kids, hundred ninety-three movies, gut is swelling, ass is sinking."

"But the camera loves your face."

"Bushwacked by time, Sis. Time's meaner than a comanchero."

"You've anchored an archetype in flesh and blood."

"Turn on that tape machine, Sis, and let's figure out how it happened. To the movies and everything else."

"It's Vietnam and My Lai and Cambodia."

"How you figure it happened, Sis?"

"It's the modern situation."

"Cappy used to throw out the script. Once he took a look at the light, decided light was perfect for a funeral, so he just put one in the movie."

"It's Watergate."

"Sixteen different setups and fifty retakes nowadays till some fireball director figures out whether I should be scratching my nose or my nuts."

"It's Kent State and the Third World."

"Build you a drink, Sis."

"Build me a drink, Luke."

"I want to say something as we finish tape three. In a way, the Luke Tyler way, you were right. I think you were right, I think politics should never stop people from shaking hands. I think politics . . . damn all politics, damn all who practice politics. Politics is the punishment of God. Also I wish . . ."

"Sis."

"Actually I don't know what I wish, but insofar as I do it's along the lines of wishing that you ran things or that you were in charge of whatever there is to be in charge of instead . . ."

"Hey, Sis."

". . . instead of the shits and the fats, the shitty fats."

"No call to cry over it."

"I'm crying because we don't have clean air or a cure for cancer or a Gavrych."

"Wouldn't shake his hand neither."

"How do you feel about Gavrych?"

"Might be a good man. Hell, why not. But being a good man don't mean he understands."

"What do you think Gavrych doesn't understand?"

"Well, things."

"What things?"

"American things. The things Utah Joe understood."

"Tell me about Utah Joe."

"A Navajo killed him off in about every movie Cappy made. Sort of for luck. Long of tooth, short of breath, little bit simple in the head. Kept a tally on things, American things. Murder-rape-mutilate things. Read newspapers all the time. Didn't matter to him from what city or how old they were. Made him laugh till he farted. Used to say, 'Stud, your U.S.A. one real *yatanamah*.' "

"*Yatanamah?*"

"That there's Navajo for a mean place. A mean and crazy place."

"Tape four, and that was a sweet, giving, comfortable kiss."

"Well thanks, Sis. Thanks a whole lot for cryin'."

"I'm crying because of a little pain and because I belong to the generation that is not used to such kisses. A respectful kiss. Didn't hear or feel a 'Let's screw' in it."

"Well, not all that respectful, Sis."

"I'm crying because all the good causes are gone and because there's no chance against the fats and the shits and because I've taken something of a beating lately that's made me hate my body and because we're at the end of tape four and . . ."

"And *yatanamah*, Sis."

"*Yatanamah*, Luke. More *yatanamah* than anything else."

"That Dolores."

"She favors you, Sis."

"Hard to believe she's seven."

"A real little honey."

"And unique. May I tell you how unique Dolores is? She has a fabulous vocabulary confined to one word, and when you can understand that word it's 'no.' I'm proudest of her inner resources. Seven years old, but she can amuse herself all day mewling under a sink. Great at clicking her teeth. Strongest arches you ever saw. Comes from walking on her toes. Just your average autistic toe walker. Superior pain threshold. Bites into herself until she bleeds. I'll show you how. May I? I need only take the skin of my upper arm, pull it, lick it and lick it awhile—"

"I'd say you had enough hurt, Sis. No need . . ."

"Suppose not. No. Don't need more than her picture. Never do. Her picture's always enough to make me angry, very angry, so very angry that . . ."

■

FROM LIVE TELECAST, WSJV NEWS, CBS FEED: ". . . seem to be some technical difficulties we're hoping to straighten out momentarily. Jane Uva should be back real soon. Meanwhile, for those who tuned us in late, let me recap this fast-breaking story: Luke Tyler, the durable, slow-speaking cowboy hero whose career spanned more than four successful decades, has been shot to death in his San Jacinto Valley home at Rimrock Ranch. A suspect, suffering from self-inflicted bullet wounds described as grave, was apprehended on the scene and is being questioned by the police. The suspect's identity has not yet been released and no motive has been established. Mr. Tyler, whose last picture, *Ringo,* was described by WSJV's own Dave Everson as a 'moving—' "

"Hear me, Marty?"

"I hear you, Jane. Okay? Okay! We can switch over now to Jane Uva for a live report from Rimrock Ranch."

"Okay, thank you, Marty. Standing by me now is Lieutenant Frank Habruska of the county sheriff's office, who's in charge of investigating this shocking tragedy. Meanwhile, I have an update on the suspect. The suspect, who's tentatively been identified as Margo or Margot Freeman—not clear on that yet—died about twenty minutes ago of self-inflicted wounds. Now may I ask you, Lieutenant Frank Habruska of the county sheriff's office, what can you tell our viewers about this tragedy?"

"Jane, your estimate of the situation as a shocking tragedy sums up what has been perpetrated here."

"Lieutenant, before we were on camera you said that though you're a seasoned law-enforcement veteran—"

"You are talking twenty-two years, Jane."

"—it would take you a long time to erase memories of the crime scene."

"Jane, I'll spare the audience of viewers by saying this only: Mr. Tyler was the recipient of head and facial wounds I would have to call personally, to me, tragically shocking. The suspect, although facially recognizable because her self-inflicted injury was in the upper trunk region—well, let me put it this way: The weapon she employed at close range was comparably equivalent in destructive capability to a nine-gauge shotgun."

"But it wasn't?"

"What?"

"It wasn't a shotgun?"

"No, Jane, it was not a shotgun. The weapon on the crime scene located near the upper trunk area of the deceased suspect was a very small and short-barreled, foreign-manufacture pistol known as a Landru."

"Easily hidden?"

"Definitely, Jane. It furthermore had large-caliber capacity, and our speculation is that it was custom made by a highly expert party or parties and machined for military G-7 cartridges with maximized explosive impact."

"Many, many more questions about this shocking and appalling tragedy, but it looks like we're out of time. This has been reporter Jane Uva, WSJV Newsline, live from the Luke Tyler murder site at Rimrock Ranch. Back to you, Marty."

"Thank you, Jane, thank you, Lieutenant Frank Habruska. And we're running so close to the wire that I've just about time to remind you about our special—'Luke Tyler, Man of the West'—coming tonight right after our expanded edition of the eleven o'clock Newsline."

SAN JACINTO VALLEY, CA. (AP)
TO ALL EDITORS, URGENT.
UPDATE LUKE TYLER STORY
POLITICAL MOTIVE POSSIBLE

COMMUNICATION FROM LEOPOLD SPANIER, PRES., AMERICAN ACADEMY MOTION PICTURE ARTS AND SCIENCES . . . SPANIER SAYS ONLY HOURS BEFORE SLAYING ACADEMY RECEIVED TAPE CASSETTE FROM WOMAN IDENTIFYING HERSELF AS MARGOT FREEMAN . . . SHE PROTESTED ACADEMY DECISION TO HONOR LUKE TYLER WITH LIFETIME ACHIEVEMENT AWARD. CALLED TYLER "HATEFUL SYM-

BOL OF PERMANENT WAR ECONOMY" . . . EXTENSIVE QUOTATIONS FROM PAVEL GAVRYCH . . .PROMISED TO SLAY TYLER AS "WARNING TO THE FATS, THE DEATH EATING AMERICAN ESTABLISH-MENT" . . . FBI EXPERT FLYING IN FROM WASHINGTON TO CHECK CASSETTE AGAINST MARGOT FREEMAN VOICE PRINTS ON TAPES IN LUKE TYLER LIVING ROOM . . .

—

METASTASES FILE
COMPUTER CODE: LEVITICUS A 779G
Freeman, Margot, 33. Hodgkin's disease. Minimal life expectancy. BA, 1979, UCLA; MFA, 1981, USC Graduate Film Center.

Film cutter, 1982–1985, Entertainment Enterprises Inc.; assistant editor in Visual Arts Department, Westway Foundation, 1985–1989; contributor of numerous articles and reviews to *Rolling Stone, Film Quarterly, Mass Culture Review, New Left Monthly.*

Married Donald Austin Freeman, October 15, 1979, a free-lance photographer. One child, daughter: Dolores Ramona, 7. Deserted by husband, November 12, 1983, after child was diagnosed as autistic.

Disposition of fee: Monthly installments to be laundered through Foxfire Fund and sent to Dr. Ernestine Devries, Director, Child's World, Redwood Lane, Monterey, California.

—

From: Joel Baskier, Office of the Press Secretary
  To: President
Draft: Message for Luke Tyler Memorial Service

I am shocked and appalled by this hideous crime which leaves me—and America—bereft of one whose films spoke throughout four decades so powerfully to the American soul and psyche. Luke Tyler celebrated the man of strength who makes his own way through a wide and free land, who fights for justice and order. His work will survive as long as there are those in America for whom the concept of honor retains its strength.

From: President
  To: Joel Baskier

Fine job as usual.
  One small suggestion.
  Let's ask Americans to let reason prevail, to guard against holding Gavrych or American followers reponsible for actions of a single mad, misguided individual. If the gun that blew away Tyler was once standard KGB issue, it's just one of those lamentable coincidences, as Harry says.

21

DICTATED, SIGNED, SWORN, AND WITNESSED STATEMENT MADE BY
LESTER HOLTZBERGER, 70-09 61ST AVENUE, FLUSHING, NEW YORK.
THIS IS NYPD TRANSCRIPTION MSI #501-47J: "I am Lester Holtz-
berger, assistant manager of Ritter Gourmet Foods, 1901 Broadway,
between 81st and 82nd Streets. I believe many of your officers are
acquainted with the store and myself as this month we had two
instances of breaking and entering.

"At about five in the afternoon of last Sunday, March 14, 1993,
Mr. Herschel Feigenbaum, the world-famous author of international
reputation, came into the store and took a number from the punch-
out machine by our smoked fish alcove. He did not need to do so
since there was only one person ahead of him. This is a fairly slow
time, ours is a heavy morning rush, and we generally stop serving
customers by number around three o'clock. His reason for such scrupulous formality of behavior I never altogether understood, but over
our many years of mutual acquaintance I have grown to accept and
enjoy these and similar old-fashioned ways he displayed. To me, considering the changing character of this neighborhood which can make
you DOA any second, it was refreshing and charming and civilized
that he called me only 'Mr. Holtzberger' and was very proper in his
English phraseology. I mean that in English he held himself back and
almost never expressed his true feelings. But as soon as we started
talking Jewish he could be murder; he could be very hard on people
and describe them so you would absolutely never think of them any

other way. One thing I particularly recall from last year. He had just gotten his Nobel prize and you saw him on every channel. I asked him what he thought of his Marlene Beard interview, how she had struck him. He called her—it's hard to translate his Jewish, which was highly superior to mine—I'll translate it as 'a fucked-out, used-up rag.'

"This Sunday last, when Mr. Feigenbaum came into the store, I noticed upon him an air of aggravation. He even gave my counterman a bad time for slicing his Nova Scotia thin. When I say a bad time I mean only that he raised his voice. But I was surprised, insofar as he was not the type to take your heart out like many of our clientele.

"Figuring to lighten his mood, I myself went behind the counter to wait on him personally. I have done so several times this year out of respect. Each time he would say, 'This is an honor, Mr. Holtz-berger,' each time I would answer, 'Hey, I do this for all my Nobel prize customers.'

"But Sunday he totally ignored me, and I felt slightly insulted until I observed his attention was concentrated only on our overhead security mirror. I told him, it was a tease, not to worry about shoplifters, that whatever we lose from shoplifters we get back from overcharging. Though he smiled a little bit his air of aggravation was even worse.

"I then turned away a few seconds to remonstrate a customer for flicking cigar ashes near an open bin of saffron; we sell saffron six dollars a half ounce, that's when we can get it. As I looked again to Mr. Feigenbaum I saw a lady standing alongside him. He said, 'God in heaven'; she said, 'Why do you run from me?'

"My absolute and immediate impression of her was that here is a negative personality type. In other words, whatever the whole world supports she wants to pull down.

"My other impression was that something about her did not altogether hang right insofar as her physical build was concerned. It was as if nature wanted her to be a big fat horse, a Bella Abzug, and that to spite nature she had starved herself on a crazy crash diet. She not only carried herself like a stout woman, but also there was a makeup thing which I am aware of from my wife. My wife has a very full face so she does what models do, she applies rouge to all the way up on her cheekbones, practically in her eyes. This is to thin out and lengthen the face, and this is what the lady had done, as if she was not yet on familiar terms with her extreme weight loss.

"Then she asked him a second time why he was running from her, and Mr. Feigenbaum answered, it was a tease, that he wasn't really running from her, he only wanted to check with his answering service because he expected a message from the Messiah about the world to come.

"She said all she wanted from him before was a satisfying answer to why his work had to do only with matters of mystery and magic in bygone times, why he did not deal with current issues and contemporary matters such as the wonderful hope Pavel Gavrych holds for the world of universal mankind.

"It then came out that an hour before, while Mr. Feigenbaum was delivering a lecture at the Kaufman Auditorium, she had pushed herself with annoying questions, that she wouldn't let up on him about Gavrych. At the end, when he saw her shoving away people and climbing over chairs to reach him, he excused himself to the chairman on a lavatory visit pretext and ran out from the nearest fire exit. Even so, she was right behind him. When he grabbed a cab she grabbed the next one and followed him to the store from all the way crosstown.

"She said, I thought by way of apology, 'The courage I had at the Kaufman Auditorium I don't have now.'

"Mr. Feigenbaum answered her with a very old saying, to the effect that a Jew with courage is at least half a fool. Also he pointed to the canvas thing she had over her shoulder, a tote bag, and he told her however foolishly she misbehaved from before she was wise at least in knowing that a Jew must keep a packed bag at all times.

"She said, 'Will you please accept an apology from one who is overenthused about Gavrych?'

"Mr. Feigenbaum said, 'No, I will accept an apology only from Laura Pauline Zucker, 323 West 94th Street, the apartment number I forget.'

"It came out then that before disturbing him at the lecture about Gavrych she had identified herself fully, to the extent of reciting her student identification number from Hunter College where she was taking a Women in Literature course.

"At this time I and my counterman and several customers remonstrated her, to the effect that New York is nowadays a metropolitan jungle with an urban beast population, that in front of hundreds and hundreds of people—Mr. Feigenbaum drew standing-room only in

his lectures—you don't give your autobiography so some potential
nut case should look you up for DOA purposes.

"She said we were all probably a thousand percent right, only this
is how it has been lately, lately thoughts of her own welfare were
secondary to thoughts of Gavrych.

"And again she said, 'The courage I had at the Kaufman Auditorium I don't have now.'

"I remonstrated her to the effect that she was worried too much
over courage, that you have to live from day to day and hope only
that you hold on first to your health, your health frankly doesn't look
that hot to me, then to your life in a neighborhood and a city that
can make you DOA any second.

"And even so she said, 'The courage I had at the Kaufman Auditorium I don't have now.'

"At this time I noticed her lips were moving, then she started
squeezing and pinching herself on the right side toward the back and
she looked like nausea was getting her. By accident she somehow gave
herself a good crack from that canvas tote bag, and from the knock
she came back to herself.

"She said, 'It's indigestion.'

"Mr. Feigenbaum told her, it was a tease, that God has two ways
to remind us of our Jewishness, that one way is by blows and the
other way is by indigestion.

"She answered that a little pain was good for her. It gave her back
some of the courage she had at the Kaufman Auditorium and reminded her of what she wanted to bring out there—that with so much
worse pain around in his world, the here and now world, Mr. Feigenbaum ought to handle and confront it more directly in his novels
and stories of fiction.

"Mr. Feigenbaum got slightly huffy and once again showed an air
of aggravation.

"He told her, 'Madam, I was not born shaking hands with the
King of Sweden and posing for Nobel prize pictures.'

"He told her, 'Madam, it happens that I was not inoculated against
a knowledge of what went on in the Holocaust.'

"She said, 'Mr. Feigenbaum, I have no complaints about your
dealings with the events of the Holocaust. I think it is time for you
to handle more current events and to say your last word on the
Holocaust.'

"He told her, 'Madam, there is no last word on the Holocaust.'

"At this time she had another indigestion spasm.

"Her canvas tote bag opened and stuff spilled out. Some customers helped her pick up and one of them commented that Pavel Gavrych has in her a real fan. From what I myself noticed she must have been carrying around a hundred clippings from every paper and magazine where there was a mention of Gavrych.

"It came out then that at the Kaufman Auditorium she had read from some of her clippings and also passed around leaflets announcing a forthcoming Gavrych rally of American supporters.

"At this time Mr. Feigenbaum told her that she seemed to him an intelligent and capable person, that he could not understand why such an intelligent and capable person of common sense wanted to call attention to herself in a disruptive way that left the Kaufman Auditorium with a negative impression of her and maybe also the type of individual who was for Mr. Gavrych.

"He told her, I doubt if it was altogether a tease, that he was jealous of the competition, that his Kaufman Auditorium audience now probably had their minds concentrated more on Pavel Gavrych and Laura Pauline Zucker than on Herschel Feigenbaum.

"At this time she closed up her canvas tote bag and she punched down some numbers on the lock, it was what they call a computerized lock. You set it according to whatever numbers you want and nobody else can open it without punching down those identical numbers. We have a similar gadget for our windows, it works fine but it never stopped them from breaking and entering three times this month alone.

"She said, 'You know, Mr. Feigenbaum, I now have my Kaufman Auditorium courage back.'

"Mr. Feigenbaum didn't answer her, he only proceeded to order sturgeon.

"She said, 'Mr. Feigenbaum, you write so much about wonderworking rabbis and East European villages and Jewish sects that died out hundreds of years ago.'

"And she said, 'I don't begrudge you your fame; your fame is deserved and did not come to you overnight. I am aware of the years you put in as a clothing cutter.'

"And she said, 'How are you not aware and how do you not speak out with your pen against what the powerful real estate interests are doing to the Upper West Side where you are also a long-term resident?'

"And she said, 'Surely you see that the powerful real estate interests have the state and city governments in their pockets and are driving out the poor and the so-called middle class from scarce apartments for the sake of swollen profit.'

"From there she went to big business and giant corporations and the military-industrial complex and how they control every breath you take.

"At this time Mr. Feigenbaum paid up and asked for two separate bags because the sable was for a friend visiting from Westchester, that's how well-known our store is.

"At this time also she started in on how Gavrych was the one hope that this country could get away from its terrible ways and have a change of heart.

"When she wouldn't stop about Gavrych, Mr. Feigenbaum, who was a tease, made her a promise that in case he needed a collaborator he would give Mr. Gavrych a ring.

"He walked out, she walked after him, I heard her from the street still going at him with Gavrych and Gavrych and Gavrych.

"I went a few steps after them because I had a thought of calling her back to give me one of her Gavrych leaflets or a newspaper clipping. The idea was that by the time she came back and by the time she would get her canvas tote bag open with the punch-out numbers, Mr. Feigenbaum might run away from her finally.

"I had my foot outside the door, I was half in the street, when my counterman whistled. I turned around, he showed me a bag and told me Mr. Feigenbaum forgot his Nova Scotia.

"By the time I got it and went outside Mr. Feigenbaum and the nut case were crossing to the other side of Broadway.

"Since they were crossing against the light and she looked like she was still going at him in the middle of traffic, I decided I should not cause Mr. Feigenbaum another dangerous distraction by yelling after.

"A Puerto Rican kid passed by, I said, 'Sonny, you want to make a quarter?' I pointed out Mr. Feigenbaum and during my pointing noticed the nut case making love to her canvas tote bag.

"A little explosion then happened, and there was like a flinging, a gushing up of pavement and smoke and human parts.

"In a way God was considerate for just then bringing about a letup in traffic and people; otherwise you would absolutely have had a devastating carnage taking more than only the lives of poor Mr. Feigenbaum and the nut case.

"Of course, if He had been slightly more considerate He could have managed that nut case and Pavel Gavrych and the whole Soviet Union never to be born."

PRELIMINARY REPORT FROM SERGEANT TIMOTHY LANGFRITSCH, NYPD BOMB SQUAD, ARSON AND EXPLOSION DIVISION, TO INSPECTOR VINCENT MAGGIORE: Tote bag fragments indicate tracings of magnetite and aluminum phosphate.
Sophisticated.
My guess: a squib circuit, probably transistorized and wired in parallel grids, was deployed through the lock and ignited with a late-model name-still-unknown fuse.
Those Jewish girls sure know how to hurt a guy.
Now climb off my back and let me finish my fucking report.

DICTATED, SIGNED, SWORN, AND WITNESSED STATEMENT MADE BY MRS. BERNICE ZUCKER, 323 WEST 94TH STREET, NEW YORK CITY, NEW YORK. THIS IS NYPD TRANSCRIPTION MSI #502-48J, MARCH 15, 1993: "Since I have many resentments to discharge I might as well start with my recent interview at the hands of your police-state psychiatrist, Dr. Eugene—'Call me Gene'—Eisenstern.

"I challenge, I protest, and I defy what he implied throughout under his guise of sympathy concerning the relationship between Laura Pauline and myself.

"No, I do not accept for this relationship his classification of 'slightly odd and a little unusual.'

"No, I did not hold Laura Pauline to my side by a silver cord. If she chose to be unmarried at the age of forty-five her reasons were sociopolitical reasons. If she chose to live with a mother she regarded justifiably as a best-pal roommate, her reasons were economic and rent-sharing reasons.

"As an only child, Laura Pauline suffered with me a long-lasting grief upon the premature death of her father caused in great part by the persecution he endured in the McCarthy witch-hunt days. From him she learned, as I did, a love of the little people and to despise those who maintained the status quo and their preferred class position.

"Had she cared less for the little people and their right to dignity, decency, and democracy, Laura Pauline would have been married many, many years ago to a now-prominent orthodontist and embraced a petit-bourgeois life of renovating and redecorating.

"Instead Laura Pauline chose as I did a life-style of higher social purpose and became as I did a teacher of English to the foreign born. Her further efforts on their behalf, particularly the Hispanic retail clerks, when she picketed this very station house for police brutality, are certainly recorded in your secret files.

"Sharing therefore a common profession and a common social purpose it might follow to anybody except Dr. Eugene—'Call me Gene'—Eisenstern that a mother and only child would choose also to share in common an apartment of four-and-a-half-room spaciousness no longer seen in these days of all-powerful real estate interests.

"Of course, it is no accident that Dr. Eugene—'Call me Gene'—Eisenstern made such a point of this apartment.

"I shall herewith make a few points about it myself, points which will show why Laura Pauline Zucker, not Herschel Feigenbaum, oh no, by no means, was the one meant for murder, the true victim and martyr of an outrage comparable to the Reichstag fire and the Lee Harvey Oswald frameup.

"It is no accident that a few months ago the tenants of our well-kept, rent-stabilized building received notice that a conversion plan had been submitted to the attorney general of the State of New York.

"In other words, thirty-five percent of the occupants with money for a heavy down payment could under the law vote to co-op the building and throw out the other sixty-five percent, including Hispanics and aged and infirm on fixed incomes.

"In other words, the powerful real estate interests who run our building would get nearly seven million for property they bought only three years ago for two million dollars.

"In other words, the powerful real estate interests who hold this city and urban centers throughout America hostage, thanks to well-planned housing shortages, can further their genocidal assault upon the poor.

"It is no accident that these powerful real estate interests soon came to regard Laura Pauline Zucker as a major obstacle to be removed at all costs in this genocidal assault.

"After all, Laura Pauline Zucker was the chairperson and well-loved leader of an alliance of neighborhood associations, a symbol of the little people.

"They could not buy off Laura Pauline Zucker, and so they maneuvered to have her dismissed from her job, even as her father was dismissed from the high school system during the McCarthy witch-hunt days.

"This dismissal and the resultant litigation put Laura Pauline Zucker into a hospital bed in Albany, where she had gone to fight the juggernaut lobby of the powerful real estate machine.

"Such was her character that she absolutely refused to let me visit her and undergo the expense of hotel and restaurants from our already depleted resources.

"Such was her character that despite what she finally admitted was a painful and lingering and complicated gall bladder infection with debilitating aftereffects requiring frequent hospital stays, Laura Pauline Zucker with her depleted economic and physical resources continued the struggle for social justice.

"Yes, we lost the battle of the building; yes, we were co-opted.

"But even during the search for an apartment that would be within our means, a smaller apartment requiring storage or probably throwing out the many beloved objects of my late husband, objects of sentiment and memory, Laura Pauline Zucker continued to be a bone in the throat of the real estate oligarchy.

"And so they made their decision.

"They would murder Laura Pauline Zucker.

"But they wished also to discredit her among the more liberal and progressive and influential Jewish elements who were coming to understand and support her cause.

"What better way to discredit her and her cause among these elements than to frame her for the killing of Herschel Feigenbaum, perhaps the most prominent and respected Jewish resident of our Upper West Side?

"I hereby pledge that during the years remaining to me I shall clear the good name of Laura Pauline Zucker, that I shall continue to further her plans, her good works on behalf of the metropolitan submerged and dispossessed.

"As for you, Dr. Eugene—'Call me Gene'—Eisenstern, my only wish, you rotten, lousy, filthy, dirty little bastard, is that you live only long enough to bury a child, or what is left of a child, an only child and best pal. This is from the bottom of my heart or what is left from my heart."

■

METASTASES FILE
COMPUTER CODE: LEVITICUS A 780F
Zucker, Laura Pauline, 47. Cancer of the liver. Minimal life expectancy.
BSS Hunter College, 1968.

Permanent substitute New York City junior high school system and executive secretary, League for Laboring Folk, 1970–1971; instructor, English language skills for foreign born under CETA program, 1972–1975.

Disposition of fee: Pay from Foxfire Fund $279,450 to 323 West 94th Street Holding Company, Pan American Building, New York City, on account of Apartment 5G in name Bernice Zucker. Also maintenance costs in perpetuity.

■

From: Joel Baskier, Office of the Press Secretary
   To: President
Draft: Message to leaders of major American-Jewish organizations

I share your grief and sorrow and consternation over the murder of Herschel Feigenbaum.
   He had few peers in world literature, in the magical ability to infuse his tales of times past with the warm breath of actuality.
   Be assured that his record of a vanished epoch will be forever inscribed in the hearts and minds of all who are sustained by the strength of our Judeo-Christian tradition.

From: President
 To: Joel Baskier

Excellent.

And next week leak out news that explosive device was of probable Soviet manufacture. See Harry for details.

22

MARCH 16, 1993
FROM EMPIRE BROADCASTING SYSTEM, COMMUNICATIONS DE-
PARTMENT
SPECIAL, ENTERTAINMENT EDITORS
FOR IMMEDIATE RELEASE

When Ricky Shane steps out to deliver opening monologue number five thousand next Wednesday night the "lord of hosts" will be experimenting with a new live format. If the ratings prove out, Ricky plans to give up all videotaping by September.

TRANSCRIPT, *RICKY SHANE SHOW*, APRIL 11, 1993: "Tonight is our first live show and you can't imagine what's going on with our guests in the Green Room. Buddy Hackett was telling Clint Eastwood how to break a wild matzo, Clint was telling Buddy how he just finished a Western in Israel called *Billy the Yid*, and Dr. Joyce Brothers was telling them both how breast-feeding brings mother and child closer. . . . What's that sign? Can we have a close-up? In the balcony. 'My wife and I are celebrating our silver anniversary tonight.' Isn't that something! Bet you and your wife had twenty-five wonderful years together—your one and her twenty-four.

"Anyway, anyway, it's tremendous to be live and to get these good vibes from the audience. I can see you're really loaded for bear. At least the first row looks loaded and the second row is bare. Last night—last night was something else. A lot of senior citizens who brought back memories of an older America—memories like small-pox, yellow fever, and scurvy. One woman claimed she was the oldest living go-go girl and you had to believe it. Because all night long she had to get up and go and go and go.

"More important, something just came over the wire. It's good news and it's bad news. The good news is that the President will soon be off overseas on a five-day, nine-nation junket. The bad news is that it's not a nine-day, five-nation junket. What worries me is the trade pact with India he's considering. I understand he'll be sending them computers and they'll be sending us begging bowls. No, listen, seriously, I can't blame the President. He's really a great negotiator. But his advisors! Last week at the cabinet meeting they were all yelling, 'We want the British back, we want the British back!' Nothing? You don't . . . ? See, this country, the British, once upon a time . . . 1776.

"Long as we're on international affairs, it's amazing how after all these years Russia and China are signing a nonaggression treaty. Although, I'm a little worried. Suppose an hour later the Russians feel they want to sign another treaty? Did you know the President sent Pavel Gavrych two cables? Why two? The first one was to con-gratulate him for bringing the world a step closer to peace. The other one was a warning not to ask the Chinese for any substitutions from Column B of the treaty.

"Look, I kid the President, but I have great respect for him. You have to respect a man who's willing to take on the special-interest groups; usually he takes them on *Air Force One*. And he does inspire trust—especially Morgan Guaranty Trust.

"As far as the country's mood is concerned—I don't want to be an alarmist, but Henny Youngman has been saying lately, 'Take my life—please!' Everybody's lying low and playing it safe. Even the tooth fairy is staying in the closet. Unemployment's up, productivity's down. Things are really grim. How grim? Well, have you noticed the drop in bank robberies? That's because the bank robbers found out they're better off being hostages. And on my way to the studio I saw this frail, elderly gentleman doing business with a hooker on Rodeo Drive. 'My price,' she told him, 'is a hundred dollars.' 'A hundred dollars is fair, reasonable. Only I should warn you, miss, that I have, oh, a little peculiarity. You see, I'd like to beat you when we're finished.'

'Thanks for the warning,' she says, 'and I'm not at all worried. After all, you're getting up there in years. How long could you beat me, anyway?' 'Not long,' he answers, 'only till I get my hundred dollars back.' Should I start over? Fixed income, bad times, Henny Youngman . . . Should have quit with Pavel Gavrych.

"Okay, let it pass because we have a great bunch of guests tonight. Also a little surprise, something new for our first live show. So stick around, everybody, and we'll be right back after this word from a sponsor."

"I'm back with another little piece of mixed news. The bad news is that an angry crowd in Detroit tossed bottles at the presidential motorcade. The good news—the good news is that the Secret Service was able to catch five of the bottles and get the deposits back on them.

"But I promised a surprise for our first live show. After all, the big reason, the main reason I'm coming on live is to be able to touch and be touched by my audience, to have direct contact, to give and take, to have the ebb and flow, the back and forth a performer needs, craves, loves, and—and if you believe that you're ready to believe the President's Council of Economic Advisors.

"So for the next few minutes I'm going into the audience and we'll play a game. We'll call it 'Punch Line.' Anybody who wants to can tell a joke. Only stop right before the punch line. I'll try to guess the punch line and if I miss it you'll get prizes. First prize is a week, all expenses paid, in downtown Burbank. Second prize is two weeks. We'll start—okay, here. With this striking young lady. And your dress—excuse my staring, but I never get to see any more good double features."

"My joke is a dental joke, it is about a dentist—"

"I use Dr. Overbite. He's wonderful on bridges. But if you have to see him in his office—forget it."

"A dentist is questioned by a patient, the patient asks, 'What is your fee for this work?' The dentist says, 'My fee for this work is seven thousand dollars.' The patient says, 'Doctor, have a heart, I am not buying a Mercedes—' "

"And the dentist answers, 'No, but I am.' Never mind, you're a good sport and you get a prize anyway. Have you ever seen the Ganges at moonlight?"

"Wooh!"

"We got something even better—Love Canal at high noon. So moving right along we'll go to this aisle and this gentleman. Because from the way he's waving he must have a biggy. Or a good case of whiplash."

"Needs work, dear boy."

"I was wondering about your hairstyle. Also your life-style."

"The better to catch your eye, dear boy."

"Mind moving back? Can you move back?"

"But I'm awfully tired of cruising."

"Either move back or start some foreplay."

"Well, if you're that hostile, dear boy, we might play show and tell instead. I shall show you this absolutely savage little machine pistol and tell you, now whatever shall I tell you . . . ?"

"Oh my God!"

"I do believe I shall tell you, oh, peace, sympathy, brotherhood, and purest joy. And while I'm at it—"

"Easy, pal!"

"—here's a kiss to a certain gentle heart and sweet soul who's always filled my life with stability."

"Easy, very easy!"

"Do please stop shaking that microphone. Not tossing salad, you know."

"Loaded? Is that thing . . . ?"

"Is it ever!"

". . . believe you."

"Fires a hundred rounds a second, or some such macho figure. Can't wait to see what it does to that dreadful suede ensemble of yours. And do you know why?"

"Digging into my throat . . ."

"Because you're a safety valve for the system, dear boy. Because your vicious, depthless patter turns the horror of our time into five fast minutes of tinny laughter. Because you divert us from the necessity of Pavel Gavrych. Because you smirk from the side of your mouth at the one man who would restore life and love to a world that stinks of death. Because you sap the strength we need to struggle against the old deceits, the old politics. Because—"

—

RECORDED 7:25 A.M., THURSDAY, APRIL 15, 1993, IN MAXIMUM SE-
CURITY WARD OF GOOD SAMARITAN HOSPITAL, EUCLID AVENUE
NORTH, LOS ANGELES, AND ASSIGNED TEMPORARY FILE NUMBER
CC 1752 PENDING CORRECTED AND EDITED TRANSCRIPT. PRESENT
WERE SHELDON LOCKHART, ALLEGED PERPETRATOR; ASSISTANT
DISTRICT ATTORNEY EUGENE CINQUENTI, LOS ANGELES COUNTY
DISTRICT ATTORNEY'S OFFICE; DETECTIVE FIRST GRADE RALPH
KONECKY; DR. GREGORY WINESONG; RESIDENTS OF THE GOOD
SAMARITAN HOSPITAL STAFF; AND NURSE FELICIA MCCHESMAY.

MR. CINQUENTI: The recorder has been activated, Mr. Lockhart, Mr.
Sheldon Lockhart, and I will therefore state for the record, in full
compliance with California State Law 1010 and its further amendments, that I am Eugene Vincent Cinquenti, an assistant to the Los
Angeles County District Attorney. This is now 7:25 A.M., Thursday,
April 15, 1993, in the maximum security ward of Good Samaritan
Hospital where you were received, official time to be obtained and
filled in from hospital emergency room records, after sustaining chest
and abdominal wounds during an exchange of gunfire with LAPD
police officers under the marquee of the Commodore Theater. Detective Konecky and I want to question you about your role in the
slaying of Ricky Shane. If you do not wish to make a statement or
desire to have the presence of counsel it is your right, but you must
so state at this time under California State Law 1011 and its further
amendments.
LOCKHART: Arro-gance.
DETECTIVE KONECKY: Shelly? Hi, guy.
DR. YU: This is disgusting.
MR. CINQUENTI: Our job. As long as he's conscious . . .
DR. WINESONG: Mind not jiggling his bed? You're jiggling the bed
of a dying man and I won't sit still for it.
LOCKHART: Arrogance of heterosexual.
NURSE MCCHESMAY: A waste. They're always the best-looking ones.
Why are the best-looking ones always . . . ?
DETECTIVE KONECKY: Shelly, I'm in sympathy with your low feeling
to Ricky Shane's comic talent. Only you have to level more on your

motivating impulse for blowing him away. You know? Shelly, Shelly, do we need more bigoted hatred toward your gay community?

DR. YU: It is the privilege of policemen to be inhuman and gross, but you're abusing the privilege.

DETECTIVE KONECKY: Lady, go and practice your acupuncture.

LOCKHART: Gentle heart. Sweet soul. They've made worm's meat of me.

DR. WINESONG: The mike is too damn close to his drainage tubes. And if Shirley, if Dr. Yu wants to make a formal complaint, I'm absolutely with her.

LOCKHART: Thou. At once my husband and my wife.

DETECTIVE KONECKY: Shelly, your husband-wife is waiting outside. And we want to let him in. Only he is very angry at you. You know why . . . ?

MR. CINQUENTI: He wants you to be more cooperative with us.

DETECTIVE KONECKY: Help us to help you. You and your gay community.

MR. CINQUENTI: Don't spend your life in prison, Shelly.

DETECTIVE KONECKY: They'll gang-bang you, Shelly. The whole prison population.

MR. CINQUENTI: All because of Pavel Gavrych.

DETECTIVE KONECKY: What did Gavrych ever do for you and your gay community?

MR. CINQUENTI: His followers are using you.

DETECTIVE KONECKY: They took advantage of your good-hearted gay nature. They did their Russian brainwash and steamed you up into homicidal mania.

MR. CINQUENTI: Who planned it? Who gave the orders? Was it the Russians?

DETECTIVE KONECKY: Shelly, I could tell you a hundred stories on how the Russians have always mistreated their gay community.

LOCKHART: Love me, Mommy, love my roommate.

MR. CINQUENTI: How'd you get hold of a late-model Vanya III? Who gave it to you? Which Soviet big shot?

DETECTIVE KONECKY: Shelly, the Russians designed it for riot quelling in their gay community.

DR. YU: Stop poking his stomach.

DR. WINESONG: What's left of his stomach.

LOCKHART: Dying, Egypt, dying.

DETECTIVE KONECKY: One name. Give us one name, Shelly, Shelly, and we let your husband-wife in.

LOCKHART: Life is a dirty trick.

DR. WINESONG: He's going into Cheyne-Stokes.

LOCKHART: No more cruising.

MR. CINQUENTI: Who planned it? Who told you Shane was going into the audience? Did you have any backup?

DR. YU: Tachycardia.

DR. WINESONG: Listen to the aorta.

DR. YU: What's left of the aorta.

NURSE MCCHESMAY: He's crying.

MR. CINQUENTI: How about a shot? Buy us another couple minutes.

DETECTIVE KONECKY: A shot, another minute. Because I'm getting to him.

DR. YU: I don't have my acupuncture kit, round-eyes.

DR. WINESONG: Good for you, Shirley.

LOCKHART: A cruiser is a loser.

DETECTIVE KONECKY: Come on, Shelly. Hang in, honeypot.

NURSE MCCHESMAY: Do you want to knock down the screen? You're . . .

DETECTIVE KONECKY: Open your mouth, Shelly. You had plenty practice, so open your mouth. Let's go. Go, mutant.

NURSE MCCHESMAY: Hands off, don't push. Don't push!

DETECTIVE KONECKY: Open your mouth, you fairy faggot prick cocksucker . . .

DR. WINESONG: Good-bye, aorta.

DR. YU: He's had it.

DR. WINESONG: Gone.

———

METASTASES FILE

COMPUTER CODE: ECCLESIASTES A 781 F

Lockhart, Sheldon, 53. Prostatic cancer, some rectal involvement. Minimal life expectancy.

Attended Harvard University, 1971–1973; no major; expelled for violation of student conduct code.

Intermittent employment Boston and Cambridge areas, 1973–1974, as messenger, waiter, Addressograph operator, dog groomer, theater usher, locker-room attendant, relief bartender.

Joined Hermes Greeting Cards Co. as designer, 1974.

Published *Furious Tiger,* collection of verse, under Goodspeed Press imprint, 1975; joined Goodspeed Press, 1975, as personal secretary to Senior Editor Glennister Pangborn; inherited, upon Pangborn's death, 1978, half interest in firm; will contested by Pangborn family; out-of-court settlement in sum of thirty thousand dollars.

Moved to Santa Cruz, California, 1979; attended University of California, Santa Cruz, as nonmatriculating student, 1979–1982; studied printmaking, textile design, ceramics.

Contributed verse, dance criticism to *Gay Blade* magazine, 1982–1984; joined magazine February 1985 as editorial director; when magazine suspended publication on June 3, 1986, formed Gay Blade Enterprises in partnership with owner, Bruce Devore.

Opened Counterculture Catering Service on August 12, 1987; forced to close on January 9, 1988, after dispute with Food Processors Union.

Opened Posh Nosh Parlor, March 3, 1988; liquor license revoked May 8, 1988.

Moved to San Francisco October 1, 1988, opened Furious Tiger Cafe; serious damage to premises from fire of unknown origin, November 14, 1988; reopened January 28, 1989, closed April 23, 1989; during this time nine charges brought against Hell's Angels for harassment of patrons; petition of bankruptcy filed July 2, 1989.

Disposition of fee: Pay $315,000 through Foxfire Fund to Bruce Devore, Creative Director, Bruce Custom Kitchen Design, 3561 Market Street, San Francisco, California.

From: Joel Baskier, Office of the Press Secretary
  To: President
Draft: Message to AFTRA for inclusion, Ricky Shane tribute

Ricky Shane was a great comic artist and social satirist whose irreverent, tough-minded humor inevitably evoked both laughter and reflection, joy and pain.

For two decades he functioned as something akin to an oral historian of our troubled times, recounting our follies and failures, our tiny and towering achievements in quest of the American dream.

I had the enormous pleasure of meeting him at my Inaugural Ball. Nothing underscored his wit and wisdom more than these moving and memorable lines: "Mr. President, let's never forget that we're all in the same boat, in steerage, still sailing on to the real America."

I share the grief and outrage of the millions who saw him ruthlessly cut down in the name of "peace, sympathy, brotherhood, and purest joy."

From: President
  To: Joel Baskier

Deeply felt, spirited, and sustained throughout.

Might not hurt to play up murder weapon, its Russian manufacture.

Maybe a contrast between historically humorless Russia and how Americans love to laugh at themselves?

23

REPRINTED FROM *THE EAST HAMPTON STAR*, EAST HAMPTON, LONG ISLAND, JUNE 21, 1993.

Chips from the Publisher's Backlog

Decaf and discourse yesterday with VIVIAN MARINER at her Sagaponack Pond beach house.

The noted dramatist, who carries her fame as graciously as her years, looked fit and feisty after surgery to repair a broken hip. (Claims she tilts to the left when she walks.) She expects to complete *Agony Time,* her personal history of "the swinish fifties," within the year. "Absolutely pouring out; 2,000 words a day, and that's on a bad day."

How does she keep going?

"I derive strength from poached eggs and old hatreds."

Talked about the forthcoming revival of *The Conspirators* at East Hampton's own John Drew Theater.

Did she think people are buying tickets to a thirty-year-old play because of the Vivian Mariner name?

"I hope not. I'd like to think it's because of *their* names—the names of Ethel and Julius Rosenberg. I'd like to think it's because I dealt honestly and passionately with their tragedy."

But are they relevant?

"The Rosenbergs are branded into the American psyche. I believe each generation must come to terms with them; each generation must find the courage to weep and rage anew, to say, 'Yes, we are all, all, all of us responsible.''

■■

ENTERED AS MATERIAL EVIDENCE IN SUPREME COURT, SUFFOLK COUNTY, AND ASSIGNED TEMPORARY DOCKET NUMBER P2091 UNTIL FINAL ADJUDICATION OF SUIT INSTITUTED BY AMERICAN CIVIL LIBERTIES UNION (ARMAND PROCTOR/*EAST HAMPTON STAR* VS. SUFFOLK COUNTY DISTRICT ATTORNEY). LITIGATION IS EXPECTED TO REACH THE SUPREME COURT OF THE UNITED STATES AND RESULT IN A LANDMARK DECISION INVOLVING FREEDOM OF THE PRESS.

NOTES OF ARMAND PROCTOR, CULTURAL CRITIC, *EAST HAMPTON STAR*: Air conditioning between abominable and execrable. Fifteen minutes late starting.

All eyes sliding sideward.

Vivian Mariner arriving.

Wearing fur-trimmed suit in this weather!

Teeth set on edge, mouth twisted (Plates or what? Can't she afford better dentistry?) as if . . . repressing a scream.

But still leonine. And awesome posture. Spine straight and true as . . . her dramatic line? Her career? Life?

One thrilling audible "Bravo."

She sits.

Among friends, yet aloof and isolate.

Another "Bravo."

Raises hand. Pretends to toast audience.

Touched. Shoulders momentarily droop. Then straight-backed again. In profile suggests T. S. Eliot.

Curtain rises. Can't they fix air conditioning?

Tony Binder's sets are marvelous. Stamp themselves on retina. Lighting . . . implacable. Wonderfully hard and grainy. Like old newsreels. Like Walker Evans photographs.

Carole Hahn's Ethel Rosenberg worrying me. Right now more Bennington than Bronx in her tones. Why must she keep sniffing every time she embraces boys? Sounds like a neurasthenic goose. Audience winced at way she delivered line: "Atlas and Jewish mothers carry the world on their shoulders." Maybe Dan Frehling's direction? His unsettled rhythm? Herky-jerky. And those kabuki-like gestures of Carole!

Better now with entrance of Harold Shacker. Brings a life-marred exactness to Julius Rosenberg. Love, love the way he sharpens pencils for the boys. Absolutely right moving blade toward himself. European, Old World. What artful artlessness! Boys are good, especially Perry Osler as Norman.

Vivian Mariner nodding, flushed as Julius says, "The best causes are the lost causes."

Applause.

Groupie girl behind me goes, "Like, all right!"

Absolutely with it now. All.

Mariner's magic (theater craft) suddenly has them.

Her Passover seder positively stops the heart. One of the finest moments in American theater as old socialist neighbor shows concentration camp tattoo and boys raise sweet young voices in "Peat Bog Soldiers."

Good use of music throughout. Groupie girl sniffled when Julius sings "Kevin Barry" in prison yard.

Carole Hahn starting to dig out nuggets of small truth. That whimpering puppy sound during boys' first visit! Paralyzingly poignant praising them to matron. Her "not because they're mine" so right, so right! Her "electric chair is practically painless" soliloquy chillingly underplayed.

Vivian M. bending head, squeezing hands white. A face of stern anger.

Intermission.

Air conditioning coming up. Temperature now merely tropical.

Groupie girl scoots over to Vivian M.

"May I fast tomorrow in your honor?"

V. M. kisses her. "It would please me more if you performed one small action to ease human suffering."

Middle-aged couple introduce themselves.

The Laskers, Emil and Helene.

Emil says, "What can we say, what can we say?"

And Helene points to her streaming eyes.

But Tony and Luba Manfritz are almost upon me. Crying, "After show come by, drop over . . ."

Therefore escape through the crowd and into the lobby.

Ushers struggling with street doors. Sticking because of humidity. Doors freed just in time for electric crackle of thunderstorm. Rain bringing new heat.

Rising voices. A stir in the crowd.

Between double line at water fountain my groupie girl is sobbing and shouting, "Greeks had a word for you; the word is 'phallus.' "

Tall, white-haired old fellow with fierce, bony nose (looks like Cotton Mather or Daumier judge) laughs into her face.

"My apologies. Perhaps Vivian Mariner is a writer. Yes, I concede. She has all the equipment a writer needs—desk, typewriter, paper."

Sunburnt neck. Heavy, blue long-sleeved workman's shirt. Old-fashioned cut. Out of *The Grapes of Wrath* by way of *Our Daily Bread*.

"Vivian Mariner is a prostitute of the pen."

Enjoying himself. Performing. Playing to crowd.

"Vivian Mariner is an alchemist liberal. Shall I tell you what alchemist liberal is?"

Short, unpleasant sound from groupie girl.

"An alchemist liberal is someone who takes another person's pain and translates it into pure gold."

Groupie girl suggests he rent a hall.

Cheers from the crowd; offers to refund price of his ticket.

"Vivian Mariner would love to change the world. If only—ah, she weren't expecting that call from the Coast. Meantime, we might as well sign a long-term lease with the Heartbreak House of Capitalism, 24-hour security, full-service garage, health club on premises."

Curtain bell.

"Vivian Mariner is the spokesman of those who have lost the appetite for struggle . . ."

House lights dimming.

Groupie girl sticks out tongue.

". . . those who tell themselves, 'At least we have our memories of Paul Robeson . . .' "

Crowd filing in.

" '. . . at least we can hope for more plays like *The Conspirators.*' "

Shower over. Heat, humidity unbearable. Everybody wilting. Yet old fellow shivers, buttons that heavy work shirt to the throat.

Back to my seat barely in time to avoid Tony and Luba.

Death cell scenes searing. Prolonged assault on conscience. (Sensibility? Soul?)

Soliloquy by Julius to unseen boys among highest moments of American theater.

Harold Shacker builds from merely inspired to shattering perfection.

Love when he addresses snapshots: "I would like you to feel clean inside. Improve your chess, your math skills, hate as little as possible."

Learlike intensity.

And his marvelous croaky off-pitch singing of "Ballad for Americans"!

Gabriel Trosten's David Greenglass too heavy on leering villainy, Myron Topper needs longer tether.

Must atone over initial reaction to Carole Hahn. Pay out tribute like public address system.

Cast leaps from stage, surrounds V. M. like warm bath.

Her friends running from row to row.

They have an announcement, a reminder, an apology.

"FORGIVE!"

Ned Romeo climbs seat.

"Forgot to slip cards into your programs. Party for Viv at Amagansett Coast Guard Beach."

Sue Ann Shevrin climbs adjacent seat.

"Everyone, all, whoever—please come. Sand, surf, starlight. Let's make this truly communal. A communal celebration honoring a great playwright, a great play, a great cast!"

But Tony and Luba Manfritz draw near. "We'll see you there—there! Come—you'll come to our blanket."

One season passeth away, another season cometh, but the Manfritzes abideth forever.

Parking lot impossible.

A hullabaloo of horns.

For the old fellow in the workman's shirt weaves drunkenly between moving cars.

"Oh Vivian Mariner, come forth and lay thy blessing upon these middlebrows."

Pushes pamphlets into windshield wipers, through side vents and sunroofs.

"Find out who's truly free and liberal."

One pamphlet falls at my feet.

Deep madder cover. Crashing black Gothic Bold typeface.

The Essential Pavel Gavrych.

I pick it up, skimming as I walk away from my car.

Which is beautifully boxed in now.

By the red Volvo belonging to—could it be otherwise?—Tony and Luba Manfritz.

Haze over breath.

Mists fogging every pair of glasses. People forced to squint. Hundreds of people, cramped, pressing one upon the other.

I prowl periphery of overlapping blankets.

Feeling rueful, melancholy.

Two vodkas or specters of seasons past?

Overheard: "This beach is where the eight Nazi saboteurs landed in 1942, when I could have bought at two dollars a foot."

Bonfires.

Thermos jugs of coffee and Benedictine.

Sand kicked in my face.

By cast which is running for Vivian.

They lift and carry her to canopied beach chair near the surf and seat her reverently.

Wind blows, stars appear.

In perfect unison cast chants, "The best causes are the lost causes."

And in nearly perfect unison: "We celebrate the life and times, the mind and heart, the fire and force of Vivian Mariner, our Vivian."

Guitars fetched.

Then Carole Hahn alone: "For Vivian, our Vivian, a musical tribute."

Sounds of tuning.

"Although nobody can play more than three chords it's from our hearts."

And strumming, humming.

Over sounds of slamming ocean cast sings "Solidarity Forever."

Vivian blows kisses off her palms.
She rises, joins in.
Eyes enlarged with tears.
Turns.
Him.
Old fellow.
Careening down dunes.
Workman's shirt.
He's got   Shouting, him   Voice like
GAVRYCH
Seagull voice?
TOMORROW BELONGS TO GAVRYCH
A pine cone? Does he hold
GAVRYCH SYMPATHY GAVRYCH BROTHERHOOD
both they boththem

—

TEXT OF FULL-PAGE BOXED NOTICE APPEARING IN THE *EAST HAMP-TON STAR*, JUNE 28, 1993, AND PAID FOR BY THE CAST OF *THE CON-SPIRATORS.*

Dearest Vivian:
  Though he was burned beyond recognition your murderer is by no means "unidentified."
  To so classify him is an insult to your precious memory!
  For you knew and had many names for him.
  Fanatic, Bigot, Witch-hunter, Racist, Fascist, Totalitarian.
  He took the guise of Franco and Hitler and McCarthy and Batista and Nixon and Somoza.
  Once he clubbed and maced you and sought to blacken your good name.
  Now he has consumed your frail flesh in the hellish fire of a white phosphorous grenade.
  But if your light is doused your afterimage lives.
  It suffuses us.
  It carries us beyond grief and bitterness.

Dearest, gentlest friend, dearest, gentlest teacher, dearest, gentlest Vivian, know this: We, like you, shall bear witness to evil. We, like you, shall use our talents for the larger good of society. We, like you, shall be relentless and inexorable so that one day, in your own words, "Men of goodwill shall not merely endure; they shall prevail."

METASTASES FILE
COMPUTER CODE: DEUTERONOMY A 385F
Gamper, Abel, 78. Rectal cancer. Minimal life expectancy.
BA, College of the City of New York, 1933.

Shipping clerk, Neptune Rainwear, 1933–35; contributor, *New Masses, Dynamo, Anvil.*

Published novel, *Underdogs,* 1935.

Screenwriter, Warner Brothers, 1936; credits: *Young Tom Jefferson, Low Life, Powerline, Sally Trent, Fugitive.*

Married Louisa Anna Wollman, dialogue director at Columbia Studios, 1937; no children.

Removed from Executive Committee, Screen Writers Guild, following opposition to Nazi-Soviet pact of August 1939; impeachment proceeding instituted by Vivian Mariner.

Warner Brothers contract canceled December 1939, while Vivian Mariner was Story Editor.

Published novel, *Seventh Avenue,* 1941.

Military service, 1942–46; eighteen months Army Signal Corps, thereafter correspondent, *Stars and Stripes,* European theater; covered liberation of Paris, became involved with family of Thérèse Dandieux, a French political philosopher murdered in London, 1942, by Nazi agents.

For two years after discharge, traveled with wife through France interviewing Dandieux's friends, collecting unpublished writings; drafted play, *The Saint,* based on last years of Dandieux's life, when she foresaw fate of European Jewry and warned that forces of both left and right were "at work producing a universal character structure capable of inflicting even worse agonies upon mankind."

Returned New York City, November 1948.

Completed play, 1950; gave readings from Dandieux's work; instrumental in postwar discovery of Dandieux by "little" magazines, newsweeklies; arranged translation and publication of *Survivor Child,* Dandieux's interviews with Lisa Bernstein; play optioned by Oliver Sanborn Enterprises, October 1952; option dropped February, 1953.

Thérèse, a musical play by Lionel and June Bluestone, opened April 1954; Gamper brought suit for theft of ideas; Vivian Mariner, testifying as expert witness on behalf of defendants, maintained Gamper's script was "graceless, untheatrical . . . turned Thérèse Dandieux from spokesman for democracy into a mouthpiece of reaction"; case dismissed, June 1955.

Bought small truck farm near Old Forge, New York, November 1958, earned modest income till 1982, when wife suffered a stroke.

Gamper hired, 1983, as a coil winder by the Utica–New Hartford Division of the General Electric Company.

Disposition of fee: Pay from Foxfire Fund $150,000 to Jacques Sevilier, Curator, Thérèse Dandieux Archives, rue Fanchon, Paris, France; and to Louisa Anna Gamper, Clinton Nursing Home, 3543 Genesee Road, Utica, New York, monthly installments of $2,550 for balance of life.

—

From: Joel Baskier, Office of the Press Secretary
  To: President
Draft: Reply to Herman Schlaufer, Chairman, International Congress of Cultural Freedom

Dear Herman:

I too am perplexed and deeply troubled by the recent disclosure that the hideous weapon which took Vivian Mariner's life was a Soviet white phosphorus grenade called the Basya-7.

Nonetheless I would urge you, and as strongly as I can, not to succumb to the present atmosphere of alarm and confusion. For I—and America—continue to count upon you and your organization as a powerful ally in our ongoing efforts to dispel the gathering darkness of these times by pressing ahead with ongoing negotiations toward permanent peace between this administration and the Russians. To my mind, there is no finer, no fitter way of memorializing Vivian Mariner than to throw ourselves wholeheartedly into the desperately critical task of building a world truly given over to "peace, sympathy, brotherhood, and purest joy."

From: President
  To: Joel Baskier

Elegant!

But wasn't Herman Schlaufer once close intimate of V. M.? Her lover till he published attack on Henry Wallace?

We can use his anti-Nazi past, have him climbing walls, maybe even denouncing Gavrych with up-front reminder that V. M. was *incinerated* at 2,900 degrees centigrade.

Give thought to pushing parallel between V. M. burning alive and name she gave work in progress. (*Agony Time?*)

24

COUNSELOR: But my notes show that you enjoyed them at first, Vidyon. Here, from Thursday last: "America's late-night radio chatter quells Orlofsky's hangover of hotshot elitism. Each talk show gives me a populist high and puts me in my rightful place on your great democratic human wheel."

ORLOFSKY: Hey, was I ever wrong! The mental health of your air-wave multitude and the loudmouth brotherhood of your jabberjockey hosts now busts my gut.

COUNSELOR: Consider, Vidyon, that most special audience served by the jabberjockeys—an audience composed, I suspect, of the solitary, the chronically ill, the agitated, the sleepless, the—"

ORLOFSKY: Call them by their right name, good buddy. And their right name is . . . losers all.

COUNSELOR: Yes? Yes, I suppose you do have a point.

ORLOFSKY: Though exhausted and ready to fold from this night's earful, I will nevertheless lay on you my news. And the news is not good for the nerve-rattled human material in your radioland limbo.

COUNSELOR: How so, Vidyon? I welcome your input. As would the President.

ORLOFSKY: Dig, therefore, that these daft, dotty outcasts are at the end of their social ropes. They cannot endure the tensions of true intimacy, but they crave the sound of intimacy. They crave it as the user craves a fix. And so they place a toll-free call to make contact with their electronic pushers.

COUNSELOR: Your insights, as ever, carry me along, involve me fully. More, please, if you will.

ORLOFSKY: I'm in an uproar when I consider how they are short-changed by these chickenshit seers. For ninety seconds, perhaps a big two minutes, of cold chitchat comfort they strip to the buff of their beings, they beat their emotional meat and spill dirt and scandal and nutty erotic practices and stamp upon the graves of mothers and fathers who bugged them and trashed their lives with too-early toilet training or bad food, mommas and poppas who gave them gender doubts. "Help me," is their cry, "heal me, light my fire so that I can hold a lover, a job, a thought!" A few hundred words of conventional American wisdom, then—then station identification, then barter and commerce, then the next sucker calls.

COUNSELOR: Sad. Pitiful. Still, as you've said, Vidyon, a big two minutes, a few hundred words, and—and they're back to the business of living. Little benefit, but no significant damage either.

ORLOFSKY: Guess again. Let me tune you in to "what if?"

COUNSELOR: What if?

ORLOFSKY: What if some jabberjockey, perhaps a hot and heavy ratings king like Gary Rambler, turns sorehead. One night, blown away by a black thought—okay, why not?—he gives not sugary benevolence to his sucker-bait losers but sets forth a screwball doctrine. At first for kicks, then power-mad kookiness takes over and he decides—okay, why not?—that he will use his misfits as mortar in the building of a hell on earth.

COUNSELOR: Yes, such an audience would be highly susceptible. Congratulations, Vidyon, on a prodigious insight which you shall one day pass on.

ORLOFSKY: There are other what ifs I would lay on you.

COUNSELOR: And so you shall once we've adjusted your ten A.M. medication.

ORLOFSKY: What if the doctors of sex should snap their anchors, let it all hang out, and sound the radio trumpets for unrestrained coupling and copulation, for a libido loosening that—"

COUNSELOR: First your medication, Vidyon. Then we'll consider how we shall communicate your findings to the secretary of health, education, and welfare and, through him, to the White House.

25

That night, after he had skimmed Orlofsky's latest transcript, the President dreamed that Eunice secretly left the bed and made a call to a famous radio talk show host.

He switched on his Nanny Dora's ancient Digby wireless so that he might listen in, and somehow it came as no surprise to hear the voice of Lewis Buntline giving Eunice counsel on matters of consequence.

Precisely what matters the President could not make out, for the wireless now and then failed, but it was plain to him they involved shameful episodes in their lives, and he was full of misgivings.

When he heard the fawning style of Eunice's questions and the spite and exultation in Buntline's answers, the President felt a clutch of dread at his heart.

"She's in danger," Nanny Dora told him.

Father and Mother spoke also of some peril to Eunice, and when the President exclaimed, "Oh, my dears, from what? Can you tell me from what?" they did not answer directly but said only, "She will soon learn the world was not made for her alone."

And so the President sought to warn Eunice.

Rushing from bed, he kicked free some sheets in which his foot had caught.

An awful odor assailed him.

Momentarily wavering, he collided with someone who had been crouching under the bed.

He tore away convulsively, crying, "Foul fiend!" and struck out with all his might, but he was borne to the ground.

When he asked, "What do you want of me?" his assailant held back, and the President decided, "Why, this is Eunice's father."

He whispered aloud, "Papa, poor Papa."

Then he forced himself to caress his assailant's face.

Nevertheless the President was being slowly dragged under the bed, and he could find nothing within himself with which to resist.

His mouth opened, at first to rage, then to lament.

"By Jesus," he said, "what will happen to Eunice? She's as blind as a stone to the ways of the world; she doesn't know shit about cruel and mischievous purpose. Oh Papa, poor Papa, make her understand that no good will come to her from Lewis Buntline, that he's a professor and, like Harry says, no good has ever come to the world from professors. By Jesus, that Buntline will put her simple uncomprehending heart into tumult and abandon her, even as he abandoned wife and son for the sake of some KGB squeeze."

He came awake when his assailant had him under the bed and started to strike the blow that would settle him forever.

26

Cheeks red and shining, the small girl in the orange velvet suit and bottle-green buskins entered the Oval Office at 11:23 A.M., strode over to the President, slid an envelope between his extended hands, and said, "My credentials, sir."

Though the President smilingly directed her to the loveseat, she sprang, with a little bound, into one of the black leather armchairs beside his desk.

"Perhaps"—she made a short horizontal gesture as if to underscore the word—"you ought to check them, the credentials."

The President laughed, largely from astonishment. Then, touched by her enormous, expectant eyes, he sat and answered, "Of course. So I should, so I should." He felt obliged to add with a mock shudder, "These days especially."

She scratched a little scab at her ankle, crossed her feet, and after a giggly sigh said, "Actually I have this terribly, terribly overpowering ego and I wanted to find out how Mr. Porlock might . . . characterize me."

"Look for yourself," the President said, passing the envelope across the desk.

In a shocked, reprimanding voice she answered, "But it's addressed to you, sir."

The President slit the seal with a fingernail, shot out a piece of onionskin paper, scanned it. "Thought Harry liked you, young lady." But he said this too severely, overpowering what he had intended as a bit of teasing, and when he heard the child's sharp intake of breath, her trembly "Oh," he was penetrated with remorse. "No, no. Listen." Bending so close that he could feel the heat on her skin, he grinned, cleared his throat musically, and read aloud:

" 'How gracious of you to find room in your crowded schedule today for my very good friend Ms. Melissa Siampa, whose wisdom, sweet gravity, and acuity of perception I shall not dishonor with the word "mature."

" 'As I mentioned, she is soon to celebrate her twelfth birthday. Since she has been named feature editor of her school newspaper, I thought she might especially appreciate the gift of an interview with the President of the United States.' "

The child's pensive face brightened.

"Don't be disconcerted if during the interview you don't see me write anything down. Really no need in my case."

She smiled ruefully.

"It simply happens, sir, that I am endowed, actually afflicted, with phenomenal and voodoolike recall."

"If you say so," the President bantered. "Although, although . . ." He looked carefully into her eyes and winked. ". . . considering your limited vocabulary range."

Melissa giggled, quickly stopped herself. "About that," she said, with a little wag of the wrist, "I'm a dreadful exhibitionist. Right now, at this moment in fact, all I can think of in your presence, at the side of the President, is how I shall employ two new words." A white spot showed on the tip of her nose. "Adumbrate and fecund."

"Awful, dreadful," murmured the President, giving one of her bangs a playful tug.

"My compulsive exhibitionism doesn't exactly endear me to people. I pay for it, do I ever, with the abiding hostility of my peer group."

Melissa shivered and there was a surge of blood to her forehead.

Taken her share, more than her share, the President reflected.

"Therefore my first question, sir. If you're ready, sir."

"All yours, at your service." He took her hand and squeezed it a shade harder than he meant to.

"Did you have, enjoy, a happy childhood? Or"—Melissa's stomach gurgled—"would you say you support Mr. Porlock's outlook? We had a luncheon the other day and when the subject arose he said, 'Melissa, you must understand that there are no happy childhoods.' "

A moment passed.

"If you'd like, sir, your answer can be off the record."

The President chuckled, shook his head. "See now," he ventured in a slightly scoffing voice, "my folks were rich."

"Then you had, you enjoyed"—Melissa puffed out her cheeks— "what was once called 'position.' "

"Oh, I'd have to say so. Definitely. I enjoyed position, I had advantages."

"Status and favored or favorable circumstances," said Melissa with a pleased smile. "Can you remember, would you care to discuss how you were favored? What, specifically, among your advantages gave you the most childhood pleasure?"

"See now, Melissa, as a child I was fascinated by the First World War. You might say more than fascinated. I . . ." He groped. "I was bananas and gaga, obsessed by the Great War."

Her tongue went around in tiny circles. "Nineteen-fourteen to nineteen-eighteen, also a false armistice.

"And, you see, because my parents had the means they would indulge me. They sent all the way to England, to a man named Hillary Dempster, for these magnificent handmade models of French eighty-eights and Big Berthas and zeppelins and soldiers, *poilus* and Tommies, whose wounds looked so real—so real you could see empty eye sockets and bits of exposed bone."

"Yuch!" went Melissa. A second later she added, "Sir."

"The wounded soldiers were special order. My father's idea."

"Maybe he wasn't really indulging you, then. Or he was indulging you with, for . . . a purpose."

Oh, what a deep little person, the President thought. Knows how to head straight at the soul. Watch yourself, best watch yourself with this one.

Nevertheless he laughed softly, passed a hand over her hair, and said, "Suppose you tell me, Melissa. What do you think my father had in mind? His purpose."

"Okay."

Melissa pulled a foot up on the chair and worked a finger under the strap of her buskin.

"Parents . . ."

For the first time she took her eyes off him.

"Ah, you know, sir."

"Ah, I don't know, Melissa," the President gently mimicked. His heart beat rapidly and he felt a stifling pressure in his throat. Yes, he reflected, Father persecuted me with those wounded soldiers. As I grew older their stumps grew bloodier. Then came dead rats and mutilated carcasses and bloated dog carcasses. He cut into my bliss like a psychic surgeon.

"As I see it, sir"—Melissa closed her eyes—"your father must have been a wonderful and resourceful parent. He was trying to show you, in a gently compassionate manner, that war is an evil."

"And how well he succeeded!" the President sonorously affirmed. Inwardly he exclaimed, "Now, isn't she something! Twelve years old and . . . and, by Jesus, she's handling me, she's sparing my feelings."

Then Melissa, flexing the soles of her buskins against the carpet, told him, "I'm interested in fathers."

She forced out a giggle.

"All except my own."

The President fought to hold an expression of humorous reserve.

"What was he like, sir? Your father? And in addition to a hatred of war's evils, did he provide you with other principles which . . . which to this day influence you?"

"My father," the President answered, folding his hands and centering them on the desk, "was an elegant and graceful and cultured man. Long, long before it was fashionable, Melissa, he had the idea that he should be a full partner in my upbringing, that besides teaching me good manners, fair play, and justice he must take a turn trimming my nails and giving me a bath and putting me to bed. I can't ever remember him honestly running out of patience with me. To give you an example, now, I had a hatred of haircuts. Maybe a fear, come to think of it. Well, Father found a barber who didn't mind working on the both of us in one chair, and while we were being clipped and scissored Father made a game of it. He pretended he was Charles I and I was a one-armed, one-eyed headsman who kept begging him to hold still for the ax."

"Charles I," said Melissa, tapping her brows significantly. "That's the Reformation, and Oliver Cromwell was his enemy."

"He respected my feelings and dignity in a way that's still rare among adults. If we were at the zoo and he sensed it just might be time I, oh, paid a visit to the washroom, he'd say, 'What about keeping me company while I refresh myself?' When he gave me something of his own, say a wonderful old fountain pen, he took care to throw in a brand-new gift-wrapped pencil box because he had the delicacy and tact to understand that newness is important to a child."

Yes, yes, he reflected, the spirit of loving kindness moved through our household. Yet I can't recall a morning when Mother failed to drink a couple of scoops of gin before breakfast. It's still beyond me. I mean . . . considering the pleasure they always took in one another and in me. Could any couple have been more completed by a child? Well then, what was the source of my chest weakness, my allergies, my mysterious fits of trembling? If you read the psychologists . . . Where's the psychology of it all?

The President took Melissa's hand, opened and closed, opened and closed her fingers. Then all at once a random thrust of feeling stabbed him, drove the breath away from his body. He longed to say, "You'll live and die and nothing, absolutely nothing in your childhood will really ever be honest and clear."

And he was about to speak of this when she plucked at his sleeve.

"Sir"—she sucked saliva through a gap between her front teeth— "there's an appallingly commonplace question which I'm compelled to bring up because I have to consider my readers and what is of interest to them. My readers," she said half to herself, "are a terrible handicap."

"So are my constituents, Melissa."

She let out a shriek of laughter.

"That will be off the record, sir. Oh, will it ever!"

She brought the tips of her fingers together.

"My faculty advisor," she said contemptuously, "thought I should ask you about the future. What's your outlook on the future, sir?"

The President pretended to scowl.

"How about"—he lowered his voice, looked at her keenly, conspiratorially—"The President regards the future as absolutely indispensable."

Melissa shook his hand.

"I'd like to make that a direct quote. Italicized, with your permission, sir."

"You have it," said the President, and he touched the pad of baby fat under her chin.

"I am further required," Melissa went on, making a fist, "to sound you out on how you . . . I'm trying to rephrase my faculty advisor's inept meandering . . . oh, how you stay abreast, aware of continually changing world events.''

He beckoned her close and whispered, "I don't.''

"Ah, Mr. President,'' she whispered discreetly, affectionately.

"Ah, Melissa . . . ,'' he began. Then he arrested himself. "A president,'' he solemnly said, "relies on his aides. On people like Mr. Porlock. See, now, early every morning these people come and brief him about world events and try to put them into perspective. To give you an idea of how this works . . .''

While he described a sample briefing, at first dryly, then with a kind of heavy satire that greatly pleased Melissa, one part of his mind went its own way.

Please, he prayed to JFK, there's something I must know. It honestly baffles me. Really, I try to stay on top of everything. Dear friend, not even you subscribed to so many obscure magazines or sucked up to more deep thinkers. Then why in blazes do I feel myself embalmed in the juices of another time? As outdated as chlorophyl toothpaste?

"Sir, you sound just like him, exactly!'' Melissa was exclaiming. She meant Harry. "Can you do him again? His sniff?''

"Sure thing,'' said the President. "What I think I'll do now is his Security Council sniff. For his Security Council sniff he'll generally use one nostril only. One nostril, he gives a twitch to his trousers, he squares his shoulders and . . . like this . . .''

Yet he was all the while meditating intensely, deeply.

And under urgent pressure he told JFK, "When I say 'Israel' I'm thinking 'Palestine.' The Katzenjammer Kids are more alive to me than most heads of state. At bottom I honest to God believe that one day India will want the British back. My balls burn, my heart aches, to see our cars getting smaller and smaller. Am I the mini-President of a mini-America? For that matter, everything conspires to somehow swindle and diminish me. If I have to smile away any more humiliations my teeth will break. In silence and strained sweetness I listen to the descendants of Arab slave traders lecturing me about how our inner fucking cities are shot to hell. Do what you can, old buddy. You could start by helping me through tomorrow, when I receive that new African minister. Don't let me forget the name of his tribe. And give me patience to withstand his platitudes. Because when the last one shook a fat finger in my face I showed my annoyance, I said—''

But Melissa had taken his hand.

"Would you care to hear how my lead is forming, emerging, sir?"

"All ears." And the President inclined his head as if to show how intently he would be listening.

Melissa sat very upright and said, "In this lead I'm playing it straight. For the first time. Usually, and this is absolutely off the record, sir, I try, I strive, endeavor, to work in some very subtle grammatical or stylistic error which my faculty advisor is never able to catch."

The President snorted. "Melissa, Ms. Siampa, you're a . . . handful," he finished lamely.

"I daresay," she answered with cool pride.

She fixed her gaze on a point beyond his head. "If we're ready, Mr. President."

He clasped his hands so tightly that they ached.

Melissa stood, hugged herself around the middle, and paced round and round the chair.

The President's heart opened. He felt his face expand.

Just what I used to do at her age, he reflected. When I was showing off I'd walk in circles and hold my breath until I got dizzy.

And in a husky, wavering voice, Melissa declaimed, "When your reporter entered the Oval Office and presented herself to the President she felt, sensed, discerned, within moments the force of his fecund mind, the firm resolve and strength of will adumbrated by a compassionate and generous nature. Born to wealth and privilege—"

The President's hands flew to his head.

" 'Fecund'? 'Adumbrate'? Those are the words"—he groaned wonderingly—"your two new words. See now . . . I see now. Warned me you'd be using them."

Melissa rose on her toes. Her eyelids fluttered a moment as she turned to say, "Hoped you'd notice, sir."

Then she added slyly, "And in one sentence."

She sat down.

"Born to wealth and privilege," she resumed, pounding away at an invisible typewriter, "he apprehended, thanks to his father's profound influence and teachings, that, as he told your reporter, 'the evils of war must never again be visited upon mankind. Yes,' he affirmed . . ."

She sighed.

"Mr. President."

"Ms. Siampa."

She looked at him with extraordinary closeness. Frowning fiercely, she said, "Mr. President, I couldn't hold back, repress . . . a thought?" She ended on a quivery, questioning note. "It's the kind of thought I don't get too often, though often enough, and to describe it . . ."

Her arms made giant circles in the air.

". . . It's highly negative, morbid, depressive, melancholy, somber. It arouses feelings such as, What is the use, the purpose, the point?"

She clicked her tongue.

"Thus, during my lead, when I came to the evils of war part, I saw or had this vision of my peer group and my faculty advisor and my readership and the thought I got was . . . Really, they are not worth saving. The evils of war is or are too good for them. Because if they represent what fills the world and goes by the name of mankind—yuch!"

"No help for it, Melissa."

"I daresay, sir."

"People are people and mankind . . ." the President floundered, ". . . is all we have."

"Stuck with it, sir."

"Everyone, Melissa, is sort of, see now, sentenced to mankind. Like it or not."

"For good or ill, sir."

"See now," he said, falling into an endearing, humble, wistful tone, "there's nothing I'd want more than a country full of Melissa Siampas. But I'm also the President of your peer group and your readership. I have to do good and wise things for them as well."

Melissa scowled.

"I wish, wish, wish I could be more sanguine about my generation. My conclusion is that goodness and wisdom for them would be a crash remedial-reading and vocabulary-building program. Do you know, sir, that even *Junior Scholastic* magazine is beyond them?"

As sincerely and solemnly as he could, the President answered, "Awful."

"Common discourse with them is . . ." She released a pent-up breath and made a negative gesture. "They say 'nuc-u-lar' instead of 'nuclear' and drop their 'G's and their current-events grasp—Mr. President, I fear the worst."

All the President could think to say was, "That bad?"

"If they represent the wave of the future or the voice of the people or even merely echo their parents—Mr. President, your efforts are for naught."

"As bad as that?"

Melissa clenched her fists before her breast. "Sir, they are ready to end life forever on this earth, planet. Their prevailing attitude during open-discussion hour last week was—"

She slitted her eyes, twisted her shoulders menacingly, and assumed an apish expression, a nasal monotone.

"What he's doin', this Gavrych, it's real cool. He figures, this Gavrych, his American pals can go round terrorizin' and it don't cost him. Long as he feeds the U.S. of A. a line about peace, the peace line, he got it made. The thing we should do is every time a famous American celebrity gets knocked off, we gotta hit 'em with a missile."

After a moment of what was clearly indecision Melissa, her face flaming, said, "During open-discussion period ten days ago they booed me. And afterward they . . . there were blows exchanged."

Her eyes opened to the full.

The President nodded and nodded.

"Because I defended your foreign policy and praised your admirable restraint in not taking hasty, precipitous action that would return us to the pre-Gavrych arms-race era."

"Thank God for Melissa Siampas," the President intoned. "Thank God for your civilized intelligence, your perception of what is in my heart."

For a few seconds, and with all his might, he believed this.

Then ambushed by other thoughts, he went on to say, "Dark times, Melissa. We live in dark times."

"Do we ever, Mr. President!"

"All the same"—he took her hands and swung them—"it's nearly twelve o'clock and we're having . . . why, by executive order, we're having chocolate milk and chocolate graham crackers and we'll just see what we can do about a special birthday present, something special."

Melissa, with an excited escape of breath, exclaimed, "Mr. President, chocolate grahams are fantastic when very, very chilled. Almost frozen!"

Whereupon the President kissed her brow, her nose, and that little roll of baby fat under her chin.

At 12:19 P.M. he made a call to Porlock.

"Mr. President."

"By Jesus, I liked your friend, Harry."

"A deep, deep child."

"But open. Open and vulnerable."

"Indeed, sir."

"Hope the world doesn't take too much out of her."

"No fear, sir. Melissa will give as good as she gets. Oh, if you had seen her handling one of those overbearing waiters at Croix Verte! 'Monsieur, I find you a bit too cheeky. Be assured that I shall recommend to my escort, Mr. Harry Porlock, that your oafish and churlish—' "

But the President cut him off, saying in a low, terse voice, "Are we on scrambler, Harry?"

"Of course."

The President's mouth was dry. "I suppose . . . Should be about fifteen, twenty minutes from now."

"More like three quarters of an hour, sir."

The President did not answer immediately.

"Mr. President?"

"Here, Harry."

He probed an eyelid and felt the beginning of a sty. "I'm thinking of the body count, Harry. Now wouldn't Macy's give us as good a body count as Bloomingdale's?"

"Indeed, sir. And good thinking, sir. But Bloomingdale's does draw such a wonderfully cosmopolitan clientele. Should have a fair chance at some middle-level UN people. Perhaps—who knows?—an ambassador or two."

"Eunice's favorite store," the President mused. "Crazy to go there whenever we're in New York. Loves the ambience. Claims it raises her consciousness."

Porlock laughed amiably.

A moment passed.

"Three quarters of an hour, then," the President said submissively.

"Around one o'clock," Porlock told him. "Optimum time. Gives us the lunch hour crowd."

"Eunice will be—" But the President trailed off. Suddenly he was murmuring inaudibly, "No children, I hope. Does Bloomingdale's get many children? Can't draw the line, though. Not now. A body count is a body count. Do what we have to do and learn to leave ourselves alone. Clemenceau or Haig said something like that."

He felt faint.

"We'll talk!" he shouted and hung up abruptly.

For an instant he could not see, and the interior of the Oval Office appeared swathed in granular, bloody colors that shimmered like gases.

And he called upon JFK and cried out to him, "Oh, what's with me and the human condition!"

But presently he got a grip on his troubled emotions.

By 1:28 P.M., after he had caught the first news bulletins on TV, after he had canceled all further afternoon appointments so that he could fly to New York and make a personal inspection of Bloomingdale's, he was clearheaded enough to call Harry again.

"This is from the top of my head, Harry, and I don't have the Metastases File on hand, but aren't the networks getting his name, the perpetrator's name, wrong?"

"Indeed, sir. And NBC continues showing the wrong photograph."

"They all keep saying, 'Sorkin,' and I know it's not Sorkin. It's not Sorkin but it's a name close to Sorkin."

"He enjoyed a certain eminence, sir."

"At the edge of my mind, the tip of my tongue."

"Cast your memory back to the sixties, sir. Consider, too, how very far we have come from those sad, silly, heady times."

Whereupon the President cried, "Dworkin!"

"Dworkin it is, sir." And Porlock went on to say, "Poor unfortunate creature."

27

METASTASES FILE
COMPUTER CODE: CORINTHIANS H 953J
Dworkin, Brian Jerome, 63. Waldenström's macroglobulinemia, some kidney atrophy. Minimal life expectancy.
Attended Brooklyn College (1960–64); early praise for long essay, "The Manifesto of a Marginal Man."

Tutor in Political Science Department, State University of New York at Albany, 1967; led march to Washington, D.C., same year; proposed a "Screamathon Day," "so that present generation could utter sounds of lamentation against their present condition."

During months that followed, debates with William Buckley; appearances on *Camera Three, Open End, The David Susskind Show;* parodies of Henry Kissinger and Lyndon Johnson in *Ramparts.*

Covered 1968 Democratic convention for *Outlook;* piece quoted by Frank Reynolds in ABC News Special *We Are Two Nations.*

Unmaking It, a collection of articles and reviews, published in 1970, immediate critical success.

Accepted appointment to Rachel Steinglass Chair of Contemporary Social Thought at CCNY, 1970.

Subleased three-room apartment near New York Eye and Ear Infirmary from Brooklyn College classmate Ned Sandberg, a member of Senator Jacob Javits's staff; bought Sandberg's 1964 Dodge Dart, parked it in street; collected thirty-seven tickets within month; mailed tickets to State Department with covering letter: "Kindly pay these fines and deduct from reparations due me as captive of this era."

Married neighbor, Mary Threethorns, Pawnee journalist, during subsequent FBI investigation; daughter, Emma Goldman Luxemburg Dworkin, born 1981.

Ignored warnings from Ned Sandberg that "IRS will be dogging you like Hound of Heaven"; continued baiting secretary of treasury, others in Nixon cabinet; CCNY salary, savings account, royalties attached by IRS.

Became monologuist at Powerless People Coffeeshop, April 4, 1972; took $8,593.81 payment in cash; failed to declare payment to IRS; arrested for violation of Federal Statute 2115R; released on own recognizance; fled New York City, August 12, 1972; expelled during next three years from five communes.

Changed name to Sheldon Silverstine; settled in Detroit; hired, with Ned Sandberg's help and forged recommendation from Senator Javits, as publicity writer, United Jewish Appeal.

Onset of symptoms six years later: depression, irritation, costly mistakes; dismissed, July 11, 1990; condition misdiagnosed by three internists; correct diagnosis at Detroit General Hospital, November 20, 1993; disposition of fee: Pay from Foxfire Fund for reissue of *Unmaking It* limited edition; and to Mary and Emma Goldman Luxemburg Dworkin $315,000 for start-up "progressive" magazine.

—

On Friday he wrote to Ned Sandberg:

"I'm in hospital.
"Something called Waldenström's macroglobulinemia. Very bad blood. Terminal. Splendid dreams of youth unfulfilled. Dealt with Rabbi Harry Waxman this morning. A big Reform honcho. Sprayed me with spittle every time he said 'Torah.' I told him the Unitarians had made me a better offer.
"He got angry.
"He said that in his capacity as hospital chaplain he had come across similar Jewish wiseguys, that with IV tubes up their noses they are not so tough and they find the six-thousand-year-old faith of their forefathers suddenly very attractive.
"And I had no answer.
"He's a prick, but he planted a thought.
"I picture myself in extremis.
"I'm wearing a paper skullcap, I'm praying from a little pamphlet in transliterated Hebrew—and at that moment my Emma walks in and has her last sight of me.
"I can do better by her.
"I mean to will her an appetite for struggle.
"Because I'm turning myself in.
"I want to go on trial and speak out.
"Will you handle arrangements with the FBI, the IRS, whomever?
"This poor sick bum is counting on you."

He was informed by registered mail that nine days hence, November 26, on or around one P.M., he was required to present and surrender himself at the baggage claims area of New York Air in Kennedy Airport.
He phoned his old editor and told him that he was turning himself in and meant to make his trial an event of great importance.
Within the hour his editor called back to say that a new edition of *Unmaking It* could certainly be brought out to coincide with the trial; the publicity people were meanwhile arranging a press confer-

ence for November 26, one P.M., at Kennedy Airport, near the baggage claims area of New York Air.

There was heavy pre-Thanksgiving air traffic at Kennedy, and so his DC-710 was stacked over Queens, cruising round and round the miles of swollen cemetery plots.

Peeping down, Dworkin gave a sigh, and the loving sorrow he felt for himself he suddenly extended to his fellow passengers.

Therefore he gazed openly and keenly at the heavyset white-haired man next to him who was writing figures on a pad. "I am Brian Jerome Dworkin," he said for the first time in many years, "and though I'm unalterably opposed to the values you probably represent I wish you luck in all your enterprises."

The man answered, "Luck to you," and hid his face.

Then two bells chimed and the captain announced that the plane was landing.

At 1:55 P.M. the blond woman from ABC ripped up her notes and said coldly, "No feds, no surrender, no story. Pack it in."

At 2:10 P.M. the CBS and NBC crews and the stringers from AP and UPI also left. Dworkin followed them a little way, strode back and forth, back and forth, before the baggage conveyor till he saw a black security guard giving him close, unblinking attention.

Unable to stare him down, Dworkin snarled and said loudly, "Do I interest you, flunky?"

He went forward, and made dangerous faces. Coming close to the guard he thought, "Here and now. Get in one good blow and make him use his gun. God give me strength for that one good blow—"

But at that moment someone smacked him across the behind and said, "Down, mad guy."

Recognizing the voice, Dworkin cried, "Oh, ye gods."

Then he turned, clasped Ned Sandberg's hand, and stooping over it, his eyes filled.

He said, "Ned, what is happening? Do you know? What is happening? Ah, Ned . . ."

Sandberg gave him a look of such powerful disclosure that it momentarily stopped his breath.

"Hey," he cried with a resonance of dread, "you weren't supposed to be here. What are you doing here?"

Sandberg lifted an arm, let it fall slackly.

"What are you doing here?" Dworkin repeated.

Sandberg glanced away. "They like to call it"—he turned down his lip—"executive recruitment."

Dworkin felt his heart shaking, knocking. A monstrous intuition pierced him and he whispered, "You work for *them*?"

"Yes, I work for *them*," said Sandberg with a faint smile. "The . . . spooks." His smile deepened. "But only part-time and not at Langley."

Dworkin held out his wrists. "Handcuffs, shackles, what? Although a first-rate betrayal calls for a bullet behind the ear."

"Part-timers"—Sandberg raised delighted brows—"get only three bullets, and I've already used my three."

"I'm still a threat to them. After all this time they won't let me stand trial, they won't let me speak out." There was a little creak in Dworkin's voice. "Death is swinging me by the ears like a rabbit, but even so they're afraid, even so."

"Actually," Sandberg said, with a nervous dodge of his wide, ruddy face, "they're hot for your body."

And he put an arm around Dworkin's waist. "Come, let's go for a drive, college chum. We'll compare sorrows. Figure out what happens to human beings and their expectations." He kissed him on the top of the head. "Come."

Sandberg steered him outside and gestured at an extended Lincoln limousine with blue plum finish. It carried U.S. government plates and was brazenly double-parked.

Sandberg made whistling noises at the sinewy little man who slouched against a fender squeezing golf balls. Instantly he bounded over, opened a curbside door, saluted, held the salute seconds after they were seated, and very formally walked behind the car, let himself in, and closed the tinted-glass partition.

Sandberg bent forward and opened it.

"Mario," he said, grinning at Dworkin, "have a look inside the trunk and see if you can find my fur gloves. Only first angle out five, ten feet and block traffic."

At 3:20 P.M., moments after they had picked up the Van Wyck Expressway northbound, Dworkin groaned, slapped the morocco-trimmed armrest, and in a small voice said, "I forgot my bag."

"Careless," said Sandberg, "but not fatal."

"Shall we go back?" Dworkin twisted around. "Only what's the sense? Ripped off by now. My best suits. And certain pills—a bottle they gave me in the hospital. Never even had the prescription. Ah, ye gods," he cried in suffocating misery.

"Do you think you're dealing with some small potatoes enterprise?" Sandberg's hands flew to his head. "They knew you had Waldenström's macroglobulinemia fifteen hours before the hospital did. Wherever you stay tonight—and there's a reservation for you at every East Side hotel in Manhattan—the pills will be waiting. Also three, let's make it five, suits from F. R. Tripler, whose special-order department will have within the hour"—he raised a finger as if it were a wand—"a printout of your size, necessary alterations, and such."

He gave Dworkin a kiss.

"They have a class act, college chum."

"I see that," said Dworkin, averting his gaze. "Yes, I believe they'd need a class act to"—he described spirals in the air—"to turn somebody like you around."

"Turn me around!"

Sandberg set his teeth. "Listen . . ." He held Dworkin with his small round eyes. "Consider my plight, college chum. First Senator Javits sickens and dies on me. Then the eighty elections blow the other liberal gasbags off Capitol Hill. No more staff jobs for marginal intellectuals. No more swollen salaries for sixty-three-page summaries of forty-one-page reports."

All Dworkin could think to say was, "Ah."

"Took stock of myself. And what was I? Another bellyaching ex-Trotskyite. Another neurasthenic Jew waiting for the world to fulfill his worst fears. Then they recruited me, made me one of them, and it was as if a spell had passed. I was delivered. True brotherhood at last among prime movers who don't know from things like alienation."

And they headed westbound on the Long Island Expressway.

Near the gas tanks in Elmhurst Dworkin whispered, "I'm at the last stage of my existence, so what do they want of me? What can your people possibly want of me?"

Sandberg thought this over a moment. "Only to make you rich and famous, college chum. You'll have a fat grant for some nothing make-work project." He closed his eyes, put his palms together. "Something, oh, in the humanities."

And presently they entered the Queens Midtown Tunnel.

CARLTON HOUSE
680 MADISON AVENUE
NEW YORK CITY

Dear Mary and Emma, Emma and Mary:

Seven-thirty and I'm trying to get you for the last half hour.
But line is busy, busy, busy.
What does Emma want in the way of a Special Daddy gift? Remember, I'll be running around, pressed for time, and Carlton House is convenient only to some broken-down boutiques and Bloomingdale's.
Dinner soon with unknown benefactor-bureaucrat.
Grant is fat, fat, fat!
Something to do with Gavrych.
I seem to be extremely well qualified.
Bath overflowing.
Try you later.

But the line was still busy when Sandberg came and hurried him out of the room, saying, "Do you want to lose the reservation? Look at him dawdle. Come!"

"I've been to good restaurants in my time," said Dworkin. "And—"

Sandberg grabbed him around the waist and whisked him down the corridor. Before the blue-tinted mirrors near the elevator he kissed him noisily. "Have a look at yourself," he cried.

Dworkin went back a step, put his hands behind his back. Yes, he was peaked, bereft of hair, ravaged about the eyes. But wearing such a suit, such a shirt of Italian silk, such snakeskin loafers, you can't acknowledge death. You can't, absolutely can't.

The elevator doors chimed open. As they entered, Sandberg

bumped him with his hip and said, "Is it so terrible having a friend in high places?"

Dworkin bumped him back. He was on the point of saying, "Satan once had a friend in high places," when he realized the elevator doors had closed, the machinery was meshing, the cables thumping.

Yet the car had not started.

He said, "Now what is this?"

Sandberg silently grinned.

Dworkin yelled, "This is no accident!"

Sandberg put a finger to his lips, made hushing sounds.

Dworkin was walking crazily about when it struck him that something was amiss with the Muzak. What noise, what infernal din! He bit the inside of his cheek as the sugary medley of "Greensleeves" and "Little Drummer Boy" whirred and squeaked and rasped.

But then he went, "Ah," and he lightly clasped hands and sighed and gasped, and he let the opening notes of Mozart's *Davidde Penitente* catch at his heart.

"Did we do right by you?" demanded Sandberg. "Isn't this your favorite Mozart?"

"Oh yes, oh yes."

Yet all the while part of Dworkin's mind was oppressed by another thought. Why have they been to such pains? Why? Is there a point they mean to make? Then what point?

But just when he believed he was close to grasping it the Mozart ended, the elevator door opened, and there entered a lean, elderly, meticulously dressed man. His face was white, straight-nosed, handsome, lively; his blue eyes were acute, and he was as bald as a gull.

He said with a genial glance, "I am Harry Porlock, Mr. Dworkin, and I hope to be your benefactor."

He and Porlock ate at DeBiasi's, on East 61st Street.

While busboys cleared their table Porlock started talking.

"When I was an adolescent and beginning to wonder what men live for," he said, "I read a sentence: 'Do not value the world more highly than it deserves.' This was in 1937, early one afternoon in Chicago. A library west of State Street. My last Christmas recess from Phillips Exeter Academy, and I had come to look Northwestern University over. The line whispered within my soul."

Dworkin said, "Yes," and with a nod of absolute assent, "I know, I know. A tremendous line makes everything clear and then—it never fails—the writer goes on and on to some nonsense."

Looking into his face, Porlock very softly said, "How perceptive you are, Mr. Dworkin. Then you will understand why I would not risk reading more, why I left the library and walked about in the deathly cold. Miles, miles. I must have been close to the stockyards, for I heard cattle. . . . Oh, Mr. Dworkin, will you take a bit more of the wild mushroom salad? The touch of goose fat is perfect."

Dworkin, wholly absorbed, made a quick negative sign.

"Well, then—" They exchanged looks, and Porlock nodded and smiled at him in a way that showed he was greatly flattered. "Well, then, Mr. Dworkin, there was a black, punishing Chicago rain, then light—such a light, I imagine, as the newly blind see in dreams. Then I passed an abandoned movie house, and a macrocephalic idiot was slamming himself again and again and harder and harder against the cashier's cage. Gave his head a curious wound. Rather like a third eye, as I remember."

He turned a knife over in his fingers.

"On that day, Mr. Dworkin, I began to understand that life is a protracted insult."

He sketched at the tablecloth with a breadstick.

"Still it always comes as a surprise to me, Mr. Dworkin. Always."

After a while Dworkin said, "My daughter"—he had to take a deep breath to go on—"once woke us up. Told us she'd seen a very bad thing that day. Wouldn't say what, but if she ever saw another such thing she'd kill herself."

"What a child you have, Mr. Dworkin, what a wonderfully sensitive child. And you're a splendid father."

He boned a slice of broiled salmon trout.

"A pity you weren't a better caretaker of your career."

"A pity?" Dworkin repeated, frowning. But then he remembered that he was here for a grant, and he checked himself. He said, "I suppose I expected America to fall into my arms." With such grace as he could muster he added, "A fallacy of the sixties."

Porlock momentarily touched his wrists.

"Mr. Dworkin, it pains me to think of you drinking the bitter cup again and again while Gavrych . . . *Leviathan's Hook* is currently in its thirty-second printing. Beloved by schoolgirl activists and ideological thrill seekers."

"I had my time in the spotlight. Maybe I wasn't Gavrych, but I wasn't a bit player either."

"How easily you might have surpassed him, Mr. Dworkin."

Dworkin made a gently scoffing sound. "Maybe I was never more than a holy terror crying bloody murder."

"Lovely!" Porlock exclaimed. "Yet I wonder if you'll feel quite resigned by"—he lowered his eyes solemnly—"March or April next."

"Why not? Henry Adams once remarked—" But at that instant Dworkin got the drift, and he thought, Biology, cell, death, I.

Nevertheless he accepted a helping of brandied apricots from Porlock and fought down an impulse to flinch when Porlock's hand accidentally grazed his hand.

"Have I made matters too plain?" said Porlock. "Forgive me."

"Actually"—Dworkin snapped his fingers—"it's good you reminded me."

"But if I'm to be your friend and benefactor I must put you in touch with fundamentals."

Porlock looked at him as if from a great distance.

"By late December, Mr. Dworkin, you'll be tried most harshly. Doubtless pride and wit should see you through what the late Dr. John Franklin Hurster spoke of as 'the staggering injustice phase.' February, though, might be the problem. How did Dr. Hurster put it? 'Our ultimate obligation at termination time is to die with a show of tranquility for the sake of our children.' "

He regarded Dworkin with a kind of amused pity.

"Have you considered the cost of tranquility, Mr. Dworkin? Can't be had nowadays with savings of some twenty-five hundred dollars and ninety-odd cents."

Dworkin shook his head.

"I'd be pleased, of course, to help your wife return to the work force."

Dworkin kept shaking his head.

"Though she might be best off free-lancing. Not all that much money, but free-lancing does allow her to be home frequently. And she'll need to be home frequently, I fear."

"Because of Emma? Ah, you have to know Emma. Her inner resources are—"

But suddenly Dworkin said, "You're not about to give me a grant, are you? There's no grant and there's no fellowship and there's no foundation, is there?"

A sigh fell from Porlock. He gave Dworkin a lingering glance, a glance of sorrow and deep quietude. But then Dworkin caught him glancing in much the same way at his watch.

Porlock was quoting Jakob Burckhardt as they left the restaurant, walking in long, sweeping strides that Dworkin could not quite match. "Only Burckhardt understood how modern urban populations hate the past and seek revenge on everything that has been."

In front of Bloomingdale's he slowed down to watch some window dressers set up a display. "Oh my!" he exclaimed. "They're giving each mannequin an old movie star's face. Isn't that Jack Oakie? And there, Fred MacMurray . . ."

But something suddenly occurred to Dworkin, and he stared hard at Porlock. A powerful ringing started up in his ears. "Listen," he cried, "listen, why should Mary free-lance? And why will she have to be home frequently? Isn't that what you said? No, need—she'll *need* to be home frequently."

"Might have had a better likeness of Fred MacMurray." Then after wincing and biting a knuckle, Porlock said, "Time you were back at the hotel, Mr. Dworkin. Should be getting a call before too long and you won't want to miss it."

He was hunched forward on the bed, swaying, muttering, "Lay off, leave me and mine alone," when the phone rang.

He instantly recognized the rhythm of Emma's breath, and he said, "Yes, hello Emma-Bemma," and she answered, "Daddy, I don't feel right."

He started to soothe her, but Mary came on and said, "Prove it's you, not some armpit doing your voice," and after a bit he answered, "Brian Jerome Dworkin here, and I'm still outraged by the ruin falling everywhere upon the world."

Though Mary kept breaking off to comfort Emma, he understood finally that they had just seen him on TV, on the big old black-and-white Zenith in the living room.

He willed himself to faint or die. But Mary's voice brought him back. "First an armpit voice goes, 'This is no dream, no hallucination.' And we can't turn the set off and we can't change channels and there you are. In an open grave. You're alive and you're trying to dig yourself out. Trying. Digging. Spitting dirt. Looks like you, sounds like you. Pushing, trying. Head is out, and neck and a shoulder. Can't make it all the way. You just can't . . ."

And he heard Emma screaming, "Because I'm pulling him under! Tell how I'm pulling him under!"

Mary screamed back, checked herself, said, "As you're going down you ask Emma to let go of your feet. 'Let go of me, bad girl. Don't pull me under, Emma, don't kill me. Emma, why are you pulling Daddy into a grave?' "

She covered the mouthpiece and murmured to Emma, who murmured back in a sickly undertone he had never before heard from her.

"Emma wants to talk," Mary said.

He heard Emma swallow and wheeze, swallow and wheeze. Then she said, "When you were going under, while I was supposed to be pulling you down down down into your grave and . . . everything . . . a message, a caption, kept appearing and flashing. 'Next time this happens again, Emma, and it will, again and again, we promise to do better, much better.' "

She's getting one of her dry throats, he thought.

"Ah," he said, and then after thinking as clearly as he could for fully ten seconds he went on to say, "Emma-Bemma, there are some people who want to weigh and measure my love for you, and they're doing it with these new, silly electronic devices and—don't worry, no problems, it's only . . ."

He made clicking, whirring, beeping noises, backed a little away from the phone, said "Hello? Hello? Hello?" and broke the connection.

He thought, Biology, cell, death, I, I, I.

He also thought, But at least I was right, all along. Yes, everything I felt about this society was dead right, dead right, and that's something.

He told this a little later to Porlock, who had let himself into the room without bothering to knock.

But Porlock did not answer directly, he only bit a knuckle and said,

"Oh, Mr. Dworkin, what a pity we couldn't have had a go at one another when we were in our prime."

Dworkin looked at him with cold hatred.

Then he lost strength in his knees, and Porlock helped him to a chair, put a pillow at his back, plumped it, said, "I'm told she's a lovely child."

For a long time Dworkin could not speak. Finally he said, "What do you want of me?"

Porlock took a chair, moved it close, and sat on the edge so that they were knee to knee.

"Bloomingdale's," Porlock began.

28

From: Joel Baskier, Office of the Press Secretary
To: President
Re: TV Taping at Bloomingdale's, November 30, 11 A.M.

Shooting begins moment you set foot on Bloomie's escalator, so remember to look up, up. Anguished but resolute. Take Eunice's hand at second floor, hold it till somewhere between floors four and five. Camera leaves you for split-screen stuff. Twenty seconds of dead silence while we show news clips of blood and butchery. Back to you in soft focus. Clench lips, shake head. As if trying to shake out blood and butchery images. Leave escalator at seventh floor. Back to anguished but resolute. Eunice might have pained-by-your-pain look. Take nine, ten steps. Stop, stare off. We cut to a bloody children's book. Back to you, torn apart by thoughts. How could Gavrych, his dogma and doctrines, his American admirers and adherents, bring this about? You and Eunice part. Camera pulls back while you walk into desolation of seventh floor. Anguished but resolute.

And please put that poll out of your mind. Trust Harry. Trust Farley Bone too. Guy's brilliant. A filmmaker's filmmaker. He and Harry have worked out a lovely surprise something. Patience, faith. Wait and see. Before day's end you'll be as universally popular as chocolate chip cookies.

—

On Lexington Avenue, a few yards south of East 60th Street, the President paused. And for a moment so brief that it passed with his next breath, he felt emanations of awe from the meager crowd. But at an open window three stories above a Citibank branch, he glimpsed a long-faced girl who seemed to be watching everything in sight but him. When she wet two fingers with her tongue and put them to her eyebrows and her nose and then sucked them, he grimaced and uttered a sharp little cry.

"Wave," Eunice hissed.

"Oh, Jack," he silently prayed, "if thou would but cause one, one only, to slide under or climb over those police barriers and approach me in love, even mild admiration, I would not harden my heart against America."

"Aren't you going to wave?" murmured Eunice. "Wave like you're good country folk come Sunday visiting."

While he waved in the direction of Cohen's Optical and Gem Sounds and Alexander's and Blarney Stone, and while he slowly thrust the balls of his thumbs at the dirty pink sky, and while he extended his arms at a precise right angle from his breast, keeping his back perfectly straight and still, he was saying to his countrymen, "You shits, you pinhead nothings, you human clutter, what's wrong with my intelligence? Suddenly not smart enough to suit them, apemeat shitkickers!"

To Eunice he said, "I'll be dealing with them. You'll see how. I promise legislation—by Jesus, I'll give them nasty, repressive, ball-busting legislation. Make their lives miserable. Dark times, from sea to shining sea."

"My grieving Lord," said Eunice, blowing kisses at Lamston's and Quiche Me-Qwik and Suede N'Stuff, "you and your thundering intellect. Worse than a peacock and his tail."

In his rage the President momentarily made a fist and bared his teeth, and he cried at Eunice, "Forty-seven percent, that's practically half of those polled, have no faith in my brainpower, my intelligence. And thirty percent have no opinion either way. By Jesus, how would you feel if that was you? If they thought, practically half of America, that you had ratty hair and chicken skin and wore cheap polyesters, and . . ."

But he saw the balding agent with tortoiseshell sunglasses staring

at him, and he lowered his voice, saying, "Well, you know," and
linking hands with Eunice he turned her to the Bloomingdale's marquee.

The blond agent with the rimless sunglasses sprang ahead, spoke
into his walkie-talkie, nodded. "If you're ready, sir. Whenever you're
ready."

"Yes, boys. Ready, boys," the President answered.

Nevertheless he lingered a bit, tilted his head toward the camera
atop the CBS mobile unit, laboring to urge into his face a look that
would tell the populace that they should be heartily sorry for him,
that he was having a hard time, that his burdens were oppressive,
that he was beset with more problems than the *Encyclopaedia Bri-
tannica* had entries. Brothers and sisters, only show mercy, gratitude,
fairness, trust in my first-rate intelligence, and I'll give you . . . Why,
what won't I give you! A time, an era, an age! I could come on, if
you let me, with the understanding of Aristotle, the humanity of . . . of
Saint Francis.

But as he entered the forlorn quietude of the Bloomingdale's mezzanine he was again downcast and bitter. "On second thought," he
whispered, "fuck 'em."

"Sweet heaven," exclaimed Eunice, "how shivery empty! Hear my
own footsteps."

"Security, ma'am," the balding agent with the tortoiseshell sunglasses told her. "Best to keep the mezzanine empty."

"Aren't you nice," said Eunice. "Gracious, like an empty planet . . .
Picturing it. Why, it's thundering scary. But scary-tingly-wicked-
delicious scary," she added, pretending to tremble all over.

Then her face flushed and her breathing altered.

"Why do I have this impulse? I just do have this impulse—"

And all of a sudden she broke away. In a kind of rapture she went
among the counters, touching gently a scarf, a glove, a gold mesh
purse, a snakeskin belt, a batlike shawl . . .

"Not here, doesn't seem to be here," she said shakily.

"Eunice," the President said, raising his voice. "By Jesus, Eunice,
the cameras are coming any second. By Jesus, for all you know they're
here already filming this, and we're supposed to be, we are, here under
awful circumstances, tragic circumstances. Enough, please. Enough,
enough, enough."

"One 'enough' will do fine," she replied archly, wrinkling her face.

Taking long, stiff-legged, graceful strides, twice stopping to twirl like a model on a runway, she came to his side, hugging him and playfully patting his cheek.

"Hope they're filming this," said the President, pulling away. "Hope this shows up in the *Enquirer*."

Yearningly Eunice said, "Why, I was looking for a music box, a certain special music box, is all."

The President tensed his lips.

"See now"—she closed her eyes, put a finger to her mouth—"Papa, poor Papa, had a nap-time story about a store named Melody Magic Mart." She smiled hard. "A real enormous store, and it caters to good girls only. Now in the darkest darkness . . ." She nodded three times and then all in a rush said, "In the darkest darkness, when it's all closed, I hide away because I must absolutely prove my worthy courage to earn a special music box."

"Marvelous," the President snarled.

After a moment Eunice, staring tranquilly into the President's eyes, said, "A special music box, a blessed special music box putting me in harmony with powers of earth and heaven, the happy powers, of course. Now to find it, I must go among the counters, and right among these counters is a mannequin, and though it's darkest darkness I will know it by the light of its eyes, which is the very nicest kind of starlight. There is just one thing more, a teeny-tiny thing more I must do to find my special music box."

White-faced, the President said, "Oh, let's go. I'm going." He turned his back on Eunice, declaiming to himself, "Thou hast my permission, Lord. Lord, take the life out of her, obliterate her. Let her know"—he thought of Orlofsky's last tape—"that this man is mortal enemy to his mate."

But Eunice stood her ground and held him by a sleeve.

"Now what needed doing for my special Eunice music box was to free the poor mannequin from the evil creatures who had imprisoned him in wax, and there is but one way to do so. What way? Why, I was to call upon the aid and comfort of my best friends from dreamland who would come swishy-swirl up to do battle against the evil creatures and set him free, the mannequin."

"Lovely, marvelous," the President said.

"All I need say was, 'Come, good friends, best friends, come from dreamland, my Honeybunch, my Five Little Peppers, my Black Beauty, my Swiss Family Robinson, my Little Mary Mixup, my Campfire Girls, my Waterbabies, my Phronsie and—' "

"By Jesus!" the President yelled. "Won't you ever? . . . Must you always? . . ." Then he considered, rejected, considered, and finished with the word he knew she hated most. "Babble. On and on, on and on. Babble-babble, babble-babble."

Her face turned an ugly red.

"Why, we do thank you for calling this customary habit to our attention. Our"—she smiled haughtily—"babbling characteristic." And in a prim, clear voice she said, "I believe, yes, I do rightly believe I have never before felt so distant from a human being."

And for a little while neither of them said anything more.

Then the President turned, contemplated her. With a mixture of contrition and reproach he said, "Eunice."

Though at this moment she looked too far gone to speak a complete sentence, Eunice said, "I could not feel more distant if you were some Third World place in the darkest darkness of Africa."

Beset by a host of feelings, the President chose to single out injustice. "Eunice," he replied, "let's say I went too far. Yes, I went too far. But when you consider, under the circumstances—"

"I have circumstances, too!"

"Sure you do. Absolutely, no question. But consider, you think about it, Eunice. On balance, Eunice, consider that I need, I have need of your"— he tried his anguished but resolute look on her —"forbearance."

"Babble. Babble-babble," went Eunice. "Seems to me as those who need forbearance should themselves . . . Truly they should . . ."

But her chin was trembling, and the President sensed that she had started moving from righteousness to simple petulance. Therefore he began slowly and quietly to reveal his deepest feelings to her, saying, "This poll, this poll. Can't shake it off, by Jesus. It's as if . . . As if, okay, as if I was still . . . When I was at St. Barnabas a couple of older boys made up this story about me. That in a biology class—and by the way, I was doing bio honors—that I'd accidentally cut off the umbilicus of a fetal pig I was dissecting and pinned it back in the wrong place. Forget exactly where . . ."

He snatched up a silvery change purse from a counter and scaled it across the mezzanine.

The blond agent with the rimless sunglasses whistled softly. "Good shot, Mr. President. An easy thirty, thirty-five feet."

Then the President realized that his head was shaking, and so he pretended to be nodding, and when he had himself under control, when he had dealt with the annihilating emptiness at the root of his heart, he said, "Now, I'm not Harry—"

"Harry would not have turned on Nell with such pissfire spite."

"I meant," said the President with a little roll of his hands, "Harry's intellect. Can't match Harry's range of intellect. Can't claim to be in his class . . ." He waited a moment for her denial, at least a small show of doubt. But Eunice only shrugged her shoulders.

"I loved history," he said. "Before I was fifteen—fifteen, Eunice!— I knew enough American history to be disappointed in it."

"Well, who isn't?" she demanded. "Whole world's disappointed in American history nowadays, but they don't turn on their mates, they don't—"

"Eunice, Eunice," he rushed to say, trying to hang on to his thought, trying to dispel a sudden suffocating vision of the endless years of unloving intimacy that awaited them, "please let's stay on the plane of ideas. And on that plane—when you choose to be"—he paused, appalled by what he was about to say next—"no one, no one is more at home."

She colored, tilted her chin, curled one side of her mouth into a wispy smile. By Jesus, got you now, he thought. He leaned forward to let her have a look at the pain in his eyes. "American history," he went on yearningly, "didn't quite . . . My feeling was once we'd conquered the Plains and had our Civil War, once we'd had our Panic of 1893, our Spanish-American War, our labor unrest and such . . . I wanted more. Things of moment, momentous things. Now at fifteen I was just getting into European history, and there was no comparison. Events, happenings, dark times—I'm sorry to say so, but American history doesn't hold a candle when it comes to dark times."

"That is such a serious thought and you are such a serious thinker," Eunice said.

"Do you see now why I fell in love with the Great War? Couldn't get enough of the Great War. If you want to know the truth, Eunice"—his voice turned deep, pleading—"I still can't. To this day."

"Don't I know! You and your Great War! You and your . . . your Fochs and your Haigs and your Ludendorffs and your . . . Gracious sakes!"

"Gets to me that they won't ever know exactly the casualties during the first and second battles of the Marne. Every soldier felt betrayed. Baa-ed like sheep in the trenches, whole regiments. In 1917 a bunch of German soldiers went crazy and blew themselves up because they thought they heard the voices of their loved ones coming from the tunnels the French were digging and mining with tons and tons of explosives."

Eunice's "Oh" was heavy with reverence.

"Lately I'm thinking about an English colonel, Colonel F. I. Robinton. He was wounded at the Battle of Lys. When they took him off to hospital he said, 'No more infinite space.' "

"What a strange thing to say. And scary." A few seconds later Eunice added, "But scary-tingly-wicked-delicious."

"Never knew exactly what it meant, never figured it out."

"However you figure it out," she said quickly, "it's going to be a deep and profound thought."

"I keep changing my mind about that infinite space. Sometimes I feel I'm almost on top of it and sometimes . . ."

"Whatever you decide it's bound to be a deep and profound thought."

He took both her arms and she came forward.

"Right now, Eunice, it wouldn't surprise me if 'No more infinite space' meant our ability, our capacity, to . . . *imagine* infinite space. Or infinite anything. Can't. In other words we can't see and maybe never will be able to see beyond the here and now of . . . crap, hokum, bull. In a way, Eunice, it's like we're still in those trenches, we're—"

But the balding agent with the tortoiseshell sunglasses distracted him by running behind and bawling, "Stand fast for a search, Mr. Bone!"

And the blond agent with the rimless sunglasses was saying into the twittering walkie-talkie, "Big famous movie director or not, I have Bone down for an A-6 clearance, and every A-6 gets searched."

A little later, standing at the escalator while grips sprayed plaster and touched up some bloodstains and strewed chips of glass around, the President had to hold himself back from a burst of unseemly laughter.

He grinned and exclaimed, "I like that. I really enjoy that, Mr. Bone."

"Delicious," Eunice murmured. "Mr. Bone, you surely do have a deliciously wicked way of stating a matter."

"No joke, sir," answered the lank, dark-bristled, squinty young man whose stoop-shouldered twitching style and restless hands seemed ill suited to the elegance of his leathers and suedes. "What do you need it for? What do you get from this presidential business?" He banged his wrists. "Do they appreciate? See how they appreciate. You eat your heart out, kill yourself for them, and you end up on the short end of some cockamamie poll."

Eunice whispered, "Cockam . . ."

"Ma'am, that means a nothing, a less than nothing. A cockamamie is a rub-on tattoo, three for a quarter around Kissena Boulevard, Queens."

"Ah, Queens," said the President, frowning with feigned concentration.

Rising on his toes, Bone said, "Queens, New York City, New York, borough of my birth and Jewish boyhood. Already past its prime— prime for Queens was a week without a synagogue desecration— when I had the family handle of Ira Brecher. Said name-change in no way occasioned by self-hatred. Who needed self-hatred when everybody else hated me?"

The President whooped with laughter, and Eunice laughed too.

"Don't run again, sir." Bone came down heavily on his heels. "Why run again with your kind of bearing, presence? Because you project— sir, ma'am, I tell the kiss-a-pinkie truth—what you project we haven't had on screen since Spencer Tracy. How many pictures did he save? God in heaven should save America the way he could save a movie! But you'd be better. I'd cast you—absolutely!—as the mill town doctor who makes a stone-heart CEO put up bread for a medical center. No? How about a priest with a classy right hook; you go into the ring to save the orphanage. You're in good shape, sir. Fit, I should be as fit . . ."

"Well, I do have to say . . ." The President paused, wondering if Brecher-Bone might be inadvertently telling him that he was really miscast as president. But he decided not to pursue the thought, and he said, a second later, "Might have looked the part of a boxer thirty years ago."

"Twenty!" cried Eunice. She took his hand and touched it to her cheek. "Gracious, we're not all *that* old."

"I'll wait. No rush. You're bankable now; you'll be two hundred times more bankable when you finish your term. And as far as that poll"—the thumb and index finger of his right hand stopped only inches from the President's lapel—"don't aggravate. After this video plays, you'll be living and laughing."

Just then a grip called his name. He ran at the escalator and went scuttling halfway up. Turning, he raised and lowered his palms, kissed them, and cried, "Mr. President, you and America will never see better plaster dust and bloodstains."

To a grip Bone sang out, "Baby, you did good on the carnage."

A bell chimed. The escalator started to move.

"All set on the seventh floor, sir. Start thinking butchery, Dworkin, massacre of the innocents, Gavrych. Can you trust the Russians? Go trust Russians! Think how you can't trust them and hold the thought . . ."

Once more the President gave way to laughter. Fully at ease now, he decided to take a modified JFK stance. Slouching a bit, he shoved his hands deep into the pockets of his jacket; in the left-hand pocket he touched a sheet of folded-down paper. Must be Joel Baskier's memo, he realized. All at once those last few lines jogged his memory, and he called out, "Now, there's a surprise, isn't there? Something's been cooked up for me, I understand."

"Sir, if I say you're in good hands will you trust me? You're in good hands, sir."

"Good hands," Eunice affirmed, smiling away.

And presently it was time for them to get on the escalator.

At the fourth floor a camera jammed.

While it was being fixed the second unit director took Eunice off to shoot some backup stills, and the President decided he would go and take a closer look at a display of oversize dolls.

They were called the Spoiled Rotten Girls and had names like Leslie and Magda and Jill and Estabrook, and each adolescent face was sculpted into revealing some aspect of complacent insolence. Posed against a backdrop of blue plush in trappings of the very rich—riding habits, satin blouses with coin buttons, leopard-skin jeans—they appeared to be yawning and stretching and caressing themselves. When the President drew near, his step activated their voices, and they one by one languidly drawled, "Damn you, Daddy" and "Caviar sucks" and "Not the Hamptons again" and "Isn't civil disobedience divine?"

Oh, I have no business in this age, the President decided, none, none, none whatever. Because if these cynical, fashionable things in some way stand for something, if they speak to a mood, if they're announcing what we are or are on the verge of becoming, why, I'm out of luck and out of date. A vacuum tube in Silicon Valley. Obsolete, low-tech. No chance, none, none, none whatsoever. Those zeppelins bombing Paris had a better chance. I'm as irrelevant as . . . as the Balkans. Wisdom in the poll. A message. Time to pack it in, pull out, sleep with your fathers.

But when Eunice returned and said, "I was selfish and mean before and I now feel as close to you as you are to the Great War," he managed to compose his face, settle his breath.

Several times as he rode up to the seventh floor, the President thought he was close to understanding why there was no more infinite space, but when he stepped off the escalator everything fled his mind.

"The camera's rolling, sir," said Bone.

"Speed," said the operator.

His face tucked a little down, his arms tight against his sides, trying to keep his breathing deep and regular and quiet, thinking Calvary, thinking Texas School Book Depository, the President went straight past the pile of blackened water-soaked mattresses, past the snack bar where a burst coffee urn still leaked, where the counter was stacked high with stale breads and defrosted meats; and making himself stiff legged and flatfooted, he climbed the four steps to the entrance of the surprisingly undersized book department. Perhaps three feet behind the topmost step was a bridge table covered with a jade green cloth and bolted to the floor. The President stooped just a little over it, assuming a posture which was neither humble nor proud, relaxed nor stiff. He lowered his head as if in deepest thought, saw that the tiny mike was clipped securely at the exact center of his tie, then fixed his gaze steadfastly on the most distant of the three teleprompters and began.

"I am here, fellow Americans, to share your grief.

"Last Wednesday, November 21, lunchtime, this, the seventh floor of Bloomingdale's, was filled with shoppers—more shoppers, it is estimated, than on any other single day of the year.

"They came, these shoppers, because there was a very special one-day sale on fine linens and because for three hours—between eleven-thirty A.M. and two-thirty P.M.—one of our nation's most respected satirists, Miles Robin, would be in this spot, at this table, autographing copies of his very newest collection.

"By one-fifteen P.M., ninety-seven of them would be dead, corpses who had to be covered with the very same linens so many of them had come happily to buy. We still have no accurate count of the wounded, though we know there were so many that five New York City buses were diverted to transport them to hospitals.

"They died without even a moment to plead for mercy from their ruthless, fanatic executioner, Brian Jerome Dworkin, another—yet another of the loners and losers, the hopelessly outclassed and alienated sociopaths whose blind, self-destructive hatred has found in the teachings of Pavel Gavrych a philosophic underpinning, a rationale, a justification for suffering and death.

"I am here, as I said, to share your grief.

"But I am also here because it is my moral obligation, as your president, to help make sure, absolutely sure, that what you are about to see—and you will see something close to the living record of those three murderous hours—is stamped indelibly into the mind's eye of America.

"Let us first meet some of the survivors—the men and women who came upon Brian Jerome Dworkin as he made ready to deal out death in the name of Pavel Gavrych. . . ."

The teleprompters went white.

"Is that a take," asked Bone, "or is that a take?"

There was a burst of applause from the crew.

Eunice held out her arms as if to embrace the President.

And Bone, pinching his own cheeks, exclaimed, "Sir, may I say to you what I said only to Spencer Tracy? You, sir, are a prince of reality."

"Ready with the witness segment," said the second unit director.
And the sound mixer said, "You won't be on camera for this, Mr.
President. Voice-over only, sir."

But Bone croaked, "No," and whistled on his fingers. Breathing
heavily, noisily, he went rushing up to the President. "A voice-over
is not you, sir. Without your face the witness segment will play—a
herring with herpes will play better. Without your face, your presence,
the segment is like—it's making a pebble stand for the Rockies. No,
sir, I think not, sir. America"—he slapped his chest, reared backward—"our screwball pill-popping slobbo population needs to see
you feeling and reacting and giving out."

Now why am I always drawn to these types? the President reflected.
To their . . . their energy? Jack used to tell me, "Boy-o, people with
energy can always pull you along in their wake."

"What do you say," the President asked Eunice.

Eunice gave him a look of shining worship and returned a whispery
"Yes."

And so the President beamed and said, "Why not?"

"That's the ticket, sir," Bone exclaimed. " 'Why not?' Like they
say in the borough of my birth, 'Look, it beats a public execution.' "

"Why him?" the President asked, wincing at the face that filled the
five small screens in close-up.

"Because," said Bone, "two hundred and thirty million Americans,
including the lowest illegal alien wetbacks, will feel superior to him.
Because, sir, the networks threw away this Everyman's footage on
grounds of justifiable yawning, giving us a chance for powerhouse
docudrama. Because, Mr. President, we'll cut with artful artlessness
if we have to—only who has to cut? Look, sir, out there in the cornball
hinterlands meatballs by the millions are fed up with the Dustin Hoff-
mans and the Robert Redfords and the Al Pacinos and the rest of the
shrimpy Hamlets. We're giving them what they need and can identify
with—a human mineral."

Bone tore down the four steps, ran in place, then turned and said,
"Sir, in the real America that is fed up and hostile to personal style,
this divine average will play. Trust me. After all, you're in—"

"—good hands," Eunice finished.

"Back," cried Bone, rising up on his toes and banging his wrists,

"We'll take it back, sir, to graph two, line one. 'Let us first meet . . .' And this time try to watch Ratner, try to open the innermost chambers of your heart to Nathan Ratner. What the heart doth feel the face must reveal. Are we ready? Oh, we're ready, I can see we're ready . . ."

Now a camera moved in close upon the President.

Now the teleprompters rolled, and the President was reading once again, "Let us first meet some of the survivors—the men and women who witnessed Brian Jerome Dworkin as he made ready to deal out death in the name of . . . Pavel Gavrych."

Now the cameras moved in much closer as the President sought once again to gaze with profound attentiveness at the heavy-lipped man on the screen, perhaps sixty, who knitted his tubular brows and blinked his lusterless brown eyes.

"I am—"

The man moved his neck, began again in a bleak, mortally fatigued monotone.

"I am Nathan Ratner and I was looking to buy a single-bed mattress for my sixteen-year-old daughter, the best. I wanted her to have no excuse about uncomfortable broken-down mattresses when she sleeps over my apartment every fourth weekend—that's how often I see her, my ex-wife having done a beautiful job of poisoning her against me. After sixteen years I am her biological father only. This situation I no longer can take, and my regret is enjoying for my age pretty good health. My secondary regret is that I was accidentally protected by mattresses when the act happened and those exploding things didn't embed in me and put me to immediate death. Because my suffering—"

But the President, feeling stifled, tuned out. Poor drab fish, he thought. He believes, I'd bet a second term on it, that he's a good man with a good heart.

"—know what a manic is? This type I got to know well from my ex-wife. They can be pleasant, charming, and when he came over to me my reaction was, This is a very pleasant, charming person who has to be definitely a manic. He tells me first thing, 'I am Brian Jerome Dworkin and I can't remember a time when ruin was not falling everywhere upon the world.' What I wanted to answer was, 'I am Nathan Ratner, and tell me what I don't know' . . . "

To his surprise, the President realized he was watching keenly. A pang of something like compassion went through him and he sought to feed it, but he could not.

"I instead asked him where he got that nice backpack he had. What I liked was the non-American style and the Russian things printed on it in Russian writing. My sixteen-year-old daughter would have loved such a backpack and I figured, biological father or not, I'd buy one and give it to her next time she slept over. . . ."

No more, no more infinite space! The President was silently screaming at him.

"Then and there is when he ran up to where the author was signing his books and carries on about the whole store, the whole country, the whole world. Only for Gavrych does he have a kind word. Gavrych is so good we should right now do a pro-Gavrych thing and get rid of some personal expensive object. I wanted to ask him if the expensive personal object could be my manic ex-wife who is costing years from an already shortened life. But that's when I finally got a salesperson and when Dworkin threw away his backpack thing which everybody figured to be his personal expensive object, his pro-Gavrych action."

Is he—by Jesus, is he what it comes down to? the President reflected.

"The first explosion I paid no attention to because I was arguing with a lady who wanted to take my turn. So I have no idea of how I got under the mattress unless my ex-wife wished me more life to deal me more suffering. That something was going on I realized when the salesperson fell on top of the mattress and proved unable to talk as there were those flying things, the slivers of metal, sticking in or out of her."

Is he what American history and Western civilization have been striving toward? No greater purpose than keeping his belly full, his air and water pure, his traffic moving, his dollar sound?

"What should I say further? You can tell me. This event I and the whole country could have done without in the sense of having already plentiful personal and national problems."

And something within the President whispered, Oh Jack, Jack, what sort of bargain have I struck? My honor, will, conscience, courage, heart, such as they were, such as they were—did I relinquish them to preside over Nathan Ratner?

He felt cold and heavy, he felt as if he had been trapped in a dream of dying and had delayed by an instant his awakening.

But he was roused by Bone, who capered about shouting, "Slow, hold, and—freeze that frame!"

And he felt Eunice's palms against his back.

"Coming to graph nineteen of the survivor segment, sir," said the second unit director.

" 'Consider the weapon . . .' "

"Be subdued but stretched taut," Bone instructed. "In repose but poised. You're all hot grief and cold rage." Bone curved his fingers and ripped at the air. "Sir, by graph twenty-three you'll have all America wishing Gavrych and sneaky Russia off the Earth."

"You will, you surely will," exclaimed Eunice.

She stared into the President's eyes, and every cell in her face seemed so urgently involved in the effort to convey love and veneration that he could only whisper, "Dearest, thank you. Thank you and bless you, my dearest."

Now the monitors showed body bags, and there were so many of them, and the shot was off the screen so quickly that the President had no time to fix the count in his mind.

Now the monitors showed a sneaker, then two very large oatmeal cookies, then a Bloomingdale's shopping bag, then a pocket calculator, then a great many books, and though these were somewhat out of focus the President strained his eyes to make out the titles, and he had the momentary impression one was named *No More Infinite Space.*

Now the monitors showed a policeman holding a brutal-looking metal sliver with tongs, and when he unexpectedly thrust it straight at the camera the President started raising an arm to protect his eyes.

Now Bone ran in place and leveled a finger at him, and the President locked his gaze upon the closest teleprompter and began graph nineteen.

"Consider the weapon.

"What Brian Jerome Dworkin used was not some crude, homemade device from the Weatherman era of the sixties—not some hastily rigged device of dynamite and fuse and timer—not even the more lethal plastic explosive favored by the modern terrorist.

"No, Brian Jerome Dworkin could do better, much better.

"For this fugitive, this bitter, poisonous sociopath who was, as he once told us, 'homeless in America,' managed—by what means we do not know—to get hold of a Marika-3.

"The Marika-3, developed by the Soviets for use in Afghanistan, was refined and improved till the ascendancy of Pavel Gavrych, when Soviet scientists embraced, presumably embraced, peace, sympathy, brotherhood, and purest joy. It is a small, fin-stabilized projectile weighing perhaps seven pounds.

"When this projectile explodes it spews out with great force, murderous force, thin, sharp fragments in all directions over a distance of at least fifty feet.

"Properly placed, a single Marika-3 can easily kill or maim most of the passengers in a New York City subway car or most of the pedestrians on an average New York City street.

"Last Wednesday, November 21, Brian Jerome Dworkin brought with him two Marika-3s, and he placed them properly, most properly—near this very table at the entrance of the book department and somewhere between where the coffee shop and the linens and bedding are.

"In the name of Pavel Gavrych, under the banner of peace, sympathy, brotherhood, and purest joy, he made sure, as *The New York Times* has said, 'to cut a wide swath of death.'

"I am aware, all too aware, that this act, of a ruthlessness matching and perhaps surpassing anything in the bloody chronicle of modern terrorism, is the fifth outrage, the fifth national tragedy America has suffered in a scant two months.

"But we must not, we dare not at this time say anything more than 'Mr. Gavrych, we are perplexed and we must finally ask—ask, not demand—that you seek to exercise over your American supporters the kind of moral authority this nation was so pleased to acknowledge a scant two months ago.'

"Let us put aside hasty anger, dangerous anger. Let us rather at this time share our grief, and in the sharing show our enemies—whoever they may be—that we have not become so powerful or so proud that we are ashamed to express our common sorrow, our common pain.

"Here, then, are more of the survivors—the men and women who witnessed Brian Jerome Dworkin as he made ready to deal out death in the name of peace, sympathy, brotherhood, and purest joy.'"

Then the President looked a little too quickly at the screens, and seeing only shaky light and hearing only a restive hum, he proffered his face to America, seeking to say with it, "Oh my countrymen, am I not calm and sure, high-minded, intelligent?"

But abruptly there was a full-faced young woman with a cradle-sling against her breast and she was pushing a pacifier toward an unseen infant. Then it fell from her hand.

She said, "He claimed he saw me shoplift. 'I'm Brian Jerome Dworkin. I saw you hide stuff in the sling, under the baby.' Radio in his hands. Whatever. Like the radios guards carry. I panicked. My state since motherhood. 'Down the escalator, sixth floor, turning you in, lady. Let's go, no scene, quiet. Right behind you, don't look, no scene, right behind you, behind you.' But he wasn't. Never was."

And there was an elderly man with splendid white hair and a splendid white goatee.

He said, "That little detonating device was absolutely foreign to him. He held it to his ear, shook it, spoke to it. No, I'm not surprised he blew himself up, though I gather it was deliberate."

And there was a patrician lady with a fur parka, a pince-nez, and a Siamese cat on a sequin-studded leash.

She said, "He kissed me; he also kissed the cat. I was disturbed, and I walked quite as far from him as I could manage. But I did hear him—not difficult, even at seventy-eight, since he was talking at the top of his voice. 'I am Brian Jerome Dworkin, and I'm announcing that Bloomingdale's will be offering something absolutely new in the 'designer' concept—designer death.' "

And there was a fat-cheeked black man with a pencil-mark moustache in a handsome belted camel's hair coat.

He said, "I must have been outshouting Dworkin—at risk to my condition since like most blacks, many blacks, I'm hypertensive, with elevated way-up blood pressure. But the only plastic I carry is MasterCard, and this they don't absolutely accept. Result, I was hit by as bad a blood pressure headache as I ever had, and in half-blind pain I left via elevator, unable to trust my balance on an escalator. How's that for a kicker? Owe my life to feelings of injustice, oppression, and stuff. Real kicker."

And there was an old couple in identical heavy black karakul coats standing hand in hand and nodding.

The woman said, "Out of Europe nothing good can come. Give them blood. Blood they understand, blood and murder is the European language of languages, and the shoe also fits Pavel Gavrych."

"Blood and murder," the President heard himself say just as the screens went white and gray.

"We keep that," cried Bone. " 'Blood and murder . . .' Perfect, sir. Like you were born to speak that line."

"Come on over," said the President.

Head low, mouth open, the big, bony young man in Levi's went up the four steps, veered, struck his side against a corner of the bridge table.

He looked stricken and penitent and absolutely guileless.

"Sir," he said, and with such awe that there was a creak in his voice.

The President put his hands deep into the pockets of his jacket and raised his left shoulder in JFK's style.

"Mr. President, the name is Dwight Pastern. I am a communications apprentice here. The union lets networks use communications apprentices, and I am the communications student they picked from Columbia. The university."

He fell into so long a silence that the President had time to murmur something about how he favored the apprentice system, how he considered it an example of sound, progressive, forward-looking trade unionism.

But the young man answered strangely. "Many thanks, Mr. President. Many, many thanks. If you run again you have my first vote. I no longer can be into the sixties. No more."

The President had an impulse to say, "No more infinite space." He said instead, "Well, we do live in dark times, Dwight," adding, "And I do appreciate your voting for me—if and when, of course."

"Mr. President, insofar as I'm now concerned, my relation to the sixties has ceased to exist. That period, as of about ten minutes ago, when you asked America to share grief, can buzz off."

The President murmured something about taking care not to throw out the baby with the bath, emphasizing that John F. Kennedy was also a figure, a representative figure, of the sixties.

Then the President was conscious of an absence of sound. Looking about, he realized that the break was over, that the crew were waiting in respectful silence.

"Thanks to you," Dwight Pastern said, "I have just grown up."

The President opened his mouth to answer, "No, not at all. It's only that your youth just died." But suddenly Bone was at his side, and he made himself say, "Well, Dwight, luck and success to you in your communications career."

At length he and Bone set about eliminating from the list of casualties those names he had trouble pronouncing, and while the names were being matched to the photographs, he happened to glance at himself in one of those tinted three-sided makeup mirrors, and he saw to his astonishment, his shame, that his face was as guileless, absolutely guileless, as Dwight Pastern's had been.

In the middle of the first photograph the screen and the teleprompters faltered.

Then an arc light blew.

While the electricians went to work, there stole over the President a bleakness, an arctic desolation.

For he could not remember when he had last had purpose or conviction.

Deceit—his soul was saturated in deceit.

And by the way, he reflected bitterly, can you please tell me why I'm left to stew in my own juice? Where's Bone now that I could use some direction, some oddball insight, some pleasant nonsense to divert me from these awful thoughts?

Then the arc light came on.

And in the instant of blinking it seemed to the President that he glimpsed Bone bending with a cupped palm toward Eunice's ear.

But before he could look again he heard the electricians cheer, and the teleprompters were whirring and clicking.

In sickening self-hatred he told JFK, I'm not up to this, to photos of the dead. I'll see only an ant swarm of Nathan Ratners. Cold cuts are going into eternity's big mouth. Act fast, old buddy. The graphs are rolling, rolling. What do I do? Help me put out some pathos.

And he spoke the words: "The dead."

He looked at his clasped hands, and from the side of his eye saw Bone and Eunice staring guardedly at one another, and there was pounding in his skull.

He made himself watch the teleprompters all the more carefully, and he was ready for graph forty-three.

"Will you join me, America, in looking at the faces of the dead—

the faces of those who were murdered in the name of peace, sympathy, brotherhood, and purest joy?"

Then the President made a half turn away from the monitors, and he could see that Bone and Eunice had moved much closer to him, and he had the impression that Bone's face carried an extraordinarily serene smile and that Eunice's face carried this smile also.

Nevertheless he fought off the impulse to look at them again, holding his eyes to the photographs, and lowering his voice so that it was only a hair away from a whisper he spoke the names of the dead.

He spoke the names of Sandy Iverson and Eveline Thoma and James Lu Chan and Morton Schapp and Cassie Ann Fenster and Abel Yurick and Robin Lanes, and he was momentarily so bored, so out of it, that he bungled the next name, saying "Fetcher" instead of "Fletcher," and—

And now what? the President thought. What's wrong? Where's the next photograph? Ah, by Jesus, do you see, Jack, how things work against me?

He bethought himself to say again, "Will you join me, America, in looking at the faces of the dead?"

But there was only the wicked, icy emptiness of the screens.

He put out a hand as if to grip and seize.

But he had not long to wait.

In blind shock he recoiled and he was deprived of breath.

Though they had done some retouching and used an airbrush on the snapshots, the forty-year-old snapshots Nanny Dora had taken, he knew them. Them!

There, Mother; there, Father.

Mother is singing at the piano. Bent a little and looking at the piano in her nearsighted way. What she sang I forget, but the words "sweet melancholy" were in her song, and she sent words always pining upwards. Father's arm is as usual on her shoulder, lightly, lightly. Both are as tall as I thought they were, and I say, I must say after all this time that they were wise and good, and none are like them, and without them I am bereft still, and I bless God that they met and mated, and now I have no excuses, I have no infinite space . . .

And within him something opened.

Tears broke scalding upon his cheeks.

He opened his mouth to speak, without concern for what he might say, but his voice failed him, and failed him again.

With brimming eyes he stepped away from the bridge table, fled down the four steps, and blundered against Eunice, and she took him in her arms.

He said, "This was the surprise? Yes, this must be what Harry and Bone cooked up for me. But they're not getting away with it. By Jesus, my life, my feelings—I won't have them worked on and used that way."

But Eunice kissed him and dreamily answered, "Yes, I do rightly believe Mr. Bone's point is awfully well-taken. My gracious, yes! What a clever, such a thunderingly clever, understanding of the body politic and such. And compliments to Harry as well."

"Are you babbling? You're babbling," the President was ready to reply. Then Bone was suddenly all around them like a warm bath.

"Mr. President, when this airs there'll be maybe one dry eye in America—and that, as they say in the borough of my birth, can belong only to a one-eyed landlord."

"Because I cried for my parents?" demanded the President.

"Because, silly"—Eunice gave him a soft slap on the arm—"you cried. Besides, all that retouching and such. Who, now just who, can possibly recognize your folks?"

"God rest them," said Bone. And he went on to say, "You'll be crying, sir, for America, for the state of the Union, for the duplicity of Gavrych, the savagery of Dworkin. But more, and most of all, you'll be crying for the dead."

"Well," said the President. "I see. I do begin to see."

"Additionally, sir, when this airs—may I predict the fate of that poll? As is said in the borough of my birth—"

Bone bowed courteously and unloosed a powerful Bronx cheer.

And by the time the three of them went down the escalator the President was at peace within, and he was moved by thoughts of life to come, of eternity, of infinite space.

29

Moscow Book Fair, Lunacharsky Plaza, December 3, 1993:

I must inform you, most regretfully, that recent terrible and tragic events have compelled the overwhelming majority of my associates to withdraw from participation in the Moscow Book Fair. Let us hope that this most meaningful exchange between our countries and our cultures will yet come to pass for the sake of peace, sympathy, brotherhood, and purest joy.

Evander M. Fells
Chairman, American Booksellers Association

Nevertheless, a surprising number of university presses had taken booths, and there were sizable delegations from Gavrych's principal American supporters, and they clumped together on the northeast quadrant to await him, and some looked fully completed, filled with thankfulness, and some looked prepared and eager and enduring, and some wept openly.

This time Gavrych came in a Volga limousine as long as a locomotive, wore the belted chocolate-brown shearling coat Belyushkin had chosen, and walked without protest among Stepanchov's big, flanky, bear-eyed marksmen.

They hurried him past the "little magazines" booth near the unfinished Universal Chapel, but he heard himself blessed.

He stopped so suddenly that two of the marksmen trod on his shoes.

While they fingered their Uzis he heard, "love," he heard, "connection," he heard, "being," he heard, "renewal."

Nerves prickling in his skin, groping from one obscure thought to another, he stood rooted.

"Mr. Secretary-General? Sir?"

A young woman with blue-black straight glossy hair was applauding him with her arms extended over her head and her palms meeting stiffly. He could not tell if she was impatient or in repose, if her gaze was turned inward or upon him.

She bowed her head, clasped her hands to her breast.

Then she held out one hand—To touch me, he wondered, or to examine her nails?—and in a voice that was decorous and dark, submissive and suggestive, said, "Mr. Secretary-General, you've bridged the gap between alienation and connection."

He tilted his head courteously.

"Sir, you're absolutely the most crucial experience of my generation."

He made his face radiate wisdom and patience and spirituality; he made his voice calm and deeply sure. "May all these books be dog-eared by the fingers of millions seeking to add richness, brilliance, and intensity to life."

But Stepanchov's marksmen were whispering harshly and pressing close, and so he walked on in the unsteady sunlight past the wild-flying spray of the new Walt Whitman Fountain and under concealed loudspeakers from which poured an Uzbek children's chorus singing of a time to come when man would command the tongue of poets, when he would put down upon the page words spelled out in letters of flame.

At the Literature and Liberation Pavilion he saw a clear reflection of himself in the golden oak radiance of the topmost stairs, and he shied away.

He had the sensation that his eyes were gummy and swollen, that his valves and sphincters were closing, that a corrupt moldering smell was in his nostrils.

I know. Have I not always known? he thought, though many seconds passed before he would confess it.

For he felt a vast penitential surge, he felt drained of faith and principle, he felt drunk with remorse.

I know. Have I not always known, he thought, that nothing will help? No system, no stratagem, will bring my species within reach of true good, true safety. Far better if I had been another doctor of men, if I had taken as a matter of course how little and low human beings are.

Far better, far better, he silently groaned to Stepanchov's marksmen. I would have been wiser to seek laughter from a bleeding ox than righteousness in politics.

But all the same he smiled, he beamed, he rounded his mouth like a child who has been caught at mischief; and all the same he took the first three steps of the platform on tiptoe and the last two in a graceful leap.

When Stepanchov's marksmen came alongside and behind, he clasped the tallest one, made as if to lift and hurl him from the platform, and the marksman could not help laughing, and the people laughed too.

He rested his hands on the Plexiglas shield, turning this way, that way, to take comfort from the absorbed and ardent faces, thinking what best to say, what would not confuse them or do them injury, thinking also that somehow he had already said too much.

His first words were lost, for in the unwitting violence of his turning he had caused the standing microphone to slide down, and he decided to adjust it himself.

When he did so he was compelled to sink his knees and sway his hips a little, and one massive pleasured breath seemed to all at once escape from the people, and he imagined that this might be because he had momentarily assumed the posture of a rock star, and he felt sick at heart. But almost within the same breath the feeling was supplanted by loving sorrow for the people, for all who sought to transcend the hardness and dryness and sickness of governments, the sad wreck of human aspiration.

Sighting along the line of grass and gravel, he took a close look at the four, five ranks near the poplars, and he looked also at the stained banners borne by the Limberlost Collective and the Earthmothers Coalition, and he turned to the left to better see the faces before the blue-and-white Judaica Pavilion, for he considered going among them to ask if they truly hated hearing the word "Jew" used even as a noun.

Then he fixed his eyes steadfastly upon the running clouds, and he was pierced by images of devastation, and with every pulse it was harder not to scream out "Bloomingdale's!"

Though his eyes were filled he tried to fix on various people, impulsively, stupidly seeking one who might transmit a message of bafflement and bereavement to the President.

"Tell him," he would instruct such a one, "that Stepanchov gives me to understand that you are a good and moral man, though in these American times goodness and morality count for less than they might.

"Make clear that I would still gladly meet with him to trade observations on World War I, on Marx and Keynes and Malthus, on the nature of business civilization.

"Carry word that if he sees fit I will put myself in American hands, a hostage at his Camp David or at the White House kitchen, among his coloreds."

His eyes cleared, his mind as well.

But another thought, an insupportable thought, immediately possessed him, and he could neither endure it nor put it aside.

"Peace, sympathy, brotherhood, and purest joy," he said at last, though he wanted to say hard and dreadful things, and most of all he wanted to say, "You do not know, you do not know. Oh, how can you not know that you are beset by a force, a demon—by one whose movement is rapid and devious and in perfect step with sin and death."

But despite the agony of his concern he said nothing of the kind.

And this time, when the microphone slid down again, he let Stepanchov's tallest marksman adjust it, for he was pressing and grinding his thumbs against the Plexiglas shield.

"Welcome in the name of literature, in the longing for life," he continued, just as he felt the bone of the right thumb sliding from the socket.

30

COUNSELOR: This doesn't seem to have been your happiest week, Vidyon.

ORLOFSKY: Beaucoup spaced out. My verbal onslaughts against your do-good population of American greeners occasioned a few bad scenes, some heavy stuff.

COUNSELOR: What's the harm, Vidyon, in their working to stop— oh, rezoning or strip mining or choked traffic or pollution or the dumping of hazardous wastes?

ORLOFSKY: Still you fail to dig what gives.

COUNSELOR: At your service, Vidyon. Do straighten me out.

ORLOFSKY: America is in danger from the Think Green anticarcin-ogenic mind-set. But the cheery ladies of Alexandria and Silver Spring did a slow burn when I presented my case. They dumped on me for cutting into their bliss.

COUNSELOR: You proposed something to them, the driver said. What did you propose, Vidyon?

ORLOFSKY: A moratorium on Mother Nature causes which have the value of czarist rubles to the world. I blew my stack to make them understand that mankind was the real genuine endangered species article. My proposal was, "Girls, good ladies, take the dollar bills from your fishbowls and jelly jars and use them not for bluer skies and trout-stocked waters and bird sanctuaries but for eyesores."

COUNSELOR: Eyesores?

ORLOFSKY: Let no suburb or exurb or smaller municipality be without such an eyesore. Let each eyesore remind your nationals of mankind's pains. Scatterings of drug paraphernalia for a start, then bits of gutted inner-city structure. I want, further, dead dogs, skulls and bones from mass graves, and when convenient, sealed railway cars from whence would issue odors of excrement and noises of suffering.

COUNSELOR: An exciting idea, Vidyon. Brilliantly conceived, brilliantly developed.

ORLOFSKY: It sends you?

COUNSELOR: And one day, Vidyon, when that blood sugar is fully stabilized, you'll make your proposal in the highest American places.

3|

MATTHEW DANA
201 BARROW STREET
NEW YORK, NEW YORK
(212) 151-0987

WRITER-EDITOR:
Presently available for permanent, part-time, or free-lance projects in diversified literary, cultural, and political areas; knowledge of all aspects of production and graphics.

BACKGROUND:

Here magazine, 1935–1940: Contributing Editor, then Associate Editor, then Senior Editor of national weekly newsmagazine. Wrote many cover stories; subjects included H. G. Wells, Clifford Odets, André Malraux, Mohandas Gandhi, Thomas Mann, Bennett Cerf.
• Singled out by Founder (1938) as "our most glorious boy."
• Assigned by Founder (1940–1942) to direct, together with Barnard (Buck) Mackenzie, launching of new monthly magazine *See*. Extensive travels throughout USSR, firsthand reports of battle scenes, interviews

with Stalin, Marshal Zhukov, Sholokhov, Eisenstein. Pulitzer Prize, 1941. Founder deeply pleased. Barnard (Buck) Mackenzie offered rather formal congratulations.
• On leave 1942–1945 for service in Office of War Information. Assigned to focus strengths of liberal magazines and writers toward war effort; extensive liaison with U.S. State Department.

Vista magazine, 1945–1948: Editor in Chief of progressive weekly seeking to revive spirit of Four Freedoms in postwar era. Consistently held up to scorn by Founder; vilified in pages of *Here* by Barnard (Buck) Mackenzie.

TESTIMONY BEFORE HOUSE UN-AMERICAN ACTIVITIES COMMITTEE, 1948: Accused by Barnard (Buck) Mackenzie of "organizing and spearheading cell of left-wing liberal writer-editors into 'transmission belt' " that funneled classified State Department information to Vladimir Shepovny, Tass Bureau Chief, Washington, D.C.

Convicted of perjury, 1950.

Atlanta Federal Penitentiary, 1951–1953: Bookkeeper.

THE DANA NEWSLETTER, 1954–1955: Publisher and Editor of eight-page biweekly devoted to political commentary.

DANA BOOKS, 1953–1954: President and Managing Editor of publishing house specializing in reprints of forgotten social science classics.

MACDOUGAL STREET BOOKSHOP, 1961–1963: Owner, then Manager.

Author, *The Third Camp,* 1971, Harbinger Press.

Subsequent experience includes: Mastercraft Comics (Copy Editor); Stoler, Danzig, Carafeola, Attorneys (Office Manager).

John M. Cuelenaere
Public Library

ITEM: Fence jumpers /   33292003504960
DUE DATE: 27 DEC 00

ITEM: Blaze /   33292006715530
DUE DATE: 27 DEC 00

Please Retain this Receipt

Married, 1936–present, to former Minerva Beatrice Atherton. No children. She was never especially robust. Childless couples were more fashionable in our time and with our set.

I am immediately available.

▄▄

SATURDAY, DECEMBER 9, 1993: Shortly after sunset, as he went south in the freezing rain from Dr. Lashman's office on West 13th Street, Dana grew increasingly certain that he was being followed.

No, it wasn't in his mind or what was left of his mind after Dr. Lashman's news. ("Well, except for pancreatic cancer you're in excellent shape.")

Though shapes were blurred by the rain and the shimmer from the inexhaustible Saturday night traffic, he had spotted them easily enough. For he was, after all, a seasoned prey (1948–1949) who had been shadowed, trailed, covered by the best, and on these very streets. *Only God has kept us under closer surveillance,* Minerva used to say. But those old-timers had worked more discreetly. So discreetly, in fact, that Dana had sent a letter to the FBI praising the day-shift agents: *They have showed us every courtesy, Mr. Hoover. Would that I might say the same for certain young congressmen.* We used to treat them to coffee in the Waldorf Cafeteria every night, and every night Joe Gould stood over their table and read to them from his "Oral History of the World." *Sweet, tame right-wing primitives,* Minerva called them. *But these two remind me of nasty altar boys. Like Princeton boxers. Like the kind Mackenzie used to hire for the front of the book.*

I'll confront them, Dana decided.

But when he turned and searched through his rain-smeared glasses they were nowhere in sight.

It was full dusk now, the rain had thinned, and Saturday tourists traipsed back and forth. The fellow travelers of bohemia. The uptown provincials. The barbarian toughs from outlying boroughs. Dana went among them, grateful for his height. It protected his eyes from the tips of their umbrellas, also from their direct gaze. Too often a derisive gaze. They take me for a Village character.

But I wish to be recognized.

I'm part of the times, Dana longed to say, I mattered. I had . . . impact. I'm entitled to your notice before I become a fact of nature.

Therefore he put himself in the path of a young couple who were laughing and kissing and stroking, and when they bumped against the plastic bag that held his box of résumés and his Tagamet capsules (400 mg., take as needed), he started to declare himself.

He said, "Matthew Dana here," and he extended his long arms.

Shaking their healthy, handsome heads they passed him by.

He was about to call after them, to shout, "For shame!" when he was diverted.

By the voice of Buck Mackenzie.

The vindictive, righteous, hanging-judge voice.

As he harried me then. As he brought me low.

He heard Mackenzie say, "I begged you to come forth, Matt, but you would not, you would not."

At first he could not locate the source. Then a bicycle, masterfully handled, mounted the curb with a soft bump and came alongside.

The bicyclist, a lion-bearded black man in natty leather, put a tiny silvery thing to Dana's ear, and all Dana could hear in this world was Mackenzie exclaiming, "I say that your sin will be heavy on us all!"

Then Dana sprinted away, but the black man moved too.

Though the street was narrow and crowded he steered serenely, making the bicycle hop and spin in small circles, pressing Dana back and back.

"Breathe," he instructed. "Do not fight against the need to respirate."

Dana raised the bag of résumés over his head, setting himself to swing with full force and strike. The black man smiled dreamily, pushed the bag a little away. "What is the need?" he whispered into Dana's face. "Such a blow would not facilitate escape. And could you escape?"

Once again he put the silvery thing to Dana's ear. And Dana heard himself as he was then (May 1950), hoarse from bronchitis, barely audible in that huge domed Senate chamber, and he was saying, "Damn you, Buck, and damn as well your distortions."

And Mackenzie answered, "Will you never understand what you

did? Or what you are? Behold, look upon him, gentlemen, senators—
the self-righteous dupe who rebels against our system like an adolescent rebelling against baths. See how he plays a game of excitation,
political excitation, how—"

With a touch the black man cut off Mackenzie's voice.

"Oh, Mr. Dana," he said, "this man has surely lived too long."

"What are you up to?" Dana demanded. "You"—he cast a glance
over his shoulder—"and those two trailing me, following. Am I supposed to be a threat? Don't you know I'm not a threat? Why, I've
been finished for years, for years . . ."

But the black man was already lost in the tumult of traffic.

On trembling legs, his heart racing, Dana hurried away.

Near Eleventh Street he tasted those awful fluids in his mouth.

But he would not take a Tagamet.

Not just yet.

For something had come to mind.

People made way for him because he was walking blindly, swinging
his plastic bag, and stumbling into them.

He had this thought. It was dim, it was fragmentary, it was remote,
but when it came to dealing with the past Dana had faith in his
memory.

Therefore he pressed himself to the limit.

And a few steps beyond the Forefront Gallery he caught it, he held
it.

That afternoon there had been no microphones in the Senate chamber.

A closed session.

Which meant . . . ? Which meant . . . ?

But the display in the window of Hi's Tech moved him to other
considerations.

He bent his knees a little so that he might better see the beautiful
old L. C. Smith typewriter on the bottom shelf below electronic things
that sent and received and tallied.

It was bolted at an angle into the reinforced lid of a child-sized
casket, and over the casket was the message MAKE WAY FOR TOMOR-
ROW.

Soon Dana's mouth opened and his nostrils grew wide, for he was
deeply offended, though he could not exactly say why. By the time
he understood, some girls had stopped to look at the display, and

when he heard their animated chatter about terminals and word processors and disks he turned to them.

He tried to speak his mind.

"Ladies," he said, "once, years back, I happened to review a book—lead piece, magenta box, two-column width—a fine little book called *The Higher Good*. It was about, among other things, many other things, the distinction between labor and work, thought and contemplation . . ."

But he recognized that they were bored and already restless. Was there ever a generation more easily bored? he reflected. With a shorter attention span?

And Dana started again, speaking more quickly.

"The word processors and such"—he rapped the window—"are fine for labor and thought. For true work and true contemplation, though, I'll take that old beauty there, that L. C. Smith."

"Oh, fine."

One girl with a thinly pretty face turned to her friends. "Doesn't he make you feel terrific, absolutely wonderful, that we're paying a hundred dollars a credit to learn the word processor?"

"Hofstra is more," someone said, "and in my office I am not paid to do thought and contemplation."

"To hail the new by ridiculing the old is mean." Dana's voice rang. "Mean and nasty."

"Mister, meanness and nastiness might also be in the eye of the beholder."

Dana drew his lips against his teeth. He thought carefully over his next words, then said, "Ladies, this encounter has been of one, one small benefit at least. Yes"—he shivered from the force of his loathing—"I see now I did Minerva a service when I convinced her we should have no children."

There was a hush. Then the girls blazed up, crying, "Can you believe this?" and "Too much!" The one with the thinly pretty face said quietly, "You're sick, mister. You know? Sick . . ."

"Ladies," said Dana, "except for pancreatic cancer I'm in excellent shape."

He waited for a reply.

But they turned and walked off rapidly.

He was about to swallow down a Tagamet when he caught sight

of those two pursuers, trackers, tails, across the street. In a little while they came over, and before he could decide how to deal with them they disconcerted him by nodding courteously and smiling very gently.

One, who had a basso voice, said, "You must never again humiliate yourself, Mr. Dana," and the other, who had a tenor voice, said, "It's not over, sir. There are things in the offing. Your résumé will carry the most memorable entry yet."

And Dana took flight.

Near Sheridan Square Park he felt faint and winded, and he went in to rest. But he had to search and wait before he could find a decently dry bench under the blemished trees where dog walkers from the new high-rises liked to congregate. While he worked to get breath again he fell to thinking that though the night was bitter, though most of the high-strung terriers and poodles had on flannel pads, their owners were minimally dressed in leisure suits, stoles, skimpy safari jackets. This brought to mind . . . There was an association . . .

And all at once Dana remembered vividly and with intense shame that when he made senior editor at *Here* (November 11, 1939) he had all winter long emulated the Founder's style—wearing no over-coat and only lightweight suits and short-sleeve shirts in the worst weather. How it pleased the Founder! Once he took me walking along Fifth Avenue in a record freeze and he said, "You'll not catch cold. No fear, Matt. You were immunized by your new office and those leather wing chairs. Those who can afford vicuña never need it. You'll find that out, my glorious boy."

But as Dana saw himself as he had been then, face aflame from the wind, from the ardor of submission to the Founder, and heard himself answer, "Why, it must be that power raises body tempera-ture," he nevertheless did not fail to notice the woman at his feet now. And how could he? For she was squatting on her heels, brushing some gummy stuff from a poodle's mouth, and so far apart were her knees, so sheer and flimsy her undergarment that Dana plainly glimpsed the roughened skin inside her thighs and straggling pubic hairs.

He marveled at her single-mindedness, her self-command. Spec-tacular! She realizes that I'm looking, knows I need only bring my head a little forward and my nose would be in her cleft. But she couldn't care less. What perfect disinterest! It's in the set of her mouth, in that hard, narrow, ruthless lower lip.

Dear lady, he mentally whispered, I get your message. You're right not to waste a glance or a thought on me. As of today I'm out of it. A corpse-to-be. Like Hector kneeling before the sword of Achilles. "Still breathing though simply matter . . ."

She got to her feet and, crying, "Bad Julia, dirty Julia," slapped the poodle several times with a glove. Not hard blows, but one landed full on the nose, and this was too much for Dana.

He bent and clasped the animal, and he rubbed it about the ears, the muzzle, the chest, saying, "What a nice sweet Julia. Ah, I know, I see. Don't you think I understand how it goes, pup? What did Hobbes say? Nasty, brutish, and short . . . A dog's life. Yes, I understand fully, fully, and you're right. Yes, the canine condition is worse than the human condition."

But the dog was abruptly pulled away.

"A little rough," Dana faltered out. "Don't you see you're hurting, the leash is . . ."

The woman stepped back, cocked her head, and gave Dana what he'd long ago named the bitch-in-power look. A specialty of employment agency and personnel office secretaries. Notification that he was a relic, a back number, a bundle of airs and pretensions, a footnote, a paltry thing. But this time he held his tongue and managed to kill the tremor in his arms.

For that explosion three weeks ago in Dr. Lashman's office was still with him.

He'd been sitting an hour, at least an hour, when he became aware that Carol, the kinky-haired fat-lipped receptionist, was scrutinizing him with hauteur and malice.

Then in betrayed, blaring tones that carried through the packed waiting room she exclaimed, "Do you intend to pay your health insurance group, Mr. Dana, Mr. Matthew Dana, 201 Barrow Street? How about it? What? Unless you pay them they don't pay us, and doctor is waitin' and waitin'."

When Dana started telling her of an error which his last employer repeatedly promised to straighten out she said contemptuously, "Aaah, your last employer is ancient history, and ancient history don't fall into my area of expertise."

"Apparently not," Dana said curtly. "Your specialty"—he pretended to give it some thought—"is more in the line of rudeness."

Lashman, far from taking his part, had turned remote, cryptic, and professional. Not a joke or a smile, though Dana had been his patient these twenty-five years. Hearing him out and answering only, "I'm afraid that when the records show I'm owed for three visits Carol gets protective."

Humiliated, sick at heart, Dana dropped his head. Trying to speak he found himself stammering, and he decided to keep quiet. But all the while he was thinking clearly, keenly, and had much to say, much to say about the bland bourgeois Lashman had become. Starting with, "I see where I stand, old chum, old 'Stay and talk a little socialism' chum." Then unsparing denunciation. "Once you were as worried about the bomb as I. Once you begged me for books that would prepare you properly for socialism. Once you subscribed to no magazines, bought no piece of office furniture, hung no print, signed no petition, till I approved, till I told you, 'This is good, this is progressive . . .' "

He was not aware that he had been shaking until the elderly woman next to him changed her seat.

"But, madam," he murmured, "except for pancreatic cancer I'm in excellent shape."

And all he could hear in this world was Mackenzie exclaiming, "I say that your sin will be heavy on us all!"

Oh, yes, thought Dana, on that day (May 3, 1950) I became a sociological phenomenon, a radical ghost, a fellow-traveling essence.

Suddenly he rose, seized his plastic bag, and pulled out some résumés. "Immediately available for full- or part-time work," he said, moving from bench to bench and passing them out. "Skilled in all aspects of production, writing, editing. Known years back, years back, as the liberal's darling. Through me, I suppose, they could cling to innocence, to innocent belief."

But people filled his hands with change, then turned away from him to talk of condos and IRAs and the crazy cost of a night at the theater. Yet unless he was greatly mistaken, it seemed to Dana that a ruddy heavyset man of about his own age was looking at him solemnly and respectfully. When Dana moved he moved too, bumping benches in his haste. On the curb outside the park he drew very close, folded Dana's résumé as carefully as if it had been a love letter, and after a long breaking sigh said, "Mr. Dana, I have friends to whom you are also a great figure."

He closed his eyes and swallowed.

"These friends"—he drew several business cards out of a billfold and waited with shaky fingers till Dana took them—"you should call immediately, right now. Do not worry that it's a Saturday night. These are my friends. Sympathizers. And together with your friends—you'll see."

He turned to hide the tears running down his face.

"You have calls to make, Mr. Dana, and I shall not keep you."

As they parted Dana told him, "You are a kind, generous man."

To himself he added, "And as much use to me as an old file of *New Republics*."

Yet moments later, passing a public phone near Lafcadio's Steak House, he began to nod slowly. The fellow was right, he reflected. Before I stifle my anger, before it all slips away from me, I should make some calls.

And the first number he dialed was Dr. Lashman's.

Breathing with open mouth he scolded the balky, clanking old answering machine and made growling sounds into the receiver.

At the ninth ring the device quavered and held, and Carol, the receptionist, came on. He caught "doctor's not in now" and "message after tone," and before the insight fled his mind he managed to say, "You gave a patient with a few weeks of life barely five minutes of your time. I understand now why you smashed me down quickly, quickly with that 'Except for pancreatic cancer you're in excellent shape.' Clean, quick, smart. Treat a patient so and there's no danger of another visit, another unpaid bill. Bastard, filth, filthy son of a bitch bastard!" he cried as the connection was broken.

Next, next, and who shall be next? Dana demanded.

He could not imagine, as he turned the pages in his tiny spiral address book, why he should feel quite so remote. Perhaps, he thought, it was the remoteness of those who—did Christ say it? Peter?—"who go whither thou wouldst not"?

Then he tried Paulette Eubrice, managing editor of *Statecraft*, preparing himself for a measured, remorseless pronouncement. He would call her a wonder, a marvel, a monument to careerist deceit and hypocrisy. Next he might say, "While you had your dear, virtuous, idealistic Matty to town-house luncheons, filling me with phony promises about a defense fund, you dug and pumped and pulled me every way. You flattered my weakness for talking, to reveal everything, everything. How'd you ever manage without taking a single note? And was "The Well-Tempered Totalitarian" your title? Must have been, since you would never take editing of any kind. No matter, the phrase finished me for good.

But the number was no longer in service.

Then he tried his old literary agent, Cleve Altmark.

A man answered, saying, "May I ask who's calling Mr. Altmark?" in such an arrogant, lisping soprano that Dana, forgetting his plan to murmur, "A friend," gave his name and spelled it out angrily.

He heard the receiver set down and then, for at least a minute, no words, only voices in spiteful contention. There was a musical chime. In fearful haste he dropped another quarter into the slot. He caught a whoop of laughter, then clearly, clearly, the theatrical resonance of Altmark's, "That one, yes, dearest heart. That Dana."

And Dana gave the phone box a backhanded slap.

He cried out, "Won't talk to me? Won't? Do pick up, Cleve, honey, dear queer Cleve. At once, at once!"

He heard now creaking and soft thumping and footsteps.

He cried out, "At once, Cleve. Here and now, Cleve."

A cough, a snicker, and the line went dead.

Rocking backward and forward Dana addressed passersby.

"On the day Cleve dropped me my wife . . . Minerva stopped . . . coping. Over . . ."

He gave a demonstrative shove.

"Over the edge as it were, as it were. The present . . . She's dim and hazy. Haphazard, her grip on things."

His glasses misted. By the time he finished clearing them with his thumbs everybody was gone.

Therefore he gave full attention to a cab stand across the street, cupping his hands and shouting at the drivers.

"Listen," he said, "if I had as many coins as, as . . . as I do cancer cells they wouldn't be nearly enough to phone everybody who dumped me. Dumped me and, as the poet says, 'sped me on my way to dreariness and disaster.' Minerva too."

His right side released a small crack of pain.

"Women like Minerva put great store, great store, in childhood friends. Best friends. So many I might call now. Among those who dropped her—dropped the traitor's wife—Minerva's favorite was that Joan . . . Joan . . . What say you, gentlemen? Shall I call? Ask her to return Minerva's college yearbook? And a certain fine blue angora sweater. What's that style? Always favored it, Minerva. With buttons in the front . . ."

"Applebee," someone whispered close to his right ear.

Dana stared into the far distance for a long while. Then he turned and saw, as he had expected to see, his two hunters, trackers, tails.

One, with a basso voice, said, "Please, Mr. Dana, don't waste the final energies of your life," and the other, with a tenor voice, said, "Soon justice and equity come."

As they walked toward the stand Dana called after them.

"Stay, why don't you? All the same to me."

Without looking back they told him their assignment was done, that they would no longer trouble him.

"More deceit?" Dana cried. He slammed the plastic bag against his knee. "If it is, take care, take care."

Then he was aware of movement in the doorway of Lafcadio's Steak House.

Something metallic sang out and snapped.

Three, four heavy paper clips struck the sidewalk at his feet.

"Jumping melonballs," he heard.

A man in a green loden coat and charcoal-gray flannels strode forward. His face, though open, childlike, trusting, eager, seemed to be laboring for a look of slyness it could not quite sustain. There was very little play about his dark-ringed eyes, which were wide open, appraising, concentrated, wistful, furtive—but ultimately, Dana reflected, unperceiving. And how is he holding that clipboard? In the center, the exact center of his breast, his being.

Under his breath Dana spoke something like a prayer.

"My hatred of Thee is beyond utterance. Thy abominable hand does not cease tightening around me. Is this Thy agent? This zilch, this anonymity? Well, see how I bow my neck to him and his, and Thee and Thine!"

And Dana spat at the clipboard. But there was a stiff wind and he did not even come close.

The man passed a hand before his face in a gesture of reconciliation.

"Yo, Mr. Dana," he said with a hurt smile, "that was a disproportionate reaction."

Dana, with a dull short nod, said, "Years, years ago, if I'd interviewed you for a copyboy's job I'd have turned you down. And now
you have the power to kill me."

He advanced a step.

"Then kill."

"Sir, Mr. Dana, if I were characterologically predisposed to killing
I'd probably be at least a—wow!—GAS-23 by now."

The man came beside him and looked mildly into his eyes.

"I'm Byron Wagonside, sir, but I'd be honored if you called me
Buzz."

"All the same," said Dana, "I'd never have had you as my copyboy."

And he added scornfully, "Buzz."

"Okay. Swell." Wagonside's lower lip trembled, and he puffed out
his cheeks. "Look," he said, more to himself than to Dana, "I finally
am used to rejection. I'm an expert in rejection by those I hold in
highest esteem. And my esteem for you is unqualified. It is so unqualified that at risk of reprimand I just took upon myself early
dismissal of operatives Sheldon and Paul because I noted they were
giving you a disproportionate anxiety reaction."

"Couldn't abide those well-born copyboys. Crewcuts, rep ties, blaz-
ers. All drawled, all affected those well-born stammers . . ."

"Sir"—Wagonside spread his fingers across the clipboard—"I have
read at this time practically everything about you and by you, and I
want to express my esteem and admiration. Jumping melonballs, Mr.
Dana, when you had it you had it all. What you wrote about Gandhi,
June 11, 1939—wow! That Gandhi made, made or turned his life
into a piece of art. Didn't you? Isn't that also you, Mr. Dana?"

Dana started to walk off, but Wagonside cried, "Won't you listen,
Mr. Dana?" so despairingly that he stopped. And Wagonside went
on to say, "The truth is—I *think* the truth is that my esteem and total
admiration of you is also envy. You never, not a single time in your
professional life, failed. When they sent you to Russia to interview
Stalin (March 10, 1939), he took you around the Kremlin for ninety
minutes, he filled you in on Russian history—not that you required
it, sir—and he gave you a sable hat for the former Minerva Beatrice
Atherton." He stroked the clipboard. "Your wife."

Touched, delighted, Dana recalled how she had worn that hat throughout the HUAC hearings and once at the trial. Brought out her rich color. My heart flooded with love, with awe.

"Mr. Dana," Wagonside was saying, twisting his mouth, "I likewise was sent to Russia, and Gavrych couldn't stand me. He said I should be an exhibit in the Museum of the Ordinary."

He looked so fallen, so pitiable, that Dana had no heart to speak his mind, to say, "Poor little functionary. Are you on the track of some essential truth? I can't imagine you recognizing it, but if you do, if you should accidentally take hold and wrestle with it—ah, God forbid. Look, have a good close look. See what the touch of truth can make of you."

Standing pigeon-toed, eyes upcast, Wagonside said, "I need to share an insight with you, Mr. Dana. The need is not entirely compulsiveness and not entirely because my girlfriend is no longer supportive—I think eating with me is now an unnatural act to her—and not entirely because of my esteem and admiration and envy of you."

"What can I offer you?" said Dana. "Paul Robeson at Lewisohn Stadium? Will you have Eisenstein, the Stanley Theater, the Jefferson School?"

"Sir, Gavrych called me an 'empty vessel,' and as an empty vessel I'm turning to you." One side of Wagonside's face flamed coarsely. "My Daddy," he said, releasing a pent-up breath, "is also . . . also nearing the end of his personal history. That may be why, during my last visit, he showed me unusual overt affection of the hugging and kissing and hair-mussing kind. Additionally, he made a remark I didn't understand. The remark was, 'Buzz, could they have been right?' Upon interrogation he explained that by 'they' he meant those who did hard and good things without self-interest motivation. In return for which they are shat upon by people like Daddy, also myself, and for their efforts and pains get the short end of everything."

He met Dana's gaze.

"That's you, sir. You definitely tried to do hard and good things without self-interest motivation. And those who do and are therefore shat upon are the characterological type to understand the problems of one who believes himself to be a victim."

His mouth sank at the corners.

"That belief, sir, that I am a victim, is my insight."

Oh, Thy abominable ways, thought Dana. Thou would have even a fool suffer to his limit.

And Wagonside said wonderingly, "I now believe, Mr. Dana, that my presidential appointment as liaison to Gavrych was for the deliberate purpose of failure. My briefing took fifteen minutes and then the Gavrych fact sheet I got was in every particular wrong. As official translator I was assigned my then supportive girlfriend. Apart from her language skill lack, she had accumulated on her record wild behavioral things that . . . Jumping melonballs . . . ."

A tear approached his eye. But this did not touch Dana quite as much as the sight of a leather thong working loose from Wagonside's loden coat.

He put a finger to the thong, hastily withdrew it, and said mildly, "What things, Buzz? I would be pleased to hear, pleased to hear."

"Would you?" Wagonside looked searchingly at him. "Jeepers, you would, I think you would. Even if," he added hoarsely, "you'd never have hired me as your copyboy."

"I'd most likely have recommended you to Buck. To old Buck, dear Buck."

"Got you, sir!" said Wagonside, going up on his toes. "Her name, Mr. Dana—and I'm about to tell you everything a security-conscious compulsive-repressive type can—is Natalie. I called her supportive, but even during her most supportive period my sexual procedures were never luridly sensational enough for her. Jeepers, oral love was more natural to her than putting on lipstick. Hence . . . hence the aforementioned accumulation of wild behavioral things on her record. And he knew. Of course he knew. What doesn't he know? I once saw his first evaluation, and they wrote he probably knows everything that happens on this planet."

"He?" Dana whispered, unaccountably stirred.

"My chief, sir, and I can only tell you"—Wagonside pointed his jaw at Dana—"that they call him Artifex. Latin, sir?"

"Latin, Buzz. It means," Dana told him, more harshly than he had meant to, "a maker of forms. A . . . creator of artifices."

"And how! Is he ever!" Wagonside tapped his forehead. "Also, he . . . he is very highly alert to the worst possibilities in a person."

As I never was to Buck's, thought Dana.

"He therefore had to pretty exactly know how I would doom myself to failure and how Natalie's wild behavioral things would nail down my doom. Apart from mistranslations wherein she would tell me 'foreign exchange' instead of 'cultural exchange,' there was her openness about bathroom and feminine hygiene functions. Listen, Mr. Dana, the one item on my briefing sheet which was underscored stressed that you don't say piss or shit or complain about the non-manufacture of tampon devices to Russian people. See, maybe they will enjoy talking Marx and Gavrych, but when it comes to bathroom and bed you're better off in some medieval monastery."

"True, true. My wife made similar observations," said Dana, feeling gentle and clear. For he remembered with great vividness Minerva squirming and wriggling in Stalin's study. Finally she wrote "potty" on my pad. Somewhere I must still have that page.

"Natalie took it into her head that Russian men had larger . . . endowment than Americans."

"Doubtful," said Dana. "Unlikely." And they both looked off across the street at the blazoned canopy of La Vie Bohème.

"Mr. Dana, while I am trying to figure out which end of Russia is up, while I am working all night on position papers, while I am gaining nine pounds from their starchy food, she . . ." His mouth gaped with rage. "Jumping melonballs, she'd come in at five in the morning, when I'm in my deepest sleep, she'd put every light on and undress in front of me. Slowly—you don't know how slowly. And she would sing a Russian song and turn this way and turn that way so I should see who had squeezed or bitten or pinched and left marks where there were no marks before."

His eyelids throbbed. "How can you clean bucks?" he said, gazing meditatively at his shoes. "That's me, sir. Buzz Wagonside all over. Shoes you can't clean and a girlfriend who can only damage me." He slapped his hand through the air. "Mr. Dana, the aforementioned events . . . Natalie's body marks . . . Sir, from your experience and readings—you're widely read—why is the human mind, anyway my mind, so peculiar? Why do I lately have trouble remembering my Daddy's face, but my mind sees Natalie's body marks clearer than my eyes did in Moscow?"

They fell silent. Dana finally said, "Bucks, as I remember, aren't meant to stay clean."

"Cape bucks. Cape! Three hundred dollars a pair, sir." His laugh was short and faint. "Jeepers, I ought to read your Marx and Engels.

They might clarify why a person able to pay three hundred dollars for a pair of impractical shoes without thinking twice is . . . relegated to the loser category. Is there something about the American social system my Daddy and my instructors held back from me?"

"I think not, Buzz. Unlikely, unlikely. They gave you what they could, as much as they knew." And how could they know, he asked himself, what America would become?

"Sir," Wagonside whispered.

"Buzz," Dana whispered back.

Wagonside showed his left fist. "Sir, did you by chance ever want to beat your face into bloody little pieces?"

"Why, Buzz," answered Dana, "by the time I was done damaging my soul there was really no need."

"I should have done so before I went to Gavrych's highbrow gum-flapping gathering. See, sir, upon that night Natalie nailed down my doom by first pulling me away from the food table that finally had what I didn't mind eating, namely Russian hard-boiled eggs. She wanted reunion with Buntee, her Buntee, full name Buntline, Lewis Jasper, formerly assistant professor of English, San Francisco State University, formerly a novelist, formerly a husband and father, formerly a traveling companion who turned her on like a faucet, her word."

Wagonside's eyes lost focus for a moment.

"Immediately, while I and Buntline are trying to shush her, she started her usual thing with Buntline's companion, Irena, full name Nikolaevna, Irena Lisette, formerly support staff supervisor, KGB Central, Moscow. This is a rigid steel vault–file folder type, sir, to who one says 'limbs' not 'legs.' In a trained voice of carrying power from her college theatrical days Natalie booms out to Irena Lisette Nikolaevna several recipes for gourmet lovemaking and erotic liberation."

Wagonside compressed his lips.

"Happily, or so I initially felt, we were joined by Gavrych, and Natalie cut it out. He, Gavrych, was as usual soon baiting and teasing and putting me down. He crushed my balls with how little I knew about the Greeks, the Romans, their civilization so-called, and why *Monsieur Verdoux* with Charlie Chaplin is the best movie ever made. At mention of Chaplin, Natalie said how she had written an A paper in college about his films. She could not keep her eyes from Gavrych, and in other body-language ways showed to me clear signs of entering a state of erotic stimulation."

Wagonside knocked his heels together; his eyes filled up.

"In addition to a certain thing with her mouth, she touched him in the same way and exactly where she has touched those who later gave body marks. She touched him first on the left wrist, then the bicep region of his right arm."

He touched the loose thong on his loden coat.

"My wish was to slap Natalie. Only, dexterity has never been my strongest asset. I somehow landed on Gavrych's face and badly gashed his cheekbone. By the time I got back to our hotel room a dismissal cable from the President awaited me. This dismissal I then thought and still do was not in the style of the President. I then thought and still do that language like 'A man's character is his fate' is more appropriate to my superior, the aforementioned Artifex, who never missed saying that and similar highbrow things when I fucked up."

His face turned puffy.

"Also, I then thought and still do that my dismissal notice was written before I ever got to Moscow. This is because it carried, bottom right, the transcribing initials 'AO,' who took a pregnancy leave eleven days before my presidential appointment."

He swayed.

"Now that I've given you the facts as I have them, Mr. Dana, and put at your mercy my security clearance and what remains of my professional career, I would appreciate insight from your life."

He extended a hand.

"Do you share my insight, sir? Namely, that for reasons still unknown I was set up, made a patsy, and picked for Moscow liaison by the President and the aforementioned Artifex because I was the one mostly likely to fail? Do I have a right to the insight that I, like you, am a victim?"

At this moment, thought Dana, looking bitterly, intently at Wagonside's loose leather thong, at his cape bucks, I must speed this stupid blank boy along to a full engagement with life. It tore his heart. But all the same he answered, "You have a right to that insight. Yes, Buzz, yes, yes, yes."

"Jumping melonballs," whispered Wagonside. He made an indeterminate gesture. "Some world."

"Nevertheless . . . ," Dana began. But he did not know how to finish.

Wagonside knitted his brows. "Do you, sir, as I do, regret it—the victimizing and betrayal?"

"Most deeply." With a contortion of his face Dana went on to say, "So deep is the resentment that I'm pleased to have learned tonight"— he fumbled out a packet of Tagamets, tossed one into his mouth— "that it is temporary. Most temporary, Buzz."

"I'm sorry about it, sir. By 'it' I mean your temporariness and that like my Daddy you are near the end of your personal history."

At length he said, "I'm not of the characterological type given to physical demonstrativeness so . . . so I therefore won't shake your hand."

He looked off, croaked, "Fuck that shit," then spread out his arms and clasped Dana; though the clipboard scratched Dana's neck he did not cry out.

At length they stirred. Wagonside pointed across the street, at the taxi stand, and waved an arm. "Kennedy Airport!" he bawled.

Only one driver, a massive woman, bothered to answer. "Forty-five bucks plus the tolls."

"Receipt requested," said Wagonside. He stepped off the curb. "Sir, you have to understand that compared to my Daddy and the afore-mentioned Artifex, who feel they are doing a dirty job on the grounds of duty, I just do a dirty job. I, Mr. Dana, am just an unmotivated dirty-job-holder. As such, you're under no obligation to walk me."

But Dana accompanied him across Seventh Avenue. They stood near the cab while the driver got into a sweater.

"Sir, my earnest hope is that you don't feel used from the spilling of my guts," said Wagonside. "Also from my figuring that you are near the end of your personal history and therefore lacked time to report my security breach."

"Buzz, you'd have made a first-rate copyboy. And probably, yes, a first-rate Marxist."

They shook hands. The driver started her engine, lightly sounded her horn. But Wagonside took his time.

He said, "Sir, I remember something the former Minerva Beatrice Atherton said at your trial. How the mediocre shall inherit the earth. I am certainly one of those mediocre . . ."

The driver sounded her horn again, and Wagonside's next words were lost.

". . . because she has paid her dues. Aforesaid dues are in memory loss up around the fifty percentile level."

He opened the door full, put a leg inside.

"Therefore I hope, most earnestly, that life doesn't have in store for her other dues."

He bounded into the backseat. The cab took off before he had fully closed the door.

"What dues?" Dana shouted.

He kicked the box of résumés toward a cluster of ash cans.

For he felt unreasoning horror. Fool? No fool that Wagonside. By no means, by no means. Same cut and cloth as the others. But a better actor. And Artifex—might he not be Artifex? He delays me, engages me, while they . . . Yes, and Minerva, my trusting Minerva would buzz them into the lobby, then open the door to them. Then? Then, then, then . . . !

Once more he crossed Seventh Avenue, spilling change and Tagamet packets on his way to the pay phone.

And as he punched out the digits he saw flat, deadly, malignant faces leaning over Minerva, and he saw with awful exactness the way she would put her hand over her eyes, as though she were shading them.

But before the third ring Minerva answered as usual, "This is Mrs. Matthew Dana."

Despite his hampered breath Dana managed to joke as usual. "So the scoundrel did marry you finally."

Then he listened intently. Static on the line? No, but something, something: a footfall? Yielding of a floorboard?

And without preliminaries Minerva said, "No mention of the trial on the news, not a single word." For she could not tolerate anything less than significant conversation over the phone. But it was the significant conversation of forty years ago.

"There was little of importance," he answered lightly. "Truly, you didn't miss a thing today. Only motions and countermotions."

"Although," said Minerva, "I recall hearing Buck's name. He's to be honored. Wrote it down, here, yes. Barnard Mackenzie . . . But this is printed, not written. And Bertolt Brecht is dead, many years dead, but Barnard Mackenzie lives on . . ."

To divert her Dana said, "The résumés are done, mailed off, and I have great expectations, great expectations."

"And so you should." Her voice rose a notch, throbbed. "Did you kiss me when you left the house? On the eyes?"

Only, he recalled, to keep her from reading my face as I prepared myself for Dr. Lashman.

Then Minerva said in a different voice, a thin, dim voice, "Did you leave me a printed notice about Buck being honored?"

Dana did not answer. Understand that I am appalled by Thee, he silently declared. If she was never robust she was always strong of mind, she could . . .

And suddenly Minerva was laughing. "I do seem to expect visitors. One of your admirers, no doubt."

"No doubt."

"Or would it be Gus?"

"Doubtful." How I wish it were, Dana reflected. Pleasure to have known you, old giant, though you never called me anything kinder than "soft-headed prick." My defense cost him his life. "Gus," he picked up, "must be terribly busy on those motions and counter-motions."

"Someone . . . Perhaps someone rather older and balder and better spoken than Gus. Oh, decidedly better spoken."

"Almost everybody," he told her softly, "is better spoken than Gus."

"Then we'll have espresso for our visitor and with the espresso— oh, I think you might pick up one of those nutted cheesecakes at Le Boulanger."

"On my way," he said. For he had no heart to tell her Le Boulanger had been out of business these eleven years.

But inside of three blocks Dana was phoning her again.

She answered immediately and without waiting to hear his voice said, "I was also thinking of Provincetown. Of a certain bed, a Provincetown cottage bed, a Saturday night premarital bed."

He blew a kiss, she blew one back.

Then she was whispering to herself.

"Yes, what?" said Dana, more fearfully than he intended.

She came back with "Villagey" and, after a moment, "Oh, my mind is miles away. But did someone say, recently, that ours is a splendid flat, a most Villagey flat?"

"Recently?" He worked to keep the bitterness out of his voice.

"Two-oh-one Barrow Street," she burst out with a pipe of pride. "Small kitchen or not, we should hold on to it."

"And we shall."

"Though we might sublet it to . . . oh, that elderly well-spoken gentleman. He thought three rooms just the right size for his needs. Did he say a widower? The climb would keep him fit. Very taken with our posters and the way we'd painted the floors."

She was still talking when Dana, convulsed with tears, turned on his heel and headed home.

Something must have been troubling Prisco, the super, for he had gotten into his National Guard bivouac greens and put on a fresh headband to restrain the long yellow hair that fell Custer-style to his shoulders. And though he never worked on Saturdays he appeared to be putting forth immense energy now as he scraped the foyer tiles with a long-handled wire brush. Between his combat boots stood two large bottles of some solvent. The floor was so thoroughly soaked with the stuff that Dana had to step carefully onto the narrow runner of carpet and walk right past Prisco. They gazed at each other.

"Evenin'," said Prisco. A vein grew thick and hard on his forehead.

"Evening," answered Dana, coming down hard on the *g*.

"Man, how come stinko pinkos always talk the best American?"

And Prisco filled his lungs and sang out:

"If you don't like your Uncle Sammy
Then go back to your home o'er the sea . . ."

The doors of A-3 and A-5 opened a crack.

"Oh man," Prisco was saying, "I sure did wait. I waited on this day plenty long and I thank you for it."

He marched to the stairs, turned, ran at Dana, and came to a powerful halt before him.

"I should like to pass." At this moment Dana felt insupportable shame. Why here's your little people, he told himself. Here's the oppressed proletariat you and Minerva sought to reconstruct and restore. Thoughts of the Priscos once moved us more than thoughts of the stars. Early, early in the morning we'd walk and hunt out the oldest factories and study the dead-looking workers. When Minerva wept I'd whisper, " 'Awake and sing, ye that dwell in the dust.' "

Only he must have spoken aloud for Prisco shouted into his face "Dust! Wanna complain over my dust to Management Fat Nose? Puh-leez do so. Call on my phone, drink a beer, be my guest."

"Gracious of you. However—"

"Great-shit of you!"

"However, I wish only to pass, not to complain."

"See, we'll do complaint for complaint."

"You have a complaint against me? Would you care"—unaccountably close to stammering Dana paused—"to voice it?"

Prisco thrust two thick fingers into Dana's line of vision. "Stickin' on you two complaints."

"Are you?"

"Number one's goin' out by mailogram to twenty-five, two-five, New York fuckin' City agencies who will dispossess you and declare you a first-class undesirable tenant. Undesirable"—he sent the wire brush slamming to the floor—"means not wanted. Means goom-bye, old Red buddy."

"Does it?"

"Complaint two's better. Uncle Sammy stuff, and I thank God as how he give me the sweet chance I been waitin' on since day one, since you first crucified me to Management Money Love."

Suddenly he pulled Dana close and said hoarsely, "446–4400." Then he moved aside and hooked his thumbs in his garrison belt. "Secret Service, New York office."

Dana stood arrested for an instant.

"Man, do they ever know you there! No waitin', patched me right through to Mister Big."

"Ah, did they?" Dana's eyes watered.

"Mister Big tendered me U.S. government gratitude for takin' pictures in evidence."

"What pictures?" Iridescent fragments of red and green seemed to float off Prisco's wicked mouth. "I'm listening. About the pictures . . ."

"Pictures?" Prisco tapped his brow. "Right, right. See, only this here low-class patriot super is beat. Bushed. Mental fatigue and memory lossage from three hours' work on these tiles."

"My compliments. A good job. But—"

"My commie-mints."

"—waiting to hear about the pictures."

"Right, right. *Them* pictures. My Polaroid pictures." Prisco stood so that his belly hung over his garrison belt. "The pictures Mister Big wants so bad he is sending a special U.S. messenger to pick up."

The doors of A-3 and A-5 opened.

"Red buddy, you got balls. You and your Gav-bitch brotherhood need balls bigger'n the Kremlin to spray paint stinko-pinko piss-on-America shit on my floors."

The door of A-3 opened wider. Bettina Wren, the dancer, showed her face, spoke up. "Mr. Dana, you should choose more carefully your friends and persuade them from strong-arm tactics in your name."

And from A-5 Dan Skriloff, the printing salesman, stepped out and said, "They rang every bell in the building, these three guys. They rang, they rang and rang even when my wife held open the door for them."

Dana's teeth clicked.

His chest rose.

For he had an insight.

"You must understand," he began with serene delight. "I'd have you know," he began again, "that my humiliation is nothing beside the amused pity I feel toward you people." He had in mind to tell them that he, he at least, had some sense, some intuition of Artifex; that Artifex was one of those who managed them; that his purpose was altogether different and more dangerous to them than anything they might possibly suppose. But when he saw how stupid and how fiercely angry their faces were he faltered.

"Can't save you now," he cried. "Never could. Should have known better than to try . . ."

He stepped over Prisco's combat boots and started climbing the stairs. But though he urged himself to hurry, to hurry, Prisco caught up with him easily, and Prisco poked the small of his back and pulled the hem of his trench coat, and tenants appeared on the landings. Prisco sprinted ahead and begged them to bear witness for him.

"What did I see?" said Lynne Ornauer, the social worker, and she answered herself with a surge of blood to her blemished forehead. "Three men. Yuppie types. Daughter thought they were cute. Me too."

Then she pushed her small bosom into the banister and told how they had taken Prisco from behind, wrenching back his arms. "Upset my daughter. Did she need to see that for her asthma, Mr. Dana?" Anyway, they were shouting. What did they shout? Stuff. Crazy stuff. Who remembers? Her mind was on her daughter. Choking, wheezing . . .

But on the third floor Dana had it straight enough.

For other tenants chimed in and gave him to understand that the loonies, the terrorist types, had gone about the building and passed out handbills. Daphne Ianiello, the copy editor, C-2, showed hers, and it read:

JUSTICE TO MATTHEW DANA
LET HIS BETRAYER, BARNARD MACKENZIE,
BEWARE THE VENGEANCE OF
THE GAVRYCH BROTHERHOOD

Two steps below the fourth floor Prisco took him by the collar, turned him, pushed a Polaroid snapshot before his face.

"See what they done on my tiles? Three fuckin' hours' work and busted knees conner you and Gav-bitch. You and your stinko-pinko brotherhood lookin' to vengeance somebody? Try me, try me . . ."

Dana was a long time peering at the snapshot. Though his eyes smarted from his need to quell tears he had finally to admire the incredible skill of those who had lettered that PEACE, SYMPATHY, BROTHERHOOD, and PUREST JOY. He guessed they had laid stencils on the tiles to get such uniformity from cans of spray paint. Yes, only stencils explained that gnarled look to each letter. The look of the old Slavic alphabet . . .

They have me, thought Dana. Once again Thy devils have me.

And he addressed his neighbors.

"You members of the House Un-American Activities Committee," he declared, "have called my testimony before you 'an epic' in this committee's history. Quite so—but only, I fear, if one remembers that the epic celebrated the primitive, the savage, the bloody minded."

He passed his hands before his head.

"Yet this is 1949 . . ."

His recollection snapped; he rambled.

"Best potentialities of the heart and mind" . . . "Violence to them" . . . "You continue Hitler's war by other means" . . .

He was overtaken by a fit of laughter.

"Why, I believe I quoted Marx to them," he informed his neighbors. "Can you imagine? To HUAC!"

But who was that murmuring, "Crazy"?

And who had hold of Prisco?

And who crooned, "Come, let's go, enough!"

But what matter? For he stood now near the peeling laths of the fourth floor and Minerva was rushing to meet him.

"Such goings-on," she said. "Noise of communality and high purpose. A charge of vitality through the air. Like the moment—don't you think?—before a strike is voted."

She kissed him three times, and three times again.

"How wet we are! But rain"—she tossed back her hair gaily, gaily—"brings us good luck. As always."

"As always."

"In P-town a few drops fell that Saturday night. If memory serves. Does it serve?"

"It does, it does."

"Close your eyes."

He closed them.

"Keep them closed. Are they closed?" She pulled him toward the apartment by his wrists. "Open them to your guest and future employer."

And he beheld a tall, bald, fastidiously tailored man with blue eyes as grave and inquisitive and skeptical and ultimately worldly-wise as a child's.

And this man inclined his head courteously and said, "Good evening. I am Harry Porlock, and I hope to be of service to you."

"Good evening," Dana replied. Bitter fluids moved into his mouth. "Time we met." A second later he added, "Don't you feel it's time we met, Artifex?"

In the living room Minerva lighted the stub of a blue candle and pushed it into the crusted mouth of a Chianti bottle. When she had finished setting the bottle exactly between two hammered copper plates on the false fireplace she turned. Her eyes were filled.

"Mr. Porlock, do you think this candle pretentious?"

"Hardly." With a faint smile Porlock settled back on the studio couch, then placed a throw pillow between his head and the wall. "Little enough light in the world as it is."

"I'm annoyed, oh"—she stroked hair away from her face—"not annoyed, upset because I found, because I *have* only this one candle, this remnant of a candle."

"But a beautiful remnant," Dana rushed to say. Leaning forward on the stuffed Moroccan hassock he gazed steadfastly at Porlock. "Last of those we bought to celebrate Adlai Stevenson's nomination."

"Still," said Minerva, rubbing her palms against her Mexican skirt, "the remnant of a candle is enough for a living room on the top floor rear, a living room measuring only fourteen by eleven."

She started pacing off the room. At the window she stopped, peeping through a broken slat in the bamboo blinds. "Always and ever that Morton Street condo. Why don't the bourgeoisie ever sit on their terraces?" She put her mouth to the blinds. "Lost a foot off our living room since that condo came."

She went to Dana and in the excited, breathy voice he feared asked, "Will our guest, our friend, drink mankind's health in espresso?"

Porlock looked at her intently, then even more intently at Dana, and he nodded slowly several times.

"Perhaps," said Dana, turning on the hassock toward her, then with knitted brows toward Porlock, "another drink."

"It is rather late for espresso," said Porlock. "And perhaps for mankind," he added ruefully.

But Minerva was sliding past the gooseneck lamp and the sling chair and talking to the bookcases and touching *Man's Fate* and *Three Soldiers*. Then she struck the wall with all her force and went off to the kitchen.

"My wife . . . ," said Porlock.

Trembling, Dana directed his gaze at the light under the kitchen screen.

Porlock adjusted his throw pillow; he found it necessary to adjust it again. "I'm reminded," he said very softly, "that my wife rather favored espresso too."

Suddenly Minerva sang out, "No problem."

Dana pulled at the skin of his neck.

"I've got the coffee mill handle working beautifully. Thought I'd have trouble. Did you think I'd have trouble?"

"That is not it," Dana whispered to Porlock. "Not the handle. That's not it."

"My wife," said Porlock, "also favored those troublesome hand mills. Forever in need of repair." He bit a knuckle.

"Not what shames her. Not at all."

The light in the kitchen went out.

Minerva came forward.

"It seems," she said in a low and shaken voice, "that we've only two proper espresso cups. You might have reminded me, Matty."

"Should have. So I should."

"And you might have stopped for a cheesecake. A Le Boulanger cheesecake." She rounded her shoulders. Tears slid from her eyes. "But my Matty was ever abstracted."

"It was those résumés," said Dana, rising. "Had my mind on those damn résumés."

Minerva twirled about so that her Mexican skirt flared. "I've a thought. Hear me!"

"Let me first dry your eyes."

But Minerva danced away. "Why, I've not been out all this day"— she was stepping out of her sandals and into a pair of desert boots— "a taste of the times when we had so many candles and so many guests and so many friends."

She turned to face Dana.

"Le Boulanger is gone," he was compelled to tell her. When her breathing had quieted he said, "You'll find only a Baskin-Robbins in its place."

"I'll try Francini's. I'll try . . . Brothers Three." She focused her eyes on a greening WPA poster. "In the Village one could always find . . . something. I'll find *something!*"

"Only a mugger." He put his hands on her arms and she moved away. "Last time you might have broken your hip."

"I'll beat them off," she said.

"Min—"

"I'll hit them with"—she gestured at the bookcase—"with a copy of *Science and Society*. Or with the remnant of a candle."

Then Porlock went to the closet and returned with her heaviest winter coat, and he settled it over her shoulders, and playfully buttoned the topmost button, and fitted the cowl over her head.

Standing behind her, Porlock gave Dana a long look, a significant and sorrowful look, and said, "You'll be safe, Mrs. Dana. My word on it. Walk as far and as long as you wish with confidence."

Dana, stripped of force, stepped back. He nodded to Porlock, then to Minerva, and said, "Best put on galoshes. It's been raining and the streets are still wet, still wet." And he took the letter Porlock handed him:

Alyse Carmichael
Corporate Affairs Division
Here, Inc.
33 Rockefeller Plaza
New York, NY 10020

December 30, 1993

Dear Fellow Staffers:
Eleven days hence, Barnard (Buck) Mackenzie closes out the January 9, 1994 issue of Here—*his last as Editorial Director.*

"All this week," says Buck, who retires after thirty-five years at our helm, "I mean to putter with, polish, and finally perfect a 'Heresay' piece pointing out, in the hope that it may do some good, how this administration has fallen into the lures and snares of accommodation with Gavrych."

Oddly tranquil, Dana smiled over that "lures and snares." Still enamored of huntsman's images. Yes, and he still has that horror of anything Russian.

That piece, like everything Buck has ever written—or rigorously coaxed and cajoled and counseled out of what he likes to call "our copysmiths"—will surely be irreverent, unsparing, acidulous, and most of all, a good and joyous read.

"Hazlitt?" said Porlock, cupping an ear.

A few seconds passed before Dana realized that he had spoken aloud. He pushed a little forward so that his knees nearly touched

Porlock's. "Buck wanted to be the American Hazlitt. Insisted that his staff, his copysmiths, follow Hazlitt's methods of composition."

"Indeed!" Porlock exclaimed, smiling upon him. "Didn't Hazlitt write each sentence on the floor? To remind himself of the rigors of composition?"

Now how the devil does he know, Dana asked himself, bitterly irritated. And how is it that I feel as callow and incompetent beside him as Wagonside?

"A touch of bursitis but"—Porlock's smile increased—"he still manages to hold up remarkably well under those rigors of composition. Fit, limber, relaxed. Even on Sunday nights, when the magazine goes to bed, he's bounding from cubicle to cubicle at three A.M. The only one with a voice left—a parade-ground voice."

Under the beam of those eyes, Dana thought, I'm only a sick old man dreaming of Guernica and the death of Spain and the disgrace of the democracies.

It would be enough, more than enough, to say of Buck Mackenzie that throughout these three and a half desperately critical decades he pushed Here *to its limit—till it would become, in his words, "an essential means of assessing and affirming life in our time, a 95-page collective enterprise that captures with humanity, intelligence, and good taste a week's worth of history.*

Falling into the straight-backed stance he always took with the Founder, Dana said, " 'Week's worth of history'—my phrase."

"In this matter," said Porlock, "and in more important matters, you'll have justice, Mr. Dana. At least"—he bit a knuckle—"within the limits fixed by fate."

"Will I?" And as quietly and casually as he could Dana said, "But a few hours ago I was taught that nothing is kind or fair in creation. As you know, surely know."

Porlock, moving his eyes from Dana, answered, "Not long ago my wife and I came to a rather similar conclusion."

But to the many hundreds of younger writers whose lives and careers he has deepened and enriched—as "Bossman Buck" at Here, *as Professor Mackenzie at the Columbia School of Journalism—he is something more than a consummately gifted editor and teacher, more even than a wise and caring mentor and master.*

"Dead ducks . . . ," Dana murmured. Though Porlock cupped an ear he held back what was on his mind. That he was a dead duck, and dead ducks should be past caring.

We decided that such a playful, irreverent, acerbic man, a man who loves the explicit and the actual, should not be forced to sit helpless and without heart at some dreary testimonial dinner where he is mythologized and turned into a bloodless abstraction: a figure.

"Picked up his hatred of testimonials from the Founder," he told Porlock. And how much else, he wondered, how much else, dear Buckie?

Let us rather tell the world about the Buck Mackenzie who wouldn't let up on us till we'd given our two million readers a good, hard, luminous look at the texture of these times from Sunday to Sunday.

Gazed and gazed at the Founder with a devotion and openmouthed ardor I could never manage. And something would pass between them. As if they'd exchanged heartbeats.

Therefore, next Wednesday night, eight P.M., you're invited, along with staffers from our dim and recent past and a host of admiring rivals, to Radio City. We picked the former picture palace because, as Buck writes in his memoir, New York Cornball, *"I developed a certain mild affection for the place when I fled the narrow minds and unlimited landscapes of Kansas."*

Bending close to Porlock Dana said harshly, "A 'certain mild affection'! Why, he loved Radio City!"
"Did he?"
"Used to say, 'May God bless Radio City.' "
"Indeed."
"Only to look into the lobby restored him, put him at perfect peace. Like a certain old pica measure the Founder kept on his desk. Reminded him how far he'd come, how well he'd done."

Porlock shook his head. "As you said, nothing is kind or fair in creation." He kept shaking his head. "Still, a certain equity does prevail."

Buck will preside—and how could it be otherwise?—over a special ninety-minute film we've put together for the occasion. It covers Buck's decades at Here *and tells, with newsreel and TV clips and in Buck's own words, what went on in the hearts and minds of men, what they said and did and how with reason and spirit, with ghastly blunder and glorious wisdom, they somehow endured and prevailed. Food, of course—buffet-style from Lutèce. For the ladies, surprise gifts; for the children, souvenir balloons blown up and passed around by the funniest and saddest-looking clowns in the business.*

As Dana lay down the letter, Porlock rose. The throw pillow wheezed from the sudden release of pressure.

In a vindictive voice Dana said, "Gifts for the ladies, clowns for the children. Of course. I see your equity at work, Artifex, I do see how your precious equity prevails."

Porlock, trying to set right the bamboo blinds, said, "But Mr. Dana, you will be one of the clowns."

And he told Dana what was expected of him.

A little past ten Minerva came in.

"Oh, Matty," she said, "I found no cheesecake, but I enjoyed a most wonderful walk, a Village walk."

"If you wish, Min, only if you wish, you can make your espresso."

From the kitchen she said, "I see our guest, our new friend is gone, and so we need two cups only."

A moment later she put her head over the screen and asked, "Was there talk of"—she started turning the handle of the coffee mill violently; nevertheless, Dana caught the last word—"employment?"

"Why, as to that—"

Then Dana went over and took her in his arms; he saw that she still had her scarf on. He said, "There is a place in Provincetown you know, have reason to know, a place where Theodore Dreiser came to join our rally for the Loyalists. There, oh there, you shall have a cottage. And such a cottage, such a cottage!"

FOUR

32

Then it seemed to the President that Radio City had put his father in an awful humor, so awful that he left suddenly by a special exit, a secret exit known only to himself, and he walked off as far and as fast as he could, and he did not look back.

Somehow the President found this exit, and though it was plain to him that he would only be doing himself dreadful harm he labored to catch up with his father.

Several times he drew close, but each time he was pressed back by a crowd, and each time he believed someone in the crowd was taunting him about a movie he would never get to see, a marvelous movie about flying aces and hell's angels and devil dogs of the air.

On a street he believed he knew well was a loudspeaker announcing arrivals and departures, and the President called out to his father, begging him to stop, asking him how he would ever find his way home again.

His father stopped, but not for him, and extended his arms to Pavel Gavrych, who moved forward calm and sure.

It stole over the President that Pavel Gavrych and his father were discussing him, and though he never once heard them he somehow knew well enough that his father did not want him home again.

He likewise knew well enough that if he did get home again he would find that his father had taken another son, a bookish, gap-toothed belly laugher, a fellow he could not quite place though he was perfectly sure he had once seen him.

"Yes, by Jesus, it's Lewis Buntline," he decided.

And he cried out to his father at the top of his voice to tell him that this would be an awful deal, a lousy trade, that he would become president and Lewis Buntline nothing more than a college professor, a second-rate novelist, a faithless husband who'd run off to Russia for a shameful, carnal purpose.

Several times he tried to make a sound, but his tongue stuck to the roof of his mouth and he was glad when he awakened.

For he knew well enough that his father would have answered, "True enough, son, but I'll have pleasure knowing that Buntline could not face the world as it is."

When she was done signing letters of condolence to what was left of the *Here* corporate family, Eunice turned her chair so that she could better watch the coming of full darkness to Washington. Then she took Amy Underhill's long, horsey, violet-eyed English face in her hands, lifted it a little toward the bay window, and exclaimed, "Why there it is, my special lovely Christmas darkness."

But suddenly Eunice had a look of hopeless desolation.

A single fat tear spilled out of her right eye, slid jaggedly down, and burst upon one of the silver barrettes that held Amy's bun.

"Sweet suffering Lord," she said, "this year I am simply not pleasuring myself in Christmas dark. Nor in Christmas either."

"Nothing to fret over, love." Amy patted Eunice's hands. "Christmas has become a season of melancholy the world over. Turns everyone into a nasty baggage. Women most especially. Indeed now, only last week I had one of those fearfully contemporary greeting cards from sister Hettie. Latest thing for the meanspirited in London. Drab expressionist woodcut on the cover. Inside the dourest bit of verse. William Blake can be dour, you know." Thinning her lips and frowning severely, Amy recited:

> "I wander thro' each dirty street,
> Near where the dirty Thames does flow,
> And mark in every face I meet
> Marks of weakness, marks of woe."

Eunice studied her earnestly awhile, then said, "I truly, truly cannot believe you got any such card or any such verse, but I bless you for trying to lift my heart."

She threw her arms around Amy and squeezed her.

"Oh, oh, do watch it, love!" cried Amy, for Eunice had leaned so far forward in the chair that she nearly fell, and Amy took her quietly and strongly under the arms and kept her upright.

"Can't even keep my seat," whispered Eunice, her mouth turning loose and soft. "This surely is the most fidgety"—she rose and walked round and round Amy's chair—"and jelly-belly, jump-in-the-skin, harshest, trying Christmas of my life."

A second later she added significantly, "My *married* life."

Amy rose, put a finger to Eunice's ear, and said into it:

> "What is it men in women do require?
> The lineaments of Gratified Desire.
> What is it women do in men require?
> The lineaments of Gratified Desire."

With a little twist of the mouth she murmured, "Rather a lot of smarts, our William Blake. As you Americans say."

They embraced, laughed, broke apart, and Eunice, hand shaking in the effort of conveying her affection, touched Amy's bun and said, "Poetry or not, Amy Underhill, I do truly believe we're setting ourselves for a real good flannel nightdress, womanly, cookies-in-bed talk."

"*Biscuits* in bed," whispered Amy.

They giggled, and when it was impossible to prolong the giggling Eunice looked intently into Amy's eyes and with her voice raised a little said, "I have been so pleasured in you, Amy Underhill, that I wish, I truly want to officially appoint and designate you as my permanent social secretary."

"Bad form." Amy enlarged her eyes, gave her head the tiniest shake. "At this time dreadfully bad form."

"Don't care one bit! And if you want to know, Miss Amy Underhill, author of skinny books—"

"Slim volumes."

"—all of whom, whom or which, are over my sweet suffering head, it is my middle of the night, down deep, and most highly private secret wish that the lady to whom you are ever so unaccountably loyal, Madam Corpsy Dry, suffer during her sabbatical absence a debilitating and most highly embarrassing female hormonal disfunction causing her already excessive facial hair to prosper and flourish and multiply and—"

A bell chimed; shrilled; chimed three times more.

Wheeling, Eunice ran on tiptoe to the double doors, opened them, stuck out her face, listened. She heard from across the hall sighing sounds, purring sounds, and she mimicked them and stamped her feet so violently that her cheeks were shaken, and she gestured at the balding agent with the tortoiseshell sunglasses and in a quietly savage tone said, "However is he doing on his adorable new Exercycle?"

"Twenty minutes, four miles, and not even worked up a sweat, ma'am."

"Now doesn't that pleasure my soul."

And the blond agent with the rimless sunglasses stepped between the busts of Walt Whitman and Julia Ward Howe and told Eunice, "Best workout the President's had this week."

Eunice gave him a glance of helpless malevolence, then slid shut the doors and returned to her chair.

She took a pen from Amy Underhill's fingers, a small pad from her desk, and drew a violent tangle of lines all over the presidential seal.

"I don't suppose," she said, bearing down even harder on the pad, "that I've reached the age, time of life, when . . . when unbeknownst and willy-nilly . . . when one may just as well give up on no less than five bubble baths daily to say nothing of sprays and powders and I-don't-know-what . . . when time and physiology are closing in and . . . one emits . . . one carries and contains odors which are no longer . . . girlish."

Her pen snapped, rolled down her lap, her knees, and onto the floor. She started to brush her lap, suddenly made a fist and struck her belly, her thighs.

"Poppa, poor dear little Poppa, called me his 'may apple,' his 'blue dew,' and every blessed morning when he'd done shaving he lifted me high to his cheeks and rubbed me around them, and he claimed I left him smelling sweeter than all the lotions of Araby."

She raised a hand to strike herself again, but Amy took it gently by the wrist and murmured, "Best not, best not." Then she tapped

Eunice's kneecap with a forefinger, stiffened and cocked her head like a bird. "Dear me, how you Americans go on about olfactory matters."

In a voice barely audible Eunice said, "Well, do I?"

"Do you what, love?"

Eunice breathed out, "Olfactory matters."

Amy sat upright, looked straight ahead, and compressed her lips. "However did you Americans manage to conquer the frontier! Still"— she shut her eyes—"if you must know . . ."

"Would feel truly grateful and pleasured," Eunice whispered. And for an instant she put her thumb deep into her mouth and scowled.

"If you must know, love"—Amy gestured at Eunice's mouth, shook her head till the thumb was withdrawn—"yes, I should say that you smell as young and expectant as a spool of toy-store ribbon."

Eunice sighed, wrinkled her nose, sighed again. With a smile that mixed playfulness and insupportable sadness she said, "How you do put things, Amy Underhill. How kind and clever. 'Young and expectant as . . .' " She wet her lips. "Well, bless you mightily for speaking half the truth at least. Because I have surely been just expectant and expectant and expectant since . . . weeks, surely."

Her mouth sank down and down.

"Near freezes my soul the way he talks of Radio City and of how he and that poor Buck Mackenzie must surely have shared some special strange feeling for the place. When he wakes up it's purely to do nothing else but tell me how he just dreamed some awful Radio City dream."

She rose, stuck out her tongue at the double doors, sat.

"We're looking straight up into the dark and lying side by side like two sleds . . . sleds in the ice. Then wriggle and squirm, flinch and freeze. Whilst I am sweetly stroking my pillow and making his favorite wifely sounds, he puts on his most shaky-deep hairy-scary voice. 'By Jesus, I must have Radio City on my mind.'

" 'Well, now,' I answer in a Nice Nellie sweet potato pie way, 'I would be most happy to serve as your ear since I can't seem to serve you with any other part.' "

"Rather too sly a rejoinder," Amy said mildly, moving the tip of her shoe against the arch of Eunice's shoe. "Sister Hettie, under somewhat similar circumstances, favors a bit of Rilke. 'Can you still play the old songs? Play, darling.' "

"That's most lovely and lyrical," said Eunice, fluttering her eyelashes, "but I am too harshly tried and screamingly, achingly bored by his Radio City dreams. How his Poppa took him there, and how his Poppa went walking away into New York City, and how that Pavel Gavrych comes by, and how when this happens—"

Eunice sat back as far and stiffly as she could, and in her very deepest voice said, " 'By Jesus, Eunice, I am smitten by mortal terror.' "

"There, love," said Amy, jouncing up and down and banging her knees together. "I do believe he presents you with a smashing opportunity to paraphrase a bit of Rimbaud. Simple line, no need to write it down. 'Terror'—and when you speak it, do please make use of that shining smile of yours—'Terror'—light on the word, love, and smiling, smiling throughout—'Terror is not American.' "

But Eunice, her elbows on her lap, said, "However do I smile when he's quivering—"

There was knocking on the double doors; feet moved.

"—and plain shaking away like he's taken by Alabama fever?"

Then the blond agent with the rimless sunglasses had his head a little inside the room, and he said, "Three hours to the press conference, ma'am."

And when he had backed away the balding agent with the tortoiseshell sunglasses also put his head inside the room, and he said, "That's three hours, ma'am, and the President's setting his Exercycle for his last mile."

A bell chimed, scraped, ran on with a rusty sound.

Eunice, laughing immoderately, went to the doors, slammed them shut, opened them, swayed, slammed them shut again, let out a little shriek, and cried, "Gelding."

She waited, and when she saw that Amy was not going to speak, said, "I don't suppose you know, Amy Underhill, as how there is a decided strain of alcoholism in my family."

Amy went over, put an arm around her waist; though she tried not to, Eunice leaned on it very heavily.

"A most decided strain touching even Poppa, poor Poppa," she said while they walked round and round in small circles. "Yes, I do expect that I shall have inherited that strain, which is a wonderfully fine thing, for you see"—she made sucking noises like a famished infant—"I truly expect that by New Year's I shall have turned myself into Washington's most notorious alcoholic and thus . . . and thereby

... with the aid of daily drunken stupors be spared ... thoughts and feelings which are ... why, since he took that Exercycle into his life ... mortifying and humiliating and take the unseemliest form of ..."

Her mouth flickered at either end and her next words came out in a rush.

"I pure and simple want to be where that Exercycle is."

She and Amy looked each other in the eyes.

Then Amy said, "And do you think of yourself as seat or handle-bars?"

Eunice murmured, "Seat *and* handlebars."

"Good show, good show!" Patting Eunice's back, Amy went on to say, "Three hours till the press conference, and my mind is absolutely inflamed with possibilities." She bent a little to examine Eunice's face. "Yes, we shall first have to shed that wintery look, those lips unsmiling and seeming to say, 'I hate!' "

But Eunice only wobbled and started to slide down.

Amy caught her about the hips and positioned her against the double doors. Stepping back, she put both forefingers to her brow. " 'So much to do, so little time to do it in.' " She underscored the air. "Cecil Rhodes, 1853 to 1902, one of the guilt-ridden colonialists we had in plentiful supply."

Eunice sang out, "Gelding, gelding, gelding."

"A most extreme situation." Amy drummed her lips. "The moment has come—oh, what is it you Americans say? To move those wagons into a circle?"

"Not really a gelding," whispered Eunice. "I do rightly remember times—"

But Amy raised a palm at her.

"Sister Hettie, during similar extreme situations, several times succeeded in awakening her mate with passages of an odd sort. Among her favorites, from John Donne's 'A Mistress Laments,' was"—she drew back her lips, clicked her large teeth—" 'Are not my pudenda/ Upon your agenda?' "

"Well . . . ," Eunice said uncertainly.

Then a light seemed to have been switched on behind her face.

" 'Pudenda' means . . . You are most wicked, Amy Underhill."

And very faintly she grinned.

"Sister Hettie," said Amy, describing a circle about Eunice's mouth, "when pressed, could make deft use of Jane Austen, who was among the first to observe that 'there's a vas deferens between the penis and the vagina.' "

"Jane Austen did not say that. Oh, she just never, never did!" And Eunice shrieked with laughter.

"Now there, oh there," cried Amy, squinting at Eunice's right cheek, "is a most fetching dimple. *And* we shall tilt our head a bit, a bitty-bit, *and* affix our lips by saying 'sweetheart' and 'silly' and give thought to Sister Hettie's most splendid thrust—one drawn from an exchange between Stella and Dean Swift. The dear old dean had inquired after her nervous state, and she quipped, 'I shall be far more quiescent/When I am rendered less tumescent.' "

Eunice whinnied, whiffed, and laughed so hard that a tear flew onto the ruffle of Amy's blouse.

"There's a love," declared Amy. "Only hold that laughter, only continue saying 'sweetheart' and 'silly'—"

She slid open the double doors a little, put a hand to the small of Eunice's back, turned her.

"—and I should not be at all surprised if you did not soon understand the true power of the state."

Eunice took a step outside the doors, turned, giggled, cried, "Sweetheart" and "Silly."

"Go, oh do go, love!"

Eunice ran as fast as she could, and though the balding agent with the tortoiseshell sunglasses told her, "The President's not done with his last mile, ma'am," she answered, "Sweetheart" and "Silly," and held her smile.

And presently the tingling of the Exercycle bell stopped.

A few minutes after the President had left her body, when he had dozed, wakened sharply, and made a forlorn sound, Eunice sang:

> "Down in the valley, the valley so low,
> Hear the wind blow, dear, hear the wind blow."

The President swung about, put his head close to Eunice's left armpit, and sang back:

"Roses are red, dear, violets are blue.
Angels in heaven know I love you."

Eunice scratched and stroked the sheet with the middle finger of her right hand and sang:

"We strolled the lanes together."

The President took a little swipe at her left breast, stopped a fraction of an inch from the nipple and sang back:

"Laughed at the rain together."

Eunice stuck out her tongue and sang:

"You're a sweetheart if there ever was one."

The President walked the fingers of his right hand along her abdomen, leaped them at her thighs, landed with a hearty smack of his palm, and sang back:

"If there ever was one, it's you."

Eunice drummed the President's chest and together they sang:

"If there ever was one, it's you."

The President pushed himself a little higher on the pillow, looked straight out at the pitch-dark oblong of the Edith Wilson Room, and silently complained to JFK, saying, "Jack, how come I'm in this strange mood, state, whatever? That Radio City dream is bad enough without all this stuff adding to my cares. Have you noticed? Certain small things . . ."

He heard the stolid, stupid ticking of the old Duluth Timetraveler.

"See, old buddy, that clock is one of those small things. Whose? Found it in Camp David. Yours? Killed an hour yesterday taking stains off the crystal. Vexes and beats the shit out of me. Suddenly I can't part with it. Piece of junk, really."

He swung his feet around to the floor as Eunice said, "I do absolutely feel most wonderfully pink in my down below."

"Ah," he answered dreamily, and he made a crooning, a contented sound, and while Eunice plumped her pillows he sensed a noiseless and invisible kind of energy about the room, and he addressed it almost aloud, saying, "Stay around, Jack, if you can, if you want to. Tell me what you can about the mind. If you consider . . . what a curious piece of work, the mind! Shouldn't I be practicing voice and gesture and timing for the press conference? No, all I want to think about is that clock. Connected somehow to my boyhood, no doubt. You don't have to tell me. Something to do with time, of course. Do you suppose time was different once, Jack? Counted for more? If you take movies—by Jesus, the movie that I watched as a child, the movie that seemed to last a lovely eternity, flew by last week at Camp David. Is time failing us? You used to say, 'Everything fails us, boy-o.' "

He stood up, shivered, warmed one foot with the other. When he had gotten his bearings in the dark he remembered to tell Eunice, "Best close your eyes."

"Always favored the dark," she said throatily.

"Eyes closed, close them, are they closed?" the President said and he switched on the light. For about five seconds he shadow-boxed, then, throwing left jabs, he tiptoed over to the rose cretonne boudoir chair and squatted to see if he had set the alarm properly on the Duluth Timetraveler. "By Jesus," he declared, hefting it and moving a little aside in case JFK was still around and wanted to see, "hand work. You can make out tool marks. How about that!"

Then Eunice said, "Making me close my eyes before the light came on was about the most thoughtful and most wonderful thing you have done in the longest while." She added shyly, tentatively, "Second most . . . ?"

The President turned, looked at her intently, understood her. Nodding to the right, to the left, he extended his arms as if over a lectern and said, "I accept this tribute with wholehearted gratitude, with pleasure and pride . . ."

"You are most surely deserving of it."

"Was I"—the President raised his eyes to the ceiling—"do I get a plaque or a medallion?"

"Plaque and medallion *and* leather-bound scroll, and . . . I am prepared . . . should decisive and resolute action be taken soon . . . speedily . . ."

Eunice scratched the sheet.

There was deep silence.

At length the President sighed and showed Eunice the Duluth Time-traveler. "Quarter to seven."

"I consider that six forty-five."

"I'd need . . . the old executive branch would require . . ."

"Executive *limb*," Eunice cried gloriously.

"Before it's up to full strength—I'd have to say twenty minutes, half hour."

"Still."

"Means we'd have to be under way, finished before eight. Then, by Jesus, shower, second shave, my makeup call at eight-forty, and suppose"—the President tried to say this playfully—"I fell asleep?"

"I do believe," Eunice answered cheerily, too cheerily, "as I am trustworthy and capable of arousing you properly."

The President smiled.

Eunice giggled.

The President went on back to bed, let Eunice push her face into his chest.

" 'Arousing you properly,' " he whispered, and neither could speak for laughing.

When she had her breath Eunice said, "I do believe I'm doing that just more and more lately. And without meaningful intent or the pleasure of knowing I'm a true wit."

"By Jesus," said the President, "what a curious piece of work, the mind."

He freed his hand from Eunice's hip, lifted it as if to wave at her. "Now about my worry over falling asleep. I wouldn't want you to have the idea that I someways don't enjoy it when I fall into one of those pleasant *aftermath* sleeps. Normally I love it." He let his hand fall to the headboard. "But right now I have an immediate, temporary problem with the thought of another aftermath sleep—"

"—before you only dozed, and no more than a big minute."

"A doze, a minute"—fearing that there had been a little rasp in his voice, the President pretended to clear his throat—"I dreamed my dream all the same."

"An aftermath dream," said Eunice, looking frightened, then petulant, "should be gold gentle, peace perfect."

"Thinking on it," the President said, "and for once I don't mind so much thinking on it, there were differences to the dream."

He backhanded the headboard.

"Differences." Eunice moved up on her elbows. "*Nice* differences? Pleasanter and happier aftermath differences?"

"Tell me, please," said the President with a ring of exasperation, "what dreams are ever happy and pleasant. Be interested, by Jesus, if you tell me who ever had them."

A tinge spread from Eunice's neck to her cheeks. She opened and closed her mouth.

"Now here's what puzzles and bothers me about dreams. Let's say you dream for the purpose of working through nasty, wakeful stuff, stick-in-the-craw thoughts." The President knuckled his brows, shivered when a long shadow close by the weighted Chinese silk draperies unaccountably stirred, dilated. "Okay, I happen to remember something from Jack. As far as the world knew, as far as he knew, Jack loved touch football."

"I," Eunice rushed to say, "also knew."

"Of course, no question. But how do you explain something I remember he told me? Sixty-one? Sixty-two?"

He looked to the draperies, but the long shadow stayed put.

"Having one of those locker room talks—"

"Women have them too."

"Wasn't in a locker room literally. I mean, we were talking . . . no bullshit things. He wanted to share, and when Jack wanted to share you could no more not listen, not remember, than you could not breathe. And Jack told me that much as he loved his touch football— why, if he happened to dream about it they never once failed to be awful dreams."

"Do you know," said Eunice, touching her palms together, "that even if you didn't play that touch football *nearly* as much as Jack you most surely were his superior at throwing *and* catching *and,* I shouldn't be surprised . . ."

She curled her toes.

". . . certain other endeavors."

The President looked a while at the drapes, mouthed, "Forgive her," to the long shadow, and he had the impression that it was moving a little toward the Leporello spinet. Then he let Eunice see that he was offended, and he said curtly, "What endeavors?"

"Executive limb"—Eunice finished on a high, plaintive interrogatory note—"pink down below endeavors?"

"By Jesus, Eunice," he cried, "there are"—quickly, quickly, he changed the tense—"there have been presidents guilty of worse sins . . . offenses . . . the magnitude of which . . . but history is happy to forgive them."

"I do believe," murmured Eunice, "that in regard to Jack you can't take a tease."

"Remember Jack's back problem," the President said, softening. "Don't you think those back spasms affected his passing and catching and made me look a lot better than I was? That was Jack's fate— falling a little short, just missing out. So he believed. More than once he told me that before he came into this world a wicked magician had him marked down for an unhappy destiny."

The President nodded to the long shadow, mouthed, "Bless you, boy-o."

"More than once, he told me that before his special unhappy destiny took him out he would fill up on pleasure. Hop from bed to bed till . . . ten thousand, Eunice; he wanted to score ten thousand times."

The President smiled, said, "Can you blame him?"

And Eunice, smiling back, answered, "Suppose not."

He became grave again. With a downward wave of the hand he said, "By Jesus, maybe Jack figured to trick history. Have the last laugh, too, on his magician. And why not, Eunice? See"—the President closed his eyes—"instead of history inscribing on him his offenses in statecraft, offenses like, oh, the Bay of Pigs . . . why, history has him down for touch football and sailing and . . . everything in skirts."

When he opened his eyes he saw that Eunice had closed hers. He touched a finger to the hard bone of her nose, but she kept them closed and said, "I do so much hate history. I do so much believe we should have . . . oh, instead of that endless and endless unconviviality . . ."

"Unconviviality," murmured the President.

Eunice gnawed on a thumb.

"Eunice, Eunice," he said, nearly singing her name, "what kind of history would you have?"

She fitted herself into the arc between his knees and his stomach. "Nice history, sweet history is all."

"Is all," he murmured, flipping the drawstring of his pajama bottom at her.

"Happy-dream history." She tapped her teeth with a thumbnail. "All the Pavel Gavrych evildoers dead and gone now and forever."

"No happy dreams in America. Not when you have to deal with . . ." The President had an impulse to say, "Jack's wicked magician," but he contented himself with "statecraft."

Moments passed.

"We live in dark times. Dark times, Eunice."

"Do we ever!"

"Headed straight for"—the President spread his mouth—"the edge of the world. Edge of the world, Eunice."

"I can get a picture," Eunice murmured. "Oh mercy, I do really see that!" Her eyes began to shine. " 'Edge of the world' gives me a silly-chilly, tingly-black, ghostly-evil picture of all the nations come alive and stepping out of this bigger-than-life map and sort of sliding down, down into bitter-cold nothing."

"Not really my line, anyway." The President's glance wandered. "Though in a way it is . . ."

"First goes China, China is sliding down, down . . ."

To the long shadow the President silently declared, "By Jesus, Jack, what if she's a bit of a ninny? A prattling ninny. Might just be that I wouldn't want her otherwise."

To Eunice he whispered, "Gavrych. 'Edge of the world' is what Gavrych said in my dream. My aftermath dream, when he—"

"Hush and hush!" Small lines suddenly branched all over Eunice's face. "Time enough for Mr. Pavel bloody-murder Gavrych at your press conference. Hear?"

"In my aftermath dream . . . before," the President started again, "Gavrych says 'edge of the world.' Also something about Russia, something . . ."

"Don't know all that much about Russia," Eunice said with an aspect of suffering and terror, "but it's a subject that's always been nasty to me."

"By Jesus, Eunice, I'll tell you something. The older I get and the more I learn about a subject, any subject—"

"And you know ever so much."

"More I learn the nastier it seems. More I learn the fewer pleasures are left me."

"I would truly hope for one exception," Eunice said wistfully.

"All the same," the President told the long shadow, "I wouldn't change her by a hair, by a cell."

In a gruff voice he said to Eunice, "By Jesus, I wouldn't change you by a hair, by a cell."

Then Eunice plumped the President's pillow and he plumped hers.

Then Eunice kissed the President's pillow, he kissed hers, and presently they were settled in such a way that each was a little shaken by the other's breathing.

"This," said Eunice, "need be no more than a cuddle. Cuddling can sometimes be quite enough."

"Nothing better in dark times, Eunice."

And Eunice's breath turned easy and regular and she sang, "You're the cream in my coffee."

And the President sang back, "You're the sugar in my tea."

"Nap-nap," Eunice said.

"Too much statecraft on my mind," the President said. "Statecraft and history."

But he must have dozed briefly, for the next thing he knew he was smiling and he felt wonderfully rested.

Then he heard a buzz, then a pleasant iron clanging, like a cowbell, and he sprang from his bed to silence the alarm of his Duluth Time-traveler.

Some two minutes later the phone rang.

It was the balding agent with the tortoiseshell sunglasses, and he said, "Time, Mr. President, time."

Though Eunice cried, "Women rightly require baths after womanly pleasure," the President pulled her into the shower with him.

"Never felt so quick, so ready, so alert," he exclaimed, and he decided to lather up in the shower and have his second shave without a mirror.

He did this so flawlessly that Eunice licked his cheeks, his upper lip, his neck.

Then when they were toweling and sprinkling lotions upon one another the President reeled off the names of the press people, making only two minor mistakes; and he reeled off also the number of Radio City casualties, including those given no chance of recovery; and he asked Eunice to try to trip him up with questions, any questions, about Matthew Dana, and she could not.

33

COUNSELOR: The driver says you were a bit depressed just now.
ORLOFSKY: Night should be illegal in your suburban shopping malls. At least the hours between two and three-fifteen A.M. Shattering—a drag, truly a downer.
COUNSELOR: Why then do you insist on so many late-night visits to the Crossroads mall? We'd scheduled—yes, I see that was to be your week for close analysis of the smaller municipalities off Interstate 301, for a meal at a thruway rest stop, for research into the customs of cookouts and lawn care and . . .
ORLOFSKY: I am too beat. Beat, thoroughly bushed, and unable to straighten my head from thoughts of Buy Fest, which I take to be your average American supermarket offering twenty-four-hour service.
COUNSELOR: Then sit, Vidyon. Let your capsule take effect.
ORLOFSKY: I fear my thoughts. They would weigh me down like a hundred Pacifics.
COUNSELOR: No need to pace, no call for trembling.
ORLOFSKY: My insights excite me so dangerously that I am now a little cracked. But if you allow me to go with it totally . . .
COUNSELOR: Of course. Have I ever done otherwise?
ORLOFSKY: Okay, man, I have news for you, and my news is that your American night has been expropriated by your unfulfilled. In

Buy Fest, during the hours between two and three-fifteen A.M., these unfulfilled revealed themselves to me, and I must tell the world before I bust a gut.

COUNSELOR: Tell me, Vidyon.

ORLOFSKY: They revealed themselves to me as weak and fearful, simple and ignorant, dazed and pained, showing on their faces a far-out solemnity. Mixed nationalities, mixed types, ageless and patient and nondescript as oxen. In their wake children . . .

COUNSELOR: In their wake?

ORLOFSKY: Try to dig that the children of the unfulfilled, perhaps from ancient custom, are never carried. They are compelled to walk behind, and the fathers and mothers will take their hands only to pull, drag, force them along at the cruelest pace.

COUNSELOR: Consider the lateness of the hour, Vidyon. Perhaps the fathers and mothers are rushing to shop and get home.

ORLOFSKY: No way. The unfulfilled of your twenty-four-hour supermarkets do not enter to buy and beat it. Torpor, gloom, and insupportable boredom drive them to the killing of your American time. Hey, man, I have charted their course and clocked them through the ceremonial hunting of a shopping cart, which is never less than seven minutes, for the one they seek is always at the farthest end of the store. Then slowly back to the cashier for some endless question about double coupon redemption. And the answer, theological, metaphysical in complexity, is measured and weighed and integrated and disputed among the unfulfilled.

COUNSELOR: I have the impression . . . Would I be right to say that you're describing a secular cathedral?

ORLOFSKY: Nice, neat, and you tune in truly on my wavelength. Go with my flow, then, if I tell you how worshipfully—worshipfully!—they congregate before the Buy Fest bulletin board. Lips moving, they forget to breathe as they spell out "Mobile Home, Priced to Sell"; "Wood and Chain-Link Fencing, Barely Used"; "Dependable Baby-sitter"; "Good Station Car." The children, however small, are wise enough not to stir, wise enough to remember how the father will shake them or twist an arm out of its socket, how the mother will cuff them on the fontanel, where the skull is most fragile.

COUNSELOR: But when they shop, what items do they seem to favor?

ORLOFSKY: Various chips and bits of cheese. Pale, pulpy breads. Instant coffees whose grains look like mouse droppings. Nothing natural, nothing that belongs to any meal on this earth. And while they could properly take an express lane their custom is to join the longest queue. Hey, and if this queue moves more slowly than a glacier they are never restive. And if the cashier gives them surly words or short change they grin and bear it with quiet fortitude.

COUNSELOR: You must intercede for them, Vidyon. You must speak out for the unfulfilled.

ORLOFSKY: If I could find some pure-souled man of American power—okay, watch my speed, see how quickly I'd bind him to my feelings.

COUNSELOR: The President is such a man, Vidyon. He will hear you, I promise; he will take account—and soon.

ORLOFSKY: Like hey, like wow!

COUNSELOR: Time, though, for our needle.

There was a thrilling click as the President closed the chromed steel binder on his notes.

His heart expanded, his breathing thinned, and some of the words he had inexplicably underscored and circled stormed his mind: power; system; international; savage; never; virulence; hideous; deception.

At "deception" the pit of his stomach turned cold.

By Jesus, he thought, a little hearty, heavy male banter might set me right.

Therefore he got up from his chair in near-perfect quiet, circled stealthily behind the makeup people, and when he was sure Joel Baskier had spotted him, declared raucously, "Your resignation as press secretary is happily accepted. Happily!" Then he massaged Baskier's neck and said in an even more raucous voice, "Might be a good time to announce a revival of the slave trade."

Baskier gave a snort of amusement and the President whinnied with laughter.

Just when the President was straining for more laughter the blond agent with the rimless sunglasses wagged four fingers at him.

And the balding agent with the tortoiseshell sunglasses cried, "Four minutes, now, Mr. President. Four!"

To loosen his muscles the President did three knee-bends.

To liberate his vocal chords he quietly crooned, "Father, rest well; Mother, rest well; Nanny Dora, rest well."

He was pressing himself terribly hard to call back their faces when Eunice came skipping over, put her mouth near his ear, and made sounds like a kitten at its saucer.

For the first time in many years he whispered to her, "You're a swell kid."

"I do rightly believe you're a swell kid, too," she whispered back.

He suddenly realized that they most likely belonged to the last generation which would say "swell" naturally and sincerely and generously; which would remember, for that matter, trolley cars, factory whistles sounding off at eleven A.M. on Armistice Day; doors with frosted glass; legless veterans wearing overseas caps, ruptured ducks; and the realization filled him with sweetness and sorrow.

". . . eagles," he heard Baskier say.

The President inclined his head.

"It's your look, sir. Hold on to that look." Baskier turned to Eunice. "The look of"—he put his hands behind him, glided them up and down and together as if they were wings—"eagles. Their pride, their angry strength."

Phones rang.

Lights twittered.

One by one the television screens went dirty white.

"Think eagles, sir," Baskier said. "Think eagles and angry strength. The silent, ominous power of America at the end of its patience."

"Sure," the President answered vaguely.

Feeling very strongly in charge, he turned the heavy silver embossed handle of the door himself and stepped out onto the mild rose carpeting.

Inside of three steps he lengthened his stride, exulting in the mystery of being, in the generations and generations of ancestors who had met and loved and mated and set him on this planet, given him this destiny.

Near that long lighted mirror on the left he commanded himself as usual to avert his eyes, and as usual he could not.

But he was pretty well pleased by his reflection. Still blessed with Mother's healthy color, with the breadth and vigor of Father's frame.

Only he was all at once bothered by that look of angry strength.

And so when he had entered the East Room and laid his chrome steel binder on the lectern, he cursed Joel Baskier.

Burn in thirty hells, you meeching, propitiating, fawning, froggy-eyed, uncoordinated fatass!

Does he think he impresses me when he sucks a cold pipe and calls me "chief" and cons me about his "mystical camera instinct"? How about bursting, imploding, crumbling to dust, next time you stick me with that artsy-craftsy crap!

But at that moment—oh, bless her, Jack; oh, Father, Mother, Nanny Dora, fill her years with blossoms and sunbeams—Melissa Siampa came to his rescue.

In a pure, expectant, piercing little voice, from an aisle seat, third row right, she cried, "Hi, there."

His eyes brimmed. A smile started, increased as he studied her face, her marvelous mobile face! Oh the height of that brow! How many months and corpses since she interviewed me? And the way she breezed in and made herself at home in the Oval Office. Still not thirteen, not till March, April, if I remember my private birthday gift last year.

Melissa half rose from her chair.

She's changed her look. No bangs. Pencils clipped like barrettes to her hair, and another, yes, see, tucked over her left ear.

Once again Melissa cried, "Hi, there."

Then she bit a knuckle—by Jesus, just like Harry, she's picked that up from Harry—and added, "Hi, there, *sir*."

The President counted off three seconds, and when he observed that almost everyone was having a hard time keeping a straight face he touched his teeth to his upper lip, raised a shoulder JFK style, and said, "Well, well, hi, there, Ms. . . . Ms. . . ."

He frowned and frowned at the seating plan, pretending her name was unknown to him, hard to pronounce.

"Matilda, no, Melissa . . . Melissa Siampa, representing the *Lemwell School Log*. Hi, there, Ms. Melissa Siampa."

He and Melissa cleared their throats simultaneously.

Then the President slid his opening statement from the chromed steel binder.

"Ladies and gentlemen, I have a statement I now wish to—"

But in the rear, there was a party with his hand up already. Some frazzle-faced bearded bantam. Dressed in gorgeous green velvet like a huntsman in an opera. Dressed to be noticed. And though the President did not acknowledge him, he spoke up anyway.

"Thank you, child and Mr. President, for the exchange of your 'hi.' A beautiful American word which I dig, dig absolutely, and which sends me fully."

"Does it?" the President replied, trying for measured sarcasm. "We're pleased, Mr. . . . ."

With stifled anger he searched the seating plan. But there was no name in the little box for frazzle-face. Only his affiliation: Adolphus News Bureau. By Jesus, how's that for sloppiness? Too busy thinking about your Edward R. Murrow Memorial Lecture to make sure every frigging box has proper ID? Not getting away with this, Mr. Joel Mencken Baskier, Mr. Journalism-Is-a-Sacred-Calling. My word on it. Before God, next week I'll have you swigging your Maalox at PBS. Developing documentaries on . . . on bird binding.

"It is a beautiful word," the President said.

Only since when was Baskier guilty of such bonehead blunders? Granted, the President reflected, he's a prick. A flat, self-satisfied, closet liberal prick. But a meticulous prick. Drives you crazy with stupid detail. And didn't I see him going over every box? Last night, late, late. No matter. He'd have checked twenty times before dawn, probably before taking his first piss.

"A word," he said to frazzle-face, "which we Americans also love."

Why, this has to be another bit of Baskier business, he decided. Pulls this shit every so often to make me faster on my feet.

"Is any word more American?"

How does he put it? His crazy line? "Show the six-packers you're fast on your feet and you can dance with the devil." Then help me, Father, Mother, Nanny Dora. For I'm locked in. No choice now. Let go, wing it, quickly, quickly. . . .

And the President looked at Melissa, winked, thought "folksy," thought "vox populi."

And trying for a back-country twang he said, "Looks to me like we Americans surely proved—and it did cost us, it cost us dear—how much we preferred our 'hi' to their 'heil.' "

He heard "Good, okay," he heard "All *right,*" he heard "That was the Germans, that was the forties."

And Melissa was adoring him with her eyes.

And frazzle-face was nodding and rocking.

The President thought, What about it, Baskier? Do I have them? Yes, I'd say I have them all right, the six-packers, the hoi polloi, the null and void. At this moment mine from sea to shining sea.

The President thought, Now hold them, now pour it on, now dance with the devil, now dive full throttle with the sun at your back.

And staring straight up at the violet and blue crystals of the giant chandelier, in a voice of ringing righteousness and sore oppression, he said, "I have a statement to make now." Too hard, too shivery, too vibrant? Do you think so, Jack? Then best stretch the vowels, soften the consonants. Bring them down gently, gently to Dana, to the dead.

"You'll have noticed a number of new faces tonight."

A moment of terrifying dead gray despair. But it passed, it passed.

"We've invited, for the first time in any press conference, representatives of the foreign media as well as a number of younger men and women whose writings in their school papers and magazines are among the best and brightest of this generation."

Oh, Judge and Maker of Men, Creator of History and Statecraft and what Harry calls Realpolitik, oh, do not fuck me up with doubt.

"Since both groups have rather consistently celebrated Gavrych and condemned this administration, we wish them to understand why our patience—America's patience—is nearly at an end, stretched to its limit."

He imagined Nanny Dora tweaking his nose, asking kindly and a little sternly, "Dear lad, no more fibs, I want no more fibs if you please. You've had your six for this day."

"We wish them to understand that the nature and pattern of recent events, brutal events, can no longer be met with simple diplomatic restraint, with mere expressions of shock and outrage. We wish them to understand why the most recent and brutal events in Radio City compel me to take a hard but inescapable course of action."

He heard "NATO maneuvers, what else?" He heard "Yellow alert?" He heard "All *right!*"

And Melissa's mouth twitched and trembled.

And frazzle-face gripped his beard and tugged it twice.

Then the President stretched out his hands, two strong hands, and when he was certain all present had seen how remarkably steady they were he clasped them, but not prayerfully and not so tightly that the knuckles might whiten, and thinking "edge of the world," he went on.

"This hard but inescapable course of action was taken early this morning."

Oh, didn't you tell me once, Jack, that in this business we get only a few short hours of truth, or what passes for truth?

"Our ambassador has been recalled."

Look of eagles, look of angry strength.

"As of this afternoon, earlier this afternoon, we have restricted diplomatic relations with the Soviet Union."

Some of those present did not stir.

Some drew breath as if their nostrils were burning.

Some looked fractious, cranky, like overtired children.

Oh, Father, Mother, Nanny Dora, the President thought, why did you dazzle me by the example of your exceptional virtue? For I fail to see, I honestly fail to see the use of truth and a good heart on earth. I'm sorry to have to say this, only . . . only, by Jesus, while you were training me to the potty, hymn books, public service, you might have thrown in a crash course on practical wickedness, on the elements of deceit, and given my soul a little more stamina to dance with the devil.

But after he had read in a subdued voice the brief and bitter note that had gone to Gavrych; and after he pictured the six-packers, the hoi polloi, the louts and lunkheads, moving, no, scuttling by millions and millions toward the edge of the world, the edge of the world, he felt lighter and almost at peace.

To Melissa he silently declared, Child, I pray that on this night you start learning how to believe in nothing.

To frazzle-face he silently declared, Who the fuck wants you! Needs you! Get lost, you and your fucking Europe. I hope mud and slime cover your bastard continent. I hope wild dogs shit and piss on your museums, your parliaments, your stinking mobs, your crazy idea-merchants who just won't let up on us, who keep busting our balls and spilling our blood with their sinister notions of statecraft and history. . . .

Then disseminating an air of heroic authority and almost, almost believing that everything he was about to set forth had happened or might as well have happened in just that way, the President gazed grandly upon all present and took the first question.

"I am . . . Leon Pirenne."

Teeth like long thorns. Nasty little twitch to the nose. As if he's been sniffing wine corks for a thousand years.

"Of . . . *Aujourd'hui.*"

As if he's the only significant human event of this age.

"The restriction of diplomatic relations with the Soviet Union— no doubt, most surely a momentous and consequential act."

He's ready to spill satire. I know you'd match him, Jack, but I'm best off displaying self-containment, inner vulnerability.

"A momentous and consequential act . . . ."

Good, perfect. Advantage mine. Shouldn't have repeated that phrase, you Gallic shit. Frowns of reprimand on five, six brows. Yes, Jack, I still count for something, and not just with the press. O Shining Republic, O Democratic Vista, I'm not much, but can you do better?

"The act, Monsieur President, the restriction of relations, causes me . . . certain bafflement."

Here it comes. Take your best shot, fuckhead!

"Such a step, you understand, is formal announcement by a nation that it has been pushed to the last extreme."

The President stretched his face and, playing to all present, said, "It is formal announcement by *this* nation, Mr. Pirenne, of its anger— and of its angry strength."

A happy little noise came out of Melissa's mouth.

Frazzle-face tipped an imaginary hat.

"Such a step, Mr. President, is to be viewed as the prelude to armed hostilities. I hold this to be . . . a logical view."

You do? Oh, what a logic-loving race! By Jesus, how you love logic! Yes, nearly as much as Jack claimed.

"However, since Soviet military power has been from the ascendancy of Pavel Gavrych in shambles, what purpose to such a step? Do you not consider that the world must see it as a piece of empty aggressive . . . theater? Do you not consider that the posture of . . . a nuclear Rome must surely preclude fruitful political dialogue with Pavel Gavrych and the Soviet people?"

Pirenne sat, crossed his legs, and jiggled a knee.

"Do I think," the President said with the strong frown JFK used for deepest reflection, "that this step, the restriction of diplomatic relations, precludes dialogue with Gavrych, the Soviet people?"

But I do, he longed to say.

And he longed to say, Father, Mother, Nanny Dora, this is how the cross of history and statecraft is borne upon me, this is the consummation of all these months, all these corpses.

And he longed to say, Wait and see, only wait and see how the Soviet people start asking themselves what awful things Gavrych must have done to so provoke America.

And he longed to say that presently American bombers and warships would be violating Soviet airspace, Soviet territorial waters, that these incidents would multiply in audacity till the powerless Gavrych-fuddled Soviet masses suffered confusion and alarm, till they started asking themselves, "How much longer will we endure this shaming of our motherland?"

And he longed to say that they would pine for the old ways, the old bureaucrats, the old tyrants, the old war dogs, the old fierce military might that had locked the West, the world, into holy terror.

And he longed to say that they would rearm frantically, frantically, that before too long, please God before the next election, everything would be exactly, exactly, exactly as it had been, that from sea to shining sea the six-packers would settle back into the sweet boring bliss of the permanent war economy.

Nevertheless as the cameras moved in for a close-up he looked gently, grievously upon Melissa.

And he turned toward frazzle-face, and he made his breathing shaky, and he spoke as if with a quailing of the heart.

Saying, "We were the first to wish Mr. Gavrych well, to pledge him absolute support in the building of what he called 'a righteous politics, a righteous human order.' "

Saying, "In the months that followed . . . terrorism."

Saying, "We held back, restrained ourselves, while he and his American supporters organized, clearly planned and organized and carried out, the murders of some of our country's most beloved and renowned."

Saying, "We believed, tried, willed ourselves to believe, that in time Mr. Gavrych might control his hard-liners. We prayed—I am not ashamed to say this—yes, we prayed that a righteous politics, a righteous human order, would somehow come to pass."

Saying, "These prayers were answered . . . how? By wanton slaughter. By the massacre of the innocents, American innocents."

Saying, "We have endured. . . . Our endurance . . . We shall not wait in confusion and alarm, asking ourselves, 'What next, what will follow the horror of Radio City?' "

Then he extended his right hand and closed it into something a little less than a fist.

Then he opened it and gestured, palm upward, at Melissa, at frazzle-face.

On his countenance he put pain, reproach, and he sought to give a sense of the loneliness of his office, of how he was sorely oppressed by the misdoings of nations.

Hey Jack, hey Harry, the President thought, this realpolitik stuff . . . I'm not Bismarck, but I'm handling it. By Jesus, I can handle it!

But all the same a bit of sad irony, a light philosophical moment might now be in order, he advised himself.

Therefore he said, "I've concluded—that Mr. Gavrych's doctrine of 'peace, sympathy, brotherhood, and purest joy' is all too characteristic of Soviet politics. It embraces the universe—except, that is, for America."

He saw Melissa nodding and waving; frazzle-face pounding a knee.

He heard, "How about that for a lead?" and "Perfect for a lead."

Then the President tucked his chin down, fluttered a hand at all present, and set himself for the next question.

Only there was shoving and disorderly shouting from the row of younger people, and someone knocked against a mike, causing such awful feedback that he grimaced and flinched and felt pangs in his teeth.

But over the next instant it seemed to the President that Jack was directing him to look pointedly at his watch, and so he did.

And when he did it he had a piercing intuition of what he would say, and so he said it.

"I haven't heard the class bell but I notice . . . Yes, I notice the students are getting restless."

Extraordinary quiet. Then pleasant laughter, and almost everybody looked well pleased.

Therefore the President took his time.

"Restless students," he declared playfully, studying the seating plan, wondering which of the five college editors would have been happiest to feed on his heart.

Poor, dumb, independent-minded, Gavrych-fuddled kids, he reflected. Don't you know, how come you don't know your excitements and affirmations and embattled postures won't make a mouse-drop's difference? Won't give you a whole life or save you from what is now being imposed upon you or put you in touch with infinite space.

Still taking his time, the President tugged an earlobe and waggled a finger straight up in the air.

He kept the finger aloft while he said in the boyish side-of-the-mouth style Jack favored for commencement addresses, "Now one of your restless students is from . . . from the Stonybrook University paper, which I understand—do I have it right?—thinks this administration's dealings with Mr. Gavrych have been dishonorable, less than honorable anyway, and wants me to return the honorable degree conferred on me."

He scowled and in his severest voice said, "Forget it."

Then in a kinder voice he said, "Can't do that. But . . . but I can at least take a question from a Stonybrook press person."

And he snapped the finger down and leveled it.

At a short, fat . . . no, you'd have to fairly say "compact," a squat, compact, stolid girl as shapeless as a hydrant. The kind Jack used to call "Thumper" and "Hormone."

"Sir," she cried from high up in her nose, "the piece you refer to, my piece, never said about your dealings with him, Mr. Gavrych, they were dishonorable or less than honorable. The word I used"—voice took flight, returned by way of her sinus cavities—"was 'dissemble.' Okay? You can dissemble and still not be really or altogether dishonorable."

For some reason her direct, humorless, ungiving way amused the President, and he uttered a little laugh. "Okay," he answered, trying to capture her cadence. "I stand corrected, Ms. Langer"—he glanced at the seating plan—"Ms. Francine Langer."

But with a sour, lidded look she let him know that his charm couldn't matter less. And why should it? the President thought.

Charm's about as much use to this Thumper, this Hormone, as lipstick or stills from *I Wanted Wings* or Eunice's happy dreams.

She started slowly, so slowly that the President wondered if she was taking her time because he had taken his. Monotonous, implacable, she said, "My question isn't directly bearing on your act of restricting diplomatic relations with the Soviet Union but on one of the causes for it, okay. I would like to hear more on the Radio City terrorism act, especially—"

She raised her palms like a waitress hoisting a tray.

"—Matthew Dana."

She scratched hard at a skin eruption that fringed her forehead. Then she curled her fingers, studied her nails, continued to study them, and suddenly spoke in a strong, deep voice.

"I understand that a Matthew Dana postmortem"—she clicked her teeth—"wasn't done or performed by New York City medical examiner authorities although it's the law, although they did everybody else's body, all the many other victims."

The President shut his eyes against her, against the red-and-black haze that was beating with his pulse.

"According to the investigative reporting series of *Daylight* magazine, his body, the corpse, was removed and mysteriously expropriated away under highly top-secret orders from where it had been put or placed with the other bodies."

"So many bodies," said the President sonorously, "so very many bodies."

Ancient of Days, he reflected, dancing devil, whoever, give me a hand. Help me divert her. For this one is trouble. Get with it, quickly, quickly. Pump fake feeling into what's left of this soul lest the six-packers smell blood.

"Lots of bodies, okay"—she moved one hand clockwise, the other counterclockwise—"but the body I was questioning about, the body wherein *Daylight* magazine has launched a highly brilliant investigative reportage series, is one body only, the Matthew Dana body."

The President thought, So be it. The bodies, then. I'll go with the bodies.

He bowed his head, shook it, kept his mouth still and strong.

And as if with his last breath of life he said, "Yes, there were so very many bodies that . . ."

He thought, Abide with me.

He thought, This is it.

"... that it was necessary to bring them to an armory, to the Seventy-first Street armory."

He was glad to see a long sobbing sigh shaking Melissa; and when he looked at frazzle-face he saw that his lips were moving, that he appeared to be saying, "Terrible, terrible, terrible."

Then the President stared at the great chandelier. Though his eyes burned he kept himself from blinking while he said, "This armory, enormous as it is ... much larger than this East Room, so much larger, ... still it could hardly hold so many bodies, so very many."

He closed his eyes. When he opened them again he felt clearsighted, hypnotic, subtle, absolutely attuned to history and statecraft.

He thought, Look, Jack. Look at this Thumper's cheeks puff out, at the way she avoids my glance. How elegantly I've addled and distracted and rattled her!

He thought, There's such a power flowing, surging through me. What say, Jack? Shall I excite the six-packers with some corny rhetoric, with a nice cheap shot at Gavrych?

"Sympathy," he began, biting down hard on the last syllable.

He tossed back his head, clawed the air in front of his chin.

"Peace, sympathy, brotherhood, and purest joy. Ah, indeed. Ah, our thanks, Mr. Gavrych. Our wholehearted thanks to you and your American followers. Yes, you've helped us understand something. ..."

Pausing, the President sent a subliminal apology to Harry. For he was about to lift a phrase from him.

"We understand, and I hope, I pray, we understand this now and forever, that the Russian character, the essential Russian character is ... as murderous as it is mystical."

He caught one, two, three sullen, reprimanding looks. Otherwise thought-clouded faces, respectful faces, awed, absolutely respectful faces laboring under the dire and powerful consequences of history and statecraft.

And at this moment the President was moved by the Thumper. Did anything, would anything, come easily to someone who stood that way? Raising one leg, now another as if ... as if her underthings were binding. An overweight, breastless by-blow of the sixties believing she could take on an old realpolitik hand. Not the likes of Jack, of course, but still a top gun of realpolitik. Ah, stupid girl, buttocky, cause-ridden, conspiracy-seeking girl, hold still. Time to finish you off.

And he wondered, Shall I use the children on her?

Can I sink so low?

The children, by Jesus, the children!

"These days, these last days," he said, "I've not slept well, Francine, Ms. Langer. Thinking, praying for—not ashamed to use the word, no—Mr. Gavrych's latest victims. So many, so very many who might have been spared had only America and the West been less open and generous and eager, had we better understood the Soviet system and character. So many, so very many . . ."

From the depths of his diaphragm he breathed out the word, ". . . children."

By Jesus, I might have made good use here and now of *The Washington Post* photos. Mounted that four-page spread on a bulletin board behind me. Or just that one shot—a toddler, ringlets, kissing his pony.

"Hundreds, those hundreds of children who, now and forever, are not to know . . . peace, sympathy, brotherhood, and purest joy."

Melissa was glowering at the Thumper.

Frazzle-face had a hand around his throat.

"Let's have, let's take . . ."

The President was about to say, "You, your question," to Zach Boardman, *USA Today,* when he heard from the Thumper again.

She was hunched over, arms hanging at her sides.

Her lips smacked together.

"Sir, I have a follow-up," she said. "Will you accept my follow-up even if I forgot the custom and protocol of immediately mentioning it before?"

Smiling, the President answered, "Sure—long as I don't have to give back that honorary degree."

This time she smiled back. Why? Ancient of Days, why?

"My follow-up question is from *Daylight* magazine also, from a forthcoming number I read"—she swung an arm toward all present—"upon my recent hiring to join their research staff."

"Good for you," the President told her, forcing a throb of loving kindness into his voice. "And good for them."

Her smile increased. A peculiar uneasiness tore at the President.

"Can you comment on the overwhelming feeling *Daylight* staff got from Dana's employers—and they went twenty years back, okay, to long before Gavrych—the feeling that Dana had absolutely no desire to change the world or be even part of it? Like he would again and again say, 'Deliver me from belief.' Can you comment on how such a personality type becomes practically an instant Gavrych true believer?"

He silently prayed, Stand by me, Jack. Help me surpass myself. Then the luster of Melissa's look renewed him.

"Sure. What you're asking . . . what you're asking," he picked up, "is really what's called nowadays by some of your higher educators, 'psychohistory.' " That little touch of down-home derision eased the pressure in his chest. "Way I see it, I guess, and I guess I see it, oh, not as a higher educator but as a simple president hoping to hold on to his poor old honorary degree, looks to me as if Dana . . . For Dana I think true belief or belief of any kind never entered into it, wasn't a real factor. I'd say, yes, it was more a matter of what he *didn't* believe in—and he sure as anything didn't believe in . . ."

Softly, softly now.

". . . America."

And pause.

"Stalin, Gavrych . . . Looks to me like it never did matter, not then, not now, under whose dogma and doctrines he could injure America, long as he could bring it suffering. And also, let's remember this: his motive of revenge. His wanting to settle a score with Barnard Mackenzie and a fine magazine, a grand *American* magazine."

Should I have dropped some "G"s? the President wondered. Did I strike the proper pitch of folksiness?

But he must have done well enough.

For all present were writing away, even Melissa and frazzle-face.

And the Thumper's look . . . By Jesus, certainly more sympathetic.

She rose on her toes, came down heavily, said, "My second follow-up point for your comment, Mr. President . . ."

Her voice! Cracking with anger. Deeply wrong then about that sympathetic look. It was meant—oh, Ancient of Days, of course—for Dana, for Dana!

". . . is about the possibility of Dana being, like, sick, and whether this possibility, if so, had a bearing upon his body's disappearance prior to postmortem."

"Dana sick?"

Under the lectern his feet moved, moved, and notions of fainting away went through his head.

"Sick?" he said again, thinking, Petty or not, I'll see you never make it beyond secretary!

And he took such pleasure from the thought that he was able to go on serenely, sarcastically. "This may be old-fashioned, I suppose, but it's my feeling, now and forever, that any American who would bring injury upon his nation is . . . sick."

But she too was serene. And she would not be trapped into sarcasm. In her absolute happiness he saw that she had no need of sarcasm.

"Old-fashioned," he threw out vaguely. "Not one of your higher educators, your psychohistorians."

She ignored this.

"Sir, I was referring to physical sickness, okay. As shown by medical group insurance blood workup forms which Dana's custodial maintenance person, Mr. Prisco, forgot to mail out for Dana's wife. He, Mr. Prisco, turned them over to our health and science editor."

Up and down, up and down on her toes.

"Our health and science editor interviewed the authorizing physician, Dana's doctor, who hinted definitely of a Dana illness, who, however, was reluctant to speak further until a medical ethics determination could be obtained."

Noise inside my head. Don't give way to the knocking, the ringing. Lost if I tune out.

"The authorizing physician, Dana's doctor, then contacted our health and science editor that he had received this medical ethics determination which was favorable and he therefore could discuss Dana's case. An appointment of two days' hence was made."

Father was right to behave as he did in my Radio City dream. Running from me, taking another son.

"Upon arrival for this appointment he heard from the doorman of a break-in and murder of the doctor, the receptionist likewise, by stabbing. Also there was total office ransacking and total disappearance of medical records."

Ah, beautiful, well done, Harry, was the President's first thought.

His second was, Father, Mother, Nanny Dora, remember me as I was then, as I was then.

"Can you comment, sir?"

She swayed, went up on her toes, and puffed out one cheek.

She filled his eyes.

She became all that he could see in the world.

". . . Dana's physical illness, Mr. President."

Take notice of the creature that can bring me down, Jack! Have a look at what terrifies me!

She clicked her teeth twice, she moved her shoulder like a wrestler.

"Likewise the break-in and the stabbing, also . . ."

And the President had an inspiration.

Mean, nasty.

Perhaps the meanest, nastiest single act of my life.

But for the sake of realpolitik, in the service of history and state-craft, he set about mimicking her.

Vindictively. Obviously. For all to see.

He too clicked his teeth, moved his shoulders, went up and down on his toes.

He too swayed and puffed out one cheek while he said, "This is a most inappropriate time to deal with the problems of our cities, even with a major metropolitan problem of crisis proportion like crime."

Again he clicked his teeth, again he moved his shoulders.

"Let's hope," he finished, "let's all hope that the perpetrators are speedily apprehended."

He heard, "Hardly blame," "Isn't she a case?" "Three credits in communications and she thinks . . ."

And when the Thumper was seated the President noticed Melissa and frazzle-face laughing to themselves and clicking their teeth.

Father, Mother, Nanny Dora, pardon. But she had me scared; she cast me into the gross darkness of terror.

A poor sort of victory, they chided.

A victory nevertheless. As Harry would say.

But no dancing with the devil. Not till I have a hold on my nerves. Right now step lightly, play it safe. Stick to the Rose Garden regulars, the brotherhood of bull.

I'll go with . . .

And there!

Glory to your gorgeous alligator loafers, your debonair stance. What's it to me if they call you the duck-billed platitude?

I'll lay odds, the President thought, extending both arms at him, that my pulse rate is down to seventy. Maybe a big seventy-five.

The strong underlip was pushed out, curled.

"Jason Axelbank, ABC News."

"Jace," the President murmured.

"Mr. President, our ABC special, *Gavrych's Undeclared War*. May I speak to one of its segments?"

George Brent used to play his type.

"The closing segment, sir. To judge by the mountains of mail from our heartland, our inner cities as well, it struck a responsive chord in Americans."

Casts forth the same kind of profound calm as George Brent. A serious, kindly American gentleman. Every hair, every thought in place. Made for long wear and hard use, like my Duluth Timetraveler.

"In that closing segment, sir, some first-graders stand with their teachers near Radio City. Each child is removing one mitten and shivering, for it's a cold afternoon."

"Brutal weather all that week," said the President. He drew a long breath, let his voice drop. "A foretaste of . . . things to come."

"Things to come," Axelbank repeated, spacing the words, investing them with solemnity and reverence. Then, eyes fixed steadfastly upon the President, he said, "Into each frozen unmittened hand the teacher puts a daisy, and each child holds the daisy against his or her heart. They recite, sir, the Pledge of Allegiance. But one lad runs off, and his teacher catches him under the Radio City marquee, close to those blackened steel shutters, those padlocks and ominous signs warning of danger. He wishes—to a child a simple, logical wish—only to enter that tragic place, to leave his daisy inside, closer to those who might one day have been his friends. 'My forever flower,' he calls his daisy."

The strong underlip was pushed out, curled.

"I must tell you, sir, that his daisy, that 'forever flower,' has taken the hearts of American parents by storm. Tens of thousands have written in the hope of seeing Radio City, presently a tragic site, re-

stored as a national shrine—a shrine where their children can enter
and leave behind forever flowers. I would like to know, Mr. President . . ."

The strong underlip was pushed out, curled.

"Sir, I think all America wants to know when that site of national
tragedy will reopen and become the national shrine our children,
America's children, long to enter with . . . their forever flowers."

Father, Mother, Nanny Dora, the President exulted, watch me
handle this. Something told me to prepare, and I did, by Jesus I did!
At every interminable briefing I demanded more, more! I pored over
papers and monographs on that awful stuff till I was long past caring,
till I was numb, then almost casual, almost a little remote. Harry's
trick. He calls it "a soul bypass."

And he had a momentary impulse to take America into his confidence, to tell the six-packers that when you understand the fragility
of lung and brain—how easily the one can burst, the other literally
boil—why, you're practically divine. At least a little more than mortal.
But he held himself to a tone of grieved uncertainty, and he began by
saying, "Nothing I want more than to have those children take their
forever flowers into Radio City."

He stooped slightly, pressed his lips shut.

"With me, please God, leading them."

Melissa's eyes were wet.

"Only I just can't say when Radio City will be safe for them.
Months probably. As much as a year."

Frazzle-face had a finger to his lips and he was shaking his head
at some whisperers.

"You see, America doesn't know certain things. Awful things. I
took upon myself . . . Yes, perhaps I took too much upon myself. . . ."

He looked at Axelbank and with a contorted face looked away.

"But if I've held back telling America the full truth about what
Mr. Gavrych put into Matthew Dana's hands, just how lethal it was,
it's only because I felt . . . with all my heart . . . Yes, I'm the President.
Let me have the awful burden. Let America be spared a while longer."

Tilt the head back a bit, he instructed himself.

"Easy enough, I suppose, to have spoken up last Tuesday. Easy
enough, over the next three days, to have added to the shock and
horror, the violation of our national soul. Out of strength or cow-
ardice we decided—No! I decided—and I pray I was right—that

America had borne about as much as it should have to bear for a while."

By Jesus, the President thought, I very nearly believe this. What a curious piece of work, the mind!

"Forgive me if I've misjudged the moral and spiritual strength of free men in a free society."

He clasped his hands before his face and nodded slowly.

"What Mr. Gavrych put into Matthew Dana's hands—the hands of a traitor who stood in court and said, 'I want to drive America out of my soul'—is known by the Soviet scientists who developed it . . . as 'hell's breath.' "

He pretended that he could not go on.

Then for perhaps three seconds he had no need to pretend.

Then there were hands, hands, and he was once again absolutely with it.

When Karen Lister, *Cleveland Plain Dealer,* twice tried and failed to pronounce the word, the President came close to saying, "Fat got your tongue?"

But he took pity on the white-on-white hair, the coarser white color she'd given her mastifflike face, and the bandy legs which had to carry that weight around.

Therefore he bestowed a glance of wistful humanity upon her and said "polyhydromethylamine" so slowly and quietly that it stopped her and made all present listen the more carefully.

Then the President stared into the far distance and in the same slow and quiet way said, "Right, quite right, Karen. One and the same, hell's breath and polyhydromethylamine. Understand, please, that if I don't congratulate you on your memory it's because . . . I suppose because I never wanted to believe, no president wants to let himself believe, that he must one day bring America . . ."

To the edge of the world, he wanted to say.

"Such news," he said instead, "news which in his experience, the experience of history and statecraft, has no place."

They looked at each other; they continued to look at each other.

"Sir . . ."

This time she was not stabbing the air with her pencil, and the haughtiness about her mouth was gone.

"Mr. President, these last few days the mood of our country . . . You must know, it will not have escaped you . . . They're united in the wish that you would give our scientists—*our* scientists, sir—permission to proceed at once and develop . . ."

They looked at each other; they continued to look at each other. Then the President folded his arms.

He said, "No, Karen. No permission, no sanction for hell's breath. Before God. Not ever, not ever . . ."

What a piece of curiosity, the mind, he thought. For only now did he remember the nine thousand kilos stored in Wyoming.

Father, Mother, Nanny Dora, I honestly welcome any suggestions. Tell me how I may keep steadfast against realpolitik.

"Only seek above all other good the kingdom and justice of our Heavenly Father," they counseled.

And he took the next question.

For once that tail-chasing cynical Amos Dempster, Media Post Network, isn't out to affront and humble me, the President noted.

No, he's a mask of misery. And so far he hasn't hoisted those hayseed suspenders or fingered his cowlick to signal his fans that he's about to get my goat.

"Hard to frame my question without a personal statement," Dempster was saying. He put his hands into his hind pockets, bent forward slightly. "My good fortune, sir, to learn my craft under Buck, as great a magazine man and teaching editor as America will ever produce. . . ."

"No doubt of it, Amos," the President declared.

Dempster's head started shaking; he smiled as if to tell the President that he was just a hardnosed old newshound unaccustomed to bringing forth such feelings.

"Sir, quite a few of us here worked for Buck Mackenzie, studied under Buck, and we remember . . . Along with most everything about Buck, we remember what he'd say after he landed on us. 'Look here,' he'd say, very seriously, 'this is your destiny. I'm only an agent of the destiny your soul was creating while you were still a babe in a blanket.' "

Blood came to his face.

"My question, two questions really, is if Buck . . . In light of Buck's personal belief about destiny, did he have a glimmer that his life was taken by Matthew Dana and that he was being . . . delivered up, he'd have thought, to *that* man? Because if he had that glimmer . . . As I and a lot of us here can't but see it . . . No matter what hell's breath did to him, that glimmer would have had to be his worst suffering."

"I can appreciate that," declared the President. And he was drifting into thoughts of destiny and babes in blankets when he noticed Dempster hoisting his suspenders and touching his cowlick.

Therefore he braced himself for trouble, but there was no need.

"My second question, Mr. President, concerns the videotapes by *Here* Metropolitan Service. I understand you've seen some of it, such portions as remain. . . ."

It should have moved me more, the President reflected. People fell, people fell and I kept thinking they don't look right. The style, the expression, the drama, the posture's simply not right. Still fixed on memories of my old movies, I suppose.

"Can you tell us, and I can certainly imagine how painful this might be for you, from your impressions of the videotapes, if Buck . . . Can you say if Buck . . . ?"

In a terrible but brave voice the President said, "Was he spared? At least spared from . . . ?"

He allowed a moment to pass, another.

He looked at Melissa, at frazzle-face, and he tried to bring to his eyes the kind of faraway desolate shining that was in their eyes.

He said at last, "I'm afraid not, Amos. No."

He moved his arm like a blind man.

"Now understand, Amos, why I watched those tapes—and if it please God neither I nor any other president will see their like again— and what I and my experts were watching for."

They fell, they fell. Nothing on their faces. Or no more than different kinds of nothingness. "Why do they look the same?" I kept asking Harry. "How can it be that they all look the same?" He said they were corporate types and the faces of corporate types suffer a paucity of expression.

"My experts and I wanted to be very, very sure that the monster Mr. Gavrych had set loose upon us, upon America, was Matthew Dana. Because hell's breath, I must tell you, does things. It does things to faces, bodies. But Dana's movements, now when you compare them with newsreels of his trial—certain patterns of movements are absolutely indisputable. Same as voice patterns, they tell me. Yes, at his trial he never appeared in court without an old briefcase, and he always held it in the way he held that box of crazy résumés he made sure to leave around. Those crazy résumés . . ."

He did not mean to be unsettled by what came next, but he was unsettled anyway.

"A few of them, the résumés, he even folded into paper gliders and sent sailing over the seats, and a bunch of them he crumpled up and tried to juggle."

He did not mean to nod, yet he nodded anyway, and his mouth went loose and soft.

By Jesus, he thought, paper gliders and juggling! What possessed me? You called Dana a monster, why, then, stick with the monstrous.

Curving his hands powerfully and lifting his eyes, the President, thinking, Grim and grizzly, plunge to the depth with grim and grizzly, continued.

"We wanted, my experts and I, to answer certain questions—reasonable questions, questions America had a right to ask. How, we wanted to know, did Gavrych and his followers here manage to get Matthew Dana into Radio City that night? With an invitation, like everybody else? But wouldn't he have considered that too many of his old colleagues were there and he was bound to be recognized? And if he was among the guests why was there no sign of him when the cameras were shooting every seat during the speeches and ceremonies? We studied the waiters. Could he have been one of the waiters serving food from the buffet tables? But he wasn't, he wasn't. Why, how could he handle those trays? With his . . ."

He mastered an impulse to mention Dana's long skinny arms.

"No, not among the guests or the waiters. Ah, sure, we did catch sight of him, my experts and I—but only on the film that closed out the programs. *The Mackenzie Years.* Old newsreel shots of his trial. Shots of Dana on the stand, denouncing Mackenzie, denouncing America."

Those old newsreels tore me up. His schoolboy face, his ineptitude. Then and there I wanted to scream and rebuke him. "Do you know what you're doing? Can't you foresee? Why can't you foresee that you'll be taking on the likes of Harry with only the strength of your convictions?"

"*The Mackenzie Years* finished, lights came back on again. And music. Circus music."

The President struck the lectern with all his might.

"And three clowns came. Dressed like cartoon characters. Superheroes, I gather, called . . . Earth-Lord and Prometheus and Dr. Justice."

A coldness overcame him.

"Matthew Dana was Dr. Justice.

"In his left hand he held what was supposed to be lists of Dr. Justice evildoers, and he handed them around to the children, and he mixed into that list some of his résumés. Those crazy résumés."

His hands were not shaking exactly, but he could not keep them still.

"On his back, strapped to his back, was the special Dr. Justice Force. Sort of, oh, a two-barreled energizer to help Dr. Justice take off fast, fast, after evildoers anywhere. One barrel poured out streams of colored sparklers."

Melissa trembled, bit a knuckle.

"The other barrel looked just a bit bigger and much more . . . machined . . . and a different curve at the top and it didn't pour out sparklers."

He gave Melissa his kindest glance. Honey, smartypants, wiseacre, I have plans. Yes, he sought to let her know, one day soon I'll have you in again and I'll tell you about the Great War and—why not?—we'll talk of infinite space.

"Gifts were being handed out to the children and souvenir journals to everybody else. But the children looked upset, very upset. Pretty soon everybody else was looking upset, and two of the clowns, the other two, Earth-Lord and Prometheus, stopped what they were doing, tumbling and such, and they were arguing with Dr. Justice, with Dana, and Dana was yelling, 'Peace, sympathy, brotherhood, and purest joy,' also about how he and Gavrych's American followers were rising up in our cities, city after city, to give us . . . through blows, through blows they'd give us the will to reconstruct and redistribute, and—"

The President, both hands before his face, rubbed and rubbed at the air.

"—around then he was wiping away his makeup, his paint and

grease and such. Pretty soon it was enough gone so that some people recognized him, and they came over, and they made such a stir and commotion that Mackenzie came over too, and he said something like, 'Do you come for trouble, Matthew?' and though he looked a little frightened—more than a little frightened, I suppose—he tried to put a good face on it. He said, 'No fear, friends, I believe I know by this time how to deal with disgruntled ex-employees,' and Dana said, 'Dear Buck, all the blows that have fallen since Adam would not give you the will to reconstruct and redistribute.' Then he sort of shrugged. Only he wasn't shrugging. He was just reaching around toward the barrel of his special Dr. Justice energizer, the one that was bigger and a little better machined . . ."

He saw Dempster, cynical tail-chasing Dempster, weeping openly.

And though his notes read, *Two, three seconds silence, reverent silence after energizer stuff,* the President's blood rose in such ugly, unreasoning hatred for Dempster that he gave a little snarl.

He gave a little snarl and said, "Why, look, Amos . . . ," and he was ready to unloose upon him such words, such a gust of eloquence as would blow him out to the edge of the world, the edge of the world.

Ah, I'll give you something to cry about, he swore. I'll fix you, no fear. I'll cut you off from man and God; I'll teach you what there is to cry about in this life.

But presently he was past caring.

Ancient of Days, do as You will.

All the same to me.

Besides there were hands, hands, hands.

By Jesus, let them wait, the President decided.

For he had just seen frazzle-face steal over to Melissa's chair and gently pull a knuckle from her trembly mouth, and his heart was lightened.

If only he'd raise a hand I'd give him a turn, the President thought. Why doesn't he raise a hand? I bet he'd have some curious, twisty, Middle European picture-book thing to ask. Which I'd welcome. Though he's probably out of some landlocked place, and the land-locked can be dreary. They're born with this dark internal geography from medieval times, from spooky twilight, monks, cobblestones, oppressive mountains, and such. As Harry says.

Then little old Merrylee Hobson, *Chicago Sun-Times,* crying, "Make way for us!" came hobbling forward, and because she carried a stout gold-handled stick, the kind Nanny Dora had favored toward the end, he decided to overlook her daffy ways, and he acknowledged her.

In a sweet, spirited voice she said, "We wonder, sir, how we may interpret your emphasis upon Dana's call to 'reconstruct and redistribute'?"

She raised her stick and brought it down so hard that the President jumped.

"We wonder, sir"—she opened and shut her sunken mouth—"if you fear, as we do, that Pavel Gavrych, using Dana as his instrument, was announcing his next move."

"Likely, more than likely," answered the President, though he was utterly confused. But it seemed to him that such awful, absolute understanding of time and age and mortality dwelt within the squiggly centers of her eyes that he took pity, and he went on to say, "Interesting thought, good thinking, Merrylee."

She turned her head slowly and proudly around at all present, then said, "We wonder, sir, if you fear, as we do, that Pavel Gavrych means at this time to broaden the base of his American followers with a Marxist-Leninist program that embraces not only intellectuals but an underclass, a permanent population of disgruntled and hopelessly alienated."

She held out a hand, rested her weight on her good leg.

"Marxist-Leninist," she said, frowning, fuddled. "In that reconstruct and redistribute we seem to find, we feel, we fear . . ."

She smiled vaguely, timorously, as if to concede that she had outrageously abused the President's patience and was now at his mercy.

By Jesus, I could shame this poor, odd, precise little person forever, he realized. I could have her as helpless as a bird blown out to sea. But he saw, or thought he saw, tears move into her eyes, and so he began his reply with tender teasing, saying, "Still refusing to use a word processor, Merrylee?"

"Still," she said, raising her stick and bringing it down.

They smiled together.

The President made his back completely straight and still.

"Now your question—about my emphasizing, stressing, that 'reconstruct and redistribute' and whether it comes from fearing that Gavrych . . . Is he, with Marxist-Leninist tactics . . . A program to appeal to the underclass and such?"

With his fingers he smudged and polished, smudged and polished, the rings of the chromed steel binder.

He breathed out a "Yes."

And at this moment it was as if his mind were entirely without capacity, as if he had years and years back used up the very last thought allotted to him.

Again he breathed out a "Yes."

And he considered talking of dark times and bad dreams, of the edge of the world, of Dana's long skinny arms, of his Duluth Time-traveler, of infinite space, of why Father had done right to take that Lewis Buntline as his son.

But suddenly Jack was on hand to rebuke and restore him, saying, "Boy-o, that permanent population of disgruntled—something's there if you can catch and hold it!"

And he caught it, he held it!

And he had a flashing of the hoi, the polloi, the louts and lumps, eating and drinking their fill at some great American trough and moving in multitudes from sea to shining sea.

Now strongly in charge he said, "Yes, it's been of concern to me, the possibility of a Gavrych program based on Marxist-Leninist tactics and appealing to . . . an underclass."

His voice was perfect, perfect—ringing but not overbearing.

"But we can all of us feel secure, Merrylee. Because, yes, if America has its problems, if there's still much to do for our inner cities, our urban blight, if, sure, there are those among us—far fewer than some claim, but too many to suit me—those on the level of poverty—"

He nodded at Merrylee, then at all present.

"—I still believe that the American people are blessed with a wisdom, a kind of fundamental good sense that rejects out of hand Marxist-Leninist tactics appealing to some . . . statistical underclass."

And more softly.

"Merrylee, is there an American who honestly and truly believes that he belongs to . . . an underclass?"

And still more softly.

"I think not. No. Not from sea to shining sea."

He felt a glorious heat rising in his face.

"Merrylee, I've no real fear of those who call to—what?—to reconstruct and redistribute. Our people know that one day, pray God, and soon, we'll be getting down to work at the reconstruction that's necessary. And they know, in their fundamental good sense, the emptiness of those calls and appeals to redistribute, those calls which have brought the world . . . oh, Lenin and Stalin and Pavel Gavrych and such. And how would we go about redistributing in America, our America? Well, all I can think of, I guess, the redistributing that comes to mind right now . . ."

He looked at Melissa, at frazzle-face, at Merrylee.

"Why, sure—a bowling alley for me, a tract house for you."

And he heard, "There's a quote"; and he heard, "Good form tonight"; and he heard, "The touch, he has the touch tonight."

The President could not stop staring into the sleek narrow face of Ron Labaschin, Kayle Features, into those depthless porcelain-blue eyes.

Why, give him another few inches along the shoulders, he reflected, a shiny pillbox hat and a gold cape, and he could be the usher in my Radio City dream.

Labaschin blinked, bared glittering teeth.

But the President, entranced, kept staring. For it was just such a rigid doll-groom type who'd seated him behind a pillar. Yes, he seated me behind a pillar and when he saw how horribly upset I was he smiled with obnoxious satisfaction.

Labaschin took a step backward and made a throat-stopped sound, like a puppy's whimper.

"My question, Mr. President, will be simple."

"I'm sure of that," the President wanted to say, but he held himself to "Sure."

His tone must have betrayed him, though, for Labaschin averted his head as if dodging a blow. Relenting, the President was soon softened utterly as he contemplated those sideburns and calculated the hours and hours it must take to shape them like Arab daggers. And the hair so perfectly parted down the middle—oh, how can you have higher emotions when you're clipping and snipping so long and purposefully? What can be left to pursue a grand soul or a significant life?

And all of a sudden he remembered how the usher had flashed his light on him and said, "You mustn't expect to be president of grand souls and significant lives."

What a piece of work, the mind, he thought.

With good humor he said, "I'll have your question, Ron." Smiling at Melissa and frazzle-face, he added, "Which needn't be . . . oh, all *that* simple."

"I want to sort of follow up on Merrylee Hobson's previous question from before."

Labaschin filled his lungs.

"Sir, if Pavel Gavrych's Marx and Lenin appeal to an underclass in poverty . . . if the appeal catches on to meet success of any kind . . ."

"Unlikely, Ron. Unlikely and, I would pray God, impossible."

"No argument there, sir. I join you in those prayers."

Labaschin put a finger to his tie and to each of his lapels.

"My concern, sir, is of the 'worst scenario' category. And I hope, sir, that my question is not too . . ."

"Hardly," said the President, soothingly. For it would have been indecent, given that twitching neck, to take a harsher tone. But this generation—he wondered if this generation had been trained to dullness in the way certain Africans had been trained to magic and begging and storytelling.

"See, sir—"

Labaschin struck his temple a blow, as if to dislodge something within.

". . . What if those who are broke *go* for broke and we get a contagion of terrorism such as Bloomingdale's or Radio City wherein nobody can enjoy the security of feeling safe? My question, sir . . ."

He lowered his head and scowled so fiercely that his hair seemed to scowl also.

". . . Do you have contingency plans of deterrence or prevention for such a situation?"

The President's answer was slow in coming—so slow that he noticed Melissa's knuckle gliding in and out, in and out of her mouth.

Finally he shut his eyes tightly and proudly for a moment and said, "No."

He said, "No," in a voice that reverberated like a ceremonial bell.

And he opened his eyes, and he labored to fix upon his face a gaze of unfathomable sorrow and love, and he went on to say, "Sure, yes, I've considered the options—curfews, martial law, National Guard, and such, and . . . rejected them. Absolutely!"

Fear not, he said to himself, speak whatever nonsense you please. For all the same the six-packers will rise on time tomorrow, and all the same they will drop their "G"s and break wind, all the same they will be bitter and bewildered.

"For I won't allow myself to enter the wilderness, the moral wilderness of your 'worst scenario' fears—and they're legitimate fears, Ron. As president, I must not allow myself to single out a group, a class, people whose incomes are less than they or we might wish them to be and decide that they're *potential* dangers, *potential* threats, because they've lost their jobs or their farms and might *potentially* turn to Gavrych tactics, terrorist tactics and such. I can't allow myself to even think that what's good for us—oh, laws, rights, and such—isn't good for them, that their . . . their temporary economic distress allows us to decide that we can't risk taking a chance on their humanity . . ."

Now how did this happen? he asked himself.

". . . their common humanity."

For I might be on the verge of something deep, I might have accidentally wandered into the realms of blessed truth.

"Appears to me that all we have is this common humanity to stop us from stuff like . . . sure, yes, like one fine day deciding, oh, I can't stand the variety of mankind and, oh, I've had it with this overcrowded planet and, oh, I'm tired of measuring things by right and wrong, good and evil . . ."

He heard a voice within him repeat, "Good and evil, right and wrong," and thinking, Keep it up, just keep it up if you want to be a one-term president, he closed his heart to hungers of worthiness.

But oh, my dear ones, he silently whispered, I need a finish and I am so deeply tired. What would you have me say that can do me some good?

"Child, child, consider the Psalms," answered Father, Mother, Nanny Dora. "Verses thirty-nine through forty-two nearly always gave you peace and thanksgiving during your chest weakness."

Therefore the President looked upon all present with brightened eyes, and he tried to remember, and then he was quite sure, and he said, "Doesn't it, hasn't it always come down to this? Who knew better than that psalmist what was right and good? 'No man may deliver his brother or make agreement unto God for him.' "

Am I off the hook? he wondered.

By the humbled backs, by the transfixed eyes and instantaneous tears, he saw that he might be, he just might be.

But all the same, he thought, the six-packers will rise on time tomorrow and they will drop their *g*'s and break wind, and all the same they will try to voice their bitterness and bewilderment, but they will say only "Fuck," and they will say only "Shit."

And Melissa was on her feet.

She looked new to life but age-worn, playful but grave, withdrawn but watchful, timorous but grandly, gloriously sure.

She said, "Sir, you've driven agnosticism and pseudoradical ideologies from me forever."

Then she looked heavenward, snapped her shoulders back, and saluted.

The President laughed a little. "Ah, Ms. Siampa, Ms. Siampa . . ."

But all the same, he thought, the six-packers will rise on time tomorrow, and they will drop their *g*'s and break wind, and they will wonder who has taken from them their rightful place in the world.

And when Melissa was back in her seat, when she was done double-knotting each shoelace, the President said, "I pray God, Ms. Siampa, that Pavel Gavrych and his American followers get the message. Let them understand here and now and forever that we will endure this harsh trying and, more than that, oh far more . . ."

He looked at his clasped hands.

"We shall do more than endure. Yes, we shall . . ."

He waited until all present were absolutely watchful. Then he uttered the last word.

"Prevail."

He heard sighing; he heard palates lock; he heard remorseful, heart-stopped sounds.

By Jesus, I'm off the hook, he told Jack. No fear, old buddy. I have it made.

"Prevail," he said again, with a perfect sinking of his voice.

Only is there another hook? A greater hook about which I'm not too clear, about which I'm altogether ignorant?

Then he heard hissing cries, then a small tumult.

And all present looked incredulous and amused as frazzle-face, slapping down several hands and jabbing with his head like a bearded bird, spoke up.

"Permitted to rip off a turn, sir?"

"Now what do you think, Ms. Siampa?" said the President.

Melissa nodded.

And the President, nodding also, said, "Permission granted, Mr. . . . ."

Frazzle-face, wringing his hands, tried twice to give his name. But he could not find his full voice. Only a whisper came out. Then he spread his arms, bent his knees a little, and cried, "Sir!"

Well, who needs his name? the President reflected. I can just imagine it. Some twisty, lumpy syllabic mess that I'd probably break my teeth pronouncing.

"Sir, during such time as you can spare do you take stock of your countrymen? For they need work. Their act is not together."

The President laughed in astonishment.

"Bad vibes. A blue funk. None walk whole upon your American scene. Warriors unarmed before an adversary could not be in worse shape or less straight of head. No feeling of children for parents, husbands for wives. Loveless intimacy, life like a desert . . . ."

He pulled his beard, mumbled to himself in a light, rapid voice, then, too loud, said, "What gives? For I must tell you, sir . . . ."

He hopped backward and fell straight-legged into his seat.

". . . I was high on America and once had greater expectations."

"Ah," said the President.

To himself he said, "Bless you, fellow, little European fellow. May that high return, as it never can to me, not ever again."

Something in the President stretched, quivered.

He had it in mind to have frazzle-face speak a little more, to get his ideas on history and statecraft and realpolitik.

But he heard snickering; he heard, "Weirdo"; he heard, "Crank."

All the same he stared hard at frazzle-face, trying to let him understand that before long he would set something up so they could talk away and make connection.

Then Karen Lister rose, cleared her throat as was her custom, capped her pen, said, "Thank you, Mr. President," and it was over, it was over.

As he moved from the lectern the balding agent with tortoiseshell sunglasses came to his right side and told him, "Beautiful, sir."

And the blond agent with rimless sunglasses came to his left side and told him, "Tremendous, sir."

Rapping each one on a bicep he murmured, "Ah, maybe, boys, maybe."

But he saw Joel Baskier raising hands high over his head and applauding with all his might.

And he saw Eunice mouthing "Love," mouthing "Proud," mouthing "Swell."

And even the sharpest and most cynical among the brotherhood of bull looked touched, stirred, choked with thought, and several spoke gently to him for the first time, and several others saluted him, as Melissa had done, and he longed to linger with them a little while, to loosen up, hold forth, show off, but the boys pressed them back, saying "Move along, okay," and "Can we move it along, please," as they had to, as they must.

"Where to, sir?" asked the balding agent with tortoiseshell sunglasses.

"What's your pleasure, sir?" asked the blond agent with rimless sunglasses.

"Oval Office, boys," he answered. "A few minutes of summary from"—he playfully bumped each one with a hip—"Rather and Brokaw and Jennings."

He saw Eunice waiting between the double doors and the mild rose carpet.

Yes, for once he would forgo them so that he and Eunice could hold hands and sneak off to, say, the Blue Room and there eat Perugina chocolates while they watched any old movie she wanted to watch, and they would pet and neck and exchange love's first kiss, and he would sing, "Did you ever see a dream walking?" and she would sing back, "Well, I did."

And while he did some new things with her breasts, her nipples, her right underarm, her fleecy part, he would excite her further with whisperings of his deepest secrets—war room stuff about where and when the B-52s would violate Soviet air space.

He felt a warmth in his remotest nerves.

By Jesus, we might just sneak away to watch them take off at dawn or whenever. We'll stand together in the middle of the airfield, and no matter how powerful the backwash of those engines we'll keep our feet, we'll wave both hands and lift our faces higher and higher to the sky as they climb, and when the last B-52 is out of sight I'll put an arm around Eunice's shoulder and we'll walk off, and now and then we'll look at one another as . . . as John Garfield and Eleanor Parker looked at one another in *Pride of the Marines*.

Then the balding agent with tortoiseshell sunglasses seemed to stumble.

Then the blond agent with rimless sunglasses sprang forward to help him, and he too seemed to stumble.

And the President was somehow pulled aside with them, but he managed to right himself, and the boys seemed to have unusual trouble getting back on their feet, and the President pranced a bit, and laughed, and wondered whether to say, "Getting old, boys?" or "Boys, we're all getting older."

But even before he heard, "Peace, sympathy, brotherhood, and purest joy," something within him told him that it would be wise to half turn and look to the left.

And there, close upon him, he saw frazzle-face.

"Easy, easy on him, boys," said the President.

But they made a mad rush forward and bumped against the President, and the bumping somehow sent him even closer to frazzle-face, who said, "Sir, do you wish my name?"

And with a supreme straining of all his strength he bellowed, "Orlofsky, Vidyon Yezel Orlofsky!"

The President reached out to grab, to grapple.

But he had first to deal with his ears, with a noise so loud that it burst blood vessels and membranes.

By Jesus, Harry. Ah, Harry, Harry, Harry.

His eyes grew dark.

Do I have any chest left, Father, Mother, Nanny Dora?

Ancient of Days, I wish, I feel, I think, I and I.

Oh Jack, Jack, see what they have done to me.

34

"I believe she's ready, now," Amy Underhill told the Marine captain.

Morning had not yet arrived but darkness was lifting.

"Yes, ma'am," said the Marine captain. His eyes, bright with the lateness of the hour and the reflected sanctuary lamps, gleamed earnestly into Amy Underhill's, and his mouth opened foolishly. He started to say several things, and finally, stiff and hesitant, said with a nervous qualm, "Ma'am, orders are to take the honor guard beyond earshot."

A furnace kicked on, became a smooth, easy drone.

The lights of the Great Rotunda rose a notch. They made the busts behind the President's coffin white as sugar, but they brought out the imperfections in the enormous painting of James Oglethorpe in Savannah and gave it a bitter green aspect.

Sad and unsure, chin straining upward, the Marine captain went on to say, "Beg pardon, ma'am. *Earshot? Beyond* earshot?"

"Quite so, quite so!" Amy Underhill snapped. She looked at him with extraordinary closeness and severity. "Does the word 'earshot' displease you? Dear me, oh dear! But the secretary of defense put his signature to my request readily enough."

"He was right to, ma'am. And no displeasuring intended, surely not."

There was an iron moaning from the basement; there was a dog's bark from miles away.

"Why, ma'am, it's only as I don't know where that would exactly be. Where 'tis, how fur. *Beyond* earshot."

"Just far enough, Captain, so that you hear nothing of what may be said here at the President's coffin. Nothing. Not a single syllable. Not a sound."

A rooster screamed.

"The lifts should do nicely. Lifts"—Amy Underhill tapped his wrists—"are elevators."

Smiling, his jaw slipped to one side, the Marine captain said, "Lifts are elevators. Guess I knew that, ma'am."

"I suspect," said Amy Underhill with a short trembling laugh, "that you knew also, and perfectly well, the distance needed to take you . . . beyond earshot."

There was a ferment from a diesel horn.

A sanctuary lamp guttered and seemed to empurple the coffin stand.

The blackened rifle barrels of the honor guard shone like coal.

"I suspect"—Amy Underhill closed one eye, enlarged the other— "that you are seeking to hold me till . . . oh yes, my man, till you can bring yourself to speak of certain matters. These matters, I should guess, are troublesome. You cannot quite abide them and wish to, as best you can, spill your guts. Is that not the proper, the now, idiom?"

"Good enough, ma'am."

The Marine captain put a finger to his lips, jerked his head toward the coffin, took a step forward.

"Way back when he was a senator he pushed through this law as cut three, four square miles off the Tennessee interstate spur. Forget rightly how it ruined my pa, only it ruined him and a couple uncles real well, worse'n I can decently tell you, ma'am."

The Marine captain turned down his underlip.

"I wished him the same, ma'am. Prayed he'd be taken in the meanest way. About what came to pass, wouldn't you say, ma'am?"

"Sad, silly boy," said Amy Underhill.

To herself she murmured, "Yes, that should do, oh my."

She put her hands gently on his shoulders. "Consider this bit of verse," she said close by his ear. " 'We are lived by powers we pretend to understand . . . it is they who direct at the end the enemy bullet, the sickness, or even our hand.' "

Both looked at the east bank of windows, at the last tired stars.

Vague and shy, the Marine captain said, "That's a comfort, ma'am."

Amy Underhill shook her head. "But not all that much of a comfort, is it?"

In a fierce and forlorn voice the Marine captain said, "Savin' time of war, no man should wish another man taken afore his time, no ma'am, surely not, ma'am."

He gazed sidelong at the coffin. There was a palpitation in his throat. "Sir," he said with a submissive shrug, "I beg your pardon most powerfully. Pa and my uncles likely ruin themselves anyway, even if he'd let that Tennessee interstate be."

He turned, fixed his eyes a little over Amy Underhill's head.

"Ma'am."

He put three fingers of his right hand to the hilt of his ceremonial sword.

In a curiously shrouded voice he said, "Ma'am, is the visitor ready, *ma'am*?" and he sent the last word pining upward.

"She is, Captain. The visitor," said Amy Underhill submissively, "is ready."

Then the Marine captain stepped back smartly and marched the honor guard off.

Amy Underhill counted to fifty, and fifty again.

"Come, love," she cried.

She and Eunice met and kissed between the busts of Ewing Young and John C. Fremont.

Then Amy Underhill said, "I shan't be far," and sprinted to the Northeast Stairs, and Eunice, peering as if into a smudged mirror and speaking to herself disconnected words and nonsense syllables, moved to the coffin.

A blue dew frosted over the glass of the Rotunda.

With a crooked movement of the shoulders Eunice shook back the hood of her parka and unzipped both the zippers.

"Here I am," she said.

She dropped to her knees, blurted, "Poor baby!" and got up from her knees.

She moved her lips.

She ran her hands slowly up and down the cocoa-colored peignoir and set them low on her abdomen and pressed inward.

"Hurts there," she mumbled, and her mumbling was like the sleepy fretting of a child. "Near"—she moved her fingers as if over a keyboard—"thirty-six hours, isn't that properly a day and a half? Right after or maybe just before I had a last look at my poor baby. Simply mentioning it, end of internal matters, because I surely have not forgotten your mortal shyness in matters of feminine you-know-what. Eased the least bit when Harry came by and tried so very sweetly and so very thundering hard to keep himself strong for my sake. Though I could never imagine kissing Harry, I simply had to kiss him for something he said. He said as how something of you would always color his feelings about virtue and honor. There, that's it, poor baby, only wanted you to know how the hurt has been at me this day and a half, these thirty-six hours."

She dropped to her knees, exclaimed, "I've had the shakes!" and got up from her knees.

Groaning weakly, she said, "I've had the shakes and what I feel is about enough for groaning but nowhere near enough or right enough to set me crying for natural grief. Might it be, poor baby, that you tied yourself to a prattling ninny immersed in fleshly pleasure thoughts and without capacity for softer feelings? Where, oh where, are my softer feelings? You had them sufficient to fill a hundred years of your precious *Jane's Fighting Ships* and Harry envied you for them. He most surely did, you know. When I took him by to his last look he said, 'I envy you, dear friend. You could leave these times with your softer feelings still intact.' Sweet suffering Lord, I never had trouble crying before. Might be the human condition is over my prattling ninny head. Nothing in me this day and a half, these thirty-six hours, but annoyance."

She closed one zipper of her parka, snarled the other.

"I am most thunderingly annoyed that you did not talk less about Gallipoli and Tobruk and more about why I honestly believe I should have been more than I was, though I can't say for sure what I was. I am most awfully annoyed and have not put out of my mind how I was required to praise your Gary Cooper and Henry Fonda imitations, but you never once said a nice thing about my lovemaking intentions which I can assure you took forethought and planning womanly logic. I continue to remain mortally offended at your scorning of my Honey-bunch doll collection while I wasn't allowed a flaming word against your dumb old Duluth Timetraveler."

She grumbled and waved her hands as if putting aside an objection.

"But I am also remorseful, and you'd best know why."

She struck herself heavily across the mouth.

"Eternal shame on me, for I was hornet mad and murder in my heart when your beloved Secret Service guardians, your precious pair, your boys, came to pay their respects. Cursed them out like one of those old prophets for not staying closer to you. Will you let me know why they didn't stay and shoot down that ugly little Russian sucker a couple seconds sooner? Tripping as well over some dumb old chairs when I've seen them leaping round like lizards along your Olympic balance beam. Hadn't they tripped, why, I'd not be a brave little former First Lady widow woman with nothing ahead save collecting your presidential papers and setting up your presidential library and accepting awards from interfaith people."

She pressed into her eyeballs with the tips of her fingers.

"My remorse is not from cursing and striking them and shattering their dumb old sunglasses to which I hold myself rightly privileged, but from a certain wish I put on them that sent them off all shaky and shivery like they'd been touched by the five holy terrors."

She walked three steps forward nodding, then three steps backward shaking her head.

"Wished them old prophet things. Scabs and pox and withered limbs. No more. Truly no more. Only it was wished loud and wild and crazy and afore many people, and I guess it shamed and disgraced them terrible, maybe more than they could properly bear. Dead now, the both of them, from some brake failure and steering thing. Harry says they had the satisfaction of knowing they'd done the state some service, but I don't know if it's all that much satisfaction."

She raised her hands at the coffin in such a fashion that none of her fingers touched each other.

"Poor baby, you also did the state some service, and just see what it's got you, and just see what it's got me."

She shook a finger at the coffin.

"Thanks to you and your precious state it's farewell forever to that tenderly touching deathbed scene I had in mind for us, and let me tell you some such scene is in the mind of every woman and every wife."

She clasped both hands over her head.

"I'd have read to you *Ash Girl* and *Rapunzel* and a bit of poetry, and while you were taking passage from me to the edge of the world, I'd have one special poem saved, and this is the poem."

She swung her hands to and fro, to and fro:

> "Full fathom five thy father lies;
> Of his bones are coral made;
> Those are pearls that were his eyes:
> Nothing of him that doth fade . . ."

She screamed with a supreme straining of all her voice.

Moments later, when Amy Underhill lifted her from the floor, there was solemn wonder on her face, and she was weeping profusely, proudly.

"Didn't rightly understand all that much," Eunice said, "but it appeared to be filled with human condition matters and gave me the most rightful ease."

"Pity to leave out the refrain," said Amy Underhill. "Filled with the sound of unshed tears, don't you know. Shall we have it? Follows, if you remember, 'Sea-nymphs hourly ring his knell.' "

"Together," said Eunice.

And together they recited, " 'Ding-dong! Hark! now I hear them,—Ding-dong, bell.' "

As they neared the bust of James K. Polk, Eunice whispered something to Amy Underhill.

"I can't imagine he'll mind, love," Amy Underhill said, kissing her.

Then Eunice went round in tiny circles and her eyes filled up again.

She stopped and said, "I'm remorseful again for having told you a womanly or wifely lie. See now, there are times beyond calculation when I surely did not tell all the truth, but I did not directly lie as I did now in claiming I had that 'Full fathom' poem saved for you when you were taking passage from me. It's Amy's special poem, a special magic poem meant to free a prattling ninny heart for natural grief. So please take your rest forever and ever clear of lies, and don't be too surprised if you see me fairly soon, sweet darling, darling husband."

Then she stood still while Amy Underhill combed out her hair and freed the snarled zipper on her parka.

And in the first light of morning they left the Great Rotunda.

35

On the unexpectedly mild afternoon of January 3, 1994, ten kinder-garteners of mixed racial and religious backgrounds were passed through the magenta velvet ropes that hung diagonally and to the left of the Arlington National Cemetery amphitheater.

They carried marigolds and asters and other forever flowers, and they strewed them as they went, and each guileless face showed such humility and such a hunger to be worthy that many in the dense crowd set up soft, grieved murmurs of admiration.

Just before the amphitheater the ten halted and held hands and recited without self-consciousness, without the slightest clearing of their throats, the first stanza of "The Battle Hymn of the Re-public."

Still holding hands, nine of the children walked off toward the chartered bus idling its motor between the picket fence and the two sentry boxes.

An exquisite little Mexican girl stayed behind, and she was lifted a few feet off the ground by an Eagle Scout who held her till another Eagle Scout brought a small electronic device with a single white button, which she pushed with both her index fingers and which set loose from a long rank of silvery cages flocks of fiery-breasted Ches-apeake warblers, long known to have been the President's favorite bird.

While the warblers, momentarily blinded by the reflectors and smoking arc lights, labored with much sweet shrilling to catch the air currents, Eunice lifted her veil, turned to the right, and whispered to the Chief Justice of the United States Supreme Court, who leaned forward and nodded and closed his eyes tightly behind his glasses.

Presently the two Eagle Scouts led the little Mexican girl to the amphitheater stage and handed her over to Eunice, and Eunice kissed her on both eyes and on her nose and set her on her lap in such a way as to shade her from the sun.

Then the ceremonies began with invocations delivered by three celebrated clergymen representing America's major faiths.

Near a little rise swollen with new burial mounds, Melissa put her right hand into the pocket of Porlock's dove-gray chesterfield.

Decisively and without preliminaries she said, "Yes, it was a form of symbolic protest against death."

Porlock shortened his stride.

Melissa stopped to gaze at a mechanical mower moving in perfect circles, shook some cuttings from her hair, and told him, "Look, Harry, I expect to give a whimper or a sniffle soon. Quite soon."

"Silly goose," said Porlock, pushing her hand a little deeper into his pocket.

They passed a sprinkler, climbed a stubby hill, and took the graveled walk between the memorial to the Fighting Seabees and a piece of high-polished, still unlettered granite.

Melissa stooped, made as though to dry her streaming eyes on Porlock's sleeve. Then she straightened and stamped a foot. But Porlock only looked toward some locust trees.

"See here, Harry," said Melissa, her eyes filling again, "it behooves you to ask about my symbolic protest against death."

Some moments passed, and then she murmured, "Do you know I nearly said 'behests,' that it *behests* you?"

"Hardly surprised." Porlock leaned deeply toward her. "Indeed, the sort of baby blunder I'd expect from a silly goose who sheds such fat tears."

He removed her hand from his pocket and steered her by an elbow to a stone bench into which was chiseled, FOR MICKEY, MY FLY-BOY, MY PILOT, WHO LEFT THE AIR SIGNED WITH HIS YOUTH. And when she had seated herself he told her, "You have my full attention," and he seated himself very straight backed beside her.

Melissa nodded and looked toward him and bit a knuckle.

"You know"—Porlock stopped his breath for an instant—"I did notice, oh, some fifteen minutes ago I should say, about when the ceremonies were done and you'd shaken Eunice's hand, that you were . . . limping. Rather suddenly limping a bit. And I'm taken by the thought, you see, that your protest against death and that limp . . . I did wonder . . ."

Several seconds went by.

Then Melissa, slowly wagging her head, said, "You are like me in respect to noticing. You notice. Immodest or not, you are like me in that nothing of the world's human nature and conduct escapes your notice or . . . or," she added in a voice a good deal less certain, "overly pleases you."

"Now and then an immodest silly goose who sheds fat tears manages to please me."

Melissa crossed her legs, bent a bit to her Wellington boots.

"What I did when we left the car did not escape your notice. What you saw me pick up was in no way like a dime, but you did not abash me and instead let my impulse fulfill itself. Therefore—"

She held the left boot upside down by the heel, shook it, and a bloody pebble fell to the ground.

"—so behold, and don't please exclaim over my slightly bleeding heel."

Porlock picked up the pebble, placed it into the center of Melissa's left palm and closed her fingers around it. "I should certainly keep this."

But she let it fall, and wincing, worked her foot back into the boot.

"Did no good, of course," she whispered.

Porlock looked keenly into the sky and said, "See here, Melissa, it *behooves* me to ask you . . ."

"Okay." She bit a knuckle.

And head down she said, "So. So I knew I would do something with the pebble but I didn't quite know what. I heard, I *thought* I heard you speaking to yourself quietly; I spoke even more quietly to myself and way under my breath went, Unworthy, unworthy, all, all."

They looked at each other, looked away, and Porlock said, "About when the birds were in the air, I'd guess."

"About when the birds were in the air." Melissa took his hand gently and as gently let it go. "Only they failed me. The birds."

"Not surprised. Even birds aren't quite what they used to be."

"They wouldn't obey my silent command to strike out the eyes of the unworthy."

"Just too many unworthy for them."

"I don't suppose . . . Harry, when you talked to yourself could you by coincidence have been giving my 'Strike out their eyes' command?"

"No. The beak of a Chesapeake warbler, you see, is far too fragile."

"So. So I decided what to do with the pebble right after that Rabbi Lobell cah-hah-halled upon the Supreme Judge of all nations."

"Poor man, whom else was he to call upon?"

"I then put the pebble into my heel and as hard as I could I pressed down. My idea was . . . The harder I pressed down the harder the President's life-force could fight death's dominion and maybe do something against all the unworthy."

"And how long did you . . . ?"

"A minute? A minute maybe."

"Not long enough. Not quite. Far too many unworthy about, even for the President."

"I might, *might* have held out longer, but it did hurt and I thought you'd stopped talking to yourself and would hear me whimper or sniffle."

She brought her head forward and with a little ring of exasperation said, "Well, were you?"

"Was I . . . ?"

She smiled. "It behooves you"—her smile became shaky—"to tell me if you were talking to yourself."

"Indeed I was." Porlock directed his gaze reflectively at an old slow couple opening and shutting their mouths and walking as if each were obscurely ashamed of the other.

Melissa rose, sat down, folded her hands into her lap. At last she said, in a peculiarly abstracted voice, "No need" and "Truly not" and "Don't have to."

"But I do, indeed I do." Porlock knit his fingers around a knee. "One confidence deserves another." A tremor went through his cheeks. "I quoted Falstaff and said among other things, many other things, 'Who hath honor? He who died o' it on Wednesday.' "

He pressed at a spot between his brows. Melissa kissed the spot, saying, "But among other things, many other things. And mostly, most of all, more than anything else, much more, you were saying good-bye to an old friend, a dear friend."

"Much more, more than anything else."

They rose, and that was all that either of them said till they reached the car.

EPILOGUE

Everything that was truly interesting in the minds of Americans happened in the darkness of their movie houses.

       —*From* Leviathan's Hook, *by Pavel Gavrych*

SATURDAY, FEBRUARY 5, 1994, SEMYON SQUARE, MOSCOW: I write these lines in the Dovzhenko Ciné to which Irena and I have traveled nine kilometers by three taxis and shelled out an obscene fifty-one rubles. Irena is in a rage and will not stop cursing like a muzhik or kicking my ankles or pummeling my back. And with good reason. For on Saturdays this dismal bughouse is nearly always filled with what's left of the American crowd—Fulbrights, bohemians, State Department grinds, dog-faith Gavrychoids left high and dry since "the troubles" and waiting for the gun butt to rap upon their doors. She wonders if I seek another coed, if . . .

"Do you have horniness, Bunty, sweet Bunty?" said Irena, twisting his nose. "Do you seek for cohabitation another Natalie? Perhaps another coed?"

Buntline gave her his gap-toothed grin, his fawn-eyed gaze.

"Should I have understood how insufficient I would be for one who is a writer and a teacher?"

"See here"—Buntline pumped up one of his belly laughs—"do you consider me a writer who teaches or a teacher who writes?"

She shook a fist at him. "I would wish to once again see you abject and helpless in KGB hands. And myself—an unsexed functionary, an apparatchik taking joy in sublimation."

"Didn't you notice me turn whispery and soulful? Ah, you noticed, you—"

"But such a time does not return. As your Jimmy Cagney will not. As Gavrych will not, I fear and foresee."

Then gray, stout Rob Hillveld, the film historian, was suddenly stomping up and down and back and forth along the aisles and pulling bloody patches from his billy-goat beard.

"Followed, followed," he cried. "Whistle if you believe you were followed here."

The din brought out the fat-backed manager.

He boosted himself onstage, centered his face between his cocked thumbs, and in his deepest register went, "Kumboom, kumboom!" As he scuttled to the wings he slapped both hands hard against his breast. He twirled three times, doubled over deeply, righted himself, and rapped out a Russian sentence.

Irena flinched.

"I made out 'corpses,' " said Buntline. "The rest, though . . ."

With something like a smile on her face Irena said, " 'Corpses . . . corpses or cadavers have no use for whistling.' "

House lights lowering.

Down, down, then they stay put and cast an odd, shaky orange glimmer. About as dark as it ever gets here at the Dovzhenko Ciné. I used to complain. Pompous, disdainful, sucking in my cheeks. "Look here, don't you know—high time you knew darkness in the theater is important to Americans, important to the kind of old American movies you show."

But that was before the troubles.

That was while I still set store in style, in wit, in turn of phrase and shading of words, in the importance of putting things as no man had ever put them before.

That was before I made my great discovery, took five fast credits in "truth."

Truth is sickening submission, bowing the neck, castrating all ego.

Truth is rooting out of yourself the notion of an unlimited future.

Truth is the vile, hateful, implacable, fanatic voice of sovereign authority that croaks, "You count for nothing."

So who knows?

Maybe I drew some benefit from that second B-52 overflight, when

I watched the leaflets flutter down, when I heard righteous wrath crack the throat of every Muscovite.

For I touched bottom.

At the sight of those blind, skinny, sublimely beautiful silver machines I touched ordinary nonacademic, nonliterary misery.

Human misery.

I was bared, pared down, ready, even eager, for Washington or Moscow to assign me my real place in the world.

So let's hear it for the naked force that cleansed the Buntline soul of false pride.

I fear death; therefore I am.

And it's made me a better mate these last five weeks. No more boring, compulsive discourse to Irena about:

1. My early promise.
2. The way my father failed me.
3. The way I failed wife, son, students, country.
4. The belief that somehow, with an observant eye, a sensitive ear, I would nevertheless prevail, I would nevertheless

But there it goes again—the pipe of false pride.

Enough, down with the vertical pronoun.

Vibration throughout the theater.

Sound track coming on full blast.

And music—strident, martial, barbaric music. I imagine Hector hearing the like while Achilles chased him down before the walls of Troy.

And there's that crude montage of the great stone Russian eagle stirring its wings, setting its talons for flight.

EVENTS OF THE WEEK

Once again the unbearable tedium of peasant faces and vast Russian landscapes and workingmen shaking fists and tank turrets spinning and crowbars slicing into crated artillery pieces and the close close-up of the placard that reads HE WHO COMES TO RUSSIA WITH THE SWORD SHALL PERISH BY THE SWORD.

And a glimpse of Gavrych addressing some delegation.

Bowed shoulders, worried eyes, fallen about the face, an embattled posture.

His voice—they've speeded it up. To make him sound screechy, to turn him into a babbling hysteric.

Elizabeth and Philip Warner are booing him.

Trying to court favor with sovereign authority.

True to their natures, their craven kittenish Episcopalian natures. May they be damned for it.

"Be damned for it!" screamed Buntline. "Hey Elizabeth, hey Philip, hey craven kittenish Episcopalian shitheads!"

Spittle flew from his lips.

"But Gavrych once pleased you well enough. When he spoke—"

He forced his voice up, and in a quavering, mincing tone said, "Philip, when Gavrych speaks I feel beautiful and splendid, and my dreams are filled with stars and undiscovered planets and golden oak doors."

His nose was clogged, his throat congested.

A cold?

My last cold?

What say, Washington, Moscow, sovereign authority? Am I any less craven, kittenish than the Warners? For there's a big, strong, splendid-looking old fellow on screen, a former partisan, and I see myself in his eyes. Dreadful eyes, absolute eyes. I'm turning away, I can't bring myself to

"Look, why do you not look?" said Irena.

"I want to save my eyes for Cagney. Won't you let me save my eyes for Cagney?"

Irena took him by the hair, turned him about, and pinched the back of his neck till tears came into his eyes and he was compelled to momentarily open them. Very gently she said, "Well then . . . well then, be worthy of him."

Now.

He comes now.

My cocky, feisty bantam.

My loner, my outsider, my smartass strutting wiseguy.

Give me such consolation as you can.

Help me, please, to remember, when I am packed into a closed truck, a sealed train, how the world responds less to deep truths than it does to hard blows.

The title came on: ANGELS WITH DIRTY FACES.

During the first fifteen minutes they held hands and tickled one another's palms and did all sorts of childish, desperate loverlike things, and right after Cagney threw his first punch Irena said, "Well, then . . . well, then, I concede the beauty of your Jimmy Cagney's movements. In his hitting especially I find a queer skill and terrible daring."

"Now that you see him," said Buntline, "finally see him . . ."

"Finally. Yes, finally I fear, I foresee."

". . . do you think, thinking as a woman, that if he was now as he is there . . ."

Buntline jabbed a finger at the screen.

". . . and if it had been he, not I, who'd fallen into your hands at KGB Central—would you have felt toward him as a *woman*?"

"Oh, Buntee." Irena was shivering. "Sweet emotionally immature American Buntee."

"But how would you have felt?" He squeezed her hand.

She squeezed back and gave him an odd look. "As a woman feels, I imagine, I believe."

She went on to say, "Could I love Buntee without also loving his Jimmy Cagney?"

Then Cagney was smiling and snarling and twitching his shoulders and rocking his hands, and presently he had shot his first two men.

Almost everyone in the Dovzhenko Ciné cheered and clapped and stamped their feet.

By the time Cagney had hurled away his empty gun and picked up one that was loaded the shadow of the fat-backed manager had fallen across the screen and, it seemed to Buntline, the shadows of other men as well.

—

To Chris, my son, a few words are in order from his cold, unloving, disappointed father.

You have an excellent mind, but a limited one. I certainly cannot imagine you ever going too far or wanting more than you can get or believing for a moment that all might not be well with you or the world.

I'm not sure that you care for anything but expository prose, for books of manifestly practical slant which you can underscore and bracket with your colored felt markers—a habit, I must say, which made me sick with loathing of you.

Still, our unnatural relationship has its points. Among them:

1. We've been spared the tensions of real intimacy.
2. My fate will leave you essentially unmoved—no more than mild distress, momentary inconvenience.

In return for the above and for the modest legacy to which you will fall due—albeit reluctantly on my part—I ask a small favor.

Take a few days, no more than a week, and search through my library.

Look for the books that make you quick with life.

And read!

Read in greedy gulps till you're struck, stunned by a line that sets your mind storming, till you long to run amok and do a wild dance, till your heart is changed and your small soul that made me sick with loathing of you . . .

On second thought, fuck it!

Gross philistinism suits you better.

Stay away from the climate of ideas, live the MBA–attaché case–mildly liberal life to which you're entitled. Absolutely entitled! Forgive, don't forgive me—oxen, as the Russians say, will still be bothered by fleas.

This rough gesture of reconciliation—corny, contrived.

No more than a father's insupportable biologic urge.

So do what you can, feel what you can.

Poor Chris, you have no love to spare. Your minisecond of insupportable pity will therefore suit me fine.

—

"Pick up your pen," said Irena. "It rolls away. See how it rolls away."

Buntline only shrugged and rocked his hands. "Let Cagney have the last word."

"The last word will not be your Jimmy Cagney's I fear, I foresee."

On his way to the electric chair Cagney stopped, twitched, twisted his mouth.

His throat swelled, he howled like a wolf.

He stumbled, recovered.

A few more steps, then he let himself be dragged, and he was altogether supine.

Three, four guards ringed him in. Each guard's face transmitted the same message: You are strong but there is something even greater than your strength.

The silhouette of the electric chair is imprinted upon the cold stone floor.

They have slit Cagney's trouser cuffs and clamped down his arms and the silhouette of the executioner's arm is imprinted upon the right side of his face.

And Buntline and Irena simultaneously experienced an intuition of awful force.

They started to embrace just as Winnie Gladstone, the violinist, made gagging noises.

Justin Foxman, the geneticist, and his wife, Rosa, had their heads back, and they started to slip down slowly from their seats.

Their children, Alex and Victor and Eleanor, also started to slip down slowly from their seats, but they one by one righted themselves, and Alex struck out blindly at his parents.

Jean Doberlyne, the sculptor, spread her arms and said, "Christ Jesus, Lord God, Creator and Preserver of all mankind."

Most of the people in the first seven rows were sitting quiet and curled like fetuses till Leora Silbert, the cultural anthropologist, wailed and made a commotion.

Buntline and Irena kissed each other's hands.

They were the first to rise as the lights of the Dovzhenko Ciné came on full and scores of booted men, speaking in flat metallic voices, stood three by three beside every other row.

Buntline, as he raised his hands, said, "Peace, sympathy, brotherhood, and purest joy."

Irena raised her hands also and said, "Well then . . . well then, I have this thought—that Gavrych would have done better to leave us as we were, as we were."

—

MOSCOW REPORTS DEATH OF PAVEL GAVRYCH

Moscow, May 7 (Reuters)—The Soviet Ministry of the Interior today announced that former Secretary-General Pavel Gavrych, who was charged with the wave of terrorism which culminated in the assassination of the President and brought the Soviet Union and the United States to the brink of war, died last week as a result of complications arising from kidney failure.

Mr. Gavrych, following his arrest five months ago, had been confined in Moscow's Lefortovo Prison, Ministry sources said, and was about to be sent into permanent internal exile before the onset of an undisclosed illness.

WALLACE MARKFIELD's previous novels include *To an Early Grave* (1964), which was the basis for the movie *Bye Bye Braverman, Teitlebaum's Window* (1970), and *You Could Live If They Let You* (1974). His articles and reviews have appeared in many magazines, including *Esquire, Life, New York, The New York Times Magazine*, and *Partisan Review*.